DEAD MECH

JAKE BIBLE

Published by Samannah Media

ACKNOWLEDGEMENTS

First, let me thank all of the fans of DEAD MECH that sat through hours upon hours of listening to the podcast. Without y'all, none of this would have happened.

I have to thank my wife, Marti, and my kids, Sam and Annah for living with me while I wrote, recorded, edited, wrote, recorded, edited, wrote, well, you get the picture. Thank you for being so patient. I love you very much.

I also have to thank my Dad for handing me those boxes upon boxes of paperbacks when I was in middle school. The worlds he helped me discover: Robert R. McCammon, Roger Zelazny, Isaac Asimov, Anne McCaffrey, Frank Herbert.

Thanks to my Mom who loves books also, but most of all, loved to talk about books. Hours spent dissecting the cultural and historical significance of horror and scifi characters and worlds.

I want to thank all of my friends that I grew up with that challenged me artistically and intellectually. Without y'all I would have just been another bored kid with dreams, but zero motivation to act on those dreams.

Finally, I want to thank all of the teachers (my wife included). Without teachers this country would be a cesspool of bland, lifeless crap. You, teachers, are the spark that ignites the creative fires and fans those flames into greatness. I remember you all and thank you for every single word of encouragement and for never giving up on me even though I was pretty annoying and hard to deal with.

Thank you everyone!

FOREWARD

WHAT IS A DRABBLE NOVEL?

Since writing the novel and podcasting it to over 6,000 subscribers, the number one question I am asked is: what is a drabble novel?

Well, to understand what a drabble novel is, you have to understand what a drabble is. So let us start at the beginning, a drabble is a piece of micro-fiction exactly 100 words long. Not 99, not 101, but 100 words precisely.

Having to hit that kind of word count can be a bit challenging, but after a little practice it begins to flow rather easily.

So I worked on a few drabbles and became quite hooked on the style. Of course, since just writing 100 words wasn't enough, I asked myself, "Self, could drabbles be strung together in a longer narrative?"

Thus, the Drabble Novel was born!

Well, there was a little hit and miss in the beginning...

Basically I started writing character sketches, action scenes, plot twists, really, anything that popped into my head, just to see if I even had a novel in me. After a hundred or so of these disjointed snapshots of the idea in my head, I realized I actually had something. Something that I could legitimately write and call a Drabble Novel. So I dove right in.

Now, the actual process of writing the novel wasn't quite so free for all. Pretty much I would write 100 words, go over it a few times, then a few more times, then a few more times, until the pacing and wording was just right. Then I'd print out that page and move onto the next 100 words. I was pretty much do-ing what all writers say not to do: I was doing final edits as I wrote. Yep, I was polishing one piece before moving onto the next. And there really wasn't any other way to do it.

You see, in the beginning I couldn't hit 100 words on the first pass. Usu-ally I would hit 183 words or 217 words then have to chop, chop, chop. Some of my best prose was axed in order to keep the story strong. As I became more ex-perienced with the flow of the style, I would actually hit 100 words about seven out of ten times on the first try. Which actually made my job harder because I would re-read the piece and realize something didn't work and almost have to re-write the entire thing to get the right flow and pacing and still hit 100 words.

I'll tell you one thing, you learn economy of words when writing a Drabble Novel! There really ain't no space for flowery description and exposition. You have to get to the meat of the matter right away and stick with it. Don't dilly dally. Every single word counts.

So, that's the nuts and bolts of a Drabble Novel.

I put my heart and soul into this novel and went a tad cooky writing it, but I loved every word of it.

I hope you do too.

Cheers,

Jake Bible
February 2011

PROLOGUE

Part One - The Virus

It would be decades after the restructuring of human society before records were found declaring that the virus that caused the zombie apocalypse was not the first. It wasn't even the second.

According to scientific records, there had been at least four earlier outbreaks of related viruses. Government organizations had been successful in all cases until the final virus. Prevailing theory was the virus's mutations finally outran the scientists.

The final mutation was all the virus needed to survive.

It is unknown how many people were spreading the virus among the world's population before the first carrier died and re-animated.

☠☠☠

It is believed that every member of the human species became a dormant carrier of the virus. Thus, every human that died came back as a re-animated corpse. No cure could be found, no recourse.

However, worse than the fact that people knew their body would come back as a voracious nightmare, was the discovery that a bite from a zombie would mean death and re-animation within 24 hours.

And that those bitten became contagious within twelve hours, infecting friends, family, co-workers, anyone they in turn bit.

And bite, they did. No exceptions, no remorse, no reasoning.

Madness was unleashed.

☠☠☠

Only one thing could be confirmed regarding the virus: everyone infected became a zombie.

No one was spared. No matter what anti-viral drugs were used, immuno-suppressants, gene therapies, nothing worked. Nothing even slowed it down.

Once the living died it took less than twenty minutes for the corpse to re-animate with only two things on its mindless brain: kill and eat.

Killing seemed to be its first priority. Feeding would not distract the virus driven undead from their need to kill. Too many citizens learned the hard way, thinking a zombie was distracted by flesh; thinking they had a chance.

The zombies the virus created were not shuffling, foot draggers, but active, homicidal, very hungry re-animated corpses bent on killing every human they could and feasting on their flesh. They were unbelievably strong and fast.

They were driven to kill, first and foremost. This insured the supreme dominance of the virus.

Feeding was secondary. And feeding on fresh flesh was the key. While never proven substantially, the belief was that the zombie was able to feed off the energy still stored. Old, decaying, rotten flesh was of no interest to the zombies. Thus they did not feed off each other.

The zombie physiology differed greatly form its original human form. No longer were organs needed for survival, since they could not digest or process what they caught.

All energy, all sustenance went into building and maintaining connective tissues.

While bones could not be reset, they could be healed, the break fusing and strengthening. Tendons, cartilage, ligaments and muscle could be rebuilt and re-grown. As long as the zombie fed, the zombie stayed fit and deadly.

This was another triumph of the virus. It gave the zombies a sense of self, a reason to fight, to kill, to feed. To survive.

The virus learned and encouraged learning.

It had the potential to allow its victims, the zombie hordes, to process, store and analyze information. It was a stripped down, simplistic way of reasoning, but the zombies could think and learn.

They learned to hunt in packs. They learned to split up, to surround their prey, to actively catch their victims instead of just running them down.

They learned to listen, to smell, to watch.

They learned to be predators, not just scavengers.

Worst of all, they learned their limitations and adjusted accordingly.

The fast pursued, the slow waited, the broken hid.

***

The speed with which the virus took control of a dead body astonished the doctors and researchers assigned to find the cure. In minutes their test subjects would go from corpse to zombie, ready to kill, eat and kill some more.

Too many lab assistants and eminent scientists lost their lives by underestimating the power and scope of the virus. Soon many of the researchers became the researched. Their re-animated corpses dissected and studied using protocols and procedures they themselves had created.

By the time the virus was isolated nearly half the world's population had succumbed.

The other half cowered.

Part Two - Society Re-born

Population centers were the first to go. The density of people made it impossible to control the spread of the virus. Within months both the East and West coasts were lost.

Communication with Europe, Asia, the Middle East and other world regions soon amounted to sporadic info bursts from short wave stations. Eventually, those too ceased.

The seat of power was moved to deep within the Colorado Rockies. What was NORAD became the United Defense Council.

The UDC hunkered down and waited, issuing surgical, tactical strikes to the former great cities of the nation.

Most of the country became uninhabitable.

💀💀💀

Nuclear cleansing was the only option for many population centers. Up and down the East and West coast, and places in between, cities were laid to waste, their poison scoured from the planet.

New York, LA, Chicago, DC, Atlanta, San Diego, Seattle, Denver, Philadelphia, Boston, Portland, Miami. All gone.

What was left of the country was called the wasteland.

For several generations, human kind became hermits, forced into indoor seclusion to avoid the toxic air and rains that swept through.

When they emerged and the rolling skies didn't produce boils and blisters upon their exposed skin, they found themselves lost.

💀💀💀

The wasteland: deadly gas clouds, acid rain, freak mega-storms, earthquakes, scorched earth. This was what the human race had to fight through to survive.

Before the city/states, many survivors lived in caves; burrowed under buildings, adding basement levels as needed; found sanctuaries in the mountains.

Even fighting for their lives, they still fought to preserve history and society.

When they did emerge, they brought their memories with them. But, those memories were just that, memories. Not instructions, not plans, not a future.

The UDC gave them all of that.

And for their trouble, the UDC only asked for complete loyalty.

Human civilization and society had never been about money, race, gender, looks or even power. It had always been about class.

When society finally started to pull itself back together after the first dark years of the zombie virus, it pulled itself along class lines.

Small city/states formed, walls went up, armaments placed. It became the battle of the urban vs. the rural all over again.

Once those left outside realized they had been abandoned, it was almost too late.

Some pockets survived, but most didn't.

The brutal took control and ruled.

As much inside the walls as outside them.

Frontier Town. Adventure Land. Six Flags. Windy City. Foggy Bottom.

These were the city/states left under UDC control.

Each had its own set of laws, ruling structures, police/security forces, judicial systems. Each survived alone, on their own resources and the energies of their respective populations. But, the final word on all matters of survival came from the UDC. They had the troops, the guns, the bombs, the technology to effectively hold back the zombies roaming the wasteland.

There were many more city/states at one time, but most ignored the UDC, choosing to make their own way.

They chose certain death.

Even with the small size of the city/states, all it took was one or two deceased to get over looked and an epidemic quickly spread within the walls.

The Reaper chip became a necessity for human survival. And the UDC controlled the chip's application with an iron fist.

Thus the UDC ignored the rural survivor pockets and focused on the main centers of population. This left the survivors on the outside of the walls to fend for themselves, to develop their own warning systems and protocols.

Mix rural fear with religious zealotry and a new scourge was born: the Cults.

☠☠☠

Basic trade routes were established quickly between the city/states, each sending out heavily armed convoys through the wasteland that separated human society.

In the beginning, the losses that resulted from these trading expeditions were worth it. Resources were scarce and each city/state seemed to have many strengths, but no single city/state could provide everything for its populace.

However, once the Cults figured out the armed convoys' trade schedules, the losses soon outweighed any benefits. Communication and physical trade between the city/states dwindled until each became their own self-sufficient fiefdom.

Those that dared to trade did so at their own risk.

☠☠☠

The Cults only believed their people should be allowed to live. All others were heathens and infidels; the very reason the virus was brought upon humanity.

Those survivors that were unfortunate enough to cross paths with the Cults met with ends some said were a million times worse than being eaten alive by a horde of zombies.

Tales of vivisection, cannibalism, being burnt alive, weeks of rape and mutilation, were spread through the slow grapevine that worked the land. Often by the time a message reached a small group, it was too late to flee; the Cults were upon them.

PART THREE - WARNINGS AND WEAPONS

The UDC realized they needed two things to survive: better warning and better weapons.

They already had the weapons. Technology that was on the drawing board before the zombie apocalypse decimated the earth, was still viable. The mechs. Massive, armored combat robots designed to fit around a human pilot and mimic the pilot's every move and action. However, there were design flaws with the control interface.

Developing the warning wasn't very hard. The Reaper chip came about in a burst of brilliance.

That same burst of brilliance showed the chip to be the answer to the mech pilots' control issues.

The beauty of the zombie hordes was once they ran out of food they simply starved to death. This allowed the human race to bounce back from almost certain extinction.

The virus, however, did not die with the re-animated corpses. It floated in the air, waiting for the living to expire and provide the perfect host. It was a patient, indestructible virus.

Once the Reaper chip was invented and implanted in every living person, humanity had an early warning system. Trackers locked onto the recently deceased and squads dispatched to dispose of the threat.

But nothing is ever that simple.

The Reaper chip was to be the saving grace of the human race. It was to solve all of the unreported deaths, the overlooked, the lost, the underbelly.

But, that wasn't to be.

In theory, a person died and their Reaper chip activated, alerting the authorities. It also sent a lethal shock to the cerebral cortex, frying the brain and adding another safeguard that the dearly departed stayed dearly departed.

But, in order for mech pilots to connect with their mech's computer, they needed that feature disabled.

Eventually, it was and the door for the dead mechs was opened. Wide.

The mechs came online ten years after the Reaper chip. They were almost a direct extension of that technology, working on the same principal of cerebral and computer integration.

The first mech pilot died a quick, painful death, his cerebellum frying like an oyster in hot oil. It was chalked up to equipment failure.

The second mech pilot died screaming into his com that his "brain is on fucking fire!". His eyeballs melted in his head, while grey matter oozed from his ears.

The scientists and engineers went back to the drawing board. The UDC waited patiently for their army.

☠☠☠

Try as they might, none of the scientists or programmers could retain the Reaper chips' brain frying features and allow it to fully connect with the mech's computer systems without killing the pilots.

They finally had to face the fact that the feature would need to be disabled, still allowing the pilots' vital signs to be monitored and tracking signature to be located, but no longer capable of administering a final brain death.

A single assistant composed a memo about the possible risks of pilot death while still connected to their mech.

The assistant soon became a silent test subject.

☠☠☠

A mech and its pilot were designed to be one organism. The mech's AI and the pilot's consciousness were to meld easily, allowing the pilot to control the mech without any delay or hesitation. If the pilot moved, the mech moved with it like a suit of armor, but with hydraulic assistance.

This was the worry of what would one day be called the Lost Memo: that the mech and pilot were too intertwined, too enmeshed, too complete. Mechs did not know the difference between life or death. A pilot was a pilot, whether living or undead.

Monsters were born.

☠☠☠

The day the mechs came online was hailed as the end of the zombie war, the politicians crowed.

No longer would humanity have to risk sending in hundreds of soldiers against thousands of undead, hoping not to be overrun and infected then turned themselves.

Now, just two or three specially trained mech pilots could take their massive robotic war machines into the middle of the undead masses and lay waste.

Soon battles were won in minutes and hours, not days and weeks.

Of course, it all went horribly wrong the moment the first pilot died while still operating his mech.

Part Four - The Dead Mechs

Essential to a mech's operation was a modified Reaper chip which allowed the pilot to have near complete cerebral integration with all of the mech's systems, creating response times of nanoseconds. The mech became a fifty ton extension of the pilot's reflexes. Pilots didn't think, they acted.

No one foresaw that a mech could become a fifty-ton extension of a zombie. And a zombie that was as hungry as all the rest, except now equipped with city leveling armaments.

Zombie pilots did not need to sleep or piss or ever leave their cockpits. They could hunt 24/7.

And they did.

☠☠☠

The first observed dead mech was a berserker. The mech's former pilot, now zombie, raged as hard as any other zombie *not* strapped into a fifty ton machine.

It turned on anything and everything in its path, smashing, destroying, annihilating. It fired weapons at random, the zombie pilot no longer in control of its faculties, the military training lost in death.

And just like the zombies crawling the earth without mech armor, the dead mech pilot was hungry.

The need for flesh forced the mech to learn, to gain some control of itself. The metal golem was free. And starving.

☠☠☠

The dead mechs roamed the wasteland, searching for food. They could cover several square miles a day, where a zombie horde could only move so far, so fast.

This led to some of the smaller wasteland outposts, the rural survivors, to be taken by surprise when the mech approaching turned out not to be friendly, but instead hungry for their flesh.

Now a good, strong, reinforced wall couldn't hold out the horror.

Little communities had to abandon their hard work and search for others to join forces with, whether they wanted to or not, all for the sake of survival.

Part Five - The Ride And Arrival

Mech pilots weren't chosen for being the bravest, for being the smartest or for being the best fit. They were chosen because they volunteered…and no one else did.

That didn't mean that everyone that signed up was accepted. There were still minimum standards. Such as: physical ability, intelligence, resourcefulness and, most of all, sanity.

Sanity was key. They weren't going to let you be in charge of enough firepower to level a city/state without making sure you wouldn't actually level a city/state. Unless ordered to, of course.

So tests were designed. The biggest test: the ride to the mech base.

Once a pilot candidate was singled out from their city state, they boarded a train to the mech base. This train was designed to do only two things: get the pilot candidate to the base and use every tool available to break that candidate before they got there.

Once on board, the candidate was secluded in a windowless passenger car. There was one seat only, bolted to the floor in the middle of the empty car.

The candidate would be instructed to strap in and remain strapped in until told otherwise.

They would be left that way for 24 hours.

Most pilot candidates failed the first part of the test within six hours. It's why the train never left the station until the first 24 hours were up.

Movement and sound would be simulated, making the candidate think they were on their way, but at no point would they be communicated or interacted with for the entire 24 hours.

If they undid a strap, moved from the chair, begged to be let out or just flat broke down, then the test was ended immediately, they were thanked and sent home.

The majority failed because they refused to piss their pants.

If the candidate made it past the first test, then the train would start its long journey to the mech base.

This time the simulation was opposite. Instead of faking movement and sound, it faked stillness and quiet. The candidate would be told there was a mechanical issue and the train would be stopped for at least 24 hours, when in actuality it was moving at a steady clip of 85 miles per hour.

The candidate would be allowed to move about, to use the small latrine bucket provided and to eat from the ration packets attached to the chair.

For the candidate, the train ride to the mech base was a four day trip, no matter where they were coming from.

The first day they are stuck in the station, but think they are moving.

The second day, they think they are stuck in the wasteland, but are actually moving.

The third day, they think they are moving, actually are moving and are given every opportunity to relax and ask questions. The train's pilot and co-pilot are allowed to communicate with the candidate, as long as they stay on script.

The fourth day, the candidate thinks they will die.

The third day of testing is merely designed to lull the candidate into a false sense of security. Ease their minds and put them off guard.

Then they are hit with the fourth day, the day they die.

The train never stops moving once it leaves the station, but the candidate believes it does on day two and four.

When they are told the train has been attacked on day four, they feel the attack. Every last blast, ricochet and concussion.

They are watched. Watched for how they react, how they try to help and how they try to escape.

Once the train is in motion, the candidate will not be returned for any reason. They are on their way to the mech base and that is where they will be assigned and where they will stay.

Whether they become a mech pilot or not is the question.

The test is simple: if the candidate can figure out how to get out of the train car, they will become a pilot. If they don't figure it out or don't try, then there are plenty of other jobs at the mech base.

The fourth day weeds the pilots from the cooks.

On arriving at the mech base, the candidate is stripped of his or her name. They are known only as the Rookie.

Only one Rookie is allowed at the base at a time. This keeps the confusion down and also keeps valuable resources from being drained or wasted by Rookie mistakes.

Until they are given back their name, they are the lowest on the totem pole.

Even if they are training as a mech pilot, they are above no one. From food service to maintenance, the Rookie is the base's bitch.

Some make it just fine, some don't. Most don't.

CHAPTER ONE

PART ONE - INTRODUCTION & TRAGEDY

The traffic was awful. Jimmy hadn't moved more than a mile in the past hour, surrounded by cars honking, their electric motors purring in the hot summer evening.

His com phone buzzed and he casually answered it.

"Hey Sweetheart! What's up?"

"Where are you?" Michelle's voice was frantic.

"Stuck in traffic baby. It's Friday night rush hour. What's wrong? Rachel okay?"

"Yes, but you need to get home."

"What's wrong?"

"I just talked to my dad. He said we need to get out of the city right away."

Capreze woke with a start; thankful the nightmare didn't proceed any further.

🕱🕱🕱

The two mechs stood on the ridge looming over the valley below.

"You sure you picked up something?" Bisby asked over his com.

"Positive," Stanislaw responded, double checking his scanners. Nothing.

"Hmmm, guess we have to go down into that bake oven of a dust bowl and check it all out," Bisby grumbled. "You sure?"

"Yes, Biz, I'm sure," Stanislaw snapped back. "I don't know why you're bitching, this is why we're here."

"Yeah, but the Rookie comes in today. I don't want to miss the fun."

"*You* didn't think being a Rookie was much fun."

"Shit rolls down hill."

🕱🕱🕱

Chief Mechanic Jay Rind stood and stretched, his back cracking and popping into line.

"Ahhhhh, that's the shit," Jay yawned, turning to survey the mech hangar. He glanced at his watch. 0600. "Damn, did it again."

Jethro laughed, walking into the hangar holding two cups of coffee. "You fall asleep in here last night?"

"Unfortunately, yes," Jay replied, cracking his neck and taking the offered coffee mug. He nodded his thanks to Jethro and turned back to his workbench and the schematics lain upon it. Jethro sidled up next to him.

"That's some ballsy shit."

"Don't I know," agreed Jay.

"Where you want me Stan?" Bisby asked, watching Stanislaw's mech stomp down into the barren valley.

"Stay put. Keep scanners at full and watch for the ambush."

"Listen, I know you're the best and all, but I don't think anything is in this valley. We're wasting our time."

"Never assume, Biz. That's how I stayed alive this long and following that advice will keep you alive just as long." Stanislaw's scanners beeped. He checked the readings. "I just shot you my scan. You seeing that Biz?"

"Yeah...looks like some crevice off to your left. Hard to see from up here."

Mathew walked into the barracks, towel around his waist. The noises from Masters' bunk made him stop.

"Oh, for fuck's sake you two!" Mathew said, tired of walking in on Masters and Harlow going at it.

"Just...keep...walking...pilot," Harlow muttered between grunts.

Mathew swore under his breath, walked quickly to his bunk and grabbed his uniform. He turned and huffed to the barracks door, trying to ignore the lump of sweaty flesh that made up Masters and Harlow.

"Briefing in fifty, kids," he called back, walking into the hallway. "Don't be too late."

"OH GOD," was all he heard in response.

"Whatcha see Stan?"

"Not sure. This is more than a crevice. It's a fuckin' rift in the Earth's mantle. Jeezus."

Stanislaw set scanners to full spectrum. What looked like a thin opening to a crack in the valley floor, quickly opened up below into a massive cavern. A cavern able to hold any number of dead mechs. Stanislaw backed away, powering up his weapons.

"Hey Biz?"

"Yeah, Stan?"

"I'm not sure what I'm looking at here, but I think we may need back up." Stanislaw shot the data over to Bisby.

"Shit! That cavern's huge. Who knows what's down there…"

Capreze stood in the middle of the tracks, cup of coffee in hand. He watched the dawn sun lift over the far off mountains.

"Mornin' Papa Bear."

Capreze looked up at the mech to his left. The cockpit was wide open, Rachel's legs dangling over the edge. He lifted his cup in salute.

"Mornin' Baby Girl. You make this joe?"

"Yep."

Capreze took a sip of his coffee and sighed. "You have the gift."

They stayed silent, each sipping from their mugs.

Rachel looked to the distance, down the tracks.

"Rookie'll be here soon."

"Yep. Hope he's worth a shit."

"Coming to you, Stan."

"Stay up there. No point in both of us getting ambushed."

"Fuck that! How about you drop a couple plasma charges down there and just frag it all."

"What if it isn't hostile?"

"We're in the fucking wasteland! Everything is hostile!"

Stanislaw pondered this for a moment, but just for a moment. Proximity alarms blared in his cockpit, interrupting his deliberations.

"Stan?!? What is it?!?"

Stanislaw checked his scanners. He pinged a shape, large and moving. Moving fast.

"Not sure, hard to get a reading through this rock."

He aimed his plasma cannons at the opening.

Dr. Hecate Themopolous sat in her windowless office, head in her hands. She stared at the piece of paper laid out upon her desk. Tears welled in her eyes.

She sniffed and wiped at her nose, grabbing up the paper and ripping it to shreds. She tossed the bits and pieces into the trash, subconsciously wiping her hands on her uniform as if the message on the paper had somehow dirtied her physically.

Her door chime rang. She stared at the shreds lying at the bottom of her wire trashcan. The door chimed again. She quickly wiped her eyes.

"Enter."

The dead mech burst from the crevice, exploding chunks of rock in its wake. It quickly gained its footing on the valley floor, its one arm raised and glowing ready for battle.

"Jeezus…" Stanislaw whispered.

"Stan!" Bisby shouted into his com, powering up his own weapons, dropping his mech down into the valley. "I'm coming down! Push it to the left, I'll flank it."

Stanislaw stared at the dead mech, watching its zombie pilot thrash and howl in its cockpit.

"Biz, something's not right…"

"No fucking shit Stan! It's a deader with one arm, that's the definition of 'not right'!"

Masters tried handing Harlow the soap. She fumbled around, blinded by suds. Masters laughed, gripped her hand with his and carefully placed the slippery bar into her open palm.

"Thanks baby," she smiled, still blind.

"No problem your Hotness." He turned back to the water, letting the warm spray beat down on his chest. "You think Mathew was pissed?"

"Who fucking cares," said Harlow, washing the soap from her face. "They're all just jealous cause they ain't got their own fuck buddy."

"That all we are?"

Harlow stepped from her stream into Masters'. "No, baby, that's not all we are."

Stanislaw piloted his mech into a crouch, setting up the leap and slash move. He waited for his opponent to take the bait.

It didn't.

One Arm waited, watching Stanislaw, calculating the possible attacks. Coming to a conclusion, One Arm aimed its plasma cannon.

Stanislaw's eyes went wide; he'd never seen a dead mech react this way. His com crackled.

"Get the fuck out of there Stan! He's too close for you to dodge those blasts!" Bisby screamed into his ear. "I'm too far away to take him out!"

Stanislaw knew all of this. And what his fate would be.

☗☗☗

Capreze stepped next to Jay and appraised the schematics.

"You think this will work?" the Commander asked his Chief Mechanic.

"No, but I plan on putting hundreds of man-hours into it anyway," Jay sniped, never making eye contact with the Commander.

Capreze grinned and slapped Jay on the back. "That's the spirit! You need anything?"

Still not looking away from the schematics, Jay handed Capreze an empty coffee mug. "She makes it every morning and yet I'm always surprised what your girl can do with some ground beans and water."

Capreze laughed, took the mug and headed to the mess.

☗☗☗

The blasts came hard and fast. Stanislaw dodged the first wave, but couldn't side step his mech fast enough to miss the second wave. The concussion knocked his mech back 300 yards.

Stanislaw struggled to right his mech.

"Hydraulics on my left leg are out!"

"I'm coming Stan. Hold the fuck on!"

One Arm moved in, firing twice at Stanislaw, then whirled around, sending several blasts towards Bisby.

Bisby was far enough away to evade the shots, but it slowed him down, wasting precious time needed to get to Stanislaw.

"Stan! Stan?!? Jeezus fuck, can you hear me?!?" Bisby screamed.

☗☗☗

"Goddamit Jethro! What did I say about coffee mugs ON the schematics?!?" Jay barked at his assistant mechanic. "What did I fucking say?!?"

"Don't do it?" Jethro responded sheepishly, grabbing up his mug, leaving a coffee ring behind on the plans.

Jay smacked him upside the head. "Go double check Harlow's left hydraulics system, I think I heard a hiss when she docked last night."

"I already checked it," Jethro answered.

"Then go wash the fucking thing!" Jay roared.

"Wash a mech? Really?" Jethro asked. Jay's face turned beet red. "Okay, okay. Jeezus, calm down." Jethro stomped away, muttering epithets.

☠☠☠

One Arm blasted Stanislaw's mech twice more, sending mechanized limbs flying in all directions. The live mech's torso lay smoldering on the baked earth. One Arm turned its attention on Bisby.

Seeing the state of Stanislaw's mech and the dead mech's new tactics, Bisby stopped his mech and set blast anchors into the ground. He prepped the machine for full rocket launch, intending on sending the one armed abomination to hell in a million tiny pieces.

One Arm roared and charged. Bisby's blood ran cold at the inhuman sound coming from the dead mech's loudspeakers.

"What the fuck....?" Bisby croaked.

☠☠☠

"Hey Matty! Come sit here!" June called as Mathew finished loading his plate from the mess line.

Mathew glanced around, but the mess hall was empty and he was trapped. He slowly made his way to June's table.

"Mornin'," he nodded, fake smile in place.

"Wow, did you hear Harlow last night?" June asked conspiratorially. "She and Masters were non-stop."

Mathew laughed. "This morning too."

June's eyes widened. "Wow. Must be nice having someone all to yourself like that..."

Mathew kept his eyes down, preferring to look at the pile of yellowish synth-eggs, than to look into June's inquiring eyes.

☠☠☠

Bisby checked the anchors and set his mech into a squat, bringing its body to a lower center of gravity. He watched the dead mech rage towards him and braced for impact.

Twenty yards out, One Arm leapt, using its mini-rocket boosters on its legs for extra lift. It raised its arm high into the air.

Bisby, realizing what the dead mech was about to do, disengaged his ground anchors, hoping he could side step the falling mech in time.

Everything slowed. One Arm roaring, Bisby scrambling, Stanislaw dying. It all froze for a split second in the barren valley.

☠☠☠

"Man, I never get over how good this coffee is!" Masters crowed. "I mean, how do you grow something this tasty in the fucking wasteland?"

He plopped down next to Mathew and June, smelling of soap and smiling from ear to ear.

"Hey Baby? Grab me a muffin, will ya?" he called over his shoulder to Harlow, still in the mess line.

"Will do Sugar Dick!" she called back.

Mathew shook his head, but couldn't help smiling. Masters raised his eyebrows in mock innocence.

"What?" Masters took a sip of coffee. "Can't two bad ass mother fuckers be in love?"

☠☠☠

Bisby didn't make it out of the way. The impact of mech on mech was earth shattering. Literally.

One Arm came down just as Bisby had disengaged his last ground anchor and tried to execute a tight side roll. The dead mech smashed into Bisby's cockpit; putting the two close enough that Bisby could smell the rotted zombie pilot.

A massive crack appeared in the baked earth, opening the world above to the world below. Both mechs tumbled into the fissure, smashing at each other with iron fists, knees and feet. The darkness swallowed them, their battle echoing, echoing, lost.

☠☠☠

Dr. Themopolous walked into the mess hall. Finding Mathew she quickly moved to his side and bent down close. "May I speak with you for a second?"

Mathew looked at the other pilots at the table and then at the doctor. "Um, sure. I'll see you all in the briefing." He stood and followed Doctor Themopolous outside the mess.

He raised an inquisitive eyebrow when they were alone. Doctor Themopolous cleared her throat, glancing around to make sure they were unobserved. "You came from Foggy Bottom, right?"

"Yeah...?"

"Have you heard from anyone there recently? Any news of any...problems?"

Matilda placed a kiss on his cheek. "Bye Daddy!" she said, skipping out the back door into the spring rain.

Stanislaw got up from his chair, grabbing an umbrella and followed his daughter. "Take this baby."

"Awww, Daddy, the rain isn't going to hurt me," Matilda complained. "It's not like when you were a kid."

Stanislaw smiled. "It'll make your old man feel better."

Matilda laughed and reached out. Before she could grasp the umbrella her skin started to melt from her arm. She screamed, so did Stanislaw.

He was still screaming when he came to in his burning cockpit.

"What are you doing?" Jay called up to Jethro.

"I finished washing Harlow's mech and I'm working on the Rookie's mech. That's what you wanted, right?"

Jay closed his eyes and pinched the bridge of his nose. "No, what I wanted was for *me* to work on the Rookie's mech. I'm just going to have to go back over all of your work to make sure it's right."

"Fuck you, Rind," Jethro barked, lowering the lift to the ground. He handed Jay his span-wrench. "You really need to start sleeping in a bunk. You're a grouchy bitch in the morning."

A mech hand crested the newly formed crevice's side, struggling for purchase. The giant alloy fingers dug into the edge, anchoring them fully. With a groan of damaged hydraulics, Bisby pulled himself from the fissure, rolling his mech yards from the opening before standing.

"Stan?...Stan?" he croaked into his com. " Goddammit Stanislaw! Can you hear me?"

He was met with static as his damaged mech swayed its way over to the smoking debris that was Stanislaw's machine. He tried to bring up life sensors, but only basic navigation scanners seemed to cooperate.

"Shit!" he yelled, pushing his mech on.

Mathew walked back into the mess, nearly running into Commander

Capreze.

"You heading towards the hangar, Mathew?" Capreze asked.

"No, sir. Wasn't planning on it," Mathew responded.

"You sure about that," Capreze laughed, handing the mech pilot a full mug of steaming hot coffee.

Mathew took the mug, looking at Capreze, puzzled.

"Jay's thirsty…and in a mood. My time is better spent getting ready for the briefing, don't you think?"

Mathew laughed, "Sure thing, sir. I'll make sure Mr. Grumpy Pants gets his fix."

Capreze clapped Mathew on the shoulder. "Good man. Way to take one for the team."

☗☗☗

Bisby was close enough to see the extent of the damage Stanislaw's mech had taken. He gulped, prayed and swore at the same time.

"Stan?!? Come in man!" Silence.

Bisby switched on his loudspeakers, feedback squelched at ear shattering levels. "FUCK!" Bisby roared, cutting the switch. His already battle damaged hearing rang and protested.

He stopped and took a deep breath. Grabbing his binocs he peered down at the twisted cockpit below, hoping for signs of life. After focusing briefly he was rewarded with movement. Stanislaw was alive.

Bisby looked closer and gasped. He pulled the binocs away, tears welled.

☗☗☗

"Rookie arrives today," Harlow said over a mouthful of synth-eggs.

June straightened. "Really? Today?"

"Yep," Masters responded, sitting down with his second tray of food.

"Careful, Darling, don't lose that tight bod," Harlow joked.

"Don't you worry, Babycakes. It's all so I can keep up with you." He leaned in and kissed her strongly, then pulled back, licking his lips. "Mmmm….eggy."

Harlow laughed, sending bits of yellow flying. Jane recoiled.

"Jeezus, you two are fucking gross!" she snapped, getting up from the table and stalking out of the mess hall.

Harlow frowned. "What's up her twat?"

"Nothing, that's the problem."

Stanislaw could smell the acid from the fuel cells. His mech was down hard.

He tried to reach for the strap release, but his right arm wouldn't cooperate. He didn't want to look, but knew he only had moments to get his ass out.

He pissed himself when he saw his arm two feet away, wedged between hatch brackets.

The cockpit shook violently. The dead mech was on him and Stanislaw wept as he wrenched the pistol from its holster and put the barrel to his head.

A hulking shadow of death fell over him as he pulled the trigger.

Jay jumped when Mathew sat down next to him. Closing his eyes, he took two deep breaths. "Don't you pilots have a rec room to go play in?"

Mathew laughed, offering the mug of coffee. "You want this or not?"

"Thanks," Jay sighed, taking a sip from the mug.

Mathew studied the schematics, then pointed at the coffee ring. "If that works it'll change the entire battle landscape. The deaders won't stand a chance."

Jay glared at Mathew, daggers for eyes. Mathew drew back. "What? It's fucking genius."

Jay followed Mathew's gaze and saw what he did. It was genius.

Wrenching at his straps, Bisby tried to free himself from his cockpit, hoping he could reach Stanislaw in time.

"Stan! No! It's me! Don't shoot!" he screamed. "IT'S ME!!!!!"

The pistol shot rang out, seeming insignificant compared to the cacophony of battle only minutes before.

"NOOOOOOOOOOOOOOOO!!!!!!!" Bisby roared, pounding his fists against his cockpit's frame until they were cracked and bleeding.

Slowly, fearfully, Bisby lifted his binocs, looking down at Stanislaw's wrecked mech. It took him a second to focus, but when he did, he wished he hadn't.

Bisby prayed some day he could erase that image from his memory.

Masters and Harlow left the mess hall, grabbing at each other and laughing. Harlow stumbled, tripping them both up and they crashed to the hall floor. She quickly took advantage and pinned Masters, straddling his hips with hers, slowly rocking back and forth.

Masters licked his lips and let out a playful growl. Harlow leaned down, nuzzling against his neck.

"Careful what you start," Masters warned, his breath coming in short gasps as Harlow nibbled at his ear.

"Think we have time for a quick one before the briefing?" Harlow asked.

"No. You don't," Capreze said, stepping past them both.

☠☠☠

Using all his skill as a mech pilot, Bisby carefully pulled apart Stanislaw's cockpit, exposing the body of his mentor and friend.

The colossal hands lifted Stanislaw's body away from the wreckage and into the air. Bringing the body to eye level, Bisby said his silent goodbyes, then deposited the corpse in an auxiliary cargo pocket.

Bisby turned his mech 360 degrees, trying to get his bearings, not trusting the minimal info his navigation scanners were giving him.

He spotted the ridge and pushed his crippled mech in that direction. The direction of the mech base. The direction of home.

☠☠☠

"Okay, everyone settle down," Commander Capreze said. "Let's get through this as fast as possible and get on our way."

The mech pilots grabbed a seat, ready for the daily briefing. Capreze sipped at his coffee, glanced at his tablet then started in.

"Alright… Only real order for the day is to keep an eye on Balsam Ridge. Harlow noticed some activity out there yesterday and we should probably keep a watch on it. Harlow?"

"Nothing, really. Just some Rancher movement. They didn't engage, so I didn't either, but they watched my ass the whole time."

"Okay, next quick item…"

☠☠☠

Bisby pushed his mech as fast as he could without the thing falling apart. He knew the damage was bad since he couldn't engage the motor drive; he was walking the thing in to the base. Even with the hydraulics working, the long trek was starting to take its toll on Bisby's legs.

Off to his right he caught movement. He tried activating scanners, but they were shot. He was walking blind, a 50-ton target with a living meal in the cockpit and a quickly putrefying corpse in the auxiliary cargo pocket. He raised his binocs.

"Fucking great," he muttered.

Downing the last of his coffee, Jay rubbed his eyes and pushed away from his worktable. "That might actually work..." he muttered. "But first, some real work."

He crossed the hangar to a partially dismantled mech, grabbing a span-hammer on the way. He surveyed the mech, taking in the wounded behemoth.

Nodding to himself he raised the span-hammer, took aim and whacked the mech in a junction point just above its ankle. He listened carefully then whacked it again. This time he smiled and tossed the span-hammer aside.

"Jethro! Put this heap back together! Try not to fuck it up!"

Bisby watched the wave of zombies crest the hill and swarm towards him. There must have been hundreds.

"Jeezus fuck! Where did they all come from!?!" he cursed aloud.

He tried to outrun them, but his mech was not cooperating. Accepting the inevitable, Bisby double checked his weapons, turned and made a stand.

When the front of the undead horde was fifty yards out he fired up the 50mms. Scorching hot lead ripped through dead flesh, painting the wasteland grey and black.

"DIE ALL YOU MOTHER FUCKERS!!!!!" he screamed in his cockpit.

Row upon row of zombies fell, finally dead.

"Need a hand," Jethro asked, his grin filling his voice.

Jay struggled with the six cables he had hopelessly tangled around his legs. Jethro just watched him, eyebrows raised, waiting for Jay to give in.

Within seconds, Jay's shoulders slumped in defeat. "Yes."

"Yes, what?" Jethro asked enjoying Jay's torture.

"Yes, you can help me," Jay growled.

"What's the magic word?"

Jay whirled on Jethro, intending to throttle him, but his feet stuck solid and he lost his balance.

Jethro smirked and offered his hand. Jay slapped it away. Jethro offered it again, unfazed.

Jay gave up and laughed. "Thanks."

☠☠☠

The right 50mm overheated within minutes. Bisby watched it redline and swore as the gun froze up, metal fusing. He flipped switches, sending all available ammunition to the left gun without stopping the flow of bullets aimed at the overwhelming zombie masses only yards away.

Unbelievably a few zombies made it past his onslaught, climbing his mech's legs, fighting to get at the flesh taunting them above.

Bisby agilely picked off the zombies, flinging each against the ground, pulverizing them.

Eyes manic, Bisby grinned wickedly, forgetting his loss and remembering why he had always dreamed of being a mech pilot.

☠☠☠

Jay settled into the cockpit, secured his limbs and powered up the mech.

"So when do I get to do that?" Jethro asked over the com.

"When you become Chief Mechanic," Jay responded. "Only the Commander, the pilots and the Chief Mechanic have their Reaper chips altered. You know that."

"Yeah, but you know how things are way out here in the waste. Can't rules be bent, just a little?"

"Fuck that! Last thing I need is your zombie ass coming after me. I like your chip just the way it is."

Smoke poured from the mech's control panels.

"Fuck!"

☠☠☠

"Fuck this," Bisby muttered. He started flipping switches across his weapons array.

He emptied the 50mm, started in with the plasma cannons, tossed in some plasma charges, fractal grenades and a little home made napalm Jay was kind enough to fit his mech with.

75 seconds was all that passed before movement ceased on the valley floor.

The already barren terrain was now a blackened hell, littered with smoldering zombie husks.

Bisby would have laid waste to God Himself if He had been unlucky enough to be present. That wasn't an issue; Bisby had a bone to pick with God.

☻☻☻

Commander Capreze ended the briefing, dismissing the pilots to their respective duties. Mathew hung back waiting for the others to leave then approached Capreze.

"Yes, Mathew?" Capreze asked, looking up from his tablet.

"Has Doc Themopolous talked to you about Foggy Bottom?" Mathew asked.

"No, why?"

"Not sure. She asked me if I'd heard anything from there in a while. She wouldn't go into details, but, I don't know, her tone was off."

"How so?"

"More fear than worry. When did we trade with them last?"

"Not sure, check the requisitions. Let me know what you find out."

"Sure thing."

☻☻☻

Bisby crested the ridge out of the valley and turned his mech to survey the carnage he had wrought on the landscape. His breath caught in his throat.

Sifting through the wreckage of Stanislaw's mech was One Arm. It tossed pieces of debris aside, hunting for sustenance.

Bisby raised his binocs and watched in horror as One Arm found Stanislaw's severed right arm, cracked open his cockpit and tossed the morsel to the ravenous zombie pilot inside. Bisby wanted to put his binocs away, but he couldn't tear his eyes away.

One Arm turned and roared at Bisby in triumph.

PART TWO - GRIEF & ANGER

Rachel sat up in her cockpit, instinct telling her to watch the horizon. Automatically she started to strap herself in and activate weapons systems.

She watched and waited.

Nothing.

Knowing better than to trust only her eyes, she dialed up the long-range sensors and pushed them to full spectrum.

Nothing. Wait… There, miles out, something moved. A mech. But whether it was living or dead, she couldn't tell.

Not one for drama, she didn't sound the claxons right away, waiting for a closer look and a little more info.

The thing wasn't moving fast, so she figured she had time.

☠☠☠

"Doctor?" Commander Capreze inquired, knocking lightly on Themopolous' office door. He waited politely for an invitation.

Doctor Themopolous looked up from the medical charts she was reviewing on her tablet. "Yes? Oh, Commander, please come in. What can I do for you? Feeling alright?"

Capreze chuckled. "Yes, I'm fine. I am here to check on you, actually." Capreze took a seat in one of the open chairs set before Themopolous' desk.

Themopolous raised an eyebrow. "Me...?"

"Yes. Pilot Jespers mentioned you were asking about Foggy Bottom. Anything to do with the coded communiqué you received this morning?"

Themopolous looked away.

☠☠☠

"Hey, what was the name of those vids we watched?" Jethro asked around the screwdriver clenched between his teeth. He pulled it from his mouth, stretching his arm past wires and pistons, trying to reach the right spot. "The Transmogrifiers?"

"Transformers," Jay responded, reaching from the other side, helping guide Jethro's screwdriver.

"Right. Transformers. Man, that was some cool shit."

Jay stared at his assistant in disbelief. "You work on fucking mechs! I'm pretty sure these are way more cool than that made up shit."

"Yeah, but they turned into stuff like boats and cars."

"Yeah, you got a point."

☠☠☠

Harlow stood below Masters' mech, manning the initiation console, going over the start-up procedure. She checked gauges, then looked up directly at Masters' cockpit.

"You're all set Pilot, go kick some deader ass," Harlow yelled. Masters cupped a hand to his ear and shook his head. Harlow clicked her com.

"I said, you're all set. It's the same thing I say every morning."

"I know, baby. I just like hearing your sweet voice in my ear," Masters cracked. Harlow shook her head, smiling.

"Get out of here, will ya?"

"Eager for me to leave?"

"No. Eager for you to return."

Mathew sat in the control tower, built decades before when the UDC expected the mech bases to be bustling hives of activity, mechs coming and going, troops being transported in and out.

Movement below caught his eye as Rachel locked her cockpit. The tower was insulated from sound, but he knew she was powering up full systems. Immediately he scanned the horizon, trying to see what had alarmed her.

"Hey, what's up?" he said, calling Rachel's com.

"Mech. Can't tell if it's a deader or not… You watching me again?"

"Busted. I'm off shift until after the Rookie gets here."

June walked into the rec room, hoping Jay had downloaded the new batch of vids. She grabbed some couch and flicked on the wall-sized monitor. She scanned the menu, seeing the same shows she had seen a million times. She clicked off the monitor, depressed.

She wondered where Mathew was. *Probably watching* her *again*, she thought bitterly. *Spoiled little mech brat…*

June stood up, anger and jealousy suddenly motivating her. *Fuck this,* she thought.

She stomped out of the rec room, determined to find Mathew and tell him how she felt. Determined to make him feel the same about her.

The bay doors opened wide, allowing Masters' mech to exit the hangar.

"Watch yourself out there," Harlow buzzed over Masters' com.

"Don't worry, sugar. I'm good to go."

"Not worried about you, I'm worried about your partner today."

"Rachel? Why?" Masters asked.

"She only sleeps in her mech! A, that's just weird. B, no one can get a good night's sleep in one of those cockpits. If she's fatigued, then she may hesitate when she shouldn't. Just watch yourself."

"Not to worry, baby. *I* slept fine last night. Rested and ready to wipe the wasteland clean of the deader menace!"

"It was personal," Doctor Themopolous said, still avoiding Capreze's gaze.

It was Capreze's turn to raise an eyebrow. "Personal? You don't really expect me to believe that, do you?"

The doctor considered what to tell Capreze; the Commander waited.

"I was looking to transfer. To get away from" –she gestured about the office, indicating the entire base- "all of this."

"Any particular reason?" Capreze asked kindly.

"No single reason. It's just, well…"

"The isolation, the fear, the violence, the desolation, the lack of any socialization beyond a bunch of mech pilots half out of their minds?"

Themopolous laughed, smiling weakly.

Mathew climbed the spiral stairs to the tower, having grabbed his binocs from his locker, preferring the exertion of the steps to the static hum of the lift. He clicked his com. "Anything?"

"Nope, still too far out for a decent scan," Rachel's voice buzzed in his ear. "Did you get your binocs?"

"Yah, I'm almost to the- Oh, um, hey June…"

"What's she doing there?" Rachel asked, a hint of jealousy marking her words.

"Hello, Matty," June said, her voice shaking.

"Hey Rache, I'll get back to you, okay?"

"Make it quick…Mathew."

"Ahh, come on, don't be like that…"

"That still doesn't explain why it was coded…," Capreze led. Themopolous' smile faded quickly, darkness clouding her eyes.

"It was from an old colleague of mine. He's Chief Medical Officer for Foggy Bottom…," she trailed off.

Capreze waited patiently. "And…?"

"And? Well, he has been seeing some issues with the Reaper chips. Some very alarming issues."

"He's reported these 'issues' to the UDC?"

"Well, that's complicated…"

Claxons blared, the base sent into full alarm.

Capreze jumped from his seat. "We'll continue this later, Doctor."

"Of course, Commander."

Capreze tapped his com. "Full alert folks, all staff to stations. Be ready."

"Approaching mech, this is Pilot Capreze, please respond," Rachel waited, but there was no answer. "Son of a bitch…"

Rachel fired up all systems and triple checked her weapons. She slammed her hand on the console, initiating the base's alarm and defense systems then started towards the approaching mech. Her com crackled and Commander Capreze buzzed in her ear.

"Whatcha got Baby Girl?" her father's voice asked.

"Not sure. Incoming mech, but can't tell if it's friend or not. It's not responding to my hail. Scanners say it's pretty banged up and power levels are low."

"Be careful."

"Will do."

"Listen Matty, there is something I want to say," June said sheepishly. "Something I've been meaning to say for a while."

"Um, can this wait, June? Rache has an incoming mech and I'm her eyes on this."

"No! It can't wait for Rachel!"

Mathew stepped back at the force of June's words. "Whoa, whoa, take it easy. Fine, what is it you need to say?"

June took a deep breath, she couldn't help glancing out the window, down at the mech, down at *her*. She let out the breath and turned back to Mathew.

Before she could speak, claxons blared.

"I wish it was more than meets the eye! Then this piece of shit could transform into a mech that worked!" Jay yelled at Jethro.

"How'd you get those vids anyway?" asked Jethro, handing Jay the span-driver he hadn't asked for yet.

"Thanks... Some chick I was banging before the dead mechs. Her dad was new media and had a HUGE vid library."

"Wow. Did he have that one with the talking dog and those kids? Shabby Sue, I think?"

"Huh... Don't know that one."

"Nevermi-"

Proximity klaxons shook the hangar bay.

"Shit, hope that's one of ours," Jay mumbled.

Masters settled his mech next to Rachel's. "What ya got?"

"Mech. Heading straight for us. Looks damaged," Rachel replied, engaging the drive gear. "I'm gonna head out there and intercept. If my dad sends more pilots out, then you come join me. Otherwise, stay back and cover the base."

"Will do," Masters responded, checking his weapons systems and firing up long-range sensors.

Rachel started to walk her mech away from the base. Her com crackled loudly.

"Hey! Where you going all by yourself?" Mathew asked, not bothering to hide his concern.

"I'm on intercept."

Mathew grumbled, Rachel smiled at this.

�☻☻

"Fucking piece of shit!" Bisby swore, smashing his fist against the com controls. Far off he could see the mech base, two mechs standing out front, just dots in the distance.

Having a landmark in sight, he adjusted his course, heading for the funeral pyre where he would deposit Stanislaw's body. Regardless of the state of the body, all corpses were deposited at the pyre to be dealt with immediately.

It had taken him a couple hours to walk several miles, but the last mile to the pyre was the hardest.

Bisby could feel the fatigue creep into his soul.

☻☻☻

With the motor drive in gear, Rachel took the opportunity to stretch her legs as much as she could in the tight space of the cockpit. She wanted to be plenty limber if she had to be.

The terrain in the general area of the mech base was smoothed and maintained, allowing the mechs to move fast when they needed to. Rachel kept an eye on her scanners as she approached the mystery mech.

Within seconds here computer chimed, letting her know it was Bisby's mech she was seeing.

"Biz? Come in Biz!" she hailed, hoping he could still hear.

☻☻☻

Bisby struggled to keep his mech going towards the funeral pyre. The hydraulics were quickly breaking down; he wasn't sure if he would make it to the pyre and back into base.

Bisby saw a mech approaching fast, but couldn't tell whose it was. He could give a shit who came to greet him, as long as they stayed out of his way.

In seconds the mech was close enough for Bisby to see it was Rachel coming to intercept him. He immediately launched three flairs. Red, blue, red. The signal that he was alive, but his com was down.

Rachel walked her mech right up to Bisby's so they could hear each other. She opened her cockpit and motioned for Bisby to do the same. He was slow in responding, but eventually he did.

"Where's Stan?" Rachel called out.

It was all Bisby could do to keep his tears in check. He wasn't going to cry in front of another pilot, especially one that he taught himself.

"Biz! Where is Stan?" Rachel called again.

Bisby pointed down towards the auxiliary cargo pocket holding his dead mentor's body.

Rachel's eyes swept down and then she squeezed them closed, quickly understanding.

Rachel hailed Capreze, trying desperately to hold back the sobs, but the second her father's voice came on the com, she lost all control.

"Rachel?!? What's going on out there? Whose mech is that?" Capreze asked, struggling to keep his voice professional.

Rachel couldn't answer. Blinded by tears and racked with despair, she stopped her mech, letting Bisby hobble on without her. Her chest felt empty yet unbelievably heavy at the same time.

"It's okay, Baby Girl," Capreze soothed, all thoughts of protocol lost. "Let it out, let it all out."

"St-st-stan..."

"You're with Stan?"

"St-st-stan's gone, Daddy!" Rachel wailed.

Despite the massive damage his mech had sustained, Bisby was able to retrieve Stanislaw's body from the auxiliary cargo and place it gently upon the concrete pyre.

He stood there, man and machine, man as machine, staring at a corpse that was no longer his friend, but just so much flesh to be burned, to be turned to ash.

Bisby let a tear fall from his right eye, but wiped it away quickly. He switched his gaze to the direction he had come from, making himself a promise he would find One Arm.

And destroy the deader or die trying.

☠☠☠

Watching Bisby approach, Rachel gave him a thumbs up and motioned towards the base. She hoped she was far enough away that he couldn't see her grief ravaged face. Bisby's mech returned the thumbs up, the metal protesting.

"Pilot Capreze to base, we're heading in," Rachel called over her com, using every effort to keep her voice from shaking. "Stanislaw's body has been placed on the pyre. We'll need to get a watch on it right away incase there are any zombies in the area."

"Will do," her father responded, back to professional. "Just get yourself and Biz back here."

☠☠☠

"Masters?" Capreze called.

"Yeah Commander?" Masters responded over his com, still in his mech, watching his sensors as the two far off mechs made their way slowly to base.

"We're gonna need a detail out at the pyre," Caprezez stated. "Bring your mech in and grab Mathew. I need you both out there ASAP."

"Sure thing Commander," Masters responded, hesitating slightly.

"Yes, Masters?"

"Whose mech is that coming back with Rachel?"

"Bisby's."

Masters didn't need Capreze to elaborate, he knew whose body he and Mathew would find out on the pyre.

"Mech returning to hangar," Masters called over his com.

☠☠☠

The two mechs walked back to the base, Rachel hanging back in order to keep pace with Bisby's damaged machine. Groans of protest, smoke and sparks escaped the battle-ravaged mech.

Neither spoke, not that they could be heard over the clanging and grating the mechs made. But even if Bisby's com had worked they would have remained silent. Stanislaw meant too much to both of them for either to keep it together if they spoke of what happened.

Rachel was patient enough to wait until they were back in the hangar and Bisby had made his report to the Commander.

☠☠☠

Half the base staff stood at the hangar bay doors, watching as Bisby and Rachel drew closer.

"Is that Bisby or Stanislaw?" June whispered to Mathew.

"I don't know. They're too far out," Mathew responded.

Jay came up behind them, appraising the approaching mechs. "That's Biz." He turned and strode back to whatever he had been working on.

"How do you know?" June called after him.

The mech pilots in attendance each gave her a look of annoyance. June bristled at their stares. "What? It's a logical question. They have to be at least 200 yards out."

All looked away.

☠☠☠

Everyone cleared from the hangar doors as Masters brought his mech in for docking. He powered it down and popped open the cockpit.

"Hey Matty?" he called down below, undoing the straps holding him in place.

Mathew, about to leave the hangar and head back to the control tower, stopped and turned. "Yeah?"

"Capreze wants us on pyre duty."

All heads in the hangar turned to look at Mathew, he met everyone's gaze, taking in their 'better you than me' looks.

"Gotcha. I'll round up the gear while you get your mech settled," Mathew called up to Masters.

"Thanks, man."

☠☠☠

Rachel maneuvered her mech into its previous post as Bisby's lone mech lumbered into the hangar.

She fought hard to keep the tears back, but it was a losing battle. She sobbed uncontrollably, wrapping her arms about herself as she rocked in the cockpit.

Her com buzzed and she struggled to pull herself together.

"Hey, you okay?" Mathew's voice crackled. She sucked back tears, choking a bit.

"No, Matty, I'm not," she whispered.

"What happened? Where's Stan?"

"I don't know what happened. Biz wouldn't say," she responded between hiccups.

"And Stan?"

Rachel squeezed her eyes shut. "He's on the pyre."

�☗☗

Jethro pulled his head away from the cockpit, face scrunched in disgust. "Jeezus Bisby! Did you shit yourself?"

Bisby climbed down the last few rungs on his mech's right leg, glaring up at Jethro. "Just fix the god damn targeter. I was shooting by feel, which totally wasted ammo and cut things way too fucking close."

Jethro heard the tone in Bisby's voice, knowing his guess was right; Bisby did shit himself. It must have gotten pretty bad out there.

"Everyone coming back today?" Jethro asked, ignoring the stench and climbing fully into the mech's cockpit.

"No, Jethro. They aren't."

☗☗☗

"Can you give me a ride out there?" Doctor Themopolous asked, approaching Mathew and Masters as they climbed into the waiting ATV.

"Sure thing, Doc. We're just heading out to keep watch on the body," Mathew responded.

The Doctor climbed into the back of the ATV as Masters fired up the engines. Mathew double-checked the auto-carbines' clips, stowing his and Masters' in the rack between the front seats.

Masters gunned the engine and the ATV burst from the hangar. Themopolous hung on, white knuckled as they sped over the earthen terrain, past Rachel's mech, heading out to the funeral pyre.

☗☗☗

Bisby let the water run over him, washing the filth from his body.

"Biz?" Harlow's voice called from the shower room door. "You in here?"

Bisby didn't respond.

"Capreze's looking for you," Harlow continued. "He's pretty pissed you didn't report to him before cleaning up."

Bisby sighed. "Tell him I'll be right there."

Harlow stayed put. "Did he suffer?"

Bisby tensed. "Yes, Harlow, he suffered. But only until he blew his own brains out."

Bisby shut off the water, grabbed a towel and pushed past Harlow.

Harlow slumped against the wall, slowly lowering to the floor, fighting back the tears.

The ATV skidded to a halt, kicking up sand and dirt, coating the pyre and Stanislaw's body.

"Jeezus, Masters! Show some fucking respect!" Mathew yelled.

"Don't even start with me, Jespers," Masters barked, grabbing his carbine as he climbed from the ATV. He offered Themopolous a hand.

"Thanks," she muttered, still shook up by the wild ride from the base.

Themopolous started towards the corpse. Mathew grabbed his carbine and followed, Masters right behind him.

"You worried Bisby was wrong? That Stan might come back?" Mathew asked Themopolous.

When the three saw the body, they knew Stanislaw wasn't coming back.

"I am positive that you know debriefing protocol is to see me before you shower, pilot," Capreze growled at Bisby as the pilot stood at attention. "The sooner you report, the less you forget."

"With all due respect sir, I'll never forget today," Bisby responded through clenched teeth, his anger barely contained.

"I do not doubt that, pilot, but that is not your call to make. Understand me?"

Bisby ground his teeth together, trying to hold his tongue.

"I asked if you understand-"

"I SHIT MY FUCKING SUIT SIR!" Bisby roared at Capreze.

Stunned, Capreze sat down in his chair.

Doctor Themopolous didn't bother opening her medical kit, she knew the cause of death. Masters looked over her shoulder, grimacing at the sight.

"Did he do that?" Masters asked.

"It appears so. I'd say cause of death was a self-inflicted gunshot wound to the head."

"What the fuck happened out there?"

"I'm sure we'll all find out soon enough once Bisby makes his report to the Commander."

"Must have been some crazy shit to take out Stanislaw…"

"Hey Guys," Mathew called a few feet from Masters and Themopolous.

Masters turned, raising his rifle. "Whatcha got Matty?"
"Incoming. Half mile out."

☠☠☠

Bisby, seated in front of Capreze's desk, lifted his head from his hands, eyes burning. "That's it."

Capreze, fingers steepled in front of him, sighed. "That's not good."

Uncontrollably, Bisby laughed. A short, harsh bark of a laugh. "Ya think?"

"What I mean, Biz," Capreze stood. "Is that the behavior the deader was exhibiting sounds frighteningly like adaptation."

Bisby watched as the Commander paused, then continued. "The zombies have some reasoning ability, but no impulse control. *They* don't hesitate..."

"Sir?" Bisby asked, exhaustion fighting for his mind.

"Hmmm...?" Capreze muttered, lost in thought.

"Stanislaw...?"

Reality ripped Capreze from his musing.

☠☠☠

"My God, how did they get here so fast?" Masters called out, placing a fresh clip in his carbine and taking aim. He squeezed the trigger, watching as several yards away three zombie heads exploded.

Mathew flung a grenade at the approaching undead, hoping his timing was right. Within a second the grenade exploded sending pieces of zombies high into the air. He looked behind him back towards the base. He tapped his com.

"Hey Rache? Sure could use some help out here," he said, staring at the unmoving mech still positioned by the hangar.

"Hey Rache? You in there?"

☠☠☠

"Rache? Rachel!" Mathew shouted over his com. Rachel pulled herself from her grief.

"What Matty?" she answered weakly.

"Um, are you watching this at all?!?" Mathew continued shouting. "We are about to get overrun here!"

Rachel shook her head violently, painfully. She checked her scanners and gasped. "Oh, God! I'm so sorry! I'll be there in one minute!"

She set her mech to full power, not bothering with the motor drive and began to run the thing towards the pyre. "Hold on!"

"That's the idea! Hurry please!"

Rachel quickly shoved the idea of losing Mathew also out of her mind.

"She's on her way!" Mathew shouted to Masters and the Doctor, barely heard over the concussions from the carbines.

"What can I do?" Themopolous yelled.

"Grab the ammo bag from the ATV!" Masters yelled back. "Pull out all the loaded clips!" He squeezed the trigger, more zombies fell. "Toss a fresh one to us when we call out! Fill the empty ones we toss back to you!"

Themopolous dashed to the ATV and grabbed the bag, nearly pulling her shoulder out of socket from the weight. She dragged the bag closer to Mathew and Masters.

"Okay, I'm ready!" she called.

Rachel's mech ran past the funeral pyre, not bothering to wait for Masters and Mathew to stop firing. Bullets ricocheted off the battle machine's frame.

Mathew, Masters and Themoplolous watched in awe as Rachel ran her mech into the middle of the dozens of zombies still left. Furious, she lifted her metal fists and smashed down, crushing the undead beneath her. She did the same with her massive feet, mashing the creatures into pulp.

Within seconds, all was still.

Rachel's chest heaved, then seized. Far away, Mathew's voice called to her, but it all went black before she could respond.

"Commander?" Harlow called over the com.

"Yes, Harlow?" Capreze responded, walking with Bisby from his office. "Whatcha got?"

"Looks like company may have followed Bisby."

Capreze glanced at Biz and narrowed his eyes. "I wasn't aware of that. How far out?"

"At the funeral pyre. Sounds like Rachel came in and saved my boy's ass, but…"

Capreze stopped, Bisby did also, waiting, not privy to the conversation. "But what?"

Harlow hesitated, "Well, sir, it sounds like Rachel may have passed out. Want me out there?"

"I want everyone out there. Get the transport ready and get the staff loaded up."

🕱🕱🕱

Mathew lowered Rachel's unconscious form to the ground, having just retrieved her from the cockpit. "Holy crap!" he gasped, slumping to the ground from the exertion.

Checking Rachel's pulse while pulling back an eyelid, Doctor Themopolous turned to Masters. "Your turn to help. Hand me my bag."

Masters grabbed the med bag next to the pyre and handed it to Themopolous. She shook her head. "No, I need you to pull out the injector and grab the small red vial in the side pouch."

Masters did as he was told, Mathew rolled onto his side to get a better view.

🕱🕱🕱

Jay manned the transport controls, powered up the vehicle and checked the instrument panels. "Ready to go Commander."

Capreze did a quick head count. "Alright, Jay, we're all loaded. Take us out there."

"Gotcha."

Capreze clicked his com. "Mathew?"

"Yes, sir?" Mathew responded, still sounding winded.

"We are on our way. How's my girl?"

There was a slight pause. "She's coming around now, sir. Doc says she'll be fine."

"Good to hear. Site secure?"

"Yes sir. Your girl took care of that."

"Excellent. We'll be there in just a moment."

Capreze severed the communication as the transport left the hangar.

🕱🕱🕱

Mathew helped Rachel to her feet. She wobbled a little, but stayed upright.

"Easy now," Mathew said. Rachel smiled at him weakly, gently removing his hand from her arm.

"I'm fine. I got this," Rachel responded.

"Take these," Doctor Themopolous ordered, handing Rachel two red pills.

"What are those?" Masters asked.

"Just some energy pills, they'll give her a boost and also maintain her blood sugar."

"Blood sugar?" Mathew asked.

Themopolous turned to Rachel. "I am assuming all you had for breakfast was coffee?"

Rachel nodded. "Just like every morning."

"Yes, well this wasn't like every morning, now was it?"

Doctor Themopolous and the pilots stood at attention as the transport pulled up.

The side door opened and the base staff exited, forming a semi-circle around the pyre. Capreze exited last. He placed himself opposite the semi-circle on the other side of the pyre.

Capreze nodded and Jay lifted a small bag labeled "flammable" that lay by his feet. He stepped to the pyre and shook the contents out around Stanislaw's body. Small briquettes tumbled from the bag and scattered across Stanislaw's corpse.

Jay stood back as Capreze lifted a torch from the ground and lit it.

Several sobbed quietly.

"This is an unfortunate tragedy," Caprese stated solemnly. He looked at each of the pilot's faces, trying to gauge which couldn't cope with their grief. "Stanislaw was a good man, a good pilot and a dear friend."

Some of the attendees sniffed, a few brushed away tears. Most stood stone-faced, burying their pain deep down. Bisby's face raged.

"Today we set a colleague free, we send his soul above and make sure his body stays at rest."

Commander Caprese lifted the torch to the pyre, lighting the briquettes and setting the platform and what was left of Stanislaw's body ablaze.

The base crew each said their goodbyes to Stanislaw as his body became ash and the ash became smoke, adding to the trillions and trillions of particulates of burnt, dead heroes already floating in the atmosphere.

When the train whooshed by, no one turned to look, no one cared about supplies and requisitions, news and gossip from the city/states or some dumb Rookie thinking he won the lottery and was on his way to glory.

No one could take their eyes off the now smoldering pyre and the scorched pieces of melted metal that was once part of Stanislaw's uniform.

🕱🕱🕱

"As per tradition and out of respect for our lost friend and comrade, we will walk back to base. Jay, you bring back Rachel's mech," Capreze ordered.

"Yes, sir."

"Sir, if I may?" Themopolous interrupted.

"Yes, Doctor?"

"In my professional opinion, I think Pilot Capreze would do better catching a ride back to base in the transport. Just to be safe."

"I'm fine," Rachel said quickly.

"For now, but I'd hate to have you relapse."

Rachel crossed her arms, setting her feet firmly. Capreze noted his daughter's stance.

"Understood, Doctor. But, *I* think a walk is just what she needs."

🕱🕱🕱

The Rookie stood and stretched as the train came to a halt. He looked at his bloodied hands and broken fingernails, barely believing what he'd just been through. His body was exhausted, but his mind raced, going over and over the mock attack.

The pilot and co-pilot had called back on the com when the test was over to congratulate him on a job well done. They both said they hadn't seen anyone figure out how to get out of the train car that fast before. Ever.

The car door opened and the Rookie confidently stepped out onto the platform.

🕱🕱🕱

Stanislaw's voice echoed through Bisby's fatigued brain. He shook his head violently, trying to dislodge the ghostly murmurs.

"You okay, Biz?" June asked, placing a hand on his elbow as they walked back to base.

Bisby didn't answer as he glanced sideways at her, his haunted eyes rimmed with dark circles. She squeezed his arm.

"Of course you're not. Sorry. Everyone's right, I do say stupid stuff all the time," June said. "I'm here, though, if you need to talk."

Bisby smiled wanly and patted June's hand. She smiled back and let Bisby move on ahead, giving him his space.

🕱🕱🕱

"Looks like a funeral," the train's pilot said, stepping past the Rookie.

"I wonder what happened," the Rookie mused aloud, shielding his eyes from the sun, trying to see into the distance.

"Someone died, genius," the co-pilot quipped. "Happens a lot out here in the waste."

The Rookie turned to the co-pilot. "Mostly mech drivers?"

"Pilots, boy. They are pilots. You get caught calling them drivers and it'll be your corpse getting grilled out there."

"Right, pilots. But, is it? Mostly mech pilots that die?"

"Listen kid, you need to learn that Death is everyone's bunkmate out in the waste."

"Probably not the best day for a Rookie to arrive," Capreze said walking arm in arm with Rachel.

"I disagree. It's probably the best day for him to arrive. No illusions as to what it's like out here," Rachel responded. They walked along in silence for a moment, Rachel kicking stones with her boots, the Commander staring at the base, his base, lost in thought.

"Have any idea who you want to mentor the Rookie?" Rachel asked, knowing it wasn't the most appropriate thing to say, but she couldn't take the silence anymore.

"Yep."

"And...?"

"You, Baby Girl."

Rachel nodded.

"Good luck, kid," the pilot said, shaking the Rookie's hand.

"You're not staying?"

"Nope," the co-pilot answered, shaking the Rookie's hand as well. "We're all fueled up. As soon as they all clear off, we'll be gone." The co-pilot motioned towards the group coming up the tracks. "We've got two days of wasteland to cover. The sooner, the better."

"Two?" the Rookie asked. "It took four."

The pilot laughed. "The test was four. The trip was two. Better get used to things not being what they seem out here."

"Thanks, I will," the Rookie muttered as the train's door shut.

The Rookie watched from the train platform as the base crew slowly walked back up the tracks, smoke from the pyre reaching towards the sky behind them.

The first pilot to reach him was Bisby and the Rookie stepped off the platform, hand outstretched.

"Hey, there I'm-," but his greeting was cut short by Bisby's right fist connecting with his jaw. The world spun and the Rookie took a header to the ground.

"I don't give a FUCK what your name is Rookie!" was the last thing the Rookie heard before his world went black and the pain became darkness.

CHAPTER TWO

PART ONE - WELCOME TO REALITY

"Well, you check out fine, but take it easy for the day," Doctor Themopolous said, setting her tablet aside.

"Wow...Did he hit me that hard?" the Rookie asked, still groggy.

"Bisby? No, it was the concrete steps that really did the job." Doctor Themopolous handed the Rookie a packet of pills. "Take one twice a day if you start getting headaches. If the medication doesn't help, come see me right away."

The Rookie pushed himself from the exam table and took two tentative steps. "Um, Doc?"

"Mmmm...?"

"How'd I get into an exam gown?"

"Don't worry, I've seen it all."

💀💀💀

"Welcome back to the conscious world, Rookie," Rachel said, extending her hand as the Rookie exited the infirmary. "Quite a first impression. You always fall down like a girl when someone hits you?"

The large knot at the back of the Rookie's head ached, but he pushed that aside and took Rachel's hand.

"I usually try to scream a little before I pass out, but I couldn't manage it this time," quipped the Rookie.

"I'm Pilot Rachel Capreze, you're new boss," she said, walking away. The Rookie hurried to follow.

"Oh, I'm--"

"You're the Rookie. Leave it at that."

💀💀💀

"I got it," Jay said, entering the Commander's office, not bothering to knock.

Capreze set aside his tablet. "All of it?"

"Almost. About a third of the data was corrupted, but I got most. Whatever happened out there we'll be able to see Bisby's side."

Capreze set his hand out. Reluctantly Jay handed him the small, clear disc.

"Thank you, Chief Mechanic," Capreze said dismissively.

"Really?" Jay asked, offended. "I spend all night fighting this data from an almost completely fried drive and that's all I get?"

Capreze raised his eyebrows and nodded towards the door.

"Ah, man..." Jay complained.

☠☠☠

Rachel and the Rookie stepped into the empty barracks. Rachel motioned towards a bunk that held the Rookie's pack. "There's your new home for the rest of your life."

The Rookie took in the room: the grey metal of the bunks, the foot lockers, larger upright lockers.

"Huh. Festive," he said mockingly.

"Yeah, well, we don't spend much time in here," Rachel said. "You're gonna want to get cleaned up. Showers are there, latrine is there." She motioned to two doors at the end of the barracks. "I'll be back in a few minutes to take you to the mess."

☠☠☠

Capreze switched back and forth on his tablet between the multiple vid feeds recorded by Bisby's mech.

The picture was rough, but clear enough to make the Commander's gut clench. He tossed the tablet onto his desk, leaned back in his chair and sighed.

A knock at his door brought him upright. "Enter."

Doctor Themopolous came in.

"How's the Rookie, Doc?"

"Mildly dehydrated with some minor cuts to his hands from the trip," she responded. "He slept nearly eighteen hours and checked out fine this morning."

"Good, good," Capreze muttered.

The Doctor eyed him. "How are you doing this morning?"

☠☠☠

The Rookie wrapped a towel around his waist and stepped back into the barracks. Rachel was seated on her bunk, waiting.

"You know, water doesn't grow on trees around here," she smiled. "Well, nothing grows on trees, not even trees."

"Sorry, I haven't showered in a few days."

"No problem," Rachel hopped off her bunk. "Hurry up and lets get some chow." Rachel waited, watching.

The Rookie crossed to his bunk. "Umm, is this a hazing thing or do you watch all the guys get dressed?"

Rachel laughed. "Boy, we all eat, sleep, shower and shit together. Get over it."

Capreze squeezed his eyes shut, trying to make sense of the recovered data.

"Commander...?" Doctor Themopolous asked, worried by Capreze's expression.

"Hmm..? Oh, sorry, Doc. What was the question?"

"How are you feeling? Same nightmare last night?"

Capreze chuckled. "No, new nightmare. But this one's real."

Themopolous narrowed her eyes questioningly. Capreze leaned forward and handed his tablet to her. "Take a look at this for me. Tell me what you think."

Themopolous activated the data, puzzled. Within seconds she realized what she was watching. "Is this...?"

"Yes," Capreze answered solemnly. "Watch the deader. I want your opinion."

Themopolous frowned.

Rachel and the Rookie stepped into the mess. All heads turned. Mathew, Masters, Harlow, June, each quickly sized up the Rookie.

"Rookie! Glad to see you awake!" Masters boomed as he jumped from his seat, offering the Rookie his hand. "Mitch Masters, best damn mech pilot in this base. Glad to meet you."

"Um, thanks," the Rookie responded, taken aback by Masters' enthusiasm. "I'm--"

"The Rookie," Harlow said, stepping past Masters to shake hands. "That's all we need to know."

"Really? You don't want to know my name?"

"Why? You'll probably die horribly tomorrow. What's the point?" Masters winked.

"Sir, I'm really not---" Themoplous started.

"Just watch the deader," Capreze interrupted. "Watch Closely."

Themopolous continued to watch the vids. Soon it was over and she handed the tablet back to Capreze.

"Well?"

"To be honest, I don't know what you want me to say…"

"What's your take on the deader?"

"My take?"

"Its behavior, the way it acted…the way it roared."

Themopolous gathered her thoughts then cautiously started in. "Knowing nothing of dead mech behavior…"

Capreze waved her off, motioning for her to get on with it.

"Okay. Without anthropomorphizing too much, I'd say the 'deader' was…mad."

☠☠☠

The Rookie grabbed a tray and followed behind Rachel.

"Okay, so nothing here is real. Just a heads up in case you're used to something a little more…" Rachel trailed off.

"Life-like?" Masters hollered.

"Exactly," Rachel smiled. "It's all good, it's just synth."

The Rookie perused the selections. "Looks real enough. I'm used to… different." He slapped a spoonful of synth-eggs onto his tray, added some synth-bacon and finished it off with a blueberry muffin.

"Oooh, not those," Rachel said, putting the muffin back. "Steve hasn't perfected the blueberries yet."

"Gave me the shits for a week!" Masters hollered again.

☠☠☠

"Mad? Which definition?" Capreze asked.

"Insane. Whether it was driven to madness or not, I can't tell," Themopolous responded cautiously.

"Driven? How do you mean?"

"You have heard the term 'driven mad' before, correct?"

"Yes, Doctor, I have heard the term. But, what does that have to do with this deader?"

Themopolous took a deep breath then let it out slowly and fixed her gaze on Capreze. "Any animal can go mad, regardless of its intelligence. But, to be *driven* mad…"

The Commander motioned for Themopolous to continue.

"It needs a certain level of intelligence. A *high* level of intelligence."

"Okay, so when does the hazing start?" the Rookie asked, looking around the table.

"Hazing?" Mathew asked.

"Yes, hazing. Y'all have been pretty nice so far, except for yesterday's run-in with...?"

"Bisby," Harlow helped.

"Bisby, right. Should I be worried?"

"Only if you don't want your ass handed to you," Bisby's voice growled from the mess door.

The Rookie glanced at the other pilots. Mathew shrugged.

"Let it go, Biz," Masters said.

"Was I talking to you?"

"Seriously? Grab some coffee and sit the fuck down, asshole," responded Masters.

Bisby glared at the Rookie then turned to the mess line.

The Commander paced back and forth behind his desk. Themopolous waited patiently for Capreze to collect his thoughts. Finally, he stopped, placed his hands firmly on his desk and addressed the Doctor.

"So how do we know whether this thing is just basic crazy or smart crazy?"

"Observation. Collect data about the thing's behavior, analyze the data and, well, make an educated guess," Themopolous answered.

"A guess? You want me to send my pilots out there on a guess?"

Themopolous' cheeks reddened. "Sir, I'm not suggesting anything. You asked my professional opinion. The course of action is up to you."

"So are the other pilots patrolling?" The Rookie asked.

Harlow chuckled. "Other pilots? Rookie, you're *looking* at the 'other' pilots."

The Rookie was taken aback. He scanned the faces around him, looking for the joke. He quickly realized there wasn't one.

"This is it? Just us?" the Rookie asked with alarm.

Bisby slammed his tray down directly across from the Rookie. "There is no 'us' for you Rookie." He glared across the table then smiled and tossed a muffin at the Rookie's face. The Rookie easily caught the muffin, crushing it slightly. Bisby smiled wider.

"Have a muffin. It's blueberry."

☠☠☠

"There is one other thing, sir," the Doctor said grudgingly.

"This should be good," the Commander quipped. "What else you got for me Doc?"

"A sample would be helpful."

"Sample?"

Themopolous looked at the floor.

"Come on, Doc, you're a professional here. Out with it," Capreze commanded.

"I need a zombie pilot's brain," she whispered.

"Are you fucking kidding me?" Capreze laughed harshly. "That's a little more than observation."

"And I need it intact," Themopolous continued.

Caprezez stared at her, stunned. "Of course you do..."

"It's the only way to be sure, sir."

Capreze laughed again. "Of course it is..."

☠☠☠

Masters laughed at the look on the Rookie's face. "Wow, you had no idea at all, did you?"

The Rookie shook his head in disbelief. "What, that the survival of human civilization rests on only us? No. That isn't how the UDC spins it in the city/states."

"Don't make me tell you again, Rookie. *You* are not part of *us*," Bisby growled. "Eat your muffin."

The Rookie ignored Bisby. "Okay, that'll take some processing. So, if *we* are all here, then who's patrolling? Doesn't there have to be a patrol out at all times?"

"EAT THE FUCKING MUFFIN!" Bisby roared.

☠☠☠

Jethro ignored the other sixteen monitors, his eyes darting back and forth between the four he was seated directly in front of. He deftly worked a large joystick with one hand while flipping switches with his other.

"Okay, let's see what we have here...," he muttered.

"Anything fun yet?" Jay asked suddenly, making Jethro jump and yank on the joystick. The images on the monitors shook violently.

"Jeezus Fuck! Will you please knock?!? What if I had Three on a ledge or something? It would be fucking pieces right now!"

Jay smirked. "How's Three holding up?"

"Just fine," Jethro grumbled.

In an instant the Rookie and Bisby were out of their seats and face to face.

"I don't know what your fucking problem is, old man, but you better back the fuck off," the Rookie spat, his voice low and even.

Bisby laughed. "Old man? You think you can take me, you little shit?"

"Yes," the Rookie answered matter-of-factly.

"Fine then," Bisby smiled. Before the grin left his face he brought his knee up, aiming for the rookie's groin.

The Rookie countered quickly, stomping his foot down on Bisby's, stopping the nut shot.

Bisby stumbled back.

"Oh, you're dead Rookie…"

"What is that?" Jay asked, taking a closer look at the monitor.

"That's what I was trying to find out," snapped Jethro.

"Okay, sorry. No panty bunchin' required," Jay apologized.

The two mechanics remained silent, watching the monitor. Suddenly something obscured the view, then the four monitors connected to mini-mech Three's feed turned to static.

"What the fuck happened?" Jay yelled.

Jethro checked a diagnostic screen, typing madly at his keyboard. "Fuck fuck fuck fuck fuck FUCK!"

"Well?"

"It's gone."

"Gone? Nothing? Check the homing beacon," Jay ordered.

"It's gone Rind. Not a blip."

Jay sighed. "We better tell Capreze."

Masters grabbed the Rookie as Harlow shoved Bisby back.

"Knock it off Biz!" Harlow yelled. "We're all torn up about Stan, but don't take it out on the Rookie!"

"Fuck you Harlow! Get the fuck out of my way!" Bisby roared. "I'm gonna fuck him up!"

"Try it you burned out fuckstick!" the Rookie yelled back.

"Actually, I say let 'em," Rachel said casually from the table. All eyes turned on her. "I've seen his file. Apparently our Rookie has some skills. Let's take this to the gym and see what he's got."

"Perfect," growled Bisby.

"Perfect," mocked the Rookie.

☻☻☻

Capreze stood before the static filled monitors. "Okay, so what am I looking at? I thought you said you had Three back online."

"It was," Jethro answered. "Worked perfectly."

"Okay. So what then?"

"Watch," said Jay as Three's last vid feed started to play.

Capreze watched impatiently. "Gentlemen, I have a lot to do today. This had better---" Capreze stopped short as once again something moved quickly in front of Three and then the feed went dead. "What was that?"

"Not a fucking clue," answered Jay.

"Weren't there any readings? Any proximity warnings?" Capreze asked.

"No. Nothing," Jethro answered.

☻☻☻

"Give the pads to the Rookie," Bisby snorted, knocking the protective headgear from Mathew's hands.

Mathew glared at Bisby, bent down, retrieved the gear and offered it to the Rookie.

"No thanks. Only reason I'd need a pad is to soak up all the blood this asshole is going to bleed," the Rookie taunted.

"Oh, I like this guy," Masters laughed from the edge of the sparring mat.

"Okay, gentlemen. The rules are--" Mathew started, but was quickly interrupted.

"Fuck rules!" Bisby shouted.

"Fine by me," the Rookie shrugged, cracking his neck.

Mathew sighed. "Okay. Fine. Have at it."

☻☻☻

"What about the other mini-mechs?" Capreze asked, irritated.

"They're fine, sir," Jethro responded.

"Which one is closest?"

"One, I guess, although it would take it about an hour to get to Three's position."

"Then get it going," barked Capreze, turning to Rind. "Can you make anything of this Jay?"

"Not a goddamn thing," Jay said, playing the vid feed again. "Alarms should have gone off whether it's mech, zombie or other."

"Other? What other?" Capreze's eyes narrowed.

"Human," Jay said. "Waster, culter, whatever."

"Just because you put an –er at the end doesn't make it a word, Jay," Jethro joked.

☠☠☠

The Rookie dodged Bisby's first swing, shuffling to the side.

"Dancer, eh?" Bisby taunted. "Too bad, I like the arts."

The Rookie laughed, batting away another jab and slapping Bisby upside the head.

Bisby feinted right then brought his left fist up in a powerful uppercut. The Rookie crossed his arms, blocking the uppercut and sending Bisby off balance. Using the advantage, the Rookie shoved Bisby to the mat.

Bisby immediately jumped to his feet, face dark red with rage. "Stop fucking around! Come on!"

"Okay," the Rookie said, landing a lighting fast roundhouse kick to Bisby's jaw. "How's that?"

☠☠☠

"Okay, sir, One has a new directive and is heading to Three's last position," Jethro said, pushing back from the mini-mech console. "Should only take about forty minutes to get there."

"Good. Keep me posted," Capreze commanded, heading out the control room door. "Let me know the second you find anything."

Jay and Jethro watched the Commander leave then turned back to the screens. They watched them in silence, each lost in their own thought processes.

"Fuck this shit," Jay said, stepping away from the console. "You want anything from the mess?"

"Coffee. Lots of it," Jethro responded.

"Can do."

☠☠☠

The Rookie stood over Bisby's prone form. He watched the stunned pilot struggle with consciousness then turned to the rest.

"Anyone else?" the Rookie laughed.

Harlow quickly unzipped her uniform, stripping down to her boxers and bra. "Looks like I finally have a challenge."

The Rookie's eyes widened. "I was kidding. I don't have a problem with you."

"And I don't have a problem with you," Harlow said casually. "But it's my duty to hand every mech pilot their ass. It's good for character."

"Is she serious?" the Rookie asked, looking at each pilot.

"Yes," they all answered in unison.

"Fucking fuck shit he's fast!"

The words from the gym stopped Jay. "What the fuck?" Coffee retrieval would have to wait.

The scene he walked into gave him a gut clench. "Oh, this isn't good…" He sidled up to Mathew. "What the fuck is this?"

"Hey Jay," Mathew greeted the mechanic. "Just blowing off some steam. Kind of a get to know you moment for the Rookie."

"She'll kill him."

"I don't know about that," Bisby said from behind them, an ice pack on his jaw.

"What the…?"

"Fucking Rookie."

Jay turned back to the sparring match, his interest piqued.

Jethro sighed, irritated Jay hadn't returned. He clicked his com. "Where the fuck are you Rind?"

"Holy shit! You have to come see this!" Jay's voice crackled back.

"See what?"

"The Rookie is holding his own against Harlow!"

Jethro shoved away from the console, instantly on his feet. "What?!? Oh, fuck! I'll be right there!"

He typed a couple commands into the keyboard, grabbed a tablet, double-checked the vid feed had transferred and dashed out the door.

Directly into Commander Capreze. "Um, Commander…I thought you were in your office."

Capreze frowned. "Going somewhere mechanic?"

Jethro smiled weakly. "Um, well…"

Harlow grabbed the Rookie by his neck, slipping around behind him, knocking his legs out from under him and slamming him to the mat.

The audible crunch of the Rookie's nose made the spectators cringe.

"Jeezus, baby, don't kill him before he gets his first mech," Masters laughed.

"Yes, Pilot Harlow, please don't. The paperwork I would have to fill out would put me in a very foul mood," Commander Caprese said, stepping into the training room.

"Commander on deck!" Mathew announced.

All but one stood at immediate attention.

"How is that different than any other mood, Commander?" Bisby quipped.

"Jay? Jay! Come in dammit! Capreze's on his way!"

"Yeah, I know. He's here already," Jay responded. "Thanks for the heads up."

"Dude, I tried. He blocked my com. I just now got the override in place," Jethro listened for a second. "Is it bad?"

"What the fuck do you think?"

"Mechanics? Please get off the com right now," Capreze's voice barked.

"Yes, sir. Sorry sir," Jethro answered, killing his com. "Shit."

He sat before the console staring at One's vid link, watching the mini-mech make its way across the wastelands.

Movement caught Jethro's eye. "What the fuck is that...?"

"Alright. I understand yesterday was hard, which is why protocol has all mech pilots stay at base for at least 24 hours after a loss," Capreze met each pilot's eye. "But, that doesn't mean you act like caged animals."

"Sir...," Masters started. Capreze held up his hand, cutting him off.

"I'll chalk this up to letting off steam and breaking in the Rookie. You all get a freebie." A collective sigh went up in the gym. "However, I want to see Pilots Bisby and Capreze in my office right now." Capreze turned and left.

"You too Rookie!" he called back.

Jethro switched from viewpoint to view point, hoping his eyes were just playing tricks on him. They weren't.

"Jay? You still in the gym?"

"No. Heading back your way," Jay answered over the com. "What's up?"

"You have your tablet?"

"Yeah, sure."

"Good. I'm shooting over an image. This is going to freak your shit out." Jethro waited a moment. "You seeing that?"

"Hold on," Jay barked. "Oh sweet fuckin' Jeezus with eggs..."

The com was silent.

"Jay? You still there?"

"Yeah."

"Should we call Capreze?"

"No. Not until we are sure."

"Fine. Should I pull One back?"

"Not yet."

"You are confined to barracks, Pilot," the Commander ordered. Bisby's face reddened and he opened his mouth to speak, but Capreze instantly cut him off. "I don't want to hear it, Biz. You know what you did. Regardless of what happened yesterday I need to know you can keep it together out here. If I have any doubts, any doubts at all, I'll ground you and put you on KP with Steve. Are we understood?"

Emotions swam across Bisby's face before settling on furious resignation. "Yes, sir. I understand completely."

"Good. Send in my daughter on your way out. Dismissed."

"How far out is it?" Jay asked, pouring two cups of coffee from a large thermos. "Is it close enough for a full scan?"

"It's been close enough for the last ten minutes. I'm getting nothing," Jay responded.

"Is there something wrong with One's scanners?"

"No. Full diagnostic shows them working perfectly."

"What the fuck...?" Jay mused. He handed Jethro a cup and sat down. "Let's try something. Does One have short wave?"

"Sure. All the mini's do."

"Good. Start scanning the bands."

Jethro typed quickly. Static filled the speakers then a high-pitched keening began.

Jay smiled. "That sneaky bastard..."

"Okay, I know you're mad, but--"

"Sit down Rachel," Capreze interrupted. "I'm not mad."

Rachel sat down, puzzled, having expected a thorough chewing out.

"How are you holding up?" Capreze asked.

"Um, fine," Rachel answered, confused.

"Stan was like family." Capreze closed his eyes briefly. "He was our only connection to life before this base. Now, it's just you and me, Baby Girl."

Rachel stood and crossed behind Capreze's desk. She leaned down and kissed him on the forehead. "No, Papa Bear, that's not true. We've got all those assholes out there, too."

Capreze laughed and hugged his daughter.

"Mother fucker. Jam me will ya," Jay muttered, furiously typing commands. He cocked his head and listened to the screech coming from the short wave. With a flourish he tapped the enter key one last time and pushed away from the console. "Try that bitch!"

The short wave signal immediately went back to normal static. Jethro jumped as One's scanners started picking up and streaming data.

"It's a deader!" Jethro crowed. "An almost dead deader. These readings show the zombie pilot has nearly starved back to death. And…"

"What?!?" Jay asked impatiently.

"The fucking thing is carrying Three!" Jethro exclaimed.

"How are you and Mathew doing?" Capreze asked Rachel.

"What? How? You…?" Rachel stuttered.

Capreze laughed. "Don't act so surprised. I am the base Commander, it's my job to notice these things."

Rachel snorted. "Well, good job, sir."

"How's the Rookie?"

"He'll be fine. I think he's a natural. *If* he can handle a mech."

"Well, let's speed that up. I want you and Mathew out on patrol tomorrow. Take the Rookie with," Capreze held up a hand, cutting off Rachel's protest. "I need to see how he handles the waste ASAP."

"Yes, sir."

Capreze smiled. "Okay, send him in."

Jay and Jethro watched the image on the vid screen. A lone dead mech was methodically dismantling Three.

"What's it doing?" Jethro asked.

Jay stayed silent then shook his head. "My guess? He's using the thing for parts." The dead mech uncoupled a power pack and stored it in its side cargo hold, confirming Jay's guess.

"Bump up the scans. I want more details on its vitals," Jay said.

Jethro tapped at the keys, increasing the resolution. Instantly the dead mech stopped what it was doing and quickly turned towards One.

"Shit. Did it just catch us spying?" Jethro asked.

"Wasteland survival depends on one thing and one thing only: clear thinking. Panic means death. Rushing means death. Moving slowly means death. Not taking the time to assess your surroundings, resources, abilities, and limitations means death. You must think clearly to get yourself out of the wasteland."

Commander Capreze stood, offering his hand. The Rookie, still at attention, looked at the hand confused. Capreze chuckled.

"Son, I only offer my hand once."

The Rookie quickly met Capreze's grasp.

"Umm, sir?"

"Yes, Rookie?"

"Is that it?"

"Yep. That's orientation. Good luck. You're dismissed."

The Rookie left the Commander's office thoroughly confused.

"Get One the fuck out of there!" Jay yelled, watching the image from One's rear vid feed. The dead mech was in swift pursuit, running all out to catch the mini-mech.

"I'm trying, I'm fucking trying!" Jethro yelled back, his right hand on the main joystick control while his left was busy trying to switch all power to propulsion. "Come on little guy, come on…"

Jay reached past Jethro and tapped at the control panel. "Is there enough power to fire RPGs?"

Jethro checked his readings. "Yes, but we only have enough to fire once, so shoot them all!"

"Done!"

Rachel was waiting for the rookie outside Commander Capreze's office.

"Looks like you're official now Rookie," Rachel beamed.

The Rookie frowned.

"What?" Rachel asked.

"I don't know. I guess I was expecting more," the Rookie said.

"Some rousing soul inspiring speech designed to make you want to fight for God, the UDC and City/State?"

"Something like that."

"Trust me Rookie, when you get out in the waste, you won't need a speech. Just keeping your ass in one piece is motivation enough," Rachel laughed. "Alright, let's go get shit faced!"

"What?!? You have booze?"

"Best 'shine ever made."

"Thank God!"

☠☠☠

"Fuck!" Jethro cried. "It dodged all RPGs! Now what?"

"Self-destruct?" Jay said.

"Might as well."

Jay keyed in the code. "60 seconds to boom time."

They watched as the dead mech caught up, grabbing One and flipping it.

"What's it doing?" Jethro asked. "Is it...?"

The deader held something between its massive fingers. They watched it toss the object. Ten seconds later a flash filled the screen and the dead mech braced itself against the blast. When the after affects stopped, it turned back to the camera and waggled a finger. The screen went blank.

"No fucking way," Jethro whispered.

PART TWO - MOONSHINE & BLOOD

"Operating a mech is only part of your training, Rookie," Jay slurred, sloshing 'shine from a steel cup as he, the Rookie, Mathew, Rachel and June sat around the fire pit about 100 yards from the hangar. "You gotta know how to repair the mech, salvage for parts and improvise when you can't do either."

"Yeah, yeah, but when do I get to smash shit and kill some...some... deader ass?" the Rookie asked, sipping from his own 'shine. "I'm fuckin' ready now!" The Rookie leapt to his feet then quickly sat back down. "This is good shit, Jay. Good..."

🕱🕱🕱

Doctor Themopolous inserted her security chip into her tablet. With a few keystrokes she unlocked the encrypted data sent by her colleague in Foggy Bottom. She hated hiding it from Capreze, but she was told to trust no one, not even the Commander.

She had needed to go over the information yesterday, but the unfortunate death of Stanislaw and the chaotic arrival, and subsequent medical needs, of the Rookie had put her behind.

As she perused the data, her eyes widened and she instantly knew why her friend was being so paranoid.

Dear God, she thought. *What does this mean?*

🕱🕱🕱

"What the fuck is this shit made from?!?" the Rookie yelled. "It ain't synth. Where'd ya gets the grains?"

"Oh, I gots my ways," Jay answered, exaggerating a conspiratorial wink. The Rookie furrowed his brow.

"Are you hitting on me?" the Rookie hiccupped.

"What…? Fuck you. You ain't pretty enough for me, bitch!" Jay laughed.

"I don't know, Jay. I've seen you with worse," Mathew joked.

"Fuck you Jespers! He ain't got no titties. No titties, no Jay love."

"On that note I'm going to pee," Rachel laughed as she got up from the campfire and walked into the darkness.

🕱🕱🕱

In twenty years, the nightmare had never lost its impact.

Commander Capreze tossed and turned in his room, sheets tossed aside, the bed protesting his movements.

He moaned aloud, trying subconsciously to rouse himself from images and memories he kept buried during the waking hours.

Capreze fought his own mind. And as with every night, he lost that fight. Was it guilt, shame, regret? Or had his mind been trying to tell him something? Something he couldn't grasp when awake.

He flung out his arms, trying to push the nightmare away.

With a cry he awoke to an empty room…

🕱🕱🕱

Retching sounds came from the darkness. "What is that?" June asked.

"That's Steve puking his guts out," Rachel answered, returning to the campfire. "He's out there somewhere. I heard him whimpering and then out it came."

"What, did you eat one of your own muffins?!?" Jay shouted into the night. He was answered by more sounds of throwing up. "That's right! How's it feel now?"

"Hey, leave him alone. Steve doesn't get out much," June got to her feet. "I'm gonna go check on him."

"Careful, it's spooky out there," Rachel mocked.

Mathew elbowed her in the ribs. "Be nice."

💀💀💀

"Nanotech? What is the UDC thinking?" Themopolous whispered, glancing around her office suddenly aware she didn't know how extensive the base surveillance was. She had to watch what she said aloud.

She tapped at her tablet, bringing up her side notes, adding notations as she analyzed the data. By the time she was finished she was deeply unsettled.

The UDC had been injecting citizens of Foggy Bottom under the guise of testing a new retrovirus, hoping to finally bring the plague to an end. With that cover story it was easy to find volunteers.

The truth was far more sinister.

💀💀💀

"Okay, let me get this straight," the Rookie said, leaning dangerously close to the fire, then back out again. "Whoa."

Arms around each other, Mathew and Rachel grinned at the Rookie. "Careful tough guy," Rachel smirked.

"I'm...doing...fine!" the Rookie drunkenly insisted. "But, wait, I have important shit to ask."

"And you're doing a great job there," Mathew chimed in.

The Rookie jabbed a finger at Mathew. "You think you're funny? Screwing the Commander's daughter make you think you can say anything? Huh?"

"Careful," Mathew growled.

The Rookie held up his hands. "I'm sorry, I'm sorry...that was rude..."

💀💀💀

"Okay, fine," Capreze said, finally accepting the inevitable as he got up from the bed and made his way to his bathroom. He splashed some cold water on his face, trying to bring himself fully awake.

Capreze stepped from the bathroom, grabbed his tablet and sat in the overstuffed chair in the corner of his room, the one luxury he allowed himself.

"So, let's see what the base is up to at" –he glanced at the time displayed at the top of the tablet- "0130. Sweet Jeezus...," he muttered.

He tapped the security icon and scrolled to the vid feeds.

☠☠☠

"So the UDC puts killing deaders and zombies before saving humans? That's fucked up," the Rookie said.

"It's not that cut and dry, but yeah, pretty much," Mathew answered, pouring more 'shine into the Rookie's cup.

"So what if, say, Six Flags was under attack? Where does that fit into the UDC's priorities?"

"That's different. I'm talking about out in the waste. It's kill or be killed out here."

"But what about all the survivor pockets? Don't they count?"

"As far as the UDC is concerned, if you aren't city/state, you aren't people," Rachel joined in.

"That's fucked up, man..."

***

She needed to get a response to her colleague, but Capreze would know right away if she sent a secure message, so would the UDC for that matter.

She pushed away from her desk, exhausted and frustrated. Then it hit her. She quickly grabbed her tablet and started a requisition order for medical supplies she knew they could only get when they traded with Foggy Bottom. Hidden in the order would be her analysis and reply. She would give it to Capreze in the morning telling him stock was low and was urgent that a trip was made right away.

☠☠☠

Rachel stood and stretched, dusting the dirt from her backside. "Think I'll walk back and get the ATV. Looks like Jay could use it." She glanced down at the Chief Mechanic passed out on the ground. She turned from the campfire and peered into the darkness. "Haven't heard from Steve or June in a bit. Think I'll check on them first."

"Careful. They may be having a moment," Mathew quipped.

"With the way she has the hots for you, I doubt it," Rachel scoffed.

Mathew rolled his eyes. "Oh just go be responsible or something."

Rachel blew him a kiss.

☠☠☠

Capreze checked the barracks vid feed.

Masters and Harlow were actually sleeping for a change. Bisby was crashed also. Mathew, Jane, the Rookie's bunks were empty. He expected to see Rachel's empty since she preferred to sleep in her mech most nights, but where were the others?

The Commander flicked from one feed to another. The rec room: empty. Mess hall: empty. Showers, latrine: both empty. Hangar: empty also.

"Hmmm…," Capreze muttered. "What are they up to?"

He switched to external feeds and quickly found what he was looking for. Flames flickered from the fire pit as Capreze zoomed in.

"If the UDC could give a shit about the people in the waste, then why don't they order the mechs to wipe out the Cults? Just fucking wipe them off the face of the earth," asked the Rookie.

"That, I'm not sure," Mathew admitted. "My guess is it keeps the gene pool fresh. I mean, how many humans are left in the world, do you think? Three, maybe four million? All the city/states combined equals only about two million people at last count."

"Nothing fresh about the gene pool with those crazy fucks," the Rookie muttered, anger tainting his voice.

A scream came from the darkness. Mathew and the Rookie straightened, suddenly considerably more sober than before. Mathew tapped his com.

"Rache? You okay?"

"Yeah, I'm fine. I'm not sure what just happened. I heard Steve scream…"

"That was Steve? Damn, he screams like a girl."

"Focus please!"

"Okay, sorry, focused."

"By the time I got to him he was muttering 'don't take my balls'."

"Is he hurt bad?"

"Yeah, he's bleeding from his thigh quite a bit."

"Shit. Okay, you apply pressure and I'll get the ATV and the doc. Where's June?"

"Not a fucking clue. Hurry."

"Will do."

Doctor Themopolous's head nodded. She shook it hard, fighting the drowsiness. She didn't want to go against her own medical advice and drink the coffee she had set on her desk, but she really needed to finish the encrypted message.

Her com buzzed, the emergency tone bringing her fully awake.

"This is Themopolous, what's the situation?"

"Hey Doc, it's Mathew. We've got a problem out by the fire pit. Steve's cut, looks like it may have nicked his femoral artery."

Themopolous jumped from her desk and ran from her office. "I'll grab my kit and meet you in the hangar!"

💀💀💀

Capreze debated whether to zoom in on the base staff, but decided against it. He could have easily focused the sensors and heard every word they were saying, even reading them off their lips if he wanted.

But, Capreze had made a decision years ago to *not* be that Commander. He commanded by trust, he had to if his own daughter was going to be one of his pilots.

He watched for a few moments then transferred back to internal vids.

I wonder..., he thought.

Capreze switched feeds to Themopolous's quarters, but the room was empty.

The doctor wasn't in.

💀💀💀

"What'd Capreze say?" Themopolous asked, tossing her med kit into the back of the ATV as Mathew fired it up.

"Um, yeah, we haven't told him yet."

"What?!?" she yelled. "Why not?"

A sheepish grin spread across Mathew's face and he avoided the Doctor's glare. "Well, there may have been some 'shine involved."

"Sweet Jeezus! Did Steve drink also?"

"Oh, he drank..."

"Goddamit! What are you waiting for?!? Get us out there! His blood'll be thinned by the alcohol. It could already be too late."

Mathew mashed the accelerator.

Hidden in the hangar's shadows, June watched the ATV speed away.

💀💀💀

"Doctor?" Capreze called on the com, puzzled as to where she would be at 0200. There was no response.

The Commander scanned Themopolous's quarters making sure he

wasn't missing anything in the dark room. A quick search told him he wasn't.

"Doctor? This is Capreze." Again, no response.

Capreze started to set his tablet down, but thought of something first. He switched on the audio feed.

"Doctor? Doc-," he quickly stopped, hearing the tiny buzzing of Themopolous's ear com. He zoomed in on the side table, easily finding the minute com.

Capreze narrowed his eyes and strode from his quarters.

☠☠☠

"So, you want to tell me what happened?" Themopolous asked as the ATV came to a halt a few feet from Steve's prone form. Rachel squatted over him, her hands pressed firmly against his thigh.

"Not a clue," Mathew responded, handing the doctor her med kit as she stepped from the ATV.

"Keep that pressure!" Themopolous ordered Rachel as she moved in to examine Steve. "I need light!"

Mathew sprinted to the ATV and retrieved a halogen. He shone the powerful beam down on Steve's wound.

"Keep that pressure dammit!" Themopolous yelled as she cut Steve's blood soaked uniform open.

☠☠☠

When Capreze checked base stats he knew immediately where he needed to go: the hangar.

He didn't know what was going on, but his gut told him things were off. When he stepped into the hangar his feelings were confirmed.

"Pilot Lang! What the hell are you doing?!?" he yelled up at June just as she shut her mech's cockpit. "Godammit!"

The Commander clicked his com. "June, you had better have a good explanation for this!"

Refusing to respond, June finished her start up procedure. Capreze dashed to the initiation console, but he was too late.

June was already moving.

☠☠☠

"Where's everybody?" the Rookie asked, blinking blearily at the fire.

"Over there...Steve's dying," Jay mumbled, splayed out on the dirt.

"Dying? Shit...should we help?"

"Help? With what?"

"I don't fucking know. Just thought we should…"

"You go ahead…I ain't helping with shit."

The Rookie pushed himself to his feet and staggered away from the fire pit. He could see a bright light shining just a few yards away.

"Hey! Yous guys need some help?"

"No! Just sit down and stay put!" he heard someone yell back at him.

The Rookie swayed. "Gotcha! Sitting down and staying put!"

🁢🁢🁢

"Alright, careful, careful…" Themopolous commanded as Mathew and Rachel set Steve on the collapsible stretcher retrieved from the ATV. "I said careful!"

"Jeezus Doc, were trying!" Mathew yelled back.

"He's stable for now, but he needs blood ASAP. If that wound re-opens before I get him in the OR he won't make it."

"Yeah, I know Doc! Careful, got it."

Rachel and Mathew walked Steve to the ATV and *carefully* set the stretcher down and strapped it securely to the back. They all climbed in and Mathew slowly set out for the base.

"Okay, Mathew now…"

"I know, Doc. *Careful*…"

🁢🁢🁢

June wiped the tears from her eyes.

"This is it for me. Everything is over," she said to herself. "No turning back now."

June walked the mech from the hangar, ignoring the figure of Commander Capreze waving for her to stop.

She pushed the sensors to full and scanned the night. She had no idea where she was going or what she was going to do, but she had to leave, had to get away from the base, from Mathew, from everyone.

Ignoring the motor drive she engaged her legs and took off at a full run into the night.

🁢🁢🁢

Mathew swerved to avoid the mech coming right at them.

"Jeezus fuck!" Mathew yelled. He tapped his com, trying to hail June.

"She's won't pick up!" Rachel yelled, having tried her com also. "Where does she think she's going? We can track her."

"I don't know, but she won't get far. Jethro was working on her mech. It isn't fully functional."

Mathew pulled the ATV into the hangar, barely missing Commander Capreze.

Capreze turned his attention from June's mech onto the ATV. Mathew and Rachel both blanched under his glare.

"Shit," Rachel said. "Let me handle this."

"Gladly," Mathew complied.

"Holy fuck! Is that a mech?!?" the Rookie yelled.

"What?!? Where?!?" Jay sat up quickly and looked out towards the pitch-blackness of the wasteland.

"Right there! Coming from the hangar!" The Rookie pointed and Jay turned around.

"Shit! That's June's mech. Oh, well, she ain't going far…" Jay yawned, curling up to the fire.

"Should we do something? Call the Commander?"

"Sure, Rookie, you do that," Jay laughed sleepily.

"But…" the Rookie trailed off.

"Buts are for asses, boy. Buts are for asses," Jay slurred before nodding off.

The Rookie watched the shape of the mech fade into the night.

"Okay, just listen…" Rachel started, but Capreze ignored her, moving quickly to the stretcher.

"How bad, Doc?" he asked.

"Bad," she said, jumping from the ATV.

Mathew rushed to the med cart and gurney stationed against the wall, expertly maneuvering both to the ATV.

"Grab that end," Mathew barked. The Commander's eyebrows raised but he didn't hesitate. "One, two, three!"

They lifted the stretcher, placing it on the gurney.

"What'll you need, Doc?" Capreze asked.

"I'll need Harlow to assist and anyone that's O- to be ready to give blood."

"I'm on it!" Rachel said, heading off to the barracks.

"How long are we supposed to stay here for?" the Rookie asked. All he got in response was the sound of Jay's snores. He kicked out with his boot, connecting with Jay's thigh.

"Ow! What the fuck?!?" Jay yelled.

"Are they coming back for us?" the Rookie said, irritated.

"Probably not," Jay responded, rolling over and going back to sleep. The Rookie gave him a shove.

"Hey man, I'm new here. What are we supposed to do?"

"I'm going to sleep. I don't give a Rancher's tit what you do. Just throw another log on the fire if you go."

☠☠☠

"What?" Harlow groaned as Rachel shook her.

"Steve's hurt. Themopolous needs you in the OR," Rachel whispered.

Harlow sat upright and grabbed for her uniform. Rachel handed it to her helping the sleepy pilot get her arms in the sleeves.

"Thanks," Harlow muttered. "Is there coffee?"

"Shit. No. I'll do that next and bring a thermos to the infirmary."

Harlow shook her head, trying to get rid of the fuzziness. "How bad is he?'

"He's bleeding from his thigh. It won't stop."

Harlow's eyes went wide. "That could be an artery."

She pushed past Rachel and sprinted from the barracks.

☠☠☠

"Get some sleep," Capreze ordered Rachel and Mathew, both starting to protest. "Sleep. Now. We'll talk about all of this during the briefing."

The pilots looked from each other to the Commander, Mathew finally shrugging and moving off towards the barracks.

"I'm going to clean up first," he said looking at his blood and dirt stained uniform.

"Fine idea," Capreze nodded, watching Rachel.

"I'll be there in a sec," Rachel said as Mathew walked off. She turned to her father, but the look on Capreze's face stopped her words dead.

"We'll talk tomorrow," he said. Rachel nodded and followed Mathew.

☠☠☠

"I know you're all tired," Capreze started the briefing, his gaze hardening on Rachel and Mathew. "But life goes on."

Mathew started to speak, Capreze held up his hand. "This is my briefing, Pilot Jespers. Hold your questions until I'm done."

Mathew nodded and glanced at Rachel. She avoided his eyes, choosing to keep hers firmly on her father.

"Now," Capreze began. "Harlow won't be joining us since she was in surgery until an hour ago. Which means we are only missing one person. Anyone know where the Rookie is?"

Rachel's eyes widened and she risked a glance at Mathew.

💀💀💀

Jay kicked the sleeping Rookie. "I'm pretty sure you're missing your morning briefing."

The Rookie groaned, tried to open his eyes, but thought better and sat up with his lids firmly shut. "What time is it?"

"Fuck if I know," Jay said, unzipping his fly and pissing on the barely smoldering coals in the fire pit. A steam cloud of urine wafted over the Rookie making him gag and fight to keep from vomiting. "But, you better get moving if you plan on living past today."

The Rookie groaned again, this time opening his eyes and braving the bright agony.

💀💀💀

"Um, no sir. With all the confusion last night we figured he'd come back with Jay," Mathew said.

"Quite an assumption. But, that wasn't your responsibility, Mathew, was it?"

"No, sir, it was mine," Rachel spoke up.

"Yes, it was pilot. We'll speak later. Let's move on."

Capreze lifted his tablet and scanned the screen. "Steve is going to be fine, but it may be a couple weeks before he's up to speed. Until then..." Capreze smiled. "Rachel, Mathew, the two of you will be in charge of the kitchen."

Masters and Bisby sat up. "No!" they yelled in unison.

💀💀💀

Jay tapped at his tablet and the slight crackling that the Rookie had thought all night was part fire suddenly ceased.

"What was that?" the Rookie asked.

"Security containment field," Jay answered pointing out small metal rods stationed several yards out. "Anything without an active Reaper chip crosses that field and every single external light on this base goes up. Not to mention auto-cannons, smart mines and a really, really loud alarm. You didn't think we'd be outside all night without protection, did you?"

"I didn't really think about it," the Rookie replied.

"You're a strange kid, kid," Jay laughed.

☻☻☻

"Those two? Cooking? Please, sir, you can't be serious? Why punish us?" Masters complained.

"If it's any consolation, I'll be punishing myself, also," Capreze said.

"Hey, I'm not that bad of a cook," Mathew said.

Rachel reached over and patted his hand. "Yes, you are Matty. So am I. Sorry everybody."

"Okay, we are all going to be shitting our brains out. Got it. Can we move on to the important shit, now? Like who is going to go look for June?"

"That would be Mathew. Unless you have some objections, Pilot Jespers?"

"Um, no, sir," Mathew responded. "Glad to."

☻☻☻

"So... How much trouble are we in?" the Rookie asked with apprehension.

"Us? I'm not in any trouble. You? Well, you are in a world of shit," Jay laughed. He tapped at his tablet: *Rookie with me. Bringing him in. Don't be too hard on him. Good kid.* He sent the message to Capreze and waited.

Within seconds Capreze responded: *Figured. Make him sweat, he's yours today. I want to see you both in my office ASAP.*

Jay smiled. "Looks like the Commander has given me your ass for the day. You're gonna learn how shit really works around here."

☻☻☻

Capreze set his tablet aside. "Alright, I'm done holding hands. Bisby, you're on patrol. Masters, you're on escort duty."

"Escort duty, sir?" Masters asked.

"That's what I said. I need you to shadow Jay and the Rookie to Foggy Bottom. Doctor Themopolous put in a med supply req this morning after surgery. I guess we are dangerously low on essentials."

Masters nodded.

"Mathew, you need to get out there and find June. Regular reports."

"Yes, sir."

"Pilot Capreze," the Commander turned his gaze on Rachel. "I'm pretty sure you have a kitchen to run. If that isn't too much responsibility."

☻☻☻

Jay and the Rookie walked into the hangar, both glad to get out of the morning sun. Jethro looked up from his work and started laughing.

"Well, don't you two make a cute couple. Have fun last night?"

"Fuck you, Jethro," Jay growled.

"Commander told me you two need to skip cleaning up and see him right away."

"Skip cleaning up?" the Rookie asked, shocked. "Man, I could really use a shower first."

"That's tough shit, Rookie," Jethro said, returning to the circuit board he was working on.

"Come on," Jay said, walking away.

The Rookie followed, his stomach nauseous.

☻☻☻

"That's it. Dismissed," Capreze said. The pilots quickly got up and left the briefing, glad to get on with the day. Rachel paused by the door.

"Not now, baby girl," Capreze said, looking down at his tablet. "Go get the kitchen running and I'll be in the mess later." He looked up and held Rachel's gaze. "We'll talk then."

Rachel smiled weakly. "Yes, sir."

Capreze watched her leave and soon followed, heading back to his office. He looked over the Doctor's supply requisition, knowing she was hiding something. Six Flags was closer and had better medical facilities for trading with.

☻☻☻

When Capreze entered his office, Jay and the Rookie were already waiting for him.

"Good, glad to see you took this meeting seriously," Capreze said, locking eyes with the Rookie.

"Sir, I just want to say…"

"Save it." Capreze sat down. "I sent you a med req. You two are going to Foggy Bottom. Masters is escort."

"Foggy Bottom? Six Flags is way closer and they…"

"I know," Capreze interrupted. "Rookie? Go get your gear ready. It's a five day assignment. Meet Mechanic Rind in the hangar. Dismissed."

"Yes, sir," the Rookie said, leaving the office as quickly as possible.

۞۞۞

Masters leaned in and kissed Harlow softly. She stirred slightly, but didn't wake. He grabbed his pack and headed out of the barracks, nearly colliding with the Rookie.

"Whoa, slow down," Masters said.

"Sorry, sorry…I need to get packed and get to the hangar," the Rookie said, the words tumbling out of his mouth. Masters dropped his pack and grabbed the Rookie by the shoulders.

"Calm down, kid. It's only a supply run. You listen closely to me and Jay and you'll be just fine."

The Rookie took a couple of deep breaths. Masters smiled.

"Better?"

The Rookie nodded.

۞۞۞

Capreze focused on Jay. "Is he worth it?"

Jay took a seat without asking or waiting for leave. "Gut reaction? Yes. Head reaction? He needs a lot of work. But there's something to this kid. I don't know what, but he has something to prove."

"Don't they all?" Capreze quipped.

"No, this one's different. I can't put my finger on it…"

"Well, you'll have plenty of time on the supply run."

"About that, why Foggy Bottom?"

"Doc's request."

Jay raised an eyebrow. "Since when does that matter?"

"Since I've started suspecting she's up to something."

"Really?"

"Pay attention."

"Will Do."

۞۞۞

Jethro grabbed the Rookie's pack and tossed it into the salvage mech's storage compartment.

"I figured we'd be taking the transport," the Rookie said, looking up at the modified battle mech. "I didn't know we'd be traveling by mech."

"Salvage mech," Jethro informed. "We take this out on all supply runs. It's outfitted for storage and retrieval. We'll probably come across some graveyards out there and we can use the parts."

"Graveyards?"

"Mechs," Bisby answered, entering the hangar. "Ours and theirs."

"Parts don't grow on trees," Jethro added.

Bisby climbed into his mech. "Good luck, Rookie. Try not to die."

☠☠☠

"Shit!" Rachel cried, pulling her hand from the hot pan.

"Problems already?" Capreze smirked, entering the kitchen.

"I'm no good at this, you know that!" she yelled at her father. Capreze just watched her. "Sorry," she apologized.

Capreze sighed. "Do I need to say it?"

"No, I fucked up. I know."

"I'm talking about you and Mathew."

Surprise overtook Rachel's features. "Mathew? I thought this was about the Rookie."

"The Rookie is with Jay and Masters. He's taken care of for now. I just need to know that your relationship with Mathew isn't getting in the way."

"It's not."

"Good."

☠☠☠

The four mechs left the hangar.

Bisby's headed East, Mathew's West, Masters' and the salvage mech due South.

"Good luck everyone," Mathew said over the com.

"You too," Masters answered. Bisby just grunted.

"Don't play the hero, Jespers," Jay warned. "You get into any shit, you call for help."

"Not to worry. Same thing for you. We know how you can be when in the city/states."

The Rookie looked over at Jay. "What does that mean?" Jay ignored him.

"Pretty sure my credit is cut off everywhere. Not much trouble I *can* get into."

Mathews, Masters and Bisby all snorted.

☠☠☠

In the distance, but well within the base's sensors, a dead mech watched the mechs spilt up and head their separate ways. None of them noticed the observer. It waited until the live mechs were off its scanners before moving in closer to the base.

The deader desperately wanted to do a full scan of the base and all its systems, but knew they would detect him then. The dead mech stopped, realization opening up new data streams in its AI. It had referred to itself as a *him*. He had given *himself* identity other than an *it*.

  He watched.

CHAPTER THREE

PART ONE - RED LEGS & RANCHERS

Alarms sounded in the salvage mech's cockpit. Jay tapped his com. "Masters?"

"Yeah, got it. Something's on the other side of that second ridge due east."

Jay glanced at the Rookie and smiled. "Wanna take a scouting break?"

The Rookie looked around. "Out here?"

"Gotta learn sometime, Rookie," Jay said.

"Um, sure."

"Great!" Masters laughed. "This'll be fun."

"Park over by the first ridge. Shouldn't take long to hike up and get a good view," Masters said.

"Hike?" the Rookie asked.

"Yes, hike. What? Did you think we were just going to drive over and say 'Hi'?" Masters laughed again.

The heat was unbearable.

The climate processors must have finally gone, June thought. *I ain't gonna last long out in this shit.*

She flicked the thermo sensors on, scanning her surroundings. There, ten clicks out, was a cool patch. She zoomed the scanners in and saw the mouth of what she hoped was a deep ravine.

I can hold up in there until night; wait for things to cool down.

She knew the dangers of traveling at night with limited capabilities. It would be very difficult to pick out the swarms of zombies against the rapidly cooling rocks and earth.

Masters hopped from his mech's ladder and strode towards Jay and the Rookie.

Jay handed the Rookie a small backpack. "Strap that on. Anything happens and that pack will keep you alive for at least a couple of days."

The Rookie started to open the pack.

"Leave it be, Rookie. It takes forever to get it all back in there," Masters said, taking a second pack from Jay.

"What's in it?"

"Life, kid. Your tablet has a full inventory. Shall we?" Jay said, motioning to the ridge they needed to crest. "We only have a few more hours of daylight."

☠☠☠

June glanced back and forth from her control panel to the ravine, watching as her mech's systems started to shut down, and hoped it would hold together long enough to get her to cover. She didn't want to end up exposed out in the waste, not that holed up in a ravine was any more secure.

Buzzers sounded and a loud clanging, clanging, crunch signaled the end of the ride.

Her mech ground to a halt about two hundred yards from the ravine.

"Shit," June muttered. She shut down power, grabbed her gear and unlatched the cockpit.

The sun blazed.

☠☠☠

"I know you can fight and all, but I have to question why Capreze sent you with us," Masters said, handing the Rookie an auto-carbine and two magazines. "I don't even know if you're trained to use one of these."

The Rookie pocketed the extra mags, popped the one out of the carbine, cleared the chamber and slammed the magazine back in. "Not an issue."

The Rookie slung his carbine, following Jay and Masters up the ridge.

"We really are a slapdash bunch of yahoos," Jay laughed. "Good thing we're all crazy as fuck, otherwise we'd be dead by now."

☠☠☠

Sweat pouring off of her, June collapsed into the shade of the overhang that was the mouth of the ravine. She risked a shallow drink from her canteen, hoping the ravine still held the water that had cut it out of the rock.

She brought her knees to her chest and rested her forehead against them, trying to fight the sobs. Despite her military training, years of mech experience in the waste and the untold thousands of undead she had obliterated, she could never control the tears.

She gave up and rolled onto her side, letting the emotions take over.

"So why are we watching a deader instead of killing it?" the Rookie asked.

"Pay attention," Masters replied.

The Rookie focused his binocs on the dead mech in the valley below. The thing was scorched and scarred, lumbering from wreckage pile to wreckage pile, kicking at the debris. A mass of zombies followed.

"I don't-" the Rookie stopped, noticing the dead mech's legs. "Is that paint?"

"Nope."

One of the zombies came too close, enraging the machine. It stomped on the creature then turned on the others, quickly pulverizing them under its massive feet.

"That's Red Legs. He hates everything."

Bisby checked his sensors and fumed. Nothing. Not a goddamn thing anywhere.

"Jethro?"

"Yeah Biz?" Jethro answered over the com. "Whatcha got?"

"Jack shit. You?"

Jethro checked mini-mechs Two and Four's vid screens. All were void of any movement or sign of dead mech activity. "Nope."

"I should be out with Mathew looking for June, not on some wild deader chase!"

"I don't disagree, Biz, but the Doc thinks, and Capreze agrees, that we need to know what's up with the deaders more than we need to find an AWOL mech pilot that's lost her shit."

"Yeah, yeah, I know…"

"You have names for them?" the Rookie asked in disbelief. "But, don't we kill them when we see them? Why bother with names?"

Masters gave Jay and the Rookie a look of angry sorrow.

"That's the plan kid, but it doesn't always work out that way. Sometimes they kill us and all we have is vid clips of the battle. That's how most of these have been named," Masters answered bitterly.

"Most of them?" asked the Rookie, catching the disclaimer.

Jay cleared his throat. "There are a couple we've met, battled and…"

"And…?"

"And we were lucky to get away."

☠☠☠

The dead mech, (Shiner, he named himself Shiner, he didn't know why, but it was his name. Shiner.), sat in the shadow of the mesa, tucked between rock outcroppings and finished tinkering with One.

He set the mini-mech down and powered it up. Nothing.

If the dead mech could have frowned, it would have. He lifted the mini-mech up and turned it over in his hands, puzzled. He tinkered some more.

Setting One down, Shiner tried again. Still nothing. Rage started to build and Shiner had to use all of his self-control not to smash the mini-mech to tiny bits.

☠☠☠

Mathew had tried to follow the massive footprints left by June's mech, but the wasteland was already reclaiming them, the wind whipping about and the sand flowing back to its original unmarred state.

"Dammit." He pushed his sensors to full power and scanned the horizon, but as he expected, nothing showed up. She had too much of a lead and had been zig-zagging so much, deliberately making it hard to follow her, that Mathew couldn't even guess which direction she may have gone.

He sighed and pushed on, planning on covering as much ground as possible before returning by sundown.

☠☠☠

Shiner wasn't sure how to process 'frustration' and the raging hunger from the zombie pilot strapped into his cockpit wasn't helping.

Shiner fired a plasma blast into the side of the mesa, showering the area with rock and debris. The act of violence focused him and his frustration and anger subsided. It also made him acutely aware he could have just alerted any mech in the area, living or dead, to his presence.

He set all sensors to full and scanned the area. At the far edge of his readings a mech stomped through the wasteland. Curious, he continued scanning.

☠☠☠

"So what's the plan?" the Rookie asked as the three descended from the ridge.

"The plan?" Jay asked.

"To go after the deader. After Red Legs."

Masters laughed. "Kid, our only plan is to get to Foggy Bottom and *avoid* deaders at all costs."

Jay stopped and turned on the Rookie. "We have a whole base relying on us coming back supplied. Combat can wait."

"I just thought-"

"How long do you think we can last in the waste without med supplies?"

"It can be done," the Rookie grumbled, pushing on.

Jay and Masters shared a puzzled look and followed.

Shiner noted the heading of the mech as it moved out of range of his sensors.

With renewed determination he lifted One again and went back over his modifications. Nothing seemed out of order and he couldn't figure out why the mini-mech wouldn't activate.

Frustration returning, Shiner lashed out smacking One brutally and sending the mini-mech skidding across the dirt. Instantly One buzzed to life, righted itself and approached Shiner, waiting for its commands.

Shiner opened his cockpit and withdrew a cable, plugging it into One. In milliseconds trillions of bits of information transferred from one mech to the other.

June pulled herself together and stood up, brushing sand and dirt from her uniform. She hefted her pack and carbine, checking and securing each strap, readying herself for the climb down into the ravine.

"Nothing like a good cry," she said, her words echoing off the ravine's walls as she descended. She hoped to find a perch or nook, not liking the idea of being trapped down at the bottom if she needed to make a quick escape.

The weight of the pack bit into her shoulders, but she ignored the pain, paying close attention to her footing and handholds.

"Hey Biz?" Masters called over the com pushing the system to its limits.

"Yeah. What's up?" Bisby answered.

"I got Red Legs for ya if you want it."

"Shoot me the coordinates."

The com crackled and hissed from the distance between mechs. "Done. Oh and, um…"

"What?"

"Be careful. Red Legs is a tough one and if it's changed like One Arm, you'll need back up."

"Don't worry about me. Now that I know what I'm fighting ain't nothing going to stop me."

Masters was silent for a moment. "Okay. Good luck."

"Thanks." Bisby turned his mech towards Masters' coordinates.

☠☠☠

One obeyed.

It had been told what to do, where to go and it was doing just that.

Stay out of sight. So it hid.

Stay off sensors. So it did.

Follow, observe, report. Follow, observe, report. These were its commands, these were its reasons for existing; for being allowed to exist.

It observed and reported back about the live mech it was following.

One knew this mech. It had visual memory of this mech, of it being repaired, it being deployed and it returning.

But returning to and from where? That was old programming. That was wiped.

One obeyed.

☠☠☠

"Pilot Jespers to base… Pilot Jespers to base… Hey assholes! Anyone manning the com?" Mathew yelled.

"Fucking chill Matty!" Jethro barked back. "Since your girlfriend is busy plotting our deaths in the kitchen I'm having to monitor you, Bisby and Two and Four! So fuck off!"

"Sorry, man. Listen, I'm lost out here."

"Your instruments aren't working?"

"No, dumbass, I mean I have no idea which way June could have gone. The trail is cold and I'm searching blind."

"If you weren't blind wouldn't it just be called following?"

"I fucking hate you sometimes," Mathew growled.

"Fuck you too, Jespers."

☠☠☠

June splashed the cold water onto her face, lifting her head and letting it drip down her neck. She breathed deeply and started to relax a bit.

She sat on the bank of the small stream that cut the narrow ravine and wondered what her next move was. Whatever it was, she knew it wasn't sitting on her ass out in the waste.

She dipped her canteen into the water until it stopped bubbling then plopped two purification tablets into the canteen. As she replaced the canteen, something in the water caught her eye.

She leaned in close then gagged.

Bisby's sensors picked up movement.

"Alright, now we're talking," he mumbled, readying weapons as he adjusted his course to intercept. Within seconds he had solid readings and disappointment washed over him.

His sensors told him he was following a transport of some kind, highly modified and in pursuit of approximately fifty zombies. "Ranchers..."

Bisby wanted a look. He halted his mech, grabbed his binocs and carbine and just a short hike up a small hill, he had a perfect view.

Which was more than the transport had since it seemed completely unaware of the dead mech coming up on it.

"Oh God..." June placed a hand over her mouth to keep from puking. Staring up at her, just below the surface of the water, was a severed head. And surrounding the head were other heads...and arms, legs, torsos...

"Oopsy," a voice said behind June. "Looks like someone found the larder. Now what's a pretty thing like you doing down here?"

June spun around and faced a shaggy, dirty man in tattered clothes and boots. She didn't focus too long on his appearance as the click of his switchblade commanded her attention.

She glanced at her carbine.

"Try it, bitch."

"Bisby to base..."

"Yeah, go ahead Biz," Jethro responded.

"Get Rachel on the com for me."

"Will do."

A brief moment later Rachel's voice crackled. "Whatcha find Biz?"

"Looks like I've found a deader. The thing's about to take out a Rancher herding transport."

"Can you stop it?"

"Not in time, no."

"Sucks for them. What do you need from me?"

"The deader is Red Legs."

There was a brief silence. "You still there Rache?"

"Yeah," Rachel puffed. "Sorry. I'm heading to the hangar now. I'll be geared up and on my way in five."

"I ain't waiting."

"I know."

"Pilot Capreze! Report to your station immediately!" his commanding officer screamed over the com.

"I can't, sir!" Capreze responded. "I have to get home to my family!"

"Capreze you are risking court martial for this! Possibly execution for desertion! Do you understand!"

"Yes, sir. But my wife and daughter are more important, sir! I am sorry!"

"Capreze! I will send the entire UDC con-" His commander's voice was interrupted by the sound of wrenching metal, shattering glass and a massive explosion. Then the com went dead.

Commander Capreze came awake, face down on his desk, his cheek wet with drool.

One obeyed. Follow, observe and report.

One didn't understand this mech it knew, the living one. Why was it going towards the danger?

The other mech, the dead one, was a crazy mech. Not like One's…what? It searched its limited memory, but couldn't find a term. Or didn't understand the term.

The mech One knew, was going to be in trouble, even the newly (Born? Created? Altered?) reprogrammed mini-mech saw that.

One needed to get closer, but that would risk detection. That could mean disobeying, which couldn't happen.

Follow, observe, report.

One jammed all frequencies and sensors.

One obeyed.

Commander Capreze shook his head back and forth, trying to bring himself fully awake. He stretched and yawned.

"Damn. I'm getting too fucking old for these late nights," he said aloud in his empty office. "I'm also talking to myself too much." He laughed at himself then frowned, the soldier in him seriously considering his stability.

"I need coffee." Capreze stood and strode from his office, headed to the mess hall.

I'll check on Baby Girl and make sure she hasn't burned the kitchen down, he thought, rubbing at the crick in his neck the impromptu nap had given him.

"Hey Jethro?" Mathew called.

"What the fuck? Am I the base receptionist? You want me to check your calendar to see what dinner you have planned tonight too?"

"Um, I don't even know how to respond to that," Mathew said.

"Sorry. Looks like Bisby is about to get in the shit and Rachel's heading out to back him up. I've got two mini-mechs in the waste I need to get turned around and headed back to base. So what do you need?"

"Just letting you know I'm calling it for the day and coming home."

"Great. I'll pass that on."

Capreze was grateful that when he entered the mess he didn't hear his daughter cursing the world. He took that as a good sign. His happiness soon abated when he noticed that not only was there a lack of cursing, there was a lack of any noise.

He stepped behind the mess line and back into the kitchen proper. It looked like a tornado had hit the place, which was what he expected. What he didn't expect was his daughter to be missing.

"Rachel? What's your location?" Capreze asked over the com.

"Can't talk Papa Bear! Duty calls!" Rachel responded.

The switchblade slashed before June could even register the movement. She took a gash to her forearm and another to her right thigh. Stumbling backwards, trying to get away from the madman, she didn't hear the second come up behind her until he had her about the throat, immobilized.

The first attacker closed in, cutting at her uniform.

"Hold on," the second said. "We could use that fancy gear."

The first man smiled, carefully unlatching the equipment straps. Once they hit the ground, though, he began slicing her uniform off.

The second leaned close, licking June's cheek. "You taste pretty."

☠☠☠

The Commander entered the hangar too late. Rachel was already past the bay doors and engaging her motor drive.

"Dammit Baby Girl! Where the hell are you going?" Caprezez demanded to know.

"Bisby is about to engage Red Legs and isn't waiting for my ass," Rachel responded over her com. "What's gotten into you? This is standard backup procedure."

"I know, but you're supposed to keep the base Commander informed."

"Hey, I swung by your office, but you were busy. I figured you needed your snoring and drooling time."

"You saw that?"

"Yep."

Capreze chuckled. "Okay. Be careful out there."

☠☠☠

Metal began to protest, rivets popping from the hull, as the dead mech ripped the Ranchers' mangled transport apart. The following undead unfortunate enough to be too close to the carnage were shredded and decapitated from the flying debris.

The dead mech lifted the driver's limp form, ripping it limb from limb, depositing scraps into its own cockpit maw. The zombie pilot fed ravenously, while overflowing bits and pieces fell to the undead below.

Bisby lowered his binocs, stunned.

They are learning to follow the dead mechs, he thought. *Hunting in packs now, with the dead mech's as their alphas.*

☠☠☠

"Jeezus, Riley! You ever see a body like that on a breeder?" the dirty, grease ball called Chunks exclaimed.

Riley stood over June's naked, bound form. He'd just finished gagging her to keep her quiet and to keep her teeth from getting a hold of him.

"No, Chunks, can't say as I have," Riley sneered, kneeling next to Rachel, cupping an exposed breast. "She must belong to her leader to be this well fed and healthy. Is that it bitch? You the big man's breeder?"

June glared.

Riley reached between her legs. He smiled.

"Oh, that's nice. Boss'll like you"

☠☠☠

Shiner returned to the coolness of the mesa's shadows and waited for One's reports.

He curiously observed a new data path being created within his system and followed it, tapping into his database and also the remaining memory pathways of the zombie pilot.

'Anticipation' was the word his searching brought forth. Shiner was unsure how to process this new awareness and that brought back the 'frustration'.

He smashed his fist into the ground, creating an ATV size crater.

The outburst alerted him to a second new data path. The new search result troubled Shiner even more.

The word was 'loneliness'.

☠☠☠

Bisby fired up weapons systems and readied his mech for battle.

"I don't fucking care how mean you are," he growled aloud. "You're fucking dead."

He decided to flank Red Legs, hoping to take it completely off guard.

As Bisby came around the small hill he found himself in the ruins of some long ago settlement or resort. Half buried cars and transports, concrete and framing protruded from the sand and dirt.

And Red Legs stood in the middle of it. The thing reached down and lifted a massive iron girder with one of its own massive hands.

Bisby charged.

PART TWO - LITTLE FRIENDS & LARGE FOES

Rachel pushed her mech as hard as possible without red-lining systems. She double checked her coordinates, adjusted her heading and pushed harder.

"Biz?"

No answer.

"Biz? Its Rache, do you copy?"

Still no answer. "Hey Jethro? Do you have a lock on Bisby?"

"I have a lock, but not much info. Something's jamming the signal."

"What info do you have?"

"Looks like weapons systems are readied, but not active yet. I'd say he's about to get in the shit."

"How far off am I?"

"You're at least an hour if not two."

"Shit."

"Don't worry, Rache. He can handle himself."

☗☗☗

Red Legs gripped the iron girder, swinging it like a club. Bisby barely piloted out of the way, crushing husks of burnt out cars as he scrambled out of range.

He switched on his external loudspeakers. "Oh, you wanna play, do ya?" He quickly scanned his surroundings and found his weapon.

Circling right, he forced Red Legs to the left. Bisby ducked and rolled, barely dodging a massive swipe. He came up holding two short clusters of re-bar, one in each mech fist.

"Bitch, you ain't gonna take me one on one!"

The two death machines closed on each other.

☗☗☗

"This is Commander Capreze," Capreze said, answering the secure com that chimed in.

"Capreze? Good to hear your voice. This is First General Powell, UDC Command."

"General, it's an honor. Everything alright?"

"Sure, sure. I'm just calling to send my condolences over the loss of Pilot Stanislaw."

"Thank you, General. He was a great pilot and friend. He'll be missed by all."

"Of course, of course…" the General trailed off.

"Is there something else you wanted to discuss, sir?"

"Well, Commander, yes there is… You see the UDC has been working on a retrovirus."

Capreze listened, his blood running cold.

☗☗☗

Bisby ducked low, swinging the rebar at Red Legs, trying to take the dead mech out at the knees. Red Legs leapt over the attack, twisting in the air, and brought the girder down right at Bisby's cockpit. Bisby raised the two clutches of rebar up in an X, blocking Red Legs' attack.

An alarm sounded, warning of possible hydraulics failure.

Bisby ignored the alarm, putting all his attention on fending off Red Legs as the deader slammed the girder down again and again.

Red Legs roared.

"Fuck you too!" Bisby yelled, finally able to roll away from Red Legs.

"Are all of your communication security protocols in place Commander?" General Powell asked.

"Yes, sir. We are clear to speak freely."

"Good. Now, as I am sure you are aware the UDC has been implementing full inoculation programs in all of the city/states."

"No, sir, I wasn't aware."

"Really? It came to my attention Dr. Lisbon of Foggy Bottom had contacted your Chief Medical Officer regarding the program."

"I wasn't informed, sir. I'll speak with her."

"Oh, well, it's of no real consequence, Capreze. Is Dr. Themopolous available? I'd like her to join in this conversation."

"I'll hail her, sir."

Bisby came up firing, his plasma cannon glowing red hot with each successive blast.

Red Legs agilely dodged to the left, taking cover behind some debris. Chunks of ancient concrete and steel filled the air as Bisby followed Red Legs' movement, trying to aim his blasts ahead of the deader.

"Fucking stand still!" Bisby yelled. And Red Legs did, using the girder to block several of the plasma blasts. The undead machine hurled the warped and melted chunk of metal straight at Bisby.

Bisby brought an arm up to deflect the attack, the collision forcing his mech to stumble backwards.

"Themopolous," the Doctor answered, checking Steve's vital signs.

"Doctor? I have General Powell on secure com. I hope you have a few minutes for to speak privately?"

Themopolous glanced at the doorway as Harlow came in, sleepily stretching. She motioned at her com ear and Harlow nodded, shooing her away and taking over Steve's assessment. Dr. Themopolous left the infirmary quickly.

"Of course, sir. I'm almost to my office now."

"Excellent, Doctor," the General chimed in. "I have some great news regarding the newly developed retrovirus Dr. Lisbon informed you of."

Themopolous froze and forced herself not to be sick.

☠☠☠

Red Legs took immediate advantage of Bisby's faltering and opened fire. Bisby took a graze to the right shoulder, the smell of scorched metal overpowering his environmental filters, as his mech slammed to the ground. He checked systems and saw he had been lucky, sustaining only minimal damage.

Quickly, Bisby tucked his mech back behind a half buried transport, hoping the shell still had enough structural integrity left to take the onslaught. Red Legs's blasts began to slow, the concussions weakening.

Bisby checked his scanners and smiled. The deader was losing power.

"Okay," he said aloud. "No more fucking around!"

☠☠☠

"I'm ready to proceed, sirs," Themopolous said, settling into her desk chair, apprehension clawing at her, forcing her to keep her voice even.

"Excellent. I'll keep this brief as I know you are both busy," the General said. "At approximately 1700 hours tomorrow a supply train will be arriving with the inoculation for your base personnel."

"Sir?" Capreze said, stunned.

"Yes, Commander. We have already inoculated all of the city / states and security outposts. Your base is the last on the list. We didn't want to rush the process, seeing as the mechs are an integral part of our overall survival."

☠☠☠

Bisby rolled his mech to the right into a tight crouch. Red Legs circled, trying to get the advantage, its cannons glowing dully.

"Looks like you're almost out of juice, deader!" Bisby taunted. Red Legs roared.

Bisby sprang, his mech launching into the air, twisting away from the cannon blasts. Three, two, one... The two mechs collided in a ground shaking crunch.

Bisby didn't lose stride, tucking his mech's left arm up under Red Legs and lifting it into the air. He brought the right arm down fast, smashing at Red Leg's cockpit, hoping to crush the zombie pilot inside.

☠☠☠

"Is there anything I need to have prepared, sir?" Themopolous asked, her voice audibly shaking now.

"No, no, we have everything taken care of. There will be two med techs to administer the inoculations and a small security force to accompany them."

"I'll be sure and have accommodations ready, sir," Capreze said, picking up on Themopolous' faltering poise, hoping the General hadn't.

"Not necessary, Commander. They will only be there long enough for the techs to complete their work and for the train to refuel and re-supply."

"Well, sir, the Doctor and I will have the base ready for them."

Bisby raged as he pounded away at Red Legs' cockpit hatch, so close he could smell the rot and decay.

The dead mech tried to ward off the blows, but it was no match for Bisby's close combat skills. For every maneuver it tried to make, Bisby expertly countered, never letting the bludgeoning slack.

After only minutes the dead mech's power reserves gave up and the giant machine became dead weight. Bisby threw the deader to the ground and shoved his 50mm into the cracked cockpit, ready to vaporize the barely moving zombie pilot.

"Biz?!? Talk to me!" Rachel crackled.

"Now, I do need to verify all base personnel will be present," General Powell said casually.

"Well, no sir. I have a team on a supply run to Foggy Bottom as we speak. They won't return for a few days."

"Their names, Commander?"

Capreze hesitated. This wasn't protocol. There was no need for a First General to be inquiring about the roster; that was why he had an assistant.

"Pilot Masters, General Mechanic Rind and our new Rookie."

There was a slight pause. "Excellent, Commander. Thank you. I'll let both of you return to your busy schedules."

"Thank you, sir."

"Whatcha want Rache?" Bisby asked, exhausted, trigger finger itching to depress and obliterate Red Legs's zombie pilot.

"What do I want?!? WHAT DO I FUCKING WANT?!?" Rachel exploded. "I want to know that you aren't deader food! That you are still alive and in one piece! That's what I fucking want!"

Bisby took a deep breath and removed his finger from the trigger. "Yeah,

I'm in one piece. Red Legs is out of commission." Bisby undid his harness and opened his cockpit. "I'm descending now to retrieve the head for Themopolous."

"Be careful."

Bisby snorted and climbed down his mech.

☠☠☠

Capreze strode from his office. "Themopolous? What's your location?"

"I'm in my office. I was about to return to the infirmary," she answered over the com.

"Stay put. I'm coming to you."

"Of course, sir. Is this about the inoculations?"

"You're Goddamn right it's about the inoculations!" Capreze shouted. "I'm almost to your office and we are going to get a few things straight before that train arrives. Let Harlow know you may be a while before you return. Copy that?"

There was silence on Themopolous's end.

"Doctor? Did you copy that?"

"Yes, sir, I copy. I'll alert Pilot Harlow."

☠☠☠

Mathew dozed briefly, his motor drive set to auto and course plotted. A proximity alarm sounded and roused him from his nap.

Instantly he was alert and checking all systems. A quick scan showed a transport and what were possibly three ATVs about six miles out. He couldn't quite tell what they were doing, but further readings confirmed the presence of a few dozen zombies.

"What the...?"

He disengaged the motor drive and took control of his mech, adjusting his course towards the source of the readings.

"Let's see what we got going on over here," he muttered to himself.

☠☠☠

Bisby pried open the dead mech's cockpit with a short shovel. The zombie pilot squirmed in its harness, its rotted teeth gnashing and grinding, its yellow, dead eyes never leaving Bisby's.

Bisby stared down at the abomination. "You poor, sad sack of shit." He thrust the shovel blade down into the zombie's throat and through its neck, severing the head.

He stood there for several minutes, just looking at the decapitated zombie. "Who did you used to be?"

"How's your progress, Biz?" Rachel interrupted.

"Progressing fine, Mom." Bisby slipped on heavy, rubber gloves and bent down to retrieve the head.

"You want to fucking tell me why I learn from a First General that my own Chief Medical Officer has known about retrovirus inoculations, but decided not to fucking tell me?!?" Capreze screamed, exploding into Themopolous' office. "If it was to make me look like a fucking asshole, then you fucking succeeded!"

"Sir, it's not what you think," Themopolous said quietly.

"Not what I think?!? How do you fucking know what I think?!? I don't even know what I fucking think right now!"

Capreze stood there, chest heaving, his hands planted on his hips. Themopolous refused to make eye contact.

"Rache? Head's retrieved. CPU and hard drive also. All ready for Themopolous. Where you at?" Bisby said, strapping back into his harness.

"I'm still a few miles off. Head towards me, we should meet up in about 30 minutes."

"Gotcha on my scope. See ya in a few." Bisby took one last look at the dead mech that was Red Legs. "You always seemed tougher than that. Guess I'm just the better mech."

Bisby started to walk his mech away from the scene, but blaring claxons stopped him.

Hundreds of zombies swarmed from out of nowhere, heading straight for Bisby.

Capreze glared at the doctor. "Fucking look at me when I'm talking to you?"

Themopolous forced herself to meet the Commander's eyes. She studied his face for a moment and realization dawned on her. "You really don't know anything about this, do you?"

"Have I been talking to my self? For a doctor, you're a fucking idiot!"

"So you have no clue that the inoculation is just a smoke screen?"

"What the hell are you talking about?"

"Nanotech," Themopolous stated flatly.

Capreze's confidence faltered. "What are you saying?"

"The UDC is injecting nanobots into every single person within their authority."

☠☠☠

Mathew watched the ATVs surround the fifty or so zombies, driving them towards the large transport.

"Fucking Ranchers," he muttered as he lowered his binocs and slowly crawled backwards down the low rise to his mech.

He was up, strapped in and hailing Jethro within a minute.

"Whatcha need Matty?'

"Get me Capreze."

"No 'please'?"

"What is with you today Jethro? Daddy Jay not around to rebel against so you have to act out towards me? Am I your surrogate brother?"

"My brother died in my arms when I was fifteen, asshole."

"Really? Sorry."

"No, not really. I'll get Capreze."

☠☠☠

Bisby opened fire with his plasma cannon and the 50mm, taking out the first wave of zombies as they surged towards him.

"Rachel!"

"What Biz?"

"Get your ass here now! I've got hundreds of undead coming straight for me! They are too close to take out!"

The swarm overwhelmed Bisby's weapons and smashed directly into him, the weight of the dead bringing the mighty mech to the ground. Bisby sent a high voltage current through his mech's exoskeleton, hoping to fry the zombies off, but only the first few were affected, melting a layer of rotten flesh to his mech.

☠☠☠

"Capreze here. Whatcha need Jespers?"

"Sir, I have confirmation of Ranchers. They have a herd of zombies, maybe fifty, sixty total. Looks like they're heading for Timson's Bluff. Shall I pursue?"

"No, let them alone. The UDC's said that as long as the Cults don't bother us, we aren't to bother them."

"But did they say we couldn't follow them? I can do some quick recon and mark their base, in case we need to come back."

"What was that Jespers? You're breaking up. I didn't hear a word of what you just said. Copy?"

"Yes, sir. Thank you, sir."

"Are you okay, sir?" Themopolous asked, seeing the worry on Capreze's face as he severed the com connection with Mathew.

"We've got Ranchers out near Timson's Bluff."

"Timson's Bluff? Ranchers aren't usually that close to us, if I'm not mistaken."

"You aren't," Capreze said, sighing. "But, first thing's first, I need to know why you didn't come to me with this."

Themopolous paused before answering. "I wasn't sure you could be trusted, sir. I was warned that this is top level UDC."

"Fair enough. So, now what?" Capreze asked.

"I don't know," Themopolous answered. "But we have to stop them."

Bisby struggled against the weight of zombie bodies piling onto his mech, but for every few he was able to crush or toss aside, twice as many replaced them. He could hear cables snapping, hydraulics cracking and his mech groan under the weight.

A hairline crack appeared in his cockpit and he was tempted to say 'fuck it' and start firing his sidearm through the windshield at the zombie faces trying to gnash and gnaw their way in.

Suddenly, above the noise of the zombie swarm, Bisby could hear rapid gunfire. The weight on his mech began to lessen quickly.

Mathew was able to track the Rancher transport on his sensors and he guessed correctly: they headed straight for Timson's Bluff.

Unable to get any closer without his mech being observed, Mathew shut down power and climbed from the cockpit, carbine strapped to his shoulder and binocs in hand.

He stood facing the rough, steep surface of the cliff, knowing that it would be a hard climb, but worth the unobstructed, and unobserved, view of the Ranchers' activities.

"I'm gonna be fucking sore tomorrow," he sighed.

Walking back to the mech he began unloading climbing gear from a storage compartment.

☗☗☗

"So how do these nanobots work?" Capreze asked.

"I'm not sure to be honest," Themopolous replied. "The tech behind it has never been released into public knowledge. In fact, last I heard, the UDC gave up on its success years ago. Either this has been a completely classified project or there was some recent breakthrough I didn't hear about."

"Either way, it's a bit extreme to inject those things into the entire population."

"UDC population," Themopolous corrected.

"What?"

"From the info I have seen, none of the wasteland inhabitants have been injected."

"Hmmmm....," Capreze mused. "Why only the UDC population?"

☗☗☗

"Rachel?!? Is that you?" Bisby yelled into his com. "Rachel?!?"

He slammed his fist against the console. "Fucking piece of shit com! Jethro is fucking dead!"

The gunfire continued and zombies were now visibly falling away. He shoved and fought, tossing many aside.

Without warning there was a crack and then searing pain exploded in his right shoulder. "Mother fucker!"

Bisby looked down at the rapidly spreading patch of blood. He abandoned getting his mech upright and cut open his uniform. Tearing into his med kit, he slapped a compression bandage on the wound, hoping it would stop the bleeding.

☗☗☗

Rachel's legs burned from the effort of running her mech as hard as possible.

"Biz?!? Come in, Biz! Shit!"

She tried to lock onto his location, but her sensor readings were all over the place.

"Goddammit!" she yelled. "Jethro? What the hell is wrong with my systems?!?" She waited for the reply, but was only met with static. "Jethro? What the fuck?!?"

She knew she was close, but with a lack of proper sensor readings and no com, he could be just over a hill and she'd run right past him.

"This just fucking sucks!" she screamed, filled with frustration.

Bisby ignored the pain. Pain was for fucking pussies that didn't pilot 50-ton war machines. He forced his mech upright and pulled the trigger, laying waste to dozens of zombies still swarming his mech. Fluids and tissue splattered across his cockpit, streaking the windows.

The whirling machine guns clicked empty and came to a halt, barrels smoking. Bisby glanced at the weapons levels. Empty. Everything.

Movement on the horizon: a mech. He wasn't sure if it was living or dead. Or if it mattered anymore.

All he had was his sidearm and he planned on saving one bullet for himself.

"Ready to set camp?" Masters asked over the com.

"As good a place as any," Jay responded.

The Rookie stared out at the wide-open expanse of wasteland. "Aren't we a little exposed?"

"No, not really," Jay answered. "It's easier to set a security perimeter." Jay saw the look on the Rookie's face. "Listen, if you set up against a cliff or hill you have to secure elevation, which means you have gravity working against you. There really isn't any safe place in the waste. Might as well keep it open and make the zombies cover ground to get to you."

"Fucking hell!" Rachel yelled as she nearly toppled over trying to side-step the mini-mech that came out of nowhere and screamed past her. She slowed her mech and spun around, having to physically observe the machine since her sensors were still non-operational.

But, the mini-mech was gone. She came to a full stop and turned 360 degrees, trying to spot it again. Nothing.

"JETHRO!!!!"

"What?!? Jeezus, you trying to pop my eardrums?" Jethro answered.

"Thank God the com is back up. Which mini do you have out here?"

"What? I called Two and Four in. They're almost back to base."

Mathew lay belly down just at the edge of the bluff, peering through his binocs, not believing what he was seeing.

What are the Ranchers doing loading zombies onto UDC transports? he thought.

He scooted away from the edge and back to his climbing gear. He strapped on his repelling harness, tossed the rope off the cliff side and descended.

He debated whether to alert Capreze now or wait until he was secure at base. He had no idea what monitoring tech the UDC transports had. Hell, he had no idea if they already had his mech on their sensors.

💀💀💀

"Am I just hearing voices or is the com back up?" Bisby asked.

"My com was never down, it must have been just you guys," Jethro answered.

"Biz! What's your location?" Rachel asked. "Wait, never mind, sensors are operational again also. What happened?"

"I don't know, but it got pretty lonely out here. I've got a visual on your mech, Rache. Turn around, I'm five miles behind you," Bisby said, randomly stomping on the zombies that were still moving.

"Yeah, I got ya. Be there shortly."

"Don't bother. I'm doing a little clean up and then I'll head your way."

💀💀💀

The sun set quickly, turning the wasteland into an appropriate blood red landscape.

"Hey, anybody still out here?" Mathew called over an open channel.

"Matty? Why aren't you at base?" Rachel asked.

"I found something interesting. I'll fill you in back at base. You okay?"

"I'm fine. Things got weird, but nothing I couldn't handle."

"I'm fucking fine too. Thanks for asking," Bisby grumbled. "Just got shot in the shoulder, that's all."

"Damn! You okay?"

"Yeah. We stopped and Rache patched me up."

"She's good that way."

"Yep. I'll let you two talk in private. See ya back at base."

💀💀💀

June was barely conscious when Chunks threw her onto the skin rug. She knew she was in pain, but it seemed so distant, foreign. Shock had taken over hours ago after the fourth or fifth time Riley had raped her. She fought to keep her senses, knowing any bit of information she could retain could save her life.

"We found this one messing with the larder, Boss," Chunks said.

Two leather boots filled her vision as the Boss stepped closer to examine her.

"What happened, Chunks?"

"Riley couldn't wait, Boss. He had to have a taste."

"Call him in here."

☠☠☠

Rachel and Mathew walked their mechs through the night, separated by miles, but connected by their com, each listening to the other's breathing.

A shooting star shot past the horizon.

"Did you see that?" Mathew asked.

"The shooting star?" Rachel responded.

"Yeah. Better make a wish."

"It already came true."

"I'm going to be sick," Bisby interrupted.

"I thought you were going to give us some privacy," Mathew stated, slightly annoyed.

"Yeah, well I got bored. Although I'm beginning to think boredom is better than nausea."

Rachel reached out and punched Bisby's mech sending him stumbling.

"Hey!"

"Sorry. Got bored."

☠☠☠

The Rookie was actually grateful when the high-pitched keening woke him. The trip across the waste was bringing up long dead memories, making his sleep fitful. He sat up immediately, grabbing his carbine.

Floodlights from the mechs were triggered and the Rookie had to squint into the light.

"What is it?" the Rookie called out.

"Couple wanderers broke the perimeter," Masters said, checking readings on his tablet. "All clear now. Go back to sleep."

"System staying strong?" Jay asked sleepily, still wrapped in his sleeping bag.

"Everything checks out fine."

"Good...good...," Jay mumbled, already asleep before he finished speaking.

☠☠☠

"Boss?" June heard Riley say. She felt searing pain between her legs as her bladder loosed.

"What's the Law?" the Boss's voice growled.

"Huh?"

"The Law, Riley."

"Well, she ain't no virgin. I checked. I figured you wouldn't mind if I had some fun."

Through her hazy vision, June watched the Boss's boots step away. There was a small metallic sound, a wet gurgle then Riley, throat slashed and gushing, fell next to her, his eyes wide.

"Chunks!"

"Yeah, Boss?"

"Dress this asshole for tomorrow's lunch."

"Yes, Boss."

It was then June saw the various tattoos adorning the Boss's boots.

CHAPTER FOUR

PART ONE - THE COMMANDER & THE BOSS

"Couldn't sleep, huh?" Themopolous asked as Capreze stepped into the examination room.

"No. Too much going on," He answered over a mug of coffee, setting a second down for Themopolous. "I can see you're in the same boat."

"I wanted to try to have some answers before the pilot briefing."

"And?"

"I should know in a couple of minutes." Themopolous lowered her safety goggles and picked up a rotary bone saw. On the table before her was the zombie head Bisby had retrieved. Flicking the saw on, Themopolos lowered the whirring blade to the zombie's skull and began to cut.

💀💀💀

"Wake up sleepy head," Rachel whispered into Mathew's ear.

"...huh? Wha?" he dreamily responded.

"Coffee's all made, the mess is set up. Let's go for a sunrise stroll."

"What time is it?" Mathew asked sitting up from his bunk and grabbing his uniform.

"0530."

"Really? You want to take a mech for a stroll at 0530?"

"No," Rachel answered coyly, stepping close to Mathew and helping him into his uniform. "I want to take a sunrise stroll with you at 0530. Privately."

Mathew's fatigued brain finally caught up. "Oh, well in that case, let me brush my teeth."

Rachel smiled.

💀💀💀

Just before sunrise, Jay retrieved the security poles handing them to the Rookie. Several times they had to step past headless zombie corpses, their already rotted bodies quickly decomposing in the constant wasteland heat.

"What the hell happened?" the Rookie asked.

"Specially calibrated sonic frequency. Little something I rigged up a few years back," Jay responded.

The Rookie blankly stared at him. Jay sighed. "Zombie brain composition is different than ours. I figured out the frequency so that if zombies pass between two poles, their brain is vibrated until 'POP'. But, it only works on a small scale...so far."

☗☗☗

"Jethro? Are you up?" Capreze asked over the com, sipping from his coffee mug while he watched Themopolous work.

"Of course I'm up. With Jay gone I'm on double duty. I'll sleep when I'm dead," Jethro answered.

"Good to hear it," Capreze laughed. "Listen, I want you in the briefing this morning also, so don't start any huge project you can't get away from."

"Sure thing, sir."

"Also, I need you to get everyone up and let them know the briefing will be early this morning. We have a big day ahead and need to be prepared."

"Will do, Commander."

☗☗☗

Bodies intertwined, trying to become one. Hands grasped, fingers gripped. Two sets of hips interlocked.

"Hey, Rachel? Have you seen Mathew anywhere? I can't get him on his com," Jethro's voice squawked.

"Oh, shit," Rachel whispered. "Don't move an inch."

"You're the boss," Mathew responded.

Rachel ground down on him. "Damn right." She flipped a switch. "Yeah, I have sight of him. He's taking a walk and a piss."

"Roger. Wonder why he took his com off?"

"Who knows with that boy. He gets strange ideas in his head."

Rachel killed the switch, Mathew thrust hard, making her climax immediately.

☗☗☗

"Looks like Mathew's on a morning walk," Jethro said over Capreze's com.

"Without his com on?" Capreze asked.

"Guess so. You want me to go find him?"

"Yeah, go do that and let Rachel know we are moving the briefing up."

"Can't you tell her over her com?" Jethro asked.

"I could," Capreze responded, a tinge of annoyance touching his voice.

"But, I'd hate to interrupt."

"Interrupt? What do you…? Oh, yeah, right. I'll go get them right now, sir."

"Thanks, Jethro. And Jethro?"

"Yes, sir?"

"Don't let on that I sent you after them."

Jethro laughed. "Sure thing, sir."

☠☠☠

"Hey, Rache?"

"Yeah, baby?"

"Why won't you sleep in the barracks? Why do you stay in your mech all night?"

Rachel uncurled herself from Mathew's half naked form, stretched in the cramped cockpit and kissed him deeply. He embraced her, answering the kiss equally. Their lips parted and she stroked his cheek, looking into his eyes. She pecked him quickly and re-settled onto his chest.

"That's not an answer."

"Nope."

"Ever going to?"

"Yep. When we are both ready."

Mathew thought for a second, Rachel looked up at him, he smiled down at her.

"Okay. Take your time."

"Thank you."

☠☠☠

Doctor Themopolous tossed the latex gloves in the incinerator.

"So Doc, what's the story?" Capreze asked.

Turning, Doctor Themopolous stared straight at the Commander. She did not look well. Commander Caprese waited patiently.

"Memory."

"Come again?"

"The dead mechs are using the zombie brains for memory. They are like an undead hard drive for the mech's AI."

"So what does that mean tactically?" Bisby asked, having just entered the room.

Capreze ignored the interruption, wanting to know the answer as well.

"With their processing speed, the dead mechs are as intelligent, if not more, than humans."

"Fucking great," Bisby groaned.

"Take your seats, please," Capreze ordered. "Jethro is joining us today since he may have some insights."

Jethro gave an exaggerated wave to everyone seated. Capreze rolled his eyes.

"First order of business is to watch some of the vid from Bisby's encounter with Red Legs yesterday." Capreze tapped at his tablet and the room went dark as a large vid screen filled with the grainy vid feed from the battle.

"I want you to watch the deader. Watch how it moves. Don't over-analyze things. I want your gut feelings on this."

The staff sat in silence as they watched.

"So, what do you think?" Capreze asked the room.

Those seated looked around at each other, hoping someone had an answer. Dr. Themopolous cleared her throat.

"I think the dead mechs are learning. They are becoming sentient."

Most in the room gasped.

"You have to be joking, Doc," Jethro growled.

"No, I'm not, Mechanic," she stated flatly. "I believe that because of the Reaper chip, the dead mechs are using the complexities of the human brain to do something in death we couldn't do in life."

"And what is that, Doctor?" Rachel asked.

"They have created self-replicating AI. They live."

June awoke suddenly and scrambled out from under the blankets she wrapped about her and got to her feet, turning to look at the small, dingy room she was in. There was no furniture, only the pile of blankets and a bucket in the corner.

Bits and pieces of memory came to her and from the bruises and cuts on her naked body and the intense pain radiating everywhere, she knew the day before hadn't been a dream, it had been a waking nightmare.

The door to the room rattled and then opened and the Boss entered. "Morning, Sunshine. Hungry?"

"Okay, everyone settle down," Capreze said. The room hushed. "As important as this is, it isn't the most pressing thing we have to deal with today." Capreze paused. "I received word that two med techs and a team of UDC security will be arriving at 1700 hours by train."

All eyes fell on Themopolous.

"Med techs?" Harlow asked. "For Steve?"

"They don't send security for a wounded cook," Bisby sniped.

"No, they don't," Capreze continued. "The techs are supposed to inoculate the base. But the Doctor and I have found that to be a rouse. We cannot let them succeed."

☠☠☠

June grabbed for the blankets, wrapping them around her exposed skin.

"Now, there's nothing to be afraid of," the Boss said, holding his hands up, palms out. "No need for a pretty thing like you to get all worked up."

"Where am I?" June asked, eyes darting from the Boss to the door.

"No need to even try," the Boss grinned. "Hey Chunks?"

"Yes, Boss?" Chunks responded, just outside the door.

"Nothin'. Just making a point." The Boss's grin widened, showing sharp teeth filed to points. "Now before Chunks brings in breakfast, how about you tell me your name darlin'?"

☠☠☠

"Quiet down, people," Capreze commanded. The alarmed voices of the base staff ceased. "As much as I would like sentient deaders and forced inoculations to be all of our worries, they aren't. Mathew?"

"Thank you, sir," Mathew cleared his throat. "I followed some Ranchers out to Timson's Bluff. Looks like they've set up camp there."

"So?" Bisby asked impatiently.

"They were loading zombie herds onto UDC transports."

"What the fuck?" Harlow exclaimed. "Why?"

"That seems to be the question of the morning, Pilot Harlow," Capreze commented. "But we now need to prioritize threats. The train is first. I need suggestions."

☠☠☠

"I asked you a question, darlin'," the Boss said, his grin not meeting his eyes. "Around here, I ask, you answer. There ain't any way around that." He stepped closer to June, backing her against the wall. "Unless you want to be the next meal."

June remained quiet, her body shaking from cold and fear inside her blankets.

"You sure you don't want to answer? Alright then."

Lightning quick the Boss lashed out, slapping June across the face. He yanked the blankets from her and punched her in the stomach. June doubled over.

"I can do this all day, sweetheart."

☠☠☠

"So, it's not a retrovirus?" Mathew asked.

"No," Themopolous answered. "The UDC is injecting nanotech into every person under its authority."

"Why?" Rachel asked.

"We don't know," Capreze said. "But every instinct in my body tells me it isn't for the 'greater good'."

"So, we don't let them inject us," Bisby stated. "Seems pretty fucking easy."

"This is the UDC we are talking about, not some city/state PD. How do we stop them without being marked traitors?" Harlow exclaimed. "Let alone keep them from opening fire as soon as we try to stop them."

"I have an idea," Rachel said.

☠☠☠

"Rachel!" June screamed, shit streaming down her legs after the sixth stomach punch caused her bowels to loose. "Rachel...Capreze."

"Capreze? You must be the Commander's brat." The Boss stepped back, his eyes twinkling with malevolence. "Chunks!"

"Yes, Boss?" Chunks called from outside the room.

"Get me a harness," the Boss smirked. "I'm gonna show everyone my fancy new breeder."

In seconds, Chunks came into the room carrying a bundle of leather and metal. The Boss put out a hand and Chunks placed the bundle into his outstretched palm. "Thank you, Chunks. Now, Rachel, I advise you hold perfectly still."

☠☠☠

"You think this will work?" Mathew asked, handing Rachel another pitcher of water. Rachel took the water and poured it into the brewer.

"It's going to have to," Rachel responded, closing the brewer lid and turning the machine on. In seconds the water began to gurgle through the system and the smell of coffee filled the kitchen.

Themopolous entered the kitchen, three vials in her hands. "Remember, the coffee has to be cooled to room temperature or the heat will break down the sedative."

"No problem, Doc. I'll have coffee brewed, cooled and slowly re-heated before the train gets here."

The Boss led June through the village by a leash attached to a neck collar which was in turn attached to straps that were buckled below her breasts, across her mid-section and down around her thighs. The Boss smiled and waved, acknowledging those that greeted him.

June wanted to shut her eyes and pretend like nothing was happening, but she was warned she'd lose her eyelids if she didn't keep them open and hold her head up high.

From what she could see of the village, the worst slums of the city/ states were luxury compared to the squalor around her.

Commander Capreze waited as Jethro pulled the ATV back into the hangar. "Everything's set, sir. If that doesn't jam them then we're screwed."

"I don't want 'ifs' Jethro. I want certainty," the Commander said.

"Sir, the UDC gave us all this," Jethro responded, spreading his arms wide. "But they didn't give us Jay Rind's brain. Trust me his tech beats their tech any day."

"I hope so or we will all be lined up in front of a UDC firing squad." Capreze gazed out the hangar to the train platform. "I guess were as ready as we're going to be."

"Ladies," the Boss greeted a small group of women, dressed in a dirty patchwork of clothing, gathered about a massive cook pot. "This is Rachel." The women stared.

The Boss gave a strong tug on the leash, pulling June closer to the group. She fought to keep from gagging over the smell emanating from the cook pot. "Rachel will be joining our family. I need to make sure she doesn't attract any unwanted visitors our way. When you are done, let Chunks know. He'll carry her back."

The Boss handed June's leash to one of the women and strode away.

۞۞۞

"Excuse me, Bisby? Can I have a quick word?" Dr. Themopolous called down the hallway.

Bisby stopped, but didn't turn to look at her.

"Whatcha need, Doc?"

"I need to ask a few questions, if you don't mind."

Bisby didn't move. "What about?"

"Well, mainly about Stanislaw. How he died, why he died."

Bisby stiffened noticeably on top of his already rigid frame.

"Nothing to say Doc."

"Please?"

Bisby turned and looked square at the doctor. To her credit, she didn't flinch. Bisby watched her for a moment, sighed and strode passed her as she held her office door open.

۞۞۞

Two of the women conferred while June, naked and trussed up, waited and watched. Just beyond the women and cook pot stood an animal pen. June craned her neck for a better look and gasped.

"Are those children?" she asked, horrified. In the pen, she could clearly see several deformed children of varying ages, playing and sleeping in their own filth.

"Them's ain't children. Them's breed feed," one woman said quietly.

"Breed feed?" June asked, sure she didn't want to know the answer.

"Hush!" a large woman shouted, pulling a long sharp knife from behind her back. "Hold her tight!"

۞۞۞

Capreze entered the infirmary as Harlow checked Steve's vital signs. "How's he doing?"

"He's stable," she answered.

"Can we move him quickly if needed?"

"Doc did great work and I have equipment and supplies all set in the transport."

"What if we can't take the transport? Will he survive a ride in a mech?"

Harlow sighed. "I don't know, sir. But from what Themopolous has said, I don't think so. If his sutures rupture…"

"I understand, pilot."

"Sir?"

"Yes, Harlow?"

"Have we gotten word to Masters, Jay and the Rookie?"

"We can't risk it, communications are sure to be monitored."

☻☻☻

The massive walls and heavily gunned turrets of Foggy Bottom came into sight just as the mechs crested a low hill.

"Wow, hasn't changed much," the Rookie whispered.

"You been here before?" Jay asked disengaging the motor drive and taking manual control of the salvage mech.

"Yeah...when I was a kid."

"So, when was that? Last month?" Jay joked.

The Rookie didn't respond, his eyes fixed on the approaching city/state. Jay glanced down at the Rookie's hands, fists clenching and unclenching.

"You looking for a fight?"

"Huh? What? Oh, sorry. Bad memories."

"Well, we'll see if we can fix that."

☻☻☻

"What are you doing?!? Let me go!" June screamed as the women threw her face down onto a table. June's face was forced into a hole in the table and her head was strapped down tight. "What the fuck are you doing?!?"

The large woman kneeled down and put her face up close to June's. The stench of BO and rotting teeth was overpowering.

"You'll want to be still and shut up or this will go badly for you," the woman sneered then nodded. "Start cuttin'."

June felt excruciating pain as a blade sliced into the base of her skull.

☻☻☻

"You're wasting my time, Doc," Bisby growled from his seat in front of Themopolous' desk.

"I'll be brief," Themopolous responded. "Did Stanislaw engage the dead mech or did the dead mech engage Stanislaw?"

"What's the difference?"

"Quite a bit, actually."

Bisby glared. "The deader *attacked* Stanislaw."

"I guess what I'm trying to say is, did it find you or did you find it?"

"We found it. It was hiding below and when Stan was in range the thing came up and..." Bisby choked on his words. He shook his head and stood up. "Are we done?"

"Yes, Biz. Thank you."

🐱🐱🐱

Capreze activated the open com. "Alright folks the train will be here in two hours. I expect each and everyone of you to do your part. I know we have all sworn loyalty to the UDC and with good reason, but something has changed and our ultimate duty is to the safety and survival of mankind, not some generals holed up in a mountain fortress."

Capreze paused and took a deep breath as the base waited for him to continue.

"If any of you want out, now is the time to speak up. Otherwise, I wish us all good luck."

🐱🐱🐱

Jay's com crackled to life. "Attention approaching mechs. This is Defense Tower Alpha. Welcome to Foggy Bottom. Please power down weapons systems and follow the security ATV to transport entrance."

"Will do Defense Tower Alpha. That you Scoggins?"

"Hey Jay! Long time no com! You bring me anything?"

"Sure as shit did, my man. What time ya off?"

"2200. Swing by my place later. Hey Jay?"

"Yeah?"

"Stay on mission and out of the plazas and markets. There's a bug going around, hitting folks hard."

Jay glanced at the Rookie. "Thanks for the heads up, Scog. Later on."

"Roger that."

🐱🐱🐱

June groaned as she awoke. The base of her skull felt like she was on fire and searing pain overwhelmed her entire head, neck and spine.

"Well, looks like nap time is over," she heard the Boss say next to her. She tried to turn her head and screamed from the new agonies that ripped through her.

"Oh, I'd stay still for a bit," the Boss said. "You're going to hurt for a while."

Realization slammed into June's conscious mind. "I can't feel my legs," she croaked.

The Boss laughed. "Yeah, that happens. Should go away soon. If not, well..."

The Foggy Bottom transport gates opened, allowing the security ATV and mechs to enter the scan yard.

"Afternoon, pilots," a voice greeted them over the com. "I'm Security Officer Xiang. I need to run a full contaminant scan of your mechs before proceeding to the hangar. As you may have heard, we are having some type of outbreak here and we need to detect and isolate any further issues. Shouldn't take more than 30 minutes or so. Sorry for the delay."

"Got it. Thanks," Jay responded, then unlatched his harness and kicked his feet up. "Might as well get comfortable."

Proximity claxons sounded.

"UDC train ETA is 15 minutes," Jethro announced over the com.

Capreze switched to an open channel. "Okay base, I want everyone in place and ready. We have one shot at making this work or we'll end up with an entire UDC division down our throats. You know your places. Let's do this!"

"Um, let's do this?" Rachel said from Capreze's office doorway.

"I haven't had to give a rousing speech in a while. Cut your old man some slack."

Rachel crossed and hugged her father.

"What's this about?" Capreze asked, returning the hug.

"Just in case."

"Who's the new guy?" asked the security officer at the admin desk.

"Rookie," Jay answered.

"Figured that much since new guys tend to be rookies," the officer said sarcastically.

"Which is why we call him the Rookie, dumbass," Masters said, stepping around Jay to face the officer.

"Fuck, should have guessed it'd be you this time, Masters," the officer growled.

"Good to see you too, Rodriguez," Masters growled back.

Rodriguez and Masters locked eyes.

Jay cleared his throat. "If you guys are done touching dicks, can we move on?"

"You know the rules." Rodriguez buzzed them into the city/state proper.

☠☠☠

"Keep the com open until after all UDC personnel are off that train then shut it down," Capreze ordered Jethro. He turned to Mathew as the pilot was climbing into his mech. "Stay hidden. Once Jethro jams communications, you are on your own. Get to the first city/state you can and find out what's going on. We need details and data if we are going to piece this together."

"Yes, sir," Mathew responded, powering up his mech. Rachel entered the hangar and gave a slight wave. Mathew smiled and nodded then engaged his mech's legs and walked into the wasteland.

☠☠☠

"What was that about?" the Rookie asked, tossing his bag into the back of the SUV the pilots had been provided with.

Jay tossed his in behind, gave a small laugh and moved to the driver's seat. "Ask tough guy there."

The Rookie stepped aside as Masters threw his pack in with the rest. "Old acquaintance."

"Ha!" Jay barked. "That's what you're going to tell him? Holy shit! That's rich!"

"Fuck you Rind," Masters growled.

"Fine, I'll tell him," Jay said as Masters climbed into the passenger seat, the Rookie took the back seat. "That was Harlow's ex-husband."

Masters glared.

☠☠☠

"What did you do to me?" June asked, starting to shiver.

"Look at that! You have chill bumps on your skin! That's a great sign. You should be up and walking in no time," the Boss laughed, placing a rough hand on June's back. "Not to mention the other activities I have planned."

"What did-" June started, but a fierce slap on her exposed ass stopped her.

"I heard you the first time, bitch," the Boss growled. "I just made sure that little chip in your head wouldn't bring any visitors."

"You disabled my Reaper chip?"

"No, I removed it."

☠☠☠

The SUV sped through Foggy Bottom's busy streets, dodging scooters, vendor skiffs and pedestrians.

"In a hurry?" the Rookie asked Jay, holding onto his oh-shit handle for dear life.

"Med center closes in ten minutes. We need to get this supply req in ASAP or we'll end up here an extra day," Jay answered.

The Rookie turned his attention to Masters, who was staring out the side window, lost in thought.

"So Harlow was married before you met?" the Rookie inquired.

"When we met," Masters answered gruffly.

"Ahhhh...That would explain the hostility."

"Yep, that would explain it," Masters agreed.

The UDC train powered down and the doors to the two cars behind the engine opened. Twenty UDC troops stepped onto the platform from the second car and surveyed the scene. Their commanding officer walked to the first car.

"Clear. You may disembark now."

Two med techs exited the first car, each carrying a medium sized titanium case.

Capreze crossed from the hangar. "Evening. Welcome."

"Sergeant Major Crowley, sir. I'll be overseeing the inoculations," the troop officer said, offering a salute which Capreze promptly returned.

"Excellent. If you will all follow me, I'll show you where you can set up."

The Boss left June to shiver and shake on her own. She tried to huddle her body against the wall for warmth, but even the slightest movement made her head explode and she cried out.

"There, there now, dear," a woman's voice said, as June felt a blanket being draped across her. "This will help. I know how it is."

"You had this done to you? Who are you?" June asked, unable to turn her head to see her visitor.

"I was the one with the knife, sweetie. I took out your chip... I used to be a UDC doctor."

Lights flashed behind the SUV.

"Shit!" Jay yelled. "We don't have time for this."

Masters glanced back at the FBPD cycle closing in on them. Its siren sounded twice then held when Jay didn't pull the SUV over.

"Fuck 'em," Masters said. "Head to the med center. I'll talk us out of it."

Jay laughed. "You think Rodriguez hasn't put you on the 'fuck with' list? Good luck."

"Fuck 'em," Masters said again.

"Good plan. Way to think it through." Jay shook his head.

"Um, can mech pilots be arrested?" the Rookie asked.

"Yes," Masters and Jay answered in unison.

☠☠☠

"This should be enough space," Capreze stated as they entered the mess. "We have coffee ready if you'd like."

Sergeant Major Crowley surveyed the room and motioned for his team to take up positions. Two groups broke off and spaced themselves evenly about the walls, carbines lowered, but at the ready. "We aren't allowed to fraternize. Coffee won't be necessary."

Rachel approached Crowley with a steaming mug. "You don't have to talk to us, but I'd hate for you to pass up the best coffee ever."

The aroma from the mug made Crowley's eyes widen. "That does smell good, pilot."

☠☠☠

"I shot the req to your tablet. It'll tell you who to ask for," Jay said, watching the FBPD officer in the rearview monitor. "Make it quick. We got some drinkin' to do."

"I don't know. Last time I drank with you I ended up banished on this trip with you two," the Rookie laughed.

"Banished?" Masters asked, sounding pissed. "I was at the base for six months before Capreze let me make a req trip, so shut the fuck up."

"Just hurry," Jay said as the officer tapped roughly on the driver's window. Jay looked to Masters. "You're on."

☠☠☠

"Ma'am, I think I speak for all of my men: this is the best damn coffee ever," Crowley stated and each of the UDC soldiers lifted their mugs in salute.

Rachel grinned. "Well, drink up. I'll be sure and send some with you."

"Thank you." Crowley downed his coffee and the other soldiers followed suit.

"We're ready," a med tech said.

"Commander, please send in your staff."

"Of course, Sergeant Major. They should be along in 3...2...1."

One by one the soldiers began to sway then drop. Crowley tried to lift his carbine, but failed, falling unconscious to the floor.

"We're closed," the receptionist called out as the Rookie walked into the med center lobby. "Emergencies go to FB general."

"I know, sorry. I'm with...I'm a mech pilot. I just need to drop off a supply req to a Doctor..." The Rookie fumbled with his tablet, looking for the name. "...Lisbon?"

The receptionist looked up suddenly at the mention of Lisbon's name. "Oh, I'm sorry, Doctor Lisbon is no longer with us."

"Oh...transferred?"

"No, you misunderstand. Dr. Lisbon passed away last week."

"Really? Sorry to hear that," the Rookie paused. "Then who do I give the req to?"

"How long have you been here?" June asked between the waves of pain shooting up and down her spine.

"Forty three years, six months and seven days."

June gasped. "My God...You didn't try to escape?"

The woman laughed. "Of course, but there's only two ways out: death or banishment into the waste."

"No one's ever escaped?"

"One. My grandson. I was able to help him leave. But my son took my feet for it when he found out, so I couldn't follow."

June cried out as feeling returned to her legs. Pain flayed her nerves open and set them afire.

Masters was standing outside the SUV, talking with the FBPD officer when the Rookie came out of the med center.

"Here he is, Officer," Masters grinned, nodding towards the Rookie.

The Rookie stopped short as the FBPD officer came around the SUV and approached him, retinal scanner in hand.

"Let him scan you so we can get moving," Masters smiled. "He just needs complete records for his report."

"Please hold still," the officer commanded placing the scanner close to the Rookie's right eye.

The scanner bleeped sharply and the officer checked it, puzzled. "That's strange... This says you don't exist."

☠☠☠

The two med techs stood frozen.

"Rachel, would you mind showing these two to a holding cell?" Capreze asked.

"Gladly," Rachel answered, pulling her sidearm and gesturing for the techs to move.

"We are supposed to report to the train pilots within the hour," a tech stammered.

"You can report to them right now. They're waiting for you in the cell," Capreze said.

Rachel ushered the techs out the door as Bisby came in. He glanced at the soldiers. "That's some powerful coffee," he laughed.

"This plan is stretched thin, Biz. I hope we can pull it off," Capreze sighed.

☠☠☠

The officer scanned the Rookie again with the same result. "Nope, you're still a ghost. Shoot me your ID validation codes, sir."

Masters stepped next to the Rookie. "Is this necessary, Officer? I mean, we both check out" –Masters motioned towards Jay who in turn waved enthusiastically- "I'm sure it's just a record keeping glitch."

"Your code, sir?" the officer insisted. The Rookie looked to Masters who just shrugged.

"Um, sure." The Rookie tapped at his tablet. "There you go."

The officer studied his own tablet. "Looks in order. Sorry to bother you Pilot-"

"Are we done here?" Jay interrupted.

☠☠☠

"My legs are burning!" June cried out.

"That's just the nerves turning back on. The pain is a good sign," the woman soothed.

"Fuck you it's a good sign!" June yelled.

"Removing a Reaper chip is not easy. You are lucky to be alive, let alone feeling anything."

The pain subsided and June took deep breaths.

"Better?" the woman asked.

"Yes, barely."

"It'll go away." June heard a chair scrape the floor. "I'll be back with some food and water. Don't try to move. You aren't out of the woods yet."

"Woods?" June asked.

"Just something my grandmother would say."

🕱🕱🕱

"That was weird," Masters said as the three pilots drove on. "Never seen a scanner glitch like that."

"That's tech for you," the Rookie quipped. "By the way, Lisbon's dead."

"What?!?" Jay nearly shouted. "Dead? What from?"

"Don't know. Receptionist didn't say."

"Who'd you give the req to?" Masters asked.

"The receptionist. She said she'd pass it on and have everything ready by tomorrow afternoon."

"Excellent. Then let's get this show on the road!" Jay whooped.

The Rookie caught Masters eyeing him. "What?"

"I've just never seen a scanner glitch before, that's all."

"You already said that."

"I meant it."

🕱🕱🕱

"It's up to the two of you now," Capreze said, handing Jethro and Themopolous each a titanium case. "I hope you can figure this out."

"We'll try, sir," Themopolous said.

Capreze stepped to the door. "I'll be with the pilots securing the UDC troops. Com me if you find anything." He looked them both in the eye then left the exam room.

"You know anything about nanotech?" Jethro asked Themopolous.

"No. You?"

"Not a thing. Jay's the theory guy. I'm just the grunt that keeps shit running."

"Well, it's time for us both to theory-up," Themopolous said, opening her case.

🕱🕱🕱

"Here you go, gentlemen," Jay said as he pulled to the curb in front of the UDC diplomatic lodging building. "I'll be back to get you two in a couple hours."

"What? Where are you going?" the Rookie asked, confused.

"Jay's got needs to take care of," Masters laughed grabbing a bag and tossing it at the Rookie.

The Rookie raised his eyebrows. "The Commander is okay with this?"

Jay snorted. "Not a fucking clue. What I do with my time while on a req run is my business." Jay narrowed his eyes. "I'd like to keep it that way."

☠☠☠

"These mother fuckers were armed for full on fucking war!" Harlow exclaimed as Capreze entered the mess, seeing the organized piles of rifles, pistols, grenades, knives and various other weapons and instruments. Each of the soldiers was trussed up with their arms and legs tied behind their backs. All remained unconscious.

"Well, they were on security detail through the waste," Mathew said.

"No, 90% of that gear would be stored on board the train. The only reason they'd be armed like that is if they expected trouble," Rachel responded.

"They got it," Bisby smirked.

"Yes, Biz, they did," Capreze agreed.

☠☠☠

"Wow, nice digs," the Rookie whistled in appreciation as he tossed his pack on the double bed.

"We got lucky," Masters said tossing his pack on his own double bed. "Don't expect this every time, usually we're stuck in the security barracks in the basement. These rooms are pretty much occupied by UDC brass and visiting politicians from other city/states. But I ain't complaining."

Masters kicked his boots off and flopped onto the bed. "You'll want to grab a shower before we head out tonight."

"Where are we going, by the way?"

"Oh, you'll see. Jay never disappoints, trust me."

☠☠☠

"What is it?" June asked as the woman carefully positioned June's head so she could eat.

"Food," the woman answered lifting a spoon.

"What food?" June focused on the spoon, trying to figure out the contents of the stew-like substance.

The woman stayed silent.

"Why won't you answer me?"

"You don't want to know the answer."

"No. I won't eat that."

"Maybe you just need to work up an appetite," the Boss said from the doorway.

"Leave her be!"

"Just because you're my mother don't mean I won't rape you 'til sunrise!" the Boss yelled. "Now get the fuck out!"

Masters was snoring soundly when the Rookie stepped from the bathroom, freshly scrubbed. He scooped up the mini-tablet on the bedside table and switched on the vid screen, scanning for the local news feed.

"…while half the population is over the flu bug going around, the other half is still trying to recover. Local health authorities insist there is no relation to the mandatory inoculations given earlier this month.

"In other news, School Superintendent Pierce…"

The Rookie switched the vid screen off and stretched out on his bed. Exhausted, he was fast asleep in seconds, his light snores joining Masters'.

Part Two - The Cage

"HEY! WAKE THE FUCK UP!"

Both Masters and the Rookie sat upright, clawing at their coms.

"Sweet fuck!"

"What the hell?!?"

"Ah, there you two are. Put your party dresses on ladies, it's time to get in some trouble! Get your asses down here and let's go!"

"Let me piss first," Masters yawned.

The Rookie rubbed his ear. "Fuck, I think I'm deaf."

"Bullshit. Get you ass down here. Debauchery doesn't just happen, you know."

"He really gets into this shit, huh?" the Rookie asked.

"You ain't seen nothing like a night out with Jay."

"Damn fucking right! Now MOVE!"

"Where we headed?" the Rookie asked, watching the building lights wiz by as Jay swerved in and out of traffic. "And why are we in such a fucking hurry?"

"Oh, you'll see," Jay smirked. "And we are hurrying so we don't miss the first bout."

"First bout?" Masters asked. "No way! How'd you get us on the list?"

"I called in a favor. Broke my heart to do it, but figured we should show the Rookie how to live a little."

"Fucking sweet!"

"Bout?" the Rookie asked, his blood running cold. "Jay, where exactly are we going?"

Jay's smirk widened.

💀💀💀

"This is going to be fucking great! I wish Harlow could see this. Man is she going to be pissed she missed it," Masters said, literally bouncing in his seat as Jay punched in a code to the parking garage they pulled up to. The gate lifted and they drove through, circling down several levels until they were stopped by two very large, well armed guards.

"Pass code?" one guard asked.

"Legit's bitch," Jay said casually.

"Alright. Hop on out guys. Jimmy here will show you the way," the guard said, handing Jay a valet ticket.

"Fucking great!" Masters repeated.

💀💀💀

Bass boomed, shaking the narrow stairs that Jimmy led the pilots down. He pounded twice on a massive iron door at the bottom. Within seconds it opened, revealing a cavernous space crowded with people, yelling, laughing and drinking.

At the center of the space was an enormous steel cage surrounding a blood stained mat.

"Follow me, gentlemen," Jimmy said, parting the crowd with his bulk.

Masters and Jay followed eagerly, but the Rookie froze. Masters turned to say something and frowned, seeing the Rookie's face.

"What's up, kid?"

"I shouldn't be here."

Masters grabbed the Rookie and yanked him along.

💀💀💀

"Holy shit! Jay Rind! Long time, my friend!" Legit exclaimed, clasping Jay's hand and patting him on the shoulder as Jimmy excused himself, having led the three pilots to a private box set up in front of the fight cage. "How long has it been?"

"Not long enough, you ugly bastard!" Jay shouted, trying to be heard above the crowd yelling and calling for the first fight to start.

"Scoot the fuck over!" Legit ordered three spectators seated in the box. They unquestioningly got up and moved. Legit motioned for the three to sit then stopped short, eyeing the Rookie.

"Mitch Masters. Damn glad to meet ya," Mitch said extending his hand. Legit took his eyes away from the Rookie and shook Masters' hand.

"Masters you say?" Legit smiled. "You've made quite a name for yourself. I saw the vid from the Smyrna battle. Impressive."

Legit didn't wait for Masters to respond, stepping around him to the Rookie.

"You've got balls coming back," Legit said with honest surprise and a dangerous smile.

"No, Legit, that's our new Rookie," Jay said.

Legit turned to Jay. "You really don't know who this is, do you?" Legit laughed heartily. "This is fucking priceless!"

"You want the bullet between your eyes now or after you watch a fight or two?" Legit asked the Rookie, eyes cold.

The Rookie responded by cracking his neck and stepping forward.

One of Legit's bodyguards grabbed the Rookie's shoulder. With blinding speed the Rookie reached up and snapped two of his fingers back, forcing the muscled man to the floor.

"You want him to keep these?" the Rookie asked, never taking his eyes from Legit's.

Jay stepped between the two men. "I don't know what is fucking going on, but can we dial down the murder and mayhem talk?"

Legit and the Rookie locked eyes for a few moments then Legit smiled and raised his hands. "You know what? I'm a reasonable man. How about you let my man go and we have a seat and talk some business?"

The Rookie let go of the bodyguard's fingers, but didn't sit.

Jay looked from the Rookie to Legit. "Anyone gonna tell us what's going on?"

Legit sat down and lit a cigar, puffing until the end cherried red. "You really don't know?"

"Not a clue."

"Come on Jay, you've never heard of the Razor?"

The Rookie sighed and sat down.

"The Razor?" Jay sat down abruptly. "You're the fucking Razor?"

The Rookie wouldn't meet Jay's gaze. "Yeah."

"Who's the Razor? I mean, I know now, but who was he, you, who-the-fuck-ever?" Masters asked, looking from Jay to the Rookie to Legit and back again.

"Best fighter to ever enter that ring," Legit answered, nodding towards the steel cage. "284 fights. Undefeated."

Masters' jaw dropped. "Holy shit. So why the name 'The Razor'?"

"Because when I was done killing my opponents, I'd slice their face off with a straight razor and wear it for the next fight," the Rookie answered flatly.

A half-naked waitress set a tray of drinks down next to Legit. "Thanks darlin'." He tweaked a nipple, pulling her down to him and kissed her deeply. "Be available later." Legit handed each of the pilots a drink. "Not as good as Jay's shit, if I remember right, but it'll do the trick."

The pilots each took their drinks.

"So, before the fights start, let's get business out of the way," Legit puffed his cigar, slowly exhaling. "My proposal is: I'll let Razor live –no, wait, I won't have him killed- if he agrees to one more fight. Sound good?"

The Rookie stood. "I don't fight anymore."

Legit laughed. "Don't fight? You're a fucking mech pilot! What the fuck do you call that? Dancing?"

"That's different."

"BULLSHIT!" Legit roared. Several conversations stopped, but everyone had the good sense not to look their way.

"You think I can't make it out of here?" the Rookie grinned confidently.

"You? Sure," Legit said taking out a pistol and placing it against Masters' temple. "But Hot Shot will be dead before you get two steps."

"Sit down," Jay said calmly. The Rookie glared down at Jay. "Sit. Now."

The Rookie reluctantly took his seat.

"What are you thinking?" Jay asked Legit.

Legit tucked the pistol away and reached over and patted Jay on the knee. "I could always trust Jay Rind to see reason." Legit leaned back and took another drink. "The last fight tonight is between Kilroy and Crusher John. Now Crusher John is all mine, but Kilroy refuses to play along. He's also the reigning champ at 135 undefeated bouts. I need Kilroy to go down or I stand to loose a lot of money."

Legit fixated on the Rookie. "Not quite the 17.4 mill you cost me, but it's a lot."

"He fights, Kilroy goes down, you make yours and we get to go free? That the deal?" Jay asked Legit.

"Yep."

"What's this got to do with me?" Jay asked.

"You brought the Razor here. Nothing personal Jay, just business."

Jay smirked. "So even though this ain't *my* business, you're making it mine? That it?"

"If you want to see it that way, I guess so."

"Good. Then if it's business, let's talk some real business."

Legit laughed heartily. "You'll never hear me say Jay Rind ain't got balls!"

"I also have remote control of two mechs."

Legit stopped laughing.

Legit turned and stabbed his cigar at Jay. "You may be crazy, but you ain't that crazy."

"I just uploaded your DNA to my mech. My life signs go and it comes looking for you. It's done, Legit. No going back now. You want to hear my deal or not?"

"Keep talking, crazy man."

Jay tapped at his tablet. "I just sent you a list of parts I need. They're a little outside my usual budget. Get those and the kid fights."

"Tomorrow, okay?"

"Nope."

"Fine… You'll have them by the end of the night."

"Great. Deal done?"

"Deal done."

Jay leaned in close to the Rookie. "Know anything about Kilroy?"

"Nope."

"Think you can take him anyway?"

"Yep."

Jay studied the Rookie closely then laughed and took a drink. "I can't figure you out, kid. I hope we live through this so I can."

Masters stood up. "If everyone's done using me as the pawn of death I really need to piss."

Legit nodded to a bodyguard. "He'll take you. Don't try anything."

"Is he gonna hold my dick for me?"

"If that's your kink, mech boy, then sure."

"Good to know I have my options open."

"Go piss…"

☗☗☗

The first fight took Masters and Jay by surprise. The Rookie didn't bat an eye.

"Kids? Are you fucking kidding me?" Masters asked, shocked as two boys, no more than twelve were tossed inside the cage.

"Gotta start somewhere," Legit answered casually.

A buzzer sounded and the two boys stepped out ready to kill. No handshake, no greeting, just death.

It was over in a moment as one boy pinned the other and tore out his opponent's throat with his teeth. Blood sprayed everywhere as the child stood over the corpse, animalistic screams of triumph coming from his bloody maw.

☗☗☗

"You'll like this next fight, Masters," Legit taunted. "They're not quite as skilled as your woman, but they'll put on a show."

Masters turned on Legit, but Jay held him back as two women, stripped to the waist, entered the cage. "Chill," Jay cautioned.

"Don't look so surprised," Legit scoffed. "Officer Rodriguez and I are old friends. You're his favorite subject."

Although the bout lasted a little longer than the previous, it was no less gruesome as one fighter dug her sharpened nails into the other's chest and ripped a breast clean off.

The crowd exploded with cheers and bloodlust.

☗☗☗

The third fight was a much stronger contest.

The pilots watched as two evenly matched men went after each other like caged animals, which they were.

One fighter, a squat, tightly muscled man, was a strong ground fighter, but his opponent, wiry and lean, was lightning fast and flexible and able to squirm out of the other's grasp each time before getting a limb ripped off.

"Skinny goes down in four," Legit winked at Jay and sure enough the lean fighter started to wobble only seconds into the fourth round.

The slight hesitation resulted in his quick and messy decapitation.

As the fourth fight was under way, Masters leaned over to the Rookie. "Drugs?"

The Rookie nodded.

"So how did you...?" Masters asked.

"I didn't eat or drink the entire day of or during the fight. I wouldn't let anyone get near me and I watched my gear like a starving zombie."

Masters glanced down at the Rookie's cocktail, which was half way finished. Almost imperceptibly, the Rookie nodded to the floor. Below his seat was a small puddle of liquid.

Masters looked at his own drink and blanched, flagging down a passing waitress. "Hey! You guys got any coffee?"

"So where are you getting the Reaper chips?" Jay asked Legit as the latest corpse was removed from the cage.

"Huh? I don't know what you mean, Jay. UDC provides all city/state citizens with Reaper chips at birth," Legit responded with veiled sarcasm.

"Bullshit. I've lived in the waste long enough to know you aren't getting your fighters from inside the walls. Who are you buying them from? The Ranchers? Or do you just pick from the refugees trying to get in, hoping for a better life than the waste."

"I don't know what you're talking about, Rind," Legit smiled.

"If you're sticking to the same format, I'm up after this one," the Rookie said, getting to his feet, eyeing the cage as three 'offenders' were whipped mercilessly for the crowd's entertainment.

"You got it, kid," Legit smirked. "You're up. I'll be announcing this one. What do you want me to call you."

"The Rookie."

"Excellent! That'll make the odds skyrocket in my favor. No one will believe an unknown named The Rookie can take down Kilroy."

"They can believe what they want. They'll know the truth soon enough when his body is dragged from the cage."

"Love that spirit!"

�☠☠

"Ladies and Gentlemen and those in between!" Legit boomed over the PA. "I'm sorry to say that tonight's fight has changed."

A groan erupted from the crowd. Legit made a theatrical quiet down motion. He paused before bringing the old fashioned mic back to his lips, savoring the moment.

"Now you all know me, would I disappoint?"

No's and never's rang out.

"Don't worry, Kilroy *will* be fighting, but instead of Crusher John he'll be taking on a newcomer."

Legit caught the eye of the Rookie standing just outside the cage and grinned wickedly.

"Folks, I give you The Rookie!"

☠☠☠

Kilroy stepped into the cage, his muscles twitching with nervous, murderous energy. "So you're the piece of shit that's supposed to end my reign?"

"Just settling an old debt. Nothing personal," the Rookie shouted over the crowd noise. "I'll try to make it quick." Kilroy just laughed.

The bell sounded and Kilroy came out swinging, his massive arms cutting through the air like steel girders.

The Rookie danced out of reach, studying the big fighter's movements, watching for his weaknesses, his habits.

"I know what you're doing!" Kilroy yelled between swings. "But you ain't gonna find what you're looking for."

☠☠☠

"Jeezus, that guy is fucking huge," Masters said. "What's he on?"

"Everything money can buy," Legit interjected. "300 pounds and almost zero body fat. He's an unstoppable killing machine. Too bad unstoppable is bad for business."

They watched the Rookie move around Kilroy, ducking and dodging.

"Ahh, the Razor has gone soft," Legit mocked.

"Maybe he just isn't the killer you knew," Jay said. "People change."

"Bullshit. That kid's a homicidal madman. Why'd you think he became a mech pilot?"

Masters and Jay stayed silent, neither sure they wanted to explore the answer.

"Because he needed bigger prey, that's why!"

The crowd grew impatient with the Rookie's skillful dodging. Glasses and bottles started pelting the fight cage. Liquor splashed the Rookie in the face momentarily blinding him.

That moment was all Kilroy needed. He closed in quickly on the Rookie, landing two powerful gut punches and a right uppercut, simultaneously doubling the Rookie over and sending him flying backwards against the cage.

Stunned, the Rookie barely avoided a boot stomp to the face by rolling across the mat into a crouch. That was when he saw the weakness.

The Rookie stood up, dodged two more swings and cracked his neck.

Kilroy was a mat-bound ton of muscle. The Rookie smiled at this realization.

"Keep fucking smiling, dead boy!" Kilroy roared.

The Rookie stayed silent, but turned his body just right, backing himself into a corner, giving the illusion of carelessness. Kilroy took the bait, putting all his power behind a right arm punch.

The Rookie reached above, grabbing the steel cage, and pulled himself up, just clear of Kilroy's punch. While the brawler was lucky enough not to connect with one of the steel bars, he was unlucky enough to have his arm become trapped between two bars, wedged tight.

The Rookie let go of the cage, letting all of his weight fall onto Kilroy's trapped arm. The snap brought a massive groan from the crowd and then an equally massive cheer. Kilroy tried to slump to the ground, but his still trapped arm wouldn't let him, forcing him to hang and pull on the limb in agony.

The Rookie casually stepped away from Kilroy and walked to the edge of the cage to stare at Legit. "We're done!"

Legit grinned viciously and shook his head. *Finish it*, he mouthed.

"It is!"

Legit pulled his pistol and turned on Masters.

Four bodyguards pounced on Jay and Masters, holding both of them tight as Legit placed the barrel of the pistol against Masters' forehead.

"It's a shame really," Legit said. "You seem like a good guy."

Masters and Jay struggled as Legit pulled the hammer back. The Rookie raged at the cage's door, trying to force it open, the crowd oblivious to the side-show as they raged for Kilroy's head.

Legit paused as the screams of bloodlust turned to screams of agony. He glanced over his shoulder as one by one, members of the crowd grabbed at their heads in pain.

Legit's bodyguards released Jay and Masters, falling to their knees, palms pressed firmly against their skulls, their faces distorted by pain.

"What the fuck?" Legit said, turning and watching the entire roomful of people brought to the ground by some unseen torture.

The screams joined into one horrible crescendo and then...silence.

Before him, every single person laid unmoving, chests still, dead.

Legit was so distracted by the scene that the brutal rabbit punches to his kidneys took him completely by surprise, dropping him to his knees. Masters wrapped an arm around Legit's throat, locking it tight.

"Any last words?"

"Wait!" the Rookie shouted.

Masters placed a knee in the center of Legit's back and pressed, causing the man to wince and gasp as his spine was stretched. "Why?"

"Because he knows the codes to get out of here. The door is secured from the inside," the Rookie answered, motioning to the entrance they had come through earlier in the night.

"He's...right," Legit choked.

Masters hesitated then slammed Legit upside the head and shoved him to the ground. Jay stepped in quickly and picked up Legit's pistol.

"Good. Now how about someone open this fucking cage?" the Rookie yelled.

Jay shoved Legit against the cage door, pistol trained on his forehead. "Open it asshole."

"You ain't gonna shoot me, Jay," Legit smirked. "You ain't *that* kinda guy."

"But, I am," Masters called over, having retrieved Legit's bodyguards' sidearms. "In fact," Masters continued hefting a rather large auto-pistol. "I'm the kinda guy that will ass rape you with this before I pull the trigger."

Legit sized up Masters, laughed and faced the Rookie. "I knew you hadn't gone soft. These assholes are just your kind of crazy." Legit reached for the number pad and started to key in the code.

Legit had half the code typed in when movement out of the corner of his eye distracted him.

"Whatcha fuckin' waiting on?" Jay growled.

Legit glanced away from the keypad to one of the dead spectators in the front row. "Did that guy move?"

"What? You saw what happened! Everyone's Reaper chip took a shit and fried their brains. Which begs the question: why aren't you fried?"

"Had mine taken out. Ain't lettin' nobody have control over my life."

"Yeah, yeah, finish typing," Jay sneered. But before Legit could continue, every corpse in the room twitched simultaneously.

"See!" Legit shouted.

"Whoa! What the fuck is going on?" Masters yelled, watching the corpses convulse. "They shouldn't be doing that!"

"No shit!" Jay yelled back. He turned on Legit. "Finish typing in the code! Now!"

"I'm trying! Back the fuck off, Rind!"

The Rookie eyed Kilroy's corpse as it shook, still dangling by its trapped arm. Then as one, the corpses stilled.

"This is fucking weird," Masters said.

"You think it's because of the inoculation?" the Rookie mused, his eyes never leaving Kilroy's now still form.

"Let me guess," Jay said to Legit. "You didn't get inoculated, but all your people did."

The Rookie never let his eyes leave Kilroy's corpse, instinct keeping him wary.

"I don't give a fuck who got a shot in their ass! Get me out of here!" the Rookie insisted.

And then, Kilroy moved. His body no longer dangled, as the corpse stood and tried to turn towards the Rookie, but was prevented by its wedged arm. Kilroy growled low and began to pull against the arm. Flesh started to rip.

"Um, guys?!?" the Rookie gulped.

"Yeah, we know!" Masters responded.

The Rookie risked a glance away from Kilroy.

Every corpse in the room began to stand.

☠☠☠

Double fisted and taking quick, targeted aim, Masters opened fire. The zombies' heads exploded with each expertly placed shot.

Legit hit the last number and the cage lock disengaged. "Don't say I didn't do nothing for ya Razor! Now someone give me a fucking gun!"

Masters kicked a pistol over and Legit grabbed it up in time to dodge a lunging zombie, putting a bullet in its brain, the headless corpse falling against the cage door.

The Rookie dove for the door, but a loud click told him he was again trapped with the raging corpse of a trained killer.

☠☠☠

The crunch of bone and snap, pop, tear of sinew and flesh forced the Rookie to switch his focus from the once again locked cage door, to the zombie that was Kilroy.

The hulking abomination, black blood spewing from the stump of its right arm, bared its teeth and roared. The Rookie cracked his neck, readying himself for the attack.

"Anytime you want to try opening the door again, feel free!" the Rookie yelled.

"You're just going to have to suck it up, kid and deal with your one zombie! We've got a few more on our hands!" Jay yelled.

☠☠☠

"I'm almost out!" Masters hollered.

"Behind the bar! Sixth bottle from the left! Pull it!" Legit yelled back.

Masters ducked two zombies, spun and buried his empty auto-pistols into their heads. He rolled to the bar, springing up and over in one fluid motion and grabbed the bottle as he tumbled to the floor.

Even over the cacophony of zombie howls and gunfire, Masters heard gears clanging. Within seconds the entire wall behind the bar opened onto an arsenal to rival the mech base itself.

"Oh, I wish Harlow could see this," Masters muttered, grabbing a 12 gauge full-auto shotgun.

☠☠☠

The Rookie ignored the deafening shotgun blasts and focused on the newly freed zombie Kilroy.

"Okay, big boy, let's see what you-" but before he could finish Kilroy charged.

The Rookie rolled to the side, grabbing the cage for leverage and kicked out hard with his left leg, connecting with Kilroy's right calf, knocking the enraged zombie to the mat. The Rookie pulled himself upright and continued to climb the cage wall, trying to get out of reach of the already recovered zombie as it rushed him again.

"FUCK ME!" he yelled, barley swinging his legs away from Kilroy's grasp.

☠☠☠

Jay caught the A1-59 auto pistol Masters tossed him just as his own clicked empty. Opening fire he dropped three more zombies as he tried to side-step over to the bar.

Legit lifted a chair, smashing it down atop two zombies, crushing but not killing them. He grabbed another chair and swung it out in an arc, clearing away the zombies rushing him.

"A little help!" Legit screamed.

Jay hesitated briefly, but quickly opened fire, making a path for Legit to get to the bar.

"Clear! Move your ass!" Jay called out, slapping the fresh magazine home Masters handed him.

☠☠☠

"FUCK OFF!" the Rookie screamed, kicking the Kilroy zombie squarely in the face. The reanimated brawler stumbled back and roared.

The Rookie reached up and grabbed the top of the cage, swinging himself to the other side, careful to keep his legs out of Kilroy's grasp.

Kilroy leapt several times, its one arm reaching and swinging for the Rookie, becoming more and more enraged with each miss.

The Rookie knew he couldn't hang from the cage indefinitely and couldn't expect assistance anytime soon. He swore he'd never die in the fight cage and he planned on keeping it that way.

"We may need to burn this place!" Masters yelled as Legit joined him and Jay behind the bar. "Is there a back exit?"

"No!" Legit answered.

"WHAT?!?" Jay yelled dropping nine more zombies, but dozens remained. "How the fuck'd you expect to get out if you were raided?"

"I don't get raided!" Legit answered.

"Are you FUCKING KIDDING ME?!?"

"Doesn't matter!" Masters hollered. "Keep firing!"

Legit pulled down a minigun and ammo. He clicked on the motor drive and began strafing the zombies with over a thousand rounds per minute. Those stupid enough to stay standing were vaporized. "How's that?!?"

The Rookie dropped with his back against the cage wall. Kilroy charged. At the very last second, the Rookie dodged, rolled then leapt, kicking Kilroy's head into the steel bars of the cage, wedging it tightly. The zombie roared and clawed at its neck, trying to free itself.

Not losing a moment, the Rookie leapt again, using the cage wall to launch himself back to the top. He took two swings then dropped his entire weight onto Kilroy's shoulders. The zombie's wedged head ripped from its body and stayed stuck between the bars. The body twitched, fell and was still.

The minigun jammed and Legit tossed it to the ground, replacing it with a dual-mag sub-machine gun. Masters and Jay continued to fire, desperately trying to whittle down the undead's numbers.

"Hey! Over here you deader fucks!" the Rookie yelled, rattling the fight cage, trying to divert the zombies away from Masters and Jay. Legit could fuck off and die as far as he was concerned.

About 150 zombie patrons were left and more than half turned towards the cage. "Yeah! That's right! Meat in a box! Come and get it!"

The zombies swarmed and the cage began to groan.

Legit ducked underneath the arsenal and pulled open a concealed drawer. He pulled out five small, flat boxes and set them upright on the bar.

"You are gonna want to get down Razor!" Legit yelled. Masters and Jay glanced at Legit, puzzled. "These go boom and shred. You'll want to get down too." Neither needed to be told twice and they ducked behind the bar.

Legit tapped five times on a small touch he grabbed with the boxes then winked at Jay and Masters.

"3...2...1!"

The Rookie flattened himself on the mat as the room exploded in fire.

"Holy fucking shit! I've wanted to shoot those fuckers off since I got them!" Legit whooped.

"Glad we could share the experience," Jay said sarcastically. "How about we skip the encore and get the fuck out of here?"

Masters peered over the bar. "Clear."

The three stood and surveyed the scene. Shredded, smoldering bodies were everywhere. Some still moved, but none seemed capable of any attack.

"I've got the stragglers," Masters said as he vaulted the bar and immediately set to work putting down the zombies that hadn't been destroyed by the blast.

"OPEN THE FUCKING CAGE!" the Rookie bellowed.

The cage door clicked open and the Rookie shoved against it, exited and immediately stepped up to Legit, grabbed him by the back of the head and brought Legit's face to his rising knee, shattering his nose.

Legit stumbled back, tripped over the zombie corpses and fell hard. "What the FUCK?!?"

"You call me Razor again and I'll feed you your balls," the Rookie growled, walking to the only door in or out. "What's the fucking code?"

Before Legit could answer, a loud pounding from the other side of the door echoed through the room.

"UDC Security! Open up immediately!"

"That sounds like your friend Rodriguez," Legit said, winking at Masters.

"Stop winking at me asshole," Masters replied, moving to the other side of the room as he loaded shells into a pump-action shotgun. The Rookie and

Jay armed themselves also and joined Masters, putting distance between themselves and the door.

"Y'all need to relax," Legit laughed and keyed in the code. The door clicked open. "Rodriguez, my man, glad to-!" was all Legit was able to say before the back of his head exploded and Rodriguez kicked the door all the way open, his matte black 9mm still smoking.

☠☠☠

Six more UDC security officers, weapons drawn, followed Rodriguez into the room and surveyed the scene. The pilots didn't move a muscle, their own weapons raised.

One of the security officers caught sight of the three and his head cocked to an unnatural angle. "Masters, Mitchell, Mech Pilot. Rind, Jay, Chief Mechanic. Both listed for termination. Third human does not exist. Termination order authorized." The seven officers raised their weapons in unison.

"What the fuck...?" Masters muttered.

The Rookie didn't wait to find out and started firing first, racing to the cover of the bar. Masters and Jay followed suit.

CHAPTER FIVE

PART ONE - DEATH & UNDEATH

"How are they doing?" Capreze asked Themopolous while she checked monitor readings from the UDC troops.

"We have maybe an hour, possibly two before they are conscious," Themopolous answered. "What are you going to do when they do wake up?"

"Reason with them, or specifically the Sergeant Major," Capreze answered, brow furrowed.

"Will he listen?"

"No, but I have to try."

"Commander?" Jethro called over the com.

"Go ahead, Jethro."

"We just had a spike in the communication system. Something is trying to crack my jamming and get through. I'm fighting it, but it's fighting back."

"I'll be right there."

�☠☠

Well, this just sucks, Mathew thought as he dealt with the isolation of being cut off from base communications.

He also grew frustrated with the slow progress he was making, having to stay close to the mesas and hills in order to keep a low profile.

Not that a 50-ton war machine could ever keep a low profile, but at least he wasn't an open target.

An open target for *what* also bothered him. Just a few days ago life, while not safe and secure, was at least routine.

Patrol time, base time, Rachel time. It all ran like clockwork.

☠☠☠

June wanted to die.

The Boss had appetites, beyond just cannibalism, and June's body had paid the price.

The pain was so bad that she truly believed her soul was bleeding.

When he came back and undid the straps and restraints, June stayed very still, waiting for the down side.

"Go clean up," he muttered, sounding drunk. "You stink."

She heard him shuffle away, but didn't hear the door close. June attempted to push her self up, but the pain was too much and she cried out.

"Let me help," the Boss's mother said as she hobbled through the door.

💀💀💀

"What you got for me, Jethro?" Capreze asked, entering the control room.

"I honestly don't know. I've never seen anything like this before," Jethro responded, tapping away at three separate tablets while monitoring two vid screens. "This is not normal UDC programming, nor is it modified. This is brand new shit."

"What's it trying to do?"

"If I'm reading this right, and I may not be, it's trying to get a command through our jam."

"What kind of command?"

"Not a clue, but considering how malicious this program is, I don't think we want to know."

"Well, keep at it."

💀💀💀

"There're only six of them. We can take 'em!" Masters cried. Bottles exploded above his, Jay's and the Rookie's head as they used the bar for cover.

"Not with that combat armor they have!" Jay yelled back.

"Screw this!" the Rookie said, seeing a box of grenades amongst Legit's other armaments. The Rookie grabbed three grenades and handed one each to Masters and Jay. They each pulled the pin and hurled them over the bar into the fight room.

Within five seconds all three detonated and bits of debris, zombie parts and UDC security personnel uniforms, showered down on them.

💀💀💀

June, with help, stepped into the night air. "Thank you."

"Of course, dear," the old woman said.

"I'm Ju- Um, Rachel."

"I'm Olivia."

The two stayed silent as they walked over to a water trough. June shivered as she removed the blanket Olivia had wrapped about her. Olivia pulled a stool close to the trough and motioned for June to do the same.

137

"It's hard for me to stand for long," Olivia said, pulling up her long, dingy skirt to show June the prosthetic feet attached to her lower legs. "They get me around, but aren't exactly built for comfort."

☻☻☻

"This is not good, this is not good, this is not good," Jethro muttered while frantically trying to defend against the jamming breach. "Shit shit shit shit SHIT!"

Jethro typed so hard on the three tablets before him that blisters began to form on his fingertips. He stared at the two vid screens, watching line upon line of foreign code stream by. With every programming defense he put in place, the intruding software created a counter offense.

"No! You will not fucking-!" The last words were choked from him as searing pain engulfed the back of his head.

Jethro collapsed.

☻☻☻

Harlow stared in horror as each UDC trooper, Steve and Dr. Themopolous began to convulse.

"Doctor!" Harlow yelled, running to Themopolous' side.

"My... head! Reaper...chip..." Themopolous croaked, trying to fight the agony. "Cut it out!"

Harlow lifted Themopolous onto a bed and flipped her onto her stomach. Grabbing a pair of scissors she cut Themopolous' clothes down the back and tore them away, exposing the doctor's neck and back.

Harlow splashed antiseptic across the base of Themopolous' skull, grabbed a scalpel and probed for the right spot with her fingers.

Finding it, she said a silent prayer and cut.

☻☻☻

Masters wiped gore from his uniform, flicking bits of flesh off his hands while the Rookie and Jay surveyed the room.

A UDC officer twitched, tried sitting up, but was hindered by the lack of a lower half. Viscera spilled onto the floor from its ripped open torso. The officer bared its bloody teeth as the Rookie approached, pistol trained on the thing's head.

"Masters! Looks like your buddy is still kicking," the Rookie called out, staring down at the ravaged form of Rodriguez. "He's full on deader."

"Put him down," Masters called back.

The Rookie took aim and fired.

☻☻☻

June winced as Olivia carefully wiped at her skin with a wet cloth.

"Sorry. I'll try to be little more gentle," Olivia apologized.

"Don't worry about me. I've been through worse," June responded.

Olivia eyed June carefully, taking in her battered face and throat; the lacerations and cuts across her breasts and stomach; the bruising on her exposed pelvis and thighs. "Really, dear?"

June fought back the tears, her breath catching in her chest. "No," she whispered.

Olivia kept wiping, dipping and wringing out the rag after it became too soiled. "I wish I could say it won't get worse."

☻☻☻

Jethro fought through the debilitating pain, reached up from the floor and slammed his hand down on his console. Instantly the torture stopped and Jethro collapsed back to the floor, his chest heaving and blood trickling from his ears and nose.

He could hear foot falls outside the control room, but didn't have the strength to focus.

"Jethro! Jeezus fuck!" Rachel yelled, kneeling next to the stricken mechanic. "Doc! Jethro has collapsed and is bleeding badly! I need assistance immediately!" Rachel's com crackled with static, but there was no response. "Doc!"

"Don't bother," Jethro whispered. "I shut it all down."

☻☻☻

Only a few feet from where June and Olivia sat stood the pen the deformed children were kept in. June tried to ignore the sleeping forms, but her eyes were drawn back again and again. Olivia followed June's gaze as she applied some potent and pungent salve to the worst of June's wounds.

"You don't want to know," Olivia sighed. "But, if the Boss doesn't kill you, I guess you'll find out anyway."

June waited for Olivia to continue, but spoke up when she didn't. "Find out what?"

"What's in the stew," Olivia whispered.

June's eyes went wide with shock.

☻☻☻

Themopolous went still just as Harlow pulled the Reaper chip from the back of her skull. Blood poured from the wound, soaking the table and Harlow quickly packed the wound with gauze and antiseptic.

"Doc? Doc, can you hear me?" Harlow asked, tossing the Reaper chip onto a nearby tray.

Themopolous groaned slightly and Harlow took that as a good sign. She patted the doctor on the back. "I have to check the others. Just stay still." Themopolous groaned again.

As Harlow approached the UDC troops she could easily see that half of them weren't breathing anymore.

"Shit," Harlow exclaimed.

"You cook...children?" June exclaimed.

"Only the inbred and deformed," Olivia answered. "It's how we survive."

June shook her head in disbelief. "But they're children!"

"Most don't survive past three or four years anyway. We've figured out which afflictions are the worst and plan accordingly." Olivia lifted her eyes and looked June square in the face. "We have to eat. Out here in the waste, our options are limited."

"What do you mean by 'plan accordingly'?"

Olivia set the salve aside. "We keep careful records. We cross-breed to keep our numbers up and we inbreed to keep our...stocks up."

Jethro tried to sit, but Rachel pushed him gently back. "Don't try to move."

"I don't have a choice," Jethro grunted, slapping Rachel's hands away. "Get me up. We don't have much time."

"I thought you shut it off."

"Shutting off the com system only delays the signal. It can't piggyback on our system. But that signal was strong. All it will need is a power boost and it will get here on its own. I have to repair the jam before whoever is sending dials it up a notch."

Rachel helped Jethro to his chair. "I'll get the Doc."

"Don't you dare judge!" Olivia hissed. "Unless you've lived your life on the brink of starvation out in the middle of Hell itself then you have no place telling folks how to live their lives!"

June's eyes misted over and she fought another wave of tears. "But, they're just children."

"Tasty, too," Chunks grunted from behind the two women. He raised a blackened limb to his mouth and tore a piece of the flesh away, smacking his lips greedily. "Tender. Not full of those gamey hormones."

June's stomach rebelled and she vomited what little food she had eaten. Chunks laughed.

💀💀💀

"Okay, tech man, tell me how a room full of people, all with Reaper chips, fry and then still come back as zombies?" Masters asked Jay while he loaded a duffel with weapons and ammo. "And why a group of UDC officers, who I assume were dead when they came in here, were talking, walking and shooting?"

"Not a fucking clue," Jay said poking one of the UDC officers with his foot. The thing's eyes opened and Jay instantly put a bullet in its head. "Whatever caused this has changed the entire game."

"You guys hear that?" the Rookie asked.

💀💀💀

Rachel rounded the corner to the infirmary and nearly collided with her father.

"The com's down," Capreze said.

"Yeah, Jethro cut the power. Whatever signal is trying to get in almost succeeded and nearly cooked Jethro's brain."

Capreze stepped aside and gestured for Rachel to continue to the infirmary. Both were just feet from the door when gunfire erupted. The Caprezes burst into the infirmary, side arms drawn.

"Holy fucking shit!" Rachel yelled as she took in the scene.

Themopolous, bloody and half naked was crawling towards the door while Harlow emptied her pistol into the zombies lunging for them.

💀💀💀

Bisby sat in his mech, stewing. "Fucking base watch. UDC troops inside and I get fucking base watch."

He lazily stared at his sensors as they picked up nothing but an empty wasteland.

"I should be out kicking deader ass not outside babysitting," he muttered to himself. "This is royal fucking bullshit."

An alarm sounded in his cockpit, one that Bisby hadn't heard in a very long time. "Contamination breach? Seriously?"

He double checked his readings and confirmed that the base's virus sensors had been activated.

"Hey! What the hell is going on in there?" Bisby yelled over his com.

Mathew had been watching the reading on his sensors for the better part of an hour. Or more importantly, the lack of a reading. Something was trying to hide, to trick his mech's sensors into thinking there was nothing there. But, Mathew had been in the waste at night too many times not to notice the absence of information.

During the day he may never have caught the anomaly, but night navigation was by sensor and feel, making every little bit of data stand out.

Friend or foe? Was he heading into a trap? Mathew couldn't answer those questions yet.

Six of the eleven zombies came straight at Harlow, the others fell on the still living UDC troops and began to feed.

"Aww, Goddammit!" Harlow yelled as Steve's corpse leapt a gurney and sprang at her. She put two bullets in the former cook's forehead splattering blood and brains onto to the other zombie's directly behind him. No time for grief, Harlow emptied her pistol, dropping four more.

"I'm empty!" Harlow screamed. Rachel shoved her aside.

"Get the Doc out of here! I've got the rest!" Rachel ordered.

Harlow and the Commander didn't hesitate, quickly helping Themopolous out the door.

"What do you want, Chunks?" Olivia asked.

"Boss said he needs the extra room and Rachel here is to bunk with you tonight," Chunks said, between mouthfuls of flesh. Chunks leaned in close to June, drops of grease running down his chin. "He also said that if you try anything he's giving you to me. And I ain't as sweet and tender as the Boss."

June's empty stomach convulsed and she dry heaved over and over. Chunks snorted and started to walk away. "Oh, yeah, looks like we may have a storm brewin'. Probably hit sometime tonight. Better get prepared."

⚐⚐⚐

"Shut up and listen!" the Rookie shouted.

Masters rolled his eyes and started to speak. "Shhhh!" Jay hushed.

A far off clanging echoed into the room. Jay and the Rookie spread out, following the sound. They soon converged on the same spot, a large reinforced door at the back of the room.

"Where the fuck does that go?" Masters asked, joining the two.

"The holding cells," the Rookie answered. "Where the fighters are kept."

"Oh, you got to be fucking kidding me?!?" Masters said. "Are they secure?"

A wrenching crash from the other side of the door answered Masters' question.

⚐⚐⚐

"Get me to Jethro now!" Themopolous cried out, pain wracking her body as the Commander and Harlow carried her down the hallway. Gun shots echoed from the infirmary and Capreze winced.

"No, we need to stabilize you first," Harlow said.

"Bullshit!" Themopolous protested. "We need to get Jethro's chip out before it activates again!"

More shots cracked and Capreze focused his gaze on Harlow. The pilot nodded and carefully helped Themopolous into the Commander's arms.

"Got her?" Harlow asked.

"Yes, just go help Rachel! I'll get the Doc to Jethro."

Harlow took Capreze's pistol and turned back to the infirmary.

⚐⚐⚐

"Okay, we need to go!" Masters yelled, sprinting for his duffel. "Let's get the mechs and get the fuck out of this shithole!"

The Rookie and Jay followed suit, each grabbing what they could. Masters made it to the front door, stopped, pulled an auto-pistol and began firing.

"Fuuuuuuuuuuck!!" Masters roared. He kicked out with his right leg, connected with something and slammed the front door closed, the code pad turning from green to red as it locked securely. "We aren't going out that way!"

Pounding shook both doors and each began to buckle inward.

"Mother fucker," the Rookie mumbled.

⚐⚐⚐

Olivia helped June to her feet, steadying her as she swayed a bit. June, not wanting to see the feed pen, kept her eyes tightly shut as Olivia led her away from the water trough.

"You can look now," Olivia said, slightly annoyed. "You won't be able to ignore it forever though."

"I don't plan on being here forever," June responded, opening her eyes and keeping them averted.

Olivia didn't respond, just continued to help June navigate the rough ground.

A loud bell clanged from behind them and June turned quickly, painfully, to find its source.

"Storm warning," Olivia said.

"Get me the emergency med kit from the hall," Themopolous commanded as Capreze set her in the chair next to Jethro.

"Give me a second," Capreze responded, his chest heaving with exertion. "I'm not as young as I used to be."

"No time for rest, Commander. You can pass out once I get the chip out of Jethro's head."

"What the fuck?!? Chip out?!? No one's cutting my head open!" Jethro exclaimed, spinning his chair about, a look of terror on his face. "I don't do blades."

"You do if you want to live through another com breach," Themopolous stated.

"Looked like the whole fucking city/state was coming down those stairs!" Masters yelled, slinging a loaded auto-shotgun over his shoulder as he began to load a second one. "We're fucked if that door gives way and from the looks of it it's just a matter of minutes."

"How many fighters you think are on the other side of the back door?" Jay asked the Rookie.

"Couple dozen, maybe more," the Rookie answered. "Why not just call the mechs here by remote?"

Jay and Masters looked at each other then to the Rookie apologetically.

"That was a bluff, kid," Jay said.

"Hold him still while I cut," Themopolous told the Commander.

"Hold me still?!? Aren't you going to use anesthetic?!?" Jethro cried.

"No time, Jethro. Sorry," the Commander said, grasping both sides of Jethro's head firmly.

Themopolous swabbed antiseptic, tossed that aside and picked up a scalpel, her hand visibly shaking.

"You sure you can do this?" Capreze asked the doctor, seeing the tremor.

"Sure she can do this?!? What am I missing here?!?" Jethro cried again.

"Oh, shut up you big baby," Themopolous barked as she placed the scalpel to the base of Jethro's skull and sliced.

Jethro started screaming.

💀💀💀

Rachel pulled the trigger, blasting the back of the zombie's head across the infirmary's wall. "That's the last one." Rachel looked up, watching Harlow check the UDC troops that hadn't turned right away. "Any of those guys still alive?"

"The Sergeant Major is still breathing, but he's pretty shredded," Harlow answered.

Rachel crossed to the infirmary beds and systematically put a bullet into each of the newly dead troopers' heads before stepping to Harlow's side.

"Wheel that surgical cart over," Harlow said.

"Why? He's a goner."

"We may be able to keep him alive long enough to get some answers."

💀💀💀

"What the fuck are we going to do?!?" yelled Masters.

"Well we aren't going to fall apart like some UDC pansy ass! You're a mech pilot dammit, act like one!" Jay yelled back.

The Rookie eyed the fight cage. "In there."

"What?" Jay and Masters asked at the same time.

"Load all the weapons and ammo into the cage, shut the door and start blasting once the doors give." The Rookie started scooping up weapons and ammo and tossing them onto the mat.

"We'll be trapped!" Masters shouted.

"We already are!" the Rookie shouted back. "Stop whining and start helping!"

💀💀💀

Bisby stepped around the corner, auto-carbine at the ready. He approached the infirmary cautiously.

"If you aren't dead you better speak up now, 'cause I'm coming in firing otherwise!" He yelled.

"Hold your fire asshole!" Rachel yelled back. "We've got blood and shit everywhere, so stay out unless you want to go through decontamination with us!"

"Is everyone okay?" Bisby asked, just outside the doorway.

"No. Steve had to be put down and all but one of the UDC troopers are dead," Harlow answered. "Go see if Themopolous and the Commander need you in the control room."

"Control room?"

"Yeah."

"Almost have it... Almost... Shit!" Themopolous yelled as Jethro began to convulse. "The signal must have gotten through! Hold him down dammit!"

Capreze used his whole weight to try to keep Jethro stable, but the mechanic's body thrashed violently against the Commander's grip. "I can't hold on!"

"Got it!" Themopolous tossed the Reaper chip onto the control console and immediately set to work on closing the incision. "Jethro? Can you hear me?"

"Ugggh...," Jethro grunted.

"Good. There is still going to be some pain while I suture you up, but you should be fine in a few minutes."

"Fucking ugggh..."

Masters wiped more gore from his uniform. "We make it out of here alive we're going to need some serious decontamination."

The Rookie laughed. "I've swam through worse! We'll be fine."

"Swam? Who are you?" Jay grunted, hefting a flame thrower.

"If we get out of here in one piece, I'll tell you both," the Rookie said.

"I'll hold you to that, Rookie," Masters said. Masters quickly pulled the fight cage door shut, locking it tightly. "That's all of it."

The three men waited for the doors to give way, hoping they had enough ammo to out last the onslaught.

Capreze tossed Themopolous a long jacket. "You're, um, a little exposed in the back. This should cover things up. How's your head?"

"I'm fine. Harlow is pretty good with a needle and thread," Themopolous put on the jacket, feeling behind to make sure it covered everything. "Thank you."

"Of course," Capreze responded. "Jethro, can we activate the com?"

"I don't see why not," Jethro said through labored breathing. "Signal already got through. Might as well be fully operational while we figure out what the fuck is going on."

"Good. What do I do?"

"Third button from the left, center tablet."

☠☠☠

The moment the Sergeant Major stopped convulsing Harlow took aim and put three bullets in his brain, putting him out of his soon to be undead misery. "Fuck! There goes our shot at intel!"

"Jethro!" Rachel cried, activating her com. "Papa Bear! We just had to put the Sergeant Major down. Is Jethro...?"

"He's fine," Capeze responded. "Well as fine as can be expected. You and Harlow okay?"

"Yeah. We'll need a decon hose down, but we weren't exposed as far as we can tell."

"Good. Bisby just walked in. I'll have him suit up and get you cleaned up."

☠☠☠

Olivia helped June through the door into her shack. An older woman was busy packing belongings into sealed shipping containers. June couldn't help but notice the UDC stamp on the containers.

"We salvage what we can," Olivia offered, following June's gaze. "This is my partner, Rebecca. Rebecca, this is Rachel. She'll be staying with us for the evening."

Rebecca sorted out a couple of garments from the pile she was holding and tossed them to June. "You'll need a little more than just that blanket, dear."

June dropped the blanket and, with Olivia's assistance, began carefully to dress herself. "Thanks."

☠☠☠

Bisby, in full decontamination suit, aimed the water hose at Rachel and Harlow. "Drop drawers, ladies. The sooner we get this over with, the sooner we can go back to being fucked and confused."

Both mech pilots peeled their gore stained uniforms off and tossed them in a bin marked "Incineration". They removed their boxers and bras, tossing them in the same bin.

"You're lovin' this, huh?" Harlow joked, preparing herself for the blast of cold water.

"Yep," Bisby smirked turning the hose on the two women.

"Fucking fuck shit!" Rachel screamed.

Harlow and Rachel braced themselves, enduring the pain.

🕱🕱🕱

"Alright. Let's get you up and out of here. Can you stand?" Themopolous asked. Jethro tried to adjust his position in order to sit up. He gave it several attempts and slumped back to the ground.

"We've got a problem, Doc," Jethro grunted.

"Weakness is to be expected, Jethro. I couldn't stand very well either."

"Um, yeah, standing isn't the problem." He looked from the Doctor to Commander Capreze. "The fact I can't feel my legs at all, is."

"We're going to need a wheelchair from storage. I assume everything in the infirmary is contaminated?"

Capreze nodded. "I'm on it."

🕱🕱🕱

"Everything is secure. We should get below," Rebecca said.

"Below?" June asked.

Olivia and Rebecca each took hold of their bed and pushed, revealing a small trap door underneath.

"Each shack has a small storm cellar. It'll be cramped with the three of us, but it's better than up here with sand and grit coming through every crack."

June's eyes went wide. "We have to go down there?"

"You've never been caught in a waste storm, have you?" Rebecca asked.

"Not without 50 tons of metal around me."

"With what?" Olivia asked.

"Never mind," June answered. "So who goes first?"

🕱🕱🕱

"Let's hope the rear door gives first," the Rookie said. "Smaller numbers. If we can take them out, we may be able to clear a path that way."

"I thought Legit said there wasn't a back way out," Masters said.

"Not officially, no," the Rookie smiled.

Jay's shoulders slumped. "I guess there is one way out."

"What the hell are the two of you talking…? Oh. We're going to have to crawl out the shitter, aren't we?"

"If we live long enough, yes," the Rookie answered.

"Great! Nothing like the reward of crawling through shit to keep a person motivated."

☠☠☠

"Bisby? What's your location?" Capreze asked over the com.

"Just about done hosing down the ladies," Bisby responded, grinning.

"You don't have to be so fucking happy about it!" Harlow butted in. "When this is over, I swear…!"

"Yeah, yeah. Whatcha need Commander?"

"Jethro's hurt and I don't know when he'll be able to focus on getting our tech secured. Until then we need to consider evacuation. I want you to get all the mechs prepped and ready in case we have to bug out ASAP."

"Will do."

"That goes for all of you."

"Yes, sir," Rachel responded, teeth chattering.

☠☠☠

"Shit! Front door is going to give out!" Jay yelled, readying the flame thrower.

"Figures. I get a chance to escape through the sewage system and a city/state full of deaders has to go and ruin it," Masters quipped.

Jay and the Rookie both busted out laughing and Master joined right in. All three doubled over, holding their stomachs, tears falling from their cheeks. The front door groaned and began to fall from its hinges and instantly the three men were at the ready, armaments leveled and set to destroy anything and everything that came through.

And everything came through.

☠☠☠

Bisby passed a wand around Rachel's dripping body. It turned green and beeped shrilly. "You're clean. Get dressed and meet in the hangar ASAP."

Rachel hurried to the barracks as Harlow stepped up. Bisby passed the wand around her also, smiling.

"Keep your eyes on the wand, Pilot," Harlow warned.

"Oh, give it up tough girl. I've seen your tits flopping around this base a hundred times."

"Flopping? My tits don't flop, asshole."

The wand turned green and beeped for Harlow also.

"Clean. Go get…"

"Dressed and meet you in the hangar. Yeah, my tits heard you the first time."

☗☗☗

Mathew yawned and stretched, glancing at his display. "Okay, it's time to call it a night."

He focused his sensors, looking for a spot he could hole up in and get a couple hours of sleep. It took him a few minutes, but he was able to find a crack in a cliff face he could fit his mech into, keeping it semi-hidden if anyone passed by while he tried to rest.

He glanced at his sensors again, trying to find the blank space anomaly, but it seemed to have gone.

"I have a feeling you'll be back," Mathew muttered.

☗☗☗

Capreze rolled the wheelchair into the control room. "How's he doing, Doctor?"

"He'll be fine," Themopolous answered, but the look on her face said otherwise. "He just needs some rest and time."

"Well, I can't guarantee either," Capreze said. "I have Bisby readying all mechs for immediate evac if needed. I can take you two in one of the transports. Can we move him quickly if we have to?"

"No problem. He's stable and in fine health, except for, well, you know…"

"You two realize it's my legs that aren't working, right? My ears are just fine," Jethro said, grimacing.

☗☗☗

Olivia lit a small oil lamp and set it upon a hook in the cellar. June glanced about and except for a small cot in the corner, the earthen room was bare. Rebecca tossed a bag of supplies onto the cot and began to lay out blankets on the dirt floor.

"Cozy," June joked.

"Safe," Rebecca retorted.

"Of course. Sorry."

"No apologies, dear," Olivia said, latching the trap door behind them. June wrinkled her brow, puzzled. Olivia caught the look. "Some like to take the chaos of storms as an opportunity to indulge their, well, urges. Better safe than sorry."

☠☠☠

Shiner transferred the data from One. He calculated the speed and direction that Mathew was moving and concluded the pilot was heading for Windy City.

This was a mistake. Nothing waited for the living mech in Windy City. Shiner had watched that place fall; watched the UDC troops lay waste to the city/state then, after the troops had left, he watched the dead mechs descend upon the city/state, devouring any and all that may have survived.

For a living mech and pilot, Windy City was sure death.

Shiner gave One several commands and sent the mini-mech back into the waste.

☠☠☠

Mathew backed his mech into the tight crack in the cliff. Crouching down he wrapped his mech's arms about its legs, creating a defensive shield with only a small portion of the cockpit exposed.

He longed to activate his com and speak to Rachel. It wasn't the separation that was killing him, it was the uncertainty. As far as he knew everything had gone wrong and he was the only mech pilot left alive. Except for Masters, Jay and the Rookie, but who knew what had become of them.

Mathew pushed his sensors to full and tried to get comfortable.

☠☠☠

"Is that comfortable?" Themopolous asked Jethro, positioning the wheelchair in front of his control console.

"I feel like I've had the living shit kicked out of me, but yes, it's comfortable," Jethro answered, immediately setting to work on repairing the com breach.

"Good. I have a few autopsies to perform, but I'll have my com ready the whole time. Call me if you notice any change, positive or negative."

"Will do, Doc. Let me know if you need any help analyzing the findings. I know we didn't get a chance to study the nanotech inoculations before everything went to shit."

☠☠☠

Blood, entrails, limbs, shell casings, clothing, glass, metal, plastic. The air filled with bits of zombies and debris, as Jay, Masters and the Rookie never let their trigger fingers rest.

The press to get through the front door, and at the tasty meat morsels holed up in the fight cage, was so great that it actually prevented the zombie mob from rushing in. The three men watched as the undead wedged themselves in the doorway creating the proverbial fish in a barrel scenario.

Before the back door finally gave way, all three actually thought they might make it out alive.

☠☠☠

Mathew had just drifted off to sleep when a buzzing sounded in his cockpit. It wasn't a proximity alarm, just a sensor reading demanding attention.

Groggily, Mathew checked the reading and cursed.

"Great, just what I fucking need. A waste storm," he grumbled to himself.

He set about prepping his systems for full lockdown, making sure his environmental processors were going to be up to the task. The amount of dust and sand a waste storm could produce could easily overwhelm his mech if he wasn't careful.

Satisfied he would be safe when the storm hit, Mathew closed his eyes.

☠☠☠

June wrapped herself in a blanket and listened to the whistle of the wind above them. "When will the storm be here?" she asked.

"Hard to say," Rebecca answered. "Could be an hour or more."

Olivia handed June a wet rag. "Keep that near you, just in case."

"In case of what?" June asked.

"You really don't know shit," Rebecca said, in a tone that put June on her guard.

"In case too much dust gets down here. Just put the rag over your mouth and nose and you should be able to breathe just fine."

"Oh. Okay, thank you."

☠☠☠

Jethro's head killed him. The pain was nearly blinding, but he pushed on. He glanced briefly at an external vid feed and groaned. What should have been the beginnings of a wasteland sunrise was now the murky tell-tale signs of a waste storm on the horizon.

"Commander?" Jethro called over his com.

"Yes, Jethro? You holding up?"

"Yes, sir. I think we may need to batten down. Looks like a storm is about a half-day off."

"Thanks. I'll get the others on it. Hang in there."

"Yes, sir," Jethro signed off, not noticing the blood slowly trickling from his nose.

PART TWO - LEAVING HELL & LEAVING HOME

"Can you two hold the front?" the Rookie yelled.

"Yeah. The way they're wedged in there we can do this all day," Masters responded.

"Or until we run out of ammo!" Jay added.

"Great, how about we avoid both of those scenarios?" the Rookie joked, kneeling and taking careful aim. He pulled the trigger methodically, placing a bullet between the eyes of each zombie he aimed for coming through the back door. Within less than three minutes not a body was twitching behind them. "Clear back here!"

Masters glanced over his shoulder at the Rookie's handy work. "Holy fuck! Un-fucking-believable!"

☠☠☠

Themopolous set the slice of the Sergeant Major's brain upon the slide and the slide upon the scanner. She stripped the bloody gloves from her hands and tossed them into the incinerator bin.

She sat down in a nearby chair, the only chair in the autopsy room, and tapped at her tablet until she got the readings she wanted.

"That can't be right," she said to herself, double checking the readings. "Please, God, that can't be possible."

She grabbed a fresh pair of gloves, picked up her bone saw and started to remove the rest of the Sergeant Major's skull.

☠☠☠

Seated at his desk, Commander Capreze rested his head against his palm, studying what little data Jethro was able to retrieve from the UDC security personnel's tablets.

"Sir?' Bisby asked from the doorway.

"Yes, Biz?"

"All mechs and the main transport are prepped, loaded and ready for immediate evac if needed."

"Thanks, Biz," Capreze sighed.

Themopolous chimed in on the com. "Commander?"

"Yes, Doctor?"

"Where are the bodies right now?"

"Harlow and Rachel are taking them out to the pyre," Bisby answered.

"Shit! Get them on the com now! The nanotech repairs the zombie brains! They aren't completely dead yet!"

Rachel pulled the ATV in front of the funeral pyre, slung her carbine and hopped out. Harlow did the same immediately grabbing one end of a body bag as Rachel grabbed the other. They respectfully placed it and the others on the pyre, stacking one upon the other, the sunrise reflecting off the plastic.

"Should we say some words?" Rachel asked.

"You can if you-" Harlow stopped, staring at the bags.

"Baby Girl?" Capreze's voice called over the com.

"Yeah, Papa Bear?" Rachel responded while watching Harlow un-sling her carbine as the top bag wobbled and fell to the ground.

"Commander?" Jethro called.

"Not now Jethro, we've got a situation on our hands."

"Sir, I'm picking up transports right on the heels of the waste storm."

"Fuck. Are you sure?'

"Well the info is sketchy because of the storm, but I'm pretty sure we are looking at between ten and fifteen transports."

"I'll be right there." Capreze sighed. "Doctor?"

"Yes, Commander?"

"I need you on the com with Rachel and Harlow. I've got a bigger priority right now."

"Um, okay."

"Just tell them how to kill those things and then get their asses back here."

"Yes, sir. I'm on it."

"Sounds like it's passed," Rebecca said. "Should be able to go up soon."

June coughed against the dust swirling about in the earthen room. Her head was killing her and her body ached from abuse and fatigue. "Is there anything to eat?" June asked, regretting the question as soon as it came out of her mouth.

"There is, but you won't like it," Olivia answered. She pulled a pouch from her skirt pocket and took out three short, fat strips of jerky. She took one for herself, handed one to Rebecca and offered the third to June.

"I... I can't."

☗☗☗

Harlow and Rachel watched as the body bags writhed and flexed, their contents trying to escape.

"Those won't hold long," Harlow said, taking aim.

"Hey, Base? What's the order?" Rachel called.

"Rachel? Themopolous here. Listen, shooting them in the head won't permanently kill them."

"Since fucking when?" Harlow interrupted. "My reality is based on a head shot being a kill shot."

"They have been altered. I think severing the head will kill them permanently. Or burning them completely."

"So stick with the plan then?" Harlow asked sarcastically.

"Yes."

Rachel grabbed the fuel can from the ATV and began to pour.

☗☗☗

"Alright, this is how we do this," Jay said, loading and packing weapons while the Rookie and Masters held off the bottlenecked zombie horde at the front door. "We take as much gear as we can. You two go first and I'll hold them off with the flame thrower. I'll follow as soon as you are clear."

"Wrong," the Rookie shouted back. "There are two mechs and I can't drive either of them. The two of you are more important than me. I'll hold them off with the flame thrower."

"Either plan works for me!" Masters yelled as he reloaded.

☗☗☗

Harlow surveyed the landscape as Rachel poured the fuel onto the shuddering body bags. "Not a single deader heading our way."

"Storm's coming," Rachel responded tossing the can aside and pulling a lighter from her pocket. "They aren't smart, but they know enough to take cover from a waste storm."

"Yeah, I guess so."

Rachel lit a starter and tossed it, instantly igniting the fuel soaked body bags. The plastic of the bags began to melt and fuse to the zombies, freeing them from their confinement.

"Okay, maybe we should have thought that through," Harlow said.

"No shit," Rachel responded.

Capreze stared at the screen. "I'm not seeing them."

"Just watch…," Jethro grunted, closing his eyes, his face tightening in pain.

"Jethro? You okay?"

"Yeah, I'm fine. Just the excruciating head pain, that's all." He adjusted the focus on the vid screen, trying to filter through the storm's interference. "See those blips? Those are transports. The red ones are UDC for sure. I don't know what the green ones are."

"How long?"

"Storm hits in a few hours, transports are maybe another couple hours behind that."

Capreze patted Jethro on the shoulder. "Good catch. Keep me posted."

"Will do, Commander."

"Ready to do this thing?" Jay called out.

"Ready," the Rookie and Masters responded.

The Rookie lifted the flame thrower and gave a quick blast towards the front door as Masters kicked out against the cage door. The door didn't budge.

"Shit!" Masters yelled.

"Move!" Jay took aim with his shotgun and fired off four rounds, one to the lock and three to the hinges. The door tumbled to the ground and Masters and Jay opened fire, leaping from the cage. "Come on!"

The Rookie laid down a steady stream of fire, giving them a few more seconds then followed.

Mathew awoke to the sounds of a hundred rotted fingernails scratching at the metal of his mech as dozens of zombies clambered past his war machine and into the safety of the cracked cliff face. He held his breath as the last few passed over him and into the darkness behind.

Okay, don't see that everyday, he thought. He checked his sensors and watched the zombie readings disappear further into the cliff. Looking up from his instruments he stared out into the wasteland. Directly into the Hell that was one of the largest waste storms he'd ever seen.

"Oh, shit…"

ψψψ

Themopolous watched in horror as the part of the brain she cut away was quickly repaired and replaced. She had the foresight enough to secure Crowley's body and was glad she did so as the once dead undead Sergeant Major began to thrash and convulse as it's brain became active again.

"That was faster this time," Themopolous muttered.

"Hey Doc?" Rachel called over the com. "Will a head shot stop them at all?"

"Yes," Themopolous responded. "But not for long. Drop them and burn them quickly."

"Gotcha," Harlow chimed in.

Themopolous heard gunfire before the pilots switched off the com.

ψψψ

"Holy fuck! Didn't we already put those guys down!" Masters yelled as several of the former fight patrons, those still intact enough, began to get up and pursue the three men.

"What the fuck?!?" The Rookie bellowed, setting several aflame. "That ain't fucking good!"

"Come on!" Jay screamed, as he was able to shove bodies out of the way, freeing the back door enough so they could close it behind them. "We don't have time to count bodies! Let's go!"

There was a large groan and a crack as the press of zombies at the front entrance became too great.

ψψψ

"Alright, Mechanic, the Commander wants you set up in the transport," Bisby said, entering the control room.

"Hold on, I'm making progress on the source of that signal," Jethro responded, fingers rapidly tapping at his tablets.

"No time. Capreze wants it done now. We are going to need to bug out as soon as the storm allows. You can work in the transport until we bail."

Jethro rolled back from the console. "Fine. I need those three tablets and that interface box."

"What the fuck's an interface box?"

"For the mini-mechs."

"I thought you lost those," Bisby chuckled.

"Fuck you."

☻☻☻

Shiner knew the waste storm was almost on it, and could do quite a bit of damage, but the dead mech pushed on, following the live mech's trail. As the zombie pilot inside itself deteriorated, Shiner also knew it was going to need help. The living pilot might be able to provide that help.

With the storm bearing down, Shiner finally got a lock on the living mech. Satisfied the mech wasn't going anywhere until the storm passed, Shiner set to work securing itself some protection from the storm.

Shiner punched both fists into the earth and began to dig.

☻☻☻

"Whoa, don't catch your ass on fire!" Rachel cautioned as Harlow dumped the rest of the fuel on the now still deaders.

"Don't worry about me, Rache. I can take the heat."

Rachel laughed, climbing into the ATV. Harlow tossed the empty fuel cans into the back of the ATV and jumped in as well. The two pilots watched the bodies' burn, flesh melting and melding with the body bags. One zombie began to stir and Harlow readied her carbine, but the thing was still in seconds as its skull burst from the heat and its brain boiled into nothing.

☻☻☻

Mathew braced himself as the storm front smashed into the cliff. Even tucked away, surrounded by rock, the force of the storm made his mech shudder. He double, triple and quadruple checked his environmental controls, satisfying himself he wouldn't die by choking on wasteland dust and dirt.

He laughed to himself as his sensors picked up several zombies scrambling around his mech, despite the storm, drawn to the irresistible lure of fresh meat. They didn't stay long as three of their number were brought down by debris. The waste storm had already switched gears from swirling dust to flying rock.

☻☻☻

Capreze flicked through the geo-grid, debating which route and destination would be his people's best chance of survival. Gauging the direction of the storm and what lay behind it, Capreze could only come to one conclusion: follow the rail further into the waste.

"Son of a bitch," Capreze muttered.

"Commander?" Bisby asked.

"What? Oh, hey Biz. Jethro set?"

"Yes, sir and Harlow and Rache just pulled into the hangar," Bisby answered, eyeing the Commander carefully. "Any idea where we're headed yet?"

"Yeah, but no one's going to like it." Capreze turned the tablet and Bisby took a look.

"Ahhh, man…"

☠☠☠

Masters tossed the last of their grenades into the fight room as the front door bottleneck finally broke and the zombies poured in. The Rookie sent a final stream of fire into the room then tossed the flame thrower after, hoping to add fuel to the fire.

Jay yanked on the back door, almost getting it closed before the grenades went off. The concussion from the explosion slammed the door fully closed, knocking all three men off their feet.

Masters' ears rang and he felt blood trickle down the back of his neck as got back up. "We gotta move!"

☠☠☠

"You want the good news or the bad news first?" Themopolous asked as she entered Capreze's office. The Commander and Bisby looked up from their route plotting.

"Good," Capreze said.

"The nanotech is localized in the brain only. None seems present in the rest of the body."

"Okay. And the bad?"

"They get faster each time they repair the brain."

"Which means what?" Bisby asked.

"Which means any inoculated zombie can eventually rebuild *while* taking damage."

"Invincible zombies? Great…," Bisby growled.

"Not quite. Fire will work. And decapitation should put them down, also."

"I can work with that," Bisby grinned.

☠☠☠

"Down that? Are you fucking kidding?" Masters hollered, staring at the small hole in the floor of one of the holding pens. "We'll never fit!"

The Rookie flipped his shotgun around and began hammering at the hole, sending chunks of concrete flying in all directions. The opening slowly widened with every impact.

The sound of wrenching metal echoed from above as the deaders breached the door into the holding area.

"Shut up and cover us!" Jay yelled, flipping his own shotgun around and joining the Rookie.

"This is going to suck," Masters complained, taking a knee, auto-carbine at the ready.

💀💀💀

Mathew took one last look at the waste storm then wrapped his mech's arms and legs tighter together to increase the protection against the flying debris. He knew this was going to be a bad one and hoped he'd make it through. Hearing the intensity of the crashes and feeling the shudders as fragments of the wasteland were flung against his mech, Mathew's hope began to wane.

"Hey baby," he began to dictate. "In case I don't make it through this shit, I want to say a few things..."

Outside, the waste storm enveloped the land, plunging everything into darkness.

💀💀💀

Rebecca shoved against the cellar hatch with all her weight. Finally, it gave way and she was able to squeeze through.

"Hang on," she called from above. "Let me clear away some of this shit."

"How bad is it?" Olivia asked.

"It's not a total rebuild, but it ain't good."

Olivia cursed. "I'm too old for this shit." She glanced over at June, who was staring at the piece of jerky in her hand. "Girl, you have to eat. Whether you agree with our way of life or not doesn't change the fact that if you don't eat, you die."

💀💀💀

Gunshots rang out, making Masters duck. "Shit! I really fucking preferred it when deaders didn't know how to use guns!"

"Fucking understatement of the century! Now quit whining and get in the mother fucking hole!" Jay yelled.

Masters fired off several shots and turned to look back at Jay and the Rookie's handy work. "Ahhh, this is really gonna suck!"

"Shut the fuck up you big baby!" Jay barked. "Now. Get. In. The. Hole!"

"You two first!" the Rookie hollered, taking Masters' place and pushing him towards the open sewer hole. "I'll hold them off! I'll be right behind you!"

☻☻☻

June climbed from the cellar. "My God…"

Olivia and Rebecca's shack had one collapsed wall and the interior was in ruins. June looked out upon the rest of the village and gasped. Many shacks were completely destroyed. People were frantically digging through the rubble, trying to get at those trapped underneath. Small fires burned here and there adding their smoke to the already dust laden air, turning the village into a surreal dreamscape.

June stepped out of the shack and wandered among the wreckage in a daze.

"We suffer the same as everyone," the Boss whispered from directly behind her.

☻☻☻

"Remember when this base was filled with personnel? Twenty mechs lined in a row. Another twenty out patrolling…" Capreze trailed off as he entered the hangar with Rachel. "It's changed a lot since we first came here."

"It's not your fault," Rachel said.

Capreze turned to his daughter. "I know that, Baby Girl. I just never thought the day would come that we'd have to evacuate, to leave this place because we couldn't defend it on our own."

"We'll be back, don't worry," Rachel soothed, squeezing her father's arm before joining the rest of the base staff standing at attention.

☻☻☻

"They're just people," the Boss said, gesturing at the carnage. "You can hate me, and rightly so…" He leaned in close to June's neck. "I am a bit of a monster."

June squirmed away and the Boss caught her arm tightly, pulling her in close. He grabbed her chin and forced her to look out onto the village. "But don't hate them. They're just normal people trying to survive, just like you and your mech elite. Just like every living thing in the waste."

Olivia cleared her throat from behind them. "Are you about done?"

The Boss walked away laughing.

☻☻☻

"We have less than an hour before the storm hits us," Capreze said, addressing the base staff. "All initial readings show this to be one big mother fucker."

Capreze studied the faces before him. The resolve of the mech pilots, the worry of the doctor and the pain of the mechanic. "With the speed it's moving we should be able to bug out within three or four hours, depending on the intensity of the tail end."

"We're leaving before the storm passes?" Themopolous asked.

"Yes. We need the head start and the cover to beat the transports heading our way."

💀💀💀

The Rookie dropped through the hole, landing in ankle deep filth. He flicked on his halogen and sprinted down the sewer tunnel.

"I took out the first wave, but we have maybe a five minute head start, tops," he said, catching up with Jay and Masters. "Do we know where we're going?"

Jay tapped at his tablet. "Readings are sketchy down here, but if we head straight we should hit the main junction. Get topside and we are only a quarter mile from the mechs."

"Yeah, but what's waiting for us topside?" Masters asked.

"Probably the whole city/state," Jay answered.

💀💀💀

Rebecca handed June a bucket. "Here, make yourself useful."

June took the bucket and looked around. Rebecca took her by both shoulders, pointing here in the right direction. "The well's that way. Help with the fires."

Taking June by the arm, Olivia took over, holding a bucket of her own. "I can't help you forever, girl. If you don't shape up soon, the Boss will toss you aside. Trust me, it may not seem like it, but the Boss is all that's keeping you from being torn apart here. There ain't no love loss for you mechies or the UDC."

💀💀💀

"Double check time, people! We need to prioritize," Capreze stated. "Themopolous? You need to list all supplies you think essential. Rachel? You're on food. Harlow and Biz? Weapons and ammo. We have limited space and weight means energy used, so be careful and precise. The transport can recharge as we go, but the mechs will need down time to recharge weapons sytems. We may end up traveling at night and recharging and resting during the day," Capereze looked about at his staff. "Any questions?"

"Where are we headed, sir?" Harlow asked.

"Deep, pilot," Capreze answered. "As deep as we can."

☠☠☠

The villagers watched June like wild dogs: wary, expecting her to hurt them, but ready to rip her throat out if threatened.

June tried to ignore the stares, tried to ignore her own pain and hunger, and focused on the task of fetching water. She willed herself into mission mode, to put away her fear and hesitance.

She stepped up to the well and filled her bucket, but when she turned to leave she was relieved of her bucket and handed an empty.

June took the hint and stayed by the well, filling buckets as they were thrust at her.

☠☠☠

"Hey Rookie?" Masters asked as the three men made their way through the sewage tunnel. "Can I ask you something?"

"What?" the Rookie responded.

"Back at base, when you and Harlow were sparring?"

"Yes?"

"You let her win, didn't you?"

The Rookie was quiet for a moment. "Yeah, I did. But, not by much. She'd have been a champion in the fight cage."

Masters laughed. "Yeah, I'm sure she would be. Hey, can you do me a favor?"

"Ummm, sure, whatcha need?"

"If we make it out of this, please never tell her you took a dive."

"You got it."

☠☠☠

June worked at filling and handing off buckets until her arms refused to work. She slumped against the well and someone pushed past her, taking her place as if she wasn't there.

"Come on," Olivia said, once again coming to June's aid. "The fire's are out, they're just smothering the coals so there aren't any flare ups."

June let Olivia help her to her feet and took a drink of the water she was offered. "Thank you."

"Over here," Rebecca called and Olivia directed June to a group of women, all busy working over a huge cookpot. "Dinner's almost ready."

Mathew checked systems as he walked his mech from the sanctuary of the cliff face and back out into the open of the wasteland. There was some minor damage, but nothing that would keep him from his mission or from defending himself if the time came.

He calculated the timing of when the storm hit him and when it passed by, figuring the mech base was right in the middle of a world of shit of their own right now. Nothing he could do about that now.

Mathew got his bearings and engaged his motor drive. Next stop: Windy City.

Masters, Jay and the Rookie stood in the sewer's central junction. All three stared at the ladder that would lead them up to the streets of Foggy Bottom.

"Who's first?" the Rookie asked.

"Don't look at me, I never thought this was a good idea to begin with," Masters said.

"Yeah, but you'll think it's a good idea when we make it out alive," Jay growled.

"And I'll be proven right when we're ripped apart as soon as we're topside. Funny how neither option fills me with a warm and fuzzy feeling."

The three stood there staring at the ladder.

"Sir?" Jethro called from the transport, already in place for the evacuation. "We should be able to bug out in twenty."

"Thank you, Jethro," the Commander responded. "Okay, folks, time to get ready. Rachel, Harlow? Get in your mechs and take point. Bisby, Doctor? You two are with me. We have one last task to take care of."

Themopolous sighed and grabbed a med kit. Bisby double checked his side arm then slung an auto-carbine over his shoulder. The three left the hangar and made the short journey through the base to the holding cells. To the zombies held within.

The odor emanating from the cookpot made June's empty stomach churn and her mouth water at the same time.

The women began to ladle out portions of the stew and hand them out to villagers patiently lined up and waiting. June averted her eyes, fighting her rebellious hunger.

"Here, girl," Rebecca said pushing a steaming bowl of stew into her hands. "You've been coddled enough. Now eat."

"I won't eat this," June protested, setting the bowl aside.

"Won't eat?" the Boss mocked, stepping next to June. "You hear that everyone? Rachel, our mech pilot guest, won't eat!" the Boss bellowed.

💀💀💀

"Sir? Do we have time for this?" Themopolous asked Capreze as they stood before the holding cells containing the deaders that once were the UDC med techs and train pilots. "I mean, they are already dead."

"I agree with the Doctor, sir. Fuck 'em," Bisby chimed in.

"Do they look dead?" the Commander asked, gesturing at the uncharacteristically docile zombies. "You saw how they calmed down over the past couple hours. They are different."

"So what do we do?" Themopolous asked.

Capreze pulled his pistol and shot each zombie between the eyes. "Let's bag 'em up and load them up."

💀💀💀

Two massive fists emerged from the storm swept earth of the wasteland. Shiner reached up and pulled himself from his hole, shaking the dirt and debris out of his limbs.

He scanned the surrounding area, hoping the live mech hadn't escaped him. He was relieved (another new sensation) to find the mech at the far edge of his scope. He made sure his jamming was in place and set off to pursue the live one.

He calculated the heading, knowing what he'd find. The live mech was still traveling to Windy City. And almost certain death. Probably for them both.

💀💀💀

The street was deserted. Not a car was moving nor a pedestrian walking. The sounds of the city/state were absent completely.

Jay, Masters and the Rookie noticed this immediately as they emerged from the manhole.

"Um, I think I would have preferred a zombie horde," Masters whispered. "This shit's creepy."

"No shit," agreed the Rookie.

Jay checked his tablet. "We're only about five blocks from the UDC hangar. This way."

The three men set out in the direction Jay indicated, their entire beings listening for the sounds of approaching death.

"I mean it. This is fucking creepy," Masters whispered again.

☠☠☠

"This mech brat, this privileged, spoiled little daddy's girl, thinks that our food is beneath her, that our very way of life is beneath her. Should I stand for that?" the Boss addressed the hungry, exhausted villagers.

June sat there, terrified, waiting for the group to call for her head. But none spoke, none responded to the Boss's question. They all just glared at her, seeming to know what would come next.

"No, we can't stand for this." The Boss turned to face June "Until you eat...none eat." He grinned, wide, and swept his hands about, including the entire village.

☠☠☠

"Should you start the mechs up?" Masters asked Jay as they rounded a corner and saw the entrance to the UDC hangar.

"What?" the Rookie asked. "I thought you said you couldn't remotely control the mechs?!?"

"Not with any accurate movement control," Jay answered, tapping at his tablet. "But, I can run the start up procedure and have them both ready to go when we get in there."

"You think they're waiting for us in there?" Masters asked.

"I'd be," the Rookie responded. "Not that we can guess how these things think anymore. All bets are off on that front."

☠☠☠

Even though it was daytime, Mathew knew what he was looking for and quickly spotted the same anomaly on his sensors.

"What are you and why are you jamming my sensors to your presence?" Mathew asked. He figured that since the thing hadn't made a move on him it couldn't be a dead mech or hostile waster. "What the fuck are you?"

He checked his headings and figured he'd be almost to Windy City by nightfall. He wasn't exactly sure what he was going to find once he got there. He hoped the Commander was overreacting.

He'd know soon enough.

☃☃☃

Undead UDC troops poured from the hangar door. Masters, Jay and the Rookie ducked into an alleyway, hoping they hadn't been spotted.

"Guess that answers the question of where the troops are," Masters whispered. "Waiting for us."

"You say you can't *accurately* control the mechs, right?" the Rookie asked Jay.

"Yeah, so?" Jay responded.

"Well, we don't need accuracy, do we? We just need the mechs," the Rookie smiled. "Can you bring them through those walls to us?"

Jay grinned. "Sure I can. Let me check the mechs' positions...Okay, they're ready."

"Good," the Rookie said. "Bring 'em to the streets."

☃☃☃

Bisby secured the four bagged, bound and still unmoving deaders into an outer storage compartment on the transport. "How long do you think until their brains rebuild, Doc?" Bisby asked as he shut and latched the compartment hatch.

"Probably another hour or so. That seemed to be about the length of time it took Sergeant Major Crowley's brain to repair the first time," Themopolous answered.

"Good, plenty of time for us to be on our way," Capreze called from the transport.

"Speaking of 'on our way', sir, we need to get moving or we'll loose the storm cover," Jethro said.

☃☃☃

Concrete and steel exploded outward, crushing many of the UDC troops as Masters' mech burst from the hangar.

"Get it close!" Masters yelled at Jay. "I'll get up in there and give you cover to get to yours!"

Jay shakily maneuvered the mech over towards the alleyway.

"That's as close as I can get it without risking us getting squashed!" Jay said.

"Fine. You got me?" Masters asked the Rookie.

The Rookie knelt by the mouth of the alley, auto-carbine at his shoulder. "Ready."

Masters sprinted to his mech, the Rookie layed down cover fire as the UDC troops recovered.

☻☻☻

June looked into the clay bowl in her hands and then out at the villagers. None of them averted their eyes. All watched her, waiting.

"Well, Rachel Capreze? What will it be? Eat the stew now? Or be the stew tomorrow?" the Boss laughed. He leaned in close to her ear, his breath foul and hot on her cheek. "And trust me, dear, dear Rachel. I will have my fill of fun before I hand your carcass over to the cooks. Now… Pick. Up. The. Spoon. And. Eat."

June lifted the spoon, squeezed her eyes closed and opened her mouth.

☻☻☻

Masters slipped into his cockpit and strapped in just as the salvage mech burst from the wall, widening the already massive hole. The hangar began to sway and buckle from the lack of support.

"Oh, how I've missed you," he almost purred. With practiced speed and efficiency, Masters took control and began to stomp and blast away at the undead UDC troops. "Come on! Move, move, move!" he yelled into his com.

"Go! I've got you covered!" the Rookie yelled, slapping a fourth clip into his carbine. "Move ass!"

Jay sprinted to the salvage mech and clambered up the leg.

☻☻☻

Tears fell down June's cheeks and dripped from her chin into her stew, but she didn't notice as she took bite after bite.

The Boss laughed heartily. "Awww, I was looking forward to Mech Pilot stew. Oh, well, she made her choice. Let's eat!"

The villagers cheered subserviently, none of them truly overjoyed by the Boss's game, but all glad they could finally feed their bellies after a long night's confinement and a hard day's work.

Olivia began to reach out for June, but the Boss grabbed her arm and pulled her away, leaving June alone with her torturous meal.

☻☻☻

Jay punched a massive fist into the Foggy Bottom pavement, crushing a dozen UDC troops at once.

"Climb aboard, kid!" he yelled to the Rookie, who was already slinging his carbine and dashing to the salvage mech.

The Rookie gripped the massive fist and hung on tight as Jay brought it up to cockpit level.

"Let's get the fuck out-AAAAAHHH!" the Rookie yelped as a bullet tore through his chest. He collapsed halfway into the cockpit, forcing Jay to grab a hold and pull him the rest of the way in.

"Kid! Are you okay?" Jay cried.

"Yeah, just go!"

☠☠☠

Rachel and Harlow's mechs stood before the mech base's hangar doors, the transport behind them with Bisby's mech taking up the rear.

"Open them up, Jethro," Capreze ordered, seated at the transport controls.

"Yes, sir," Jethro responded, already making the key strokes necessary to override the base's storm protocols. Even though the worst of the waste storm had passed, the wind that whipped into the hangar buffeted and shook the mechs and transport.

"Stay alert and stay tight," Capreze called over the com. "Pilots? Let's move out."

The mechs and transport stepped and rolled from the base, into the wasteland.

CHAPTER SIX

Part One - Storms & Stompers

"Sensor readings are getting clearer, Bishop Wyble."

"Thank you, Deacon Montoya. And what can those sensor readings tell us?" Bishop Wyble asked, seated directly behind Deacon Montoya as the man drove the Rancher transport towards the mech base.

"Very little, your Eminence," Deacon Montoya responded. "The storm interference is still quite a bit. We can see that the base has full power and does not appear to have suffered any damage as a result of the waste storm."

"Well, that is fortunate. The Archbishop would not be pleased to have the new seat of his diocese ruined," said the Bishop.

💀💀💀

"Reverend Stemple? Please report," Bishop Wyble called over the Rancher com.

"Yes, Your Eminence. The convoy is in perfect order. All transports are ready for the conversion of the mech base," Reverend Stemple replied.

"And our new friends? How are they faring?"

Reverend Stemple glanced at the UDC trooper driving the transport. "Cooperating nicely, Your Grace. All transports report the same."

"Excellent. God will make you a True Disciple upon your Change. Carry on His work, Reverend. God bless."

"Thank you, Bishop Wyble. I am at His and Your service."

The Reverend glanced again at the UDC driver and shivered.

💀💀💀

The dead mech lumbered across the wasteland, past mesas and bluffs, over hillsides. This dead mech did not think, did not reason, it truly was an extension of its zombie pilot.

Cresting a hill, the deader spotted the Rancher convoy and its starving, undead pilot thrashed about the cockpit, bloodlust and hunger driving it into a frenzy.

The dead mech ran towards the transports, towards fresh meat.

From long dead training, it raised its 50mms, but to no effect, the ammunition having run out years ago.

The guns clicked empty as the dead mech bore down on the rear transport.

💀💀💀

"Masters?" Jay called over the com. "The kid's in bad shape."

"I'm…fine," the Rookie said between ashen lips, as he held a compression bandage to his chest. "Keep moving…"

"No, you aren't fucking fine!" Jay shouted. "We need to stop so I can look at that wound!"

"See that bluff over there? Due east? Half mile out?" Masters asked.

"Yeah, I see it," Jay responded.

"We can take up a defensive position there so you can check out the Razor," Masters said.

"Don't… call… me… Razor… asshole," the Rookie growled, coughing.

"Good, you still have some fight," Masters laughed.

💀💀💀

"We have an incoming Demon, Reverend Stemple," Reverend Hilldebrand called over the com. "Less than 100 yards behind us and closing fast."

Reverend Stemple turned to the UDC driver. "Show me," he ordered.

Stone faced and without response, the driver tapped at his console, bringing up the rear most transports vid feed. The feed showed a dead mech bearing down on the rear transport, arms raised, ready to attack.

"Transport Gamma Three? Do you have a lock on the Demon approaching?" Reverend Stemple called.

"Yes, Reverend."

"Release your disciples and let us send the abomination back to Hell."

"Yes, Reverend."

💀💀💀

"Reverend Hilldebrand? This is Transport Gamma Three. Bless you for alerting us to the Demon presence. We can handle it from here," Deacon Williams reported over the com.

"Of course, Deacon. It is my honor and duty," Reverend Hilldebrand responded.

"Anoint the Demon, Sister," Deacon Williams ordered his driver, a young Rancher woman.

"Yes, Deacon. It is my honor and duty," the driver responded, tapping at her console.

Deacon Williams watched on the vid as cannons fired gallons of blood and offal upon the pursuing dead mech.

"Demon anointed, sir."

"Very good, Sister. Release the disciples. God bless each one."

☠☠☠

The main rear cargo hatch of Transport Gamma Three opened wide and dozens of zombies spilled out. Their feeding instincts kicked in immediately as the smell of the blood and offal that "anointed" the dead mech wafted over them.

Nearly six dozen zombies swarmed the dead mech, believing that there was more to it than just a coating of human fluids.

The dead mech stumbled from the onslaught of the zombies, but they were not heavy enough to fully bring the machine down. It began to fling deaders about the wasteland, attempting to defend itself while still pursuing the transports.

☠☠☠

"Has the Demon been dispatched to Hell?" Bishop Wyble asked.

"Deacon Williams here, Your Grace. The disciples have been released upon the abomination, but they do not seem to have strength enough to bring the Demon down," answered Deacon Williams over the com.

"Hmmm," Bishop Wyble mused. "I'd hate to lose more disciples. Deacon Williams?"

"Yes, Your Eminence?"

"Do you have any more cargo of importance?"

"No, Your Grace. We're only carrying disciples."

"And crew? How many?"

"Um, myself, Sister Elizabeth and two disciple handlers, Your Grace."

"Excellent! Then I declare martyrdom for you all! Glory is to be yours!"

☠☠☠

Deacon Williams blanched. "Martyrdom, Your Grace?"

"Yes, Deacon Williams. Today I give you the greatest honor short of becoming a True Disciple! Do you not agree?" Bishop Wyble answered over the com.

"Of course I agree, Your Grace. You have truly bestowed a great honor upon us."

"And your families, of course. They shall be well provided for."

"Thank you, Your Grace."

"Blessings be upon you and your crew, Deacon Williams."

"Thank you, Your Grace," the Deacon severed the com connection. "Turn us about Sister. We shall send the Demon to Hell ourselves. And wipe those tears from your eyes!"

☠☠☠

The dead mech flung the last of the zombies to the dirt, stomping and crushing as many as possible without breaking stride. Despite the attack of the zombies it had gained ground. The smell of the blood still coating its structure sent it into a frenzy and it doubled its pursuit.

One of the transports split form the convoy and turned directly at the deader. The dead mech was momentarily puzzled then the bloodlust overcame it and it charged straight at the transport.

The transport began to fire all of its weapons at the deader, but within seconds they collided.

☠☠☠

Bishop Wyble watched the collision of the dead mech and transport on the vid screen. A massive explosion resulted sending a fireball thirty yards into the air. The Bishop clapped loudly.

"Spectacular! The Heavens surely saw that demonstration of faith!" he called out.

"Yes, Your grace. Those Rancher souls will have a special place in Heaven, thanks to your Eminence's charity of Martyrdom bestowed upon them," Deacon Montoya said.

"Careful, Deacon. Flattery will get you everywhere!" the Bishop chuckled. "Now, what progress have we made with the sensor readings of the heathen mech base?"

"Unfortunately, nothing more yet, Your Grace."

☠☠☠

"Just hold on, kid, we're almost to the bluff," Jay said. "Masters will cover our asses while I patch you up."

"I'm… I'm fine," the Rookie grunted. "I've been through worse."

"Yeah, yeah, yeah, you've been through worse. You keep saying that, but one day *worse* is going to turn into *dead* and I'm going to do my best to make sure today isn't that day."

The Rookie grimaced from the pain. "Okay, Jay. Thanks."

"Don't mention it, kid. You were the one that saved mine and Masters' asses back in Foggy Bottom, so it's the least I can do."

"ETA, Deacon Montoya?" Bishop Wyble asked.

"If the storm maintains the same speed as now? Approximately an hour or two," the Deacon responded.

"Splendid, Deacon, that is just splendid." The Bishop angled his seat back and covered his face with a cloth. "Wake me when we are in sight of the base, if you will, Deacon. Or unless we get any new sensor readings."

"Yes, Your Grace. It would be my pleasure."

"What would?"

"Your Grace?"

"What would be your pleasure, Deacon?"

"To wake you, Your Grace."

"Well, of course it would be! All for honor and duty, Deacon Montoya!"

"Fucking hold still!" Jay yelled as he probed the Rookie's bullet wound. "I can't see shit with all this blood and your fucking wiggling!"

"I'm… trying… OW, FUCK! To… be… still…" the Rookie groaned.

Jay splashed a generous amount of antiseptic into the wound and blotted it with gauze. "Shit! I'm gonna need to cut into there."

"Do you… have… a scalpel?" the Rookie asked.

"No," Jay said. "But I have a diamond point laser blade. Sorry about this, kid."

Jay fired up the handheld tool, its tip glowing red. He pressed a button and the laser began to slice.

"Hey guys?" Masters called over the com.

"Not now, Masters!" Jay barked.

"Yeah, I understand, just listen." Masters double-checked his sensor readings. "We have two more problems. First, it looks like we have a waste storm heading right for us. We've got maybe two hours. Second, we are going to have company in less than an hour. We've been tracked. UDC transports are on their way right now if these readings are right."

Masters listened to the Rookie's groans and Jay's curses over the com.

"Okay. Right. You're busy. I can handle this," Masters said to no one in particular.

🕱🕱🕱

"Leave me," the Rookie croaked. "Get your asses back to base. They need to know about Foggy Bottom."

"Nice try, but I ain't going anywhere. And, since we're about to have a fight on our hands, I can guarantee Masters isn't going, either. He'd never miss a fight," Jay responded.

Gripping the pair of pliers plunged deep into the Rookie's chest, Jay gave a hard tug and was rewarded with a wet pop. He held the pliers up to the Rookie's face. "Plus, I just found the bullet, so we're good…as soon as I cauterize the wound." The Rookie moaned.

🕱🕱🕱

"Any ETA on when we can get the fuck out of here?" Masters yelled over the com. "Because I'm talking minutes before the UDC are… Never mind. They just crested the hill."

Masters readied his weapons systems, double checked his energy reserves and prepped for the fight.

"You know what?" Masters continued. "You guys don't worry about this. I can handle a single transport in my sleep." Three more transports crested the hill right on the heels of the first one. "Or four. Still no worries."

Warnings blared and Masters watched as all four transports targeted missiles on his mech.

🕱🕱🕱

The Rookie, sweat dripping down his face, gritted his teeth as Jay cauterized the bullet wound.

"At least you stopped screaming like a baby girl," Jay said as he finished.

"Fuck…you…Rind," the Rookie croaked.

"Yeah, you'd like that wouldn't you, you little cage fighting freak!"

Despite his pain the Rookie laughed, wishing immediately he hadn't, as his chest shook, creating fresh waves of pain.

"Ow…"

"You act like you ain't ever been shot before," Jay said cleaning up the bloody mess that was the salvage mech's cockpit.

"I haven't."

"Really? I've been shot seven times. Deserved every bullet."

🕱🕱🕱

Deacon Montoya listened to his com intently. "Roger that. I'll alert the Bishop immediately."

Bishop Wyble removed the cloth from his face and sighed. "What is it, Deacon?"

"Two mechs escaped Foggy Bottom, Your Grace. However, UDC transports were dispatched and they have tracked and found the mechs. They are engaging as we speak, Your Eminence."

"That is wonderful news, Montoya! Please keep me posted as to the outcome of the battle! I am sure God will shine down on our new UDC brethren and make them victorious against the heathen machines!" Bishop Wyble bellowed.

"Yes, Your Grace," Montoya responded.

Masters switched on his external loudspeakers. "Attention approaching UDC transports. I will give you one chance to turn your little pussy asses around and go home. I don't know if you are all dead, undead, living, but slightly spoiled or what-the-fuck-ever! But, I'm sure none of you want my mech fist shoved up your fuckholes!"

The transports responded by firing their missiles. Masters grinned from ear to ear then broke into a full run towards the transports.

"Really? Puny little missiles? Against a mech? What fucking field manual are you guys smoking?"

The missiles and mech sped towards each other.

"Here, sip this," Jay said, handing the Rookie a flask. "It'll take the edge off."

The Rookie gladly took the offered flask and quickly downed the contents handing back the empty flask to Jay. "Thanks."

Jay stared at the empty flask then back to the Rookie. "I said 'sip', asshole."

"Oh, sorry," the Rookie apologized. "That wasn't the last was it?"

"It was in the cockpit. I'll have to climb out and down to get more out of storage."

"That would be great," the Rookie said lazily as the warmth of the shine spread through his body, numbing the pain.

Without breaking stride, Masters sprang into the air, twisting his mech about, letting the missiles fly past him. He came down on his massive fists, palms flat and immediately piloted his mech into a backwards handspring, landing just yards from the first UDC transport.

"Howdy! I see you want to play!" Masters laughed reaching down and picking the first transport off the ground. "Lift with your legs! That's how we stay healthy in the workplace!"

He swung the transport about and back the way he came, directly into the missiles that had changed course and were heading right for him.

☠☠☠

The explosion sent pieces of transport and troops flying across the wasteland. The salvage mech shuddered, nearly knocking Jay loose as he descended to the storage compartment for more shine.

"Fucking show off!" Jay yelled into his com.

"Jealous much?!?" Masters yelled back.

Jay reached the compartment, lifted the hatch and gasped. "Holy fucking shit!"

"What?" the Rookie asked over the com. "You okay?"

"You won't believe this! But, Legit actually made good on his promise! Every part I asked for is loaded in here!" Jay searched a bit more. "But the fuckers took the shine!"

"Bastards!" the Rookie yelled.

☠☠☠

The giant fist slammed down and through the closest UDC transport, crushing everything inside. Masters lifted the transport and shook it off, sending it flying 300 yards before it smashed to the ground, sending fiery shrapnel across the wasteland.

"Wooo-fucking-hoooo!" Masters crowed. "I am loving the smashy-smashy! I haven't fucked shit up with my mech in a while! Feels fucking good!"

Cannon fire brought Masters' attention back to the remaining transports. He dodged to the left, letting the artillery shells wiz past him.

"Really? That's all you got! Leave it to UDC fuckheads to bring transports to a mech fight!"

☠☠☠

Jay climbed back into the cockpit. "Hey, you're missing the show," he said, carefully helping the Rookie sit upright so he could see the action. "You should watch this, you'll learn a thing or two about how to pilot a mech."

The Rookie stared in amazement at the deftness with which Masters maneuvered his mech.

"Jeezus! It's like the transports are just toys to him. Even his mech moves with that cocky swagger," the Rookie exclaimed.

"As it should," Jay said. "A mech is not separate from its pilot, but an extension."

The Rookie stared in awe as Masters worked.

💀💀💀

"Hey, Rookie? You think that's impressive? Watch this!" Masters called over the com. He swatted away two RPGs and lifted his foot over the closest mech. Without hesitation, he stomped down, his mech foot swallowed by the transport. He did the same to the second and last transport before it could get another shot off.

Masters shifted his mech's weight, securing the transports tightly.

"I gotta dance!" Masters said in a sing-song voice.

And then, he danced.

"That's fucked up…" the Rookie said, his eyes widening as he watched 50 tons of war machine break into a soft shoe routine.

💀💀💀

"Ain't I pretty? Who's a pretty dancing mech?" Masters piloted his mech in a graceful pirouette. And stopped, his mech hands splayed and shaking. "Jazz hands, bitches!"

"You've gotta be shittin' me?" the Rookie said over the com.

"Harlow loves musicals. We've seen everything Jay has on vid. You should see the routine we put together," Masters laughed, aiming his right 50mm at the transports. He fired off the gun, slicing the fronts of the transports off then shook them from his mech's feet. "You see, kid, if you can dance in a mech, you can fight in a mech."

💀💀💀

"Um, Your Grace?" Deacon Montoya asked. "We've lost all four transport signals. It appears the mechs may have destroyed them."

"That is unfortunate, Deacon," Bishop Wyble said. He stared out the windshield as the mech base came into sight. "Oh, well. Hopefully the waste storm will take care of them for us. It's in God's hands now, Montoya."

"Of course, sir," Montoya responded. He checked his scanners. "It appears the mech base is empty, Your Eminence. I have zero life signs on my scanners. Power is up and communications are online. Shall I alert the others?"

"Yes, Deacon, please do."

☠☠☠

"Well, I hate to skip the encore, boys, but we have a waste storm to out-run," Masters said over the com.

Jay secured the Rookie's straps then strapped himself in and powered up his mech. "Well, from these readings it doesn't look like we are going to out-run it, but we can't stay here. This bluff isn't near enough cover."

"Where are we?' the Rookie asked.

"The middle of Bumfuck," Jay responded. He transferred data to his tablet and held it up so the Rookie could see.

"I know exactly where we are," the Rookie responded, eyeing the tablet's screen.

☠☠☠

"Okay, I got the heading," Masters said. "The sooner we get there the more time we'll have to get secured. You sure there's enough room for both mechs, kid?"

"Yeah," the Rookie answered over the com. "Plenty of room. I've had to hole up there before."

"Really? You know, you said you'd tell us who the fuck you are if we got out of Foggy Bottom."

"Yes, I know," the Rookie winced. "But, how about we worry about the waste storm first?"

"I swear, Rookie, if you or I die before I know your story, I'm gonna be fucking pissed."

☠☠☠

"We have entered the mech base's staging area, Your Grace," Montoya informed the Bishop.

Bishop Wyble glanced from the windshield to the vid screens and back out the windshield. "And how can you tell the difference, Deacon Montoya?" the Bishop asked. "It looks the same as all the rest of the wasteland."

The Deacon pointed at his screen. "Those dots, Your Eminence. They are part of some type of warning system, but I'm unfamiliar with the tech. Must be custom."

"Custom tech, you say? Well, it appears the mech personnel haven't been fully open with the UDC," Bishop Wyble chuckled.

☠☠☠

The UDC and Rancher transports stopped in front of the mech base hangar, the tail end of the waste storm still blowing strongly.

"Well, Deacon Montoya, what are we waiting for?" the Bishop asked impatiently. "Ring the bell."

"Yes, Your Grace," Montoya responded activating his com. "Tech crew go."

A three man team dashed from a transport to the hangar doors. One man opened a small panel and began to hack the locking mechanism. Almost instantly the man was electrocuted, his body dancing and smoking as 100,000 volts fried him.

Bishop Wyble sighed. "I guess we will have to knock.

The lead Rancher transport, Bishop Wyble's, targeted its missile launcher on the mech base's hangar bay doors.

"Now, Deacon, just a light knock. No need to break the door down," the Bishop ordered.

"Yes, Your Grace," Deacon Montoya responded. "First missile away."

They watched as the missile shot from the transport and impacted upon the door. Montoya checked his sensors since the smoke was still too thick for a visual. "Barely any damage, You Grace."

"Hmmm… Well, then, kick it in! The Archbishop will be disappointed, but I'm sure its nothing we couldn't fix later."

"Certainly, Your Grace," Montoya agreed.

"Holy shit!" Jethro yelled staring at his scanner. "Looks like the transports arrived!"

"Give me a visual," Capreze commanded as he piloted the transport. Jethro tapped at his tablet and the image he was looking at was superimposed upon the windshield in front of Capreze. "Okay, what am I looking at?"

"Well, you are looking at what used to be our hangar bay doors," Jethro responded. "I guess they gave up on the subtle approach. Probably after they found my little surprise."

"Surprise?" Themopolous asked, glancing nervously out the windshield into the wasteland.

"100,000 volts of hot death," Jethro laughed.

The three mechs stomped along, escorting the transport through the wasteland. Harlow to the left, Rachel to the right and Bisby bringing up the rear.

"How deep in do you think we're going?" Harlow asked over her com.

"Not a clue," Rachel responded, stretching in her cockpit. "Biz? You got any ideas?"

"Yes," Bisby said. "And none of them are good."

"Care to share with the rest of us?" Harlow asked.

"I'd hate to give you girls nightmares," Bisby joked. Harlow stopped her mech and took a swing at Bisby's. He easily ducked out of the way. "Hey! Watch it!"

🕱🕱🕱

"Pilot Harlow, any reason you are out of formation?" the Commander asked.

"Just swatting at flies, sir," Harlow responded over the com.

"Well, I applaud your dedication to pest control, but your mech is better suited on my left flank."

"Understood, sir."

Capreze shook his head. "So, Jethro, you are positive the Ranchers nor the UDC will pick up on our surveillance?"

"98.7% sure, sir," Jethro responded. "If Jay were here we'd have the other 1.3% covered, but I'm not quite up to speed right now."

"Fair enough. Let me know when they are fully inside the base."

"Will do."

🕱🕱🕱

Bishop Wyble stepped from his transport and began barking orders. "No, you fools! Clear it THAT way! Imbeciles, that top piece is…wonderful, just wonderful! Now see what you've done?!? MONTOYA!"

"Yes, Your Grace," the Deacon answered, directly behind the Bishop.

"Those two," Bishop Wyble said, pointing to two Ranchers scurrying away from the hangar debris as their lack of attention caused a sudden collapse of pieces of door still attached to the base. "Make an example, please."

Without a word, Montoya drew his sidearm and approached the two men, firing point blank, splattering their brains against the base wall.

🕱🕱🕱

Themoplous leaned in close to Capreze. "Sir, I am worried about Jethro. He's had three nose bleeds since we left. I need to run more tests, but…" She looked about the transport in dismay. "The facilities are lacking."

Capreze furrowed his brow. "Do what you can, Doc. We aren't stopping any time soon."

"But, sir…"

"No 'buts'. We're looking at the destruction of civilization. Again. Possibly humanity. Are you saying one life is more important?"

"You know," Jethro spoke up. "You guys have a really bad habit of talking about me like I can't hear you. Knock it off, please."

"Sir?" Harlow called over the com. "What's the plan for a recharge?"

"After sundown, Pilot," Capreze responded. "We need to put more distance between us and the base. I have no idea what their endgame is, but should it be pursuit we'll need a better head start."

"Copy that, Commander," Harlow responded checking her time display. "We'll keep our eyes peeled for a suitable campsite in a few hours."

"Excellent. All pilots on board with that?" Capreze asked.

"Yep," Bisby responded.

"Yes, sir," Rachel answered.

"Good. In the meantime I'd suggest you do a full running diagnostic on your systems."

"Your Grace? UDC troops report the base is empty," Deacon Montoya said, approaching Bishop Wyble as he lounged in an ornate and well padded chair under an oversized umbrella. The Bishop lazily set his drink down on an equally ornate side table next to his chair.

"That is splendid, Deacon. Are you sure the troops are correct?"

Montoya looked at the platoon of UDC troopers and couldn't help but shiver. "Yes, Your Grace. They may no longer be…as they were, but their training appears to be intact, if not heightened."

"Very well then it is time for the Blessing."

"Are we close, Rookie?" Masters asked over the com.

"Yeah. See those two mesas on the horizon?" the Rookie responded. "The cavern is just on the other side of the left mesa."

"Gotcha. Shouldn't take us more than… Hey Jay, are you reading what I'm reading?"

Jay glanced at his scanner. "Shit! How'd that guy sneak up on us? I'm losing my touch."

"What? What is it?" the Rookie asked.

"Deader. Big fucker. Must have been using those hills as cover. Still don't know why it didn't set off the alarms though," Jay responded activating the salvage mech's weapons systems.

☠☠☠

Masters checked and double checked his scanner readings. "Shit. That's not a battle mech is it?"

"No, it's not," Jay responded over the com. "Looks like a Hill Stomper."

"A what?" the Rookie asked.

"Didn't you learn anything before signing up?" Masters mocked. "A fucking Hill Stomper. Construction mech. Quadruple the size of our mechs and built to punch holes through mountains and take a beating like nothing else."

"They can handle up to 1000 tons of pressure before their hydraulics give out. The Earth itself can't crush them," Jay added.

"Oh, that's just great," the Rookie sighed. "Just great…"

☠☠☠

"Oh Blessed Father! Cleanse this base of the heathen influence and poison," Bishop Wyble intoned as he entered the mech hangar, incense in hand, robes adorning his shoulders. The Deacons flanked the Bishop, hands near their sidearms as the rest of the Ranchers followed behind, eyes to the heavens, hands clasped to each other, mutterings of 'Amen' and 'Glory Be' escaping their devout lips.

"Take the evil that permeates this facility and cast it out. Cast it far from here and let this base be filled with the Spirit! Let the vileness and wanton lust be forever purged from here!"

☠☠☠

"Oh, you got to see this!" Jethro said. "Shooting the feed over to everyone."

Capreze, Themopolous and the pilots all focused on the images Jethro shot them.

"What the fuck am I looking at, Jethro?" Bisby asked. "Is that guy wearing a dress?"

"Robes, Pilot," Capreze corrected. "And that 'guy' is Bishop Wyble himself. And where Bishop Wyble is…"

"The Archbishop isn't far behind," Rachel finished for her father.

"What are they playing at?" Harlow asked. "Is there any sound with this?"

"Yeah, hold on," Jethro responded tapping commands into his tablet. "There."

"And as God has commanded, there shall…"

☠☠☠

"…there shall be no other Faith than the True Faith. Let God's children and Disciples, learn from their time here, this Purgatory on Earth. Let them all learn to fear God, to worship God, to be his servant and warrior for Eternity. In the name of the Father, the Son and the True Disciple, Amen," Bishop Wyble finished.

"Amen," the Ranchers echoed.

The Bishop turned to his fellow Ranchers. "Now, who shall be the sacrifice to complete the Blessing?" The Bishop looked amongst his people and smiled, pointing to a petite woman. "Sister Amanda shall have the honor of Sacrifice."

☠☠☠

"Where's this feed coming from?" Bisby asked.

"I have Two powered down. Only audio/visual and basic sensors are operational," Jethro answered. "Four is following us acting as a relay."

"Good thinking," Bisby said.

"Well, already lost two mini-mechs, so figured I'd get the most of what was left," Jethro said, his jaw tightening in pain.

"Jethro? What is it?" Themopolous asked as she got up from her seat and rushed to the mechanic's side.

"Nothing, Doc. Just a headache."

Themopolous handed Jethro two pills. "Take these." Jethro did so and smiled weakly.

"Um, guys? What's that woman doing?" Rachel asked.

☠☠☠

Sister Amanda removed her uniform and stepped naked before the Rancher congregation. "I am honored to be chosen as the Sacrifice for this Blessing," she announced, bringing her arms above her head, fingers splayed wide. "I pray, Father, that you see fit to make me a True Disciple. But, if I am not worthy, do not let that be reason for withholding your Blessing!"

Amens rang out from the Ranchers and Bishop Wyble grinned widely as he stepped forward, handing Sister Amanda a long, ornate knife. "God has heard you, my child."

Sister Amanda put the knife to her throat.

💀💀💀

"Dear God," Themopolous gasped as they all watched Sister Amanda bring the blade of the knife across her throat and collapse to the hangar floor while blood gushed from the slit.

"God has nothing to do with it, Doctor. Not where Ranchers are concerned," Capreze growled. "They may play the part, but God doesn't look down on those freaks with favor."

"I wouldn't have figured you a religious man, Commander," Harlow said.

"I'm not, Pilot. But Faith and religion are two different things. As each of you have learned out here in the waste."

"Amen to that," Bisby chimed in.

💀💀💀

The Bishop and Ranchers stared at the still form of Sister Amanda as dark blood continued to pool about her naked body. It took less than a minute before her eyes opened and what used to be Sister Amanda sprang into a crouch, a guttural growl coming from the open wound in her neck.

Bishop Wyble sighed, withdrawing a long rod, adorned with jewels, from beneath his robe. The Bishop flicked a switch and the rod hummed to life. He stepped forward and before the zombie Sister could pounce he jabbed her, sending 10,000 volts coursing through her undead body.

💀💀💀

"So is the fucking thing following us or not?' Masters asked.

"Can't tell until it makes a move," Jay answered over the com.

"Yeah, well I'd prefer it didn't make a move," Masters said, watching his scanner closely. "I may be an amazing mech pilot, but I don't know if I'm that good."

"And modest, too," the Rookie joked.

"Hey, Rookie, my sweet moves kept your ass alive," Masters said.

"Yeah, well, I'm not sure I can ever get that image from my mind. Mechs shouldn't dance, man, that's just wrong."

"So wrong, it's right!" Masters laughed.

"No. Just wrong."

💀💀💀

Capreze watched the Bishop angrily.

"Put her with the rest of the Disciples," Wyble said. Two Ranchers stepped forward and dragged the stunned zombie from the hangar. "And cleanse that." The Bishop walked away from the pool of blood. Another Rancher stepped forward with a flame thrower and proceeded to burn the blood from the hangar floor.

Capreze shook his head.

"Are you okay, Commander?" Themopolous asked, no longer watching the vid feed.

"No, Doctor," Capreze answered. "I'm not fine. I'm not fine with that hypocritical psycho spilling blood in my base while I have to tuck tail and run."

💀💀💀

"I've never heard of a Hill Stomper," the Rookie said.

"Well before your time, kid," Jay responded. "They're what built most of the city/states and cleared a path of civilization through the wasteland. When the Reaper chip came online they only outfitted four of them for full cerebral piloting. Good thing, too."

"I thought Stanislaw took out the last one years ago," Masters joined in. "Why haven't we seen this one until now?"

"Don't know and don't really care right now," Jay answered. "Let's just steer clear of the thing and get some cover. That storm is almost on us."

💀💀💀

The two mechs rounded the mesa and the Rookie pointed to a shadow in the cliff face. "Right there."

"That?" Jay said. "Kid, we can't fit two mechs in there."

"Trust me, it looks smaller than it is. We can crawl them in. And it's deep enough. Should keep the storm debris from doing any damage."

"If you say so," Jay responded doubtfully. "You get that Masters?"

"Yeah, I got it," Masters answered over the com. "You two crawl in first. I'm staying out here until I know for sure the Stomper has passed by."

"You sure?"

"Yeah, I'm sure."

💀💀💀

"You'll wanna brace yourself, kid, I haven't had to crawl a mech in quite a while," Jay said piloting the salvage mech carefully into the gap in the mesa.

"And yet, on your knees is your favorite position. Ironic, huh?" Masters laughed.

"Hardy-fucking-har," Jay said. He powered up the mech's halogens and illuminated the inside of the cavern. Wide lines of bright reds and oranges and browns glittered with minerals as Jay stood the salvage mech upright. "Holy shit…"

"Pretty cool, huh?" the Rookie smiled. "I lived here for a while…"

Jay turned to look at the Rookie. "Lived here?"

☗☗☗

Alarms blared in Masters' cockpit. "Shit! Fuck fuck fuck!" Masters cursed. "Hey guys? Looks like big and ugly found us!"

"Get in here, Masters!" Jay shouted over the com. "You can't take that thing on!"

"Too late! It already saw me!" Masters yelled, powering up all weapons. "You two stay put!"

"What are you going to do?" the Rookie asked.

"Well, luckily Hill Stompers aren't armed. And their joints aren't blast shielded," Masters responded, taking a deep breath. "With concentrated fire and some well placed hits, I think I can take the thing down."

Master turned to face the Stomper.

☗☗☗

Jay studied the inside of the cavern, noticing several smaller caves leading off the main one. "You lived here, huh? Don't worry, I don't want details… yet."

"Yeah, for a year," the Rookie answered.

"A year?!? Are you fucking…? Never mind. So, where do those lead?" Jay asked pointing to the caves.

"Most are dead ends. Some lead deeper into the mesa, some lead further down."

"Any of them a way out if we need it?"

"Out? No…well, maybe."

Jay raised his eyebrows, waiting. "Okay, what do you mean by 'maybe'?"

"There's an underground river. It comes out somewhere."

☗☗☗

Masters watched as the Stomper lifted a boulder that was easily half the size of Masters' mech. "Whatcha gonna do with that?"

The Stomper pulled its colossal arm back then threw the boulder straight at Masters.

"FuckingJeezusfuckshitfuck!" Masters yelled, barely piloting out of the way. The boulder flew past him and collided with the mesa, shearing part of the cliff face right off.

"What the fuck is going on out there?!?" Jay hollered over the com.

"I think this one is a thinker!" Masters yelled. "It's trying to play dodgeball with me."

The Stomper found another boulder and took aim.

"About that way out?" Jay yelled as the mech shook and shuddered.

"I don't really know if it is a way out," the Rookie said.

"Which cave is it?" Jay insisted.

The Rookie eyed the cavern wall then pointed to a lower cave. "I think it's that one."

Jay piloted the mech over, settling into a crouch so the cockpit was level with the cave mouth. The cavern shuddered again. "Masters?" Silence. "Masters?!? Come in!" Silence. "Shit!" Jay yelled.

"Maybe his com is down," the Rookie offered.

Jay turned on the Rookie. "You sure are optimistic for a brutal killer."

"Jay?!? JAY?!?" Masters screamed into his com, but was met with only static. Masters tried to right his mech after the last boulder clipped his leg, knocking him to the wasteland dirt. "FUCK!"

The Stomper bore down on Masters and was on him in seconds. Masters opened up on the colossal mech with his plasma cannons. The Stomper stumbled back, but quickly regained its ground, reaching down and lifting Master's mech into the air.

Masters was shaken about in his cockpit, stunned. He fought the grogginess and launched a missile directly into the Stomper's mid-section. Metal and fire exploded outward.

Jay undid the Rookie's straps and opened the mech's cockpit.

"Why're we getting out of the mech?" the Rookie asked.

"Because if this place collapses then we are trapped. I'd like to start heading for the way out, real or not, before being buried. Plus, as strong as the mech is, it's also holding several kilotons of explosives. I really don't want to be inside if the thing goes boom."

"Okay. Works for me," the Rookie responded, letting Jay help him out of the mech and onto the cave floor. Jay tossed two packs after him and grabbed his carbine.

The Stomper stumbled back, flinging Masters' mech away.

Masters watched the mesa get closer and closer as he and his mech tumbled through the air. The impact was enormous. Alarms blared, claxons rang and every warning light in the mech's cockpit lit up as Masters hit the ground.

Spots swam before his eyes and he verged on unconsciousness. He helplessly watched the mouth of the cavern crumble and collapse, sealing it off from the wasteland.

"Oh, shit... No..." he whispered, but before he could think further, all light was blocked out and Masters watched the Stomper reach for him again.

PART TWO - PIT FIGHTS & PITFALLS

Jay choked on the rock dust filling the now dark cavern. He switched on his halogen. "Hey kid, you okay?"

"Get that shit out of my eyes!" the Rookie coughed painfully. "Yeah, I'm fine."

Jay turned about and pointed the light at what was the cavern entrance. "Shit, that's not good." He tapped his com. "Masters? You there?" Silence. "Well, I don't know if Masters is alive or not, but if we plan on being part of the census count we had better find that river of yours." Jay turned and hopped back in the mech. "Just one more thing."

Masters found himself and his mech flying through the air once more and then impacting with the ground so hard the armored windshield shattered. Masters tucked his head down, but shards of windshield still drove gouges across his face.

"...mother...fucker...," he rasped. All alarms and warnings were cut short as Masters' mech died. "...that...sucks..."

He unstrapped and struggled to open his cockpit, but the hatch was too damaged. "Great. Gonna die in my mech. Not how I wanted to go. I always assumed there'd be sex involved, but I guess we can't choose how we go out, huh?"

The Rookie watched Jay step from the cockpit with a long steel tube in his hand. "What the hell is that?" the Rookie asked.

"Blueprints," Jay responded casually.

"Blueprints? You mean, like *paper* blueprints?"

"Yep, good ole fashioned blueprints. It's how I do all of my designing." Jay saw the look on the Rookie's face. "Blueprints can't be lost with a hard drive wipe or memory dump, now can they?"

"No, I guess not," the Rookie responded. "But, why are you bringing them with us?"

"Because I've worked two years on these fuckers and I'm not fucking losing them now."

☠☠☠

The dead Hill Stomper lifted Masters' broken mech off the wasteland ground as the waste storm began to intensify.

"Hey! Fucker! You suck! Yeah, I said it! You fucking suck! I'm way too much meat for you to handle! You mother fucking deader piece of shit!" Masters screamed as the Stomper brought the mechs cockpit to cockpit.

Masters held his breath as the stench coming off the zombie pilot reached him, despite the raging winds. "Jeezus! You've gone off there buddy!" The zombie pilot weakly groaned. "And you ain't lookin' so good."

Waste storm debris began to pelt the mechs.

☠☠☠

"You sure you can do this?" Jay asked the Rookie.

"Yeah, my legs are fine," he answered as the two left the main cavern and entered the mouth of the cave. "Give me my pack."

"No, I'll carry both. I'm not a doctor and your chest could start bleeding again at anytime."

The Rookie smiled. "Jay Rind, are you worried about me?"

"Yeah, I'm worried about you! You're the only one that knows how to get to the river!"

"Admit it. You want me to live."

"Are you fucking kidding me? Of course, I... you're an asshole."

The Rookie laughed.

☠☠☠

Masters watched the Stomper's other hand come at him. He grabbed the edge of his cockpit and waited.

The Stomper's cockpit opened in anticipation of the meal that would be thrust inside. Masters drew his side arm. "Night, night stinky."

Masters aimed and fired, the shriveled head of the zombie pilot exploding in a mass of rotted flesh and bone. The Stomper shuddered and stumbled causing Masters to almost lose his grip. He felt his own mech shake and leapt to the deader's cockpit just as the Stomper let go of Masters' mech.

Masters watched it plummet to the ground.

☠☠☠

June stared at the empty bowl in her hands knowing it wouldn't be the last meal she would be forced to eat. She took a deep breath and set the bowl aside. A hand gripped her shoulder and she jumped, looking up to see Olivia once again at her side.

"Come on, dear," Olivia said, her eyes sad and apologetic. "You need to come with the others."

June looked about and realized most of the villagers had left and were walking to the other end of the village. "Where are we going now?"

"I told you it would get worse."

☠☠☠

"How far down do you think it is?" Jay asked.

"I don't know, it's been years since I was here last," the Rookie answered. "But, if I had to guess-"

"Which you do," Jay interrupted.

"If I had to guess," the Rookie continued. "I'd say maybe three or four hundred yards down."

"Okay, we should get there in a few minutes then," Jay calculated.

The two men walked a few more paces then Jay held up his hand. "Hold on. Be quiet. Do you hear that?"

"Hear what?"

"Shhh! Listen." Faintly, behind them, came a series of quick scratching sounds.

☠☠☠

Masters yanked the zombie corpse free from its harness and tossed it out of the cockpit. It was so incredibly emaciated it weighed nothing and was blown nearly a quarter mile away by the storm winds before it hit the ground.

Masters studied the cockpit and the controls. It was very similar to his mech, but with some major differences. Mainly the lack of weapons systems. It was equipped with a wide sensor array, though, which would have been handy back in its construction days.

Masters felt the Stomper sway, buffeted by the winds. "Hmmm... Looks like I'm still fucked."

"I can hear that now," the Rookie whispered. "What is it?"

"Shhhh!" Jay commanded. The scratching grew louder and became more pronounced. "Oh, fuck! That's-"

"Claws!" the Rookie finished. Both Jay and the Rookie shone their halogens back the way they came. Yards away, the mouth of the cave became obscured by bodies. Undead bodies.

"Fucking deaders must have run from the storm! I bet the entire cavern is crawling with them!" Jay yelled, lifting his carbine and firing. The zombies roared as one and charged. "Move kid! Run!"

Jay and the Rookie turned and ran through the earthen tunnel.

June and Olivia took a seat on a wide bench next to Rebecca. The entire village was seated at benches set in a wide circle looking down into an open pit.

"What's going on?" June asked.

"Shhh!" Rebecca hushed her.

"Fellow villagers, friends, family, we have worked hard today. Worked hard against the adversity the wasteland threw at us," the Boss announced stepping to the edge of the pit. "We lost some folks today to injury. More importantly we lost supplies. We lost food."

The Boss turned in a circle, watching the faces, until he found June's. And he winked.

Masters pushed the mech's sensors to full, checking the screen. He had maybe fifteen or twenty minutes before the waste storm was fully on him. "Shit."

The Stomper, some semblance of awareness still intact, reached up to the cockpit, but safety protocols kicked in preventing it from doing any damage.

Masters stood up and grabbed the cockpit hatch and tried to yank it closed, but knew it wouldn't move, not unless...

Masters eyed the cerebral integration console then looked out into the swirling maelstrom of the wasteland.

"Well, I guess I'm dead, either way," he sighed, flicking the activation switch.

☠☠☠

"Go! Gogogogogo!" Jay yelled, pushing the Rookie ahead of him. "Do not stop running!"

"I'm going! Fuck! Stop pushing! You're going to knock me- WHOA!" the Rookie came to a screeching halt. "Oh fuck!"

Jay stopped himself just before slamming full force into the Rookie. "What the fuck, kid?!? Why the hell...? Oh, shit..."

Jay and the Rookie both stood at the edge of a fifty foot drop. They shined their halogens below and the light reflected off a massive, churning river. And on the banks of that river, were several hundred zombies.

"Guess we found the river," Jay said.

☠☠☠

Masters stared out at the waste storm. He could see a cyclone had formed and would be on him in a matter of minutes. The debris inside the cyclone wouldn't completely destroy the mech, but it would shred him while the cockpit remained open. He sighed.

"Okay, Mitch. Now or never," he said to himself. "No fucking guts, no fucking glory!"

Masters activated the cerebral integration process. Immediately his head snapped back and he screamed in pain as his mind was forced to share a system with another, very foreign, very dead consciousness. Masters struggled to keep his psyche intact.

☠☠☠

"What's going on?" June whispered.

"Hush!" Rebecca scolded.

"Now, we have someone new to our ways here this evening," the Boss continued. The villagers kept their gaze on the Boss, ignoring June's presence. "So I am going to explain this to her." The Boss turned and faced June. "You see, Pilot Capreze, we don't have the luxury of regular supply shipments. We live on the edge of starvation at all times." He paused, feigning sadness. "Sometimes we do not have enough to go around. When that happens, like it has now, we have to, well, thin our numbers a bit."

☠☠☠

"How deep do you think it is?" Jay asked.

"Pretty fucking deep... I hope," the Rookie answered, eyeing the river.

He looked from the water to the zombies on the bank and then to Jay. "The real question is whether we can make the jump and survive."

The roars and growls were getting louder and Jay could smell the deaders bearing down on them. "I don't think we have much of a fucking choice, do you?" Jay responded.

The Rookie looked behind them at the zombies nearly on top of them. "No, we don't."

"Then let's do this," Jay said.

Masters struggled to keep his sanity intact against the blackness that was the dead mech.

"I AM MITCH MOTHER FUCKING MASTERS! THE BEST GODDAMN MECH PILOT IN THE MOTHER FUCKING WASTELAND!" he screamed.

He focused his will against the deader's and pushed, shoved and kicked the mental shit out of the abomination that tried to take him over.

"I DO NOT WANT TO DIE!" He pushed harder, but the deader started to push back, looking into him, into his mind, searching for the breaking point. And then it touched a place in Masters' mind it shouldn't have.

Harlow.

Masters growled.

June watched as Chunks carried an earthen jar about the circle, each villager putting their hand in and drawing a small tile.

"What's going on?" June whispered.

"Hush!" Rebecca scolded again.

"Yes, pilot, hush," the Boss mocked. "This is a seriously grave moment for us. Please show some respect."

Chunks, having made the full circuit approached Olivia and Rebecca. They each drew a tile, neither looking at them. Before Chunks offered the jar to June, the Boss stepped forward and took the jar from him.

"No, please, allow me." The Boss tilted the jar towards June and she reached in.

The Rookie hit the water and felt every bit of air squeezed from his lungs. He was thrown about like a dead twig, his body tumbling, slamming into rocks.

He struggled, lungs burning, screaming. He reached out, touched the sandy bottom and pushed, orienting himself. Reaching, he felt his hand breach the surface and he stretched, broke free and gasped in the sweet air.

He turned about, but with his halogen lost in the rapids, he was blind.

He gasped again, but this time the air was not sweet. This time it smelled like rotten flesh. It smelled like deaders.

💀💀💀

"Yeah, you see that you deader fuck?!? Big fucking mistake! You shouldn't have gone there!" Masters screamed mentally, opening up the part of himself that held Harlow. "You know what that is you fucking waste of scrap metal?!? That's love! That's devotion! THAT'S MY MOTHER FUCKING SOUL!"

Masters fought, fought within his very being and could feel the deader weaken, feel it grow confused, lost.

"You don't know love, do you?" Masters laughed aloud. "You never will!"

Masters focused all his energy. The mech's cockpit hatch began to close in stops and starts.

"That's right! I'M MITCH MOTHER FUCKING MASTERS!"

💀💀💀

June stared at the tile in her hands. It was small, and off-white, made of bone she figured, knowing this lot, knowing the Boss. On the tile was a faded red diamond etched into the bone itself. She looked at the tile and then up at the Boss. The grin on his face was so big it nearly split his head in half. He closed his eyes and lifted his head to the twilight sky above. The village remained silent.

"Now, to be fair," the Boss finally said, breaking his reverie. "I'll draw also."

He did so and grinned slyly.

💀💀💀

The Boss held his tile up for all to see. It was blank. He tossed it back in and handed the jar to Chunks who proceeded to collect all the blank tiles from the villagers. Those with marked tiles remained unmoving and June could see some of them struggle with their emotions. She looked at her own.

"What's this mean?" June asked. She looked over at Olivia, who had tears in her eyes and then looked at Rebecca, who was busy staring down at her own marked tile. A tile with a red diamond.

"It means you fight," Olivia choked.

☠☠☠

The rotten smell grew stronger and the Rookie realized he wasn't alone in the water. "Jay!" he yelled. "Jay! Where the fuck are you?"

The Rookie struggled against the noise of the rapids to hear a response. "Jay!"

He did hear a low growl directly behind him, but before he could turn he was slammed into a boulder by the current. His breath was knocked from him once again and he gulped water. His chest wound blazed with pain and he realized it had opened back up.

Oh shit, he thought. *I'm leaving the deaders a trail right to me.*

☠☠☠

Masters forced the dead mech's consciousness down, down, down until it was nothing but a dead end piece of code. His head hurt like hell and he was having trouble thinking straight.

"Keep it together, Pilot," he scolded himself aloud. "This is no time for weakness."

With the cockpit closed, Masters focused on getting the mech moving. The thing could take quite a beating, but with a cyclone heading towards him, he needed to get the hell out of there.

Stabbing pains shot through his skull, requiring all of his concentration to take one step. And then another. And another.

☠☠☠

Putrid hands grabbed the Rookie about the shoulders and pushed him under. He blindly thrashed and fought against the deader and was able to get to the surface for another breath before more hands grabbed him.

He could feel them about him and he kicked out, his foot sliding through something soft. He tried to pull back, but his foot was caught. He swung his arms wildly, his chest wound screaming, hoping he could keep the things off of him, to keep them from biting.

The current slammed him against a boulder and another and another. Then all went dark.

☠☠☠

Masters saw the boulder coming at him and he braced himself for the impact. The Hill Stomper shuddered as the waste storm drove the boulder into its right thigh. Masters' concentration faltered and he almost succumbed to the blinding pain in his head, but he fought on, forcing the mech towards a near by mesa.

Masters realized his throat was raw from yelling, but the wind was so loud he couldn't hear himself. He walked the mech up to the mesa as close as it would go, shielding the cockpit up against the cliff wall.

Then he promptly passed out.

☻☻☻

Mathew stopped his mech at the edge of a bluff that overlooked Windy City and gasped.

"Sweet Jeezus. What the fuck happened here?" he whispered.

Before him, what was left of the city/state, burned and smoldered, a red hazy glow against an early night sky.

"Oh, that's not good," he muttered. He powered up his weapons systems and jumped his mech off the bluff, rolling into a crouch as he landed, his plasma cannon ready.

He checked his scanners, but the destruction was so great that he couldn't get a clean reading. Cautiously, he walked towards the city/state, guns up.

☻☻☻

"You see, dear Rachel," the Boss started, seating himself between June and Olivia. "It's simple supply and demand. When we run low on supplies, the people demand blood."

"The people demand nothing," Olivia muttered. "It's you that wants blood."

"Mother, mother," the Boss said, wrapping a hand around the back of Olivia's neck and squeezing. "You just don't get me do you? I love my people." He squeezed harder. "And my people love me...or else."

He stood suddenly. "First two in the pit!"

"Green triangles!" Chunks called out. Two villagers, an older man and a young woman stood up.

☻☻☻

Mathew walked his mech to the edge of the burning city/state. He tried his scanners again, but still no decent readings.

"Damn!" he swore. "What the fuck happened here?"

He thought he saw movement through the collapsed city/state walls and moved closer, opening all com channels.

"Attention! This is Mech Pilot Mathew Jespers. Can anyone hear me? Is anyone alive? I can offer assistance." He was met with nothing but static.

Then, again, movement. He switched to loudspeakers. "Attention! This is Mech Pilot-" Mathew stopped short as the bulk of a dead mech stood up from the rubble.

"Ah, shit..."

☠☠☠

The older man began to weep and looked up at the Boss. "Please, sir, please don't make me do this," he pleaded.

The young woman wasted no time, though, punching the man in the stomach, doubling him over. She immediately brought her knee up into his face, knocking him to the ground. With intense determination she brought her bare foot down on his face, again and again, until his features were nothing but pulp.

Chunks leapt into the pit and checked the man's pulse. "Dead."

The woman pulled a tooth from her heel then helped Chunks drag the body away.

☠☠☠

The deader stood there, watching Mathew, a burnt corpse dangling from its fist, its cockpit open and zombie pilot thrashing inside. The deader ripped the corpse in half and tossed the torso into the cockpit. The zombie fed ravenously, bits of charred skin falling to the ground like fleshy crumbs.

Mathew watched for a moment then fired his plasma cannon. The zombie pilot disintegrated instantly. Mathew watched the dead mech stumble back, sway and then finally collapse to the ground.

"And that's how you... do... that? ...fuck me..."

Four more dead mechs revealed themselves, all in various stages of feeding.

☠☠☠

"Black circles," Chunks announced.

"How many have to fight?" June asked, fingering the diamond on her tile over and over again.

"Four fights," the Boss said. "That's how many we need to die to live."

"We could all just eat less," Olivia said.

The Boss backhanded her across the face. "Or you could shut your fucking face!"

Two young men dropped into the pit.

"Oooh, now this looks like an even match. Should last a bit longer," the Boss said, smiling.

The men greeted each other and embraced. "Boo! Get a shack!" the Boss joked, elbowing June in the ribs.

☠☠☠

All weapons ready, Mathew backed away from what was left of Windy City. The dead mechs followed, walking through collapsed walls and broken buildings without a thought.

"Hey fellas, I was just passing by," Mathew called over the loudspeaker. "Sorry about your friend there, it wasn't anything personal."

One of the deaders dropped its meal and picked up the pace towards Mathew.

"Whoa, there big fella! I wasn't trying to interrupt your snack. You guys just carry on."

The other dead mechs dropped their meals also.

"Okay, now you're just making me feel bad." Mathew eyed the deaders and fired.

☠☠☠

"Commander, I'm picking up solid geothermal readings directly below this area," Jethro said.

Capreze looked out onto the nighttime landscape, assessing the location. "Well, looks like as good a place any. Pilots? Any thoughts?"

"We've been awake for over 24 hours, so this looks fucking perfect," Rachel answered over the com, yawning.

"Fine by me," Harlow agreed.

"As long as I get first watch," Bisby added.

"That means you're on breakfast duty," Capreze said.

"Better me than Rachel," Bisby joked.

"Hey!" Rachel responded good naturedly.

"Okay, then let's set camp," Capreze said, stopping the transport. "Biz, you set the perimeter."

☠☠☠

The villager that won the fight wept openly as he clambered from the pit. He strode past the circle and away from the rest of the villagers, his sobs slowly fading into the night.

"They were born the same day. They've been best friends since birth," Olivia said. "I helped deliver them both."

"Boo fucking hoo," the Boss mocked. "Get on with it!"

Chunks waited until the body was removed from the pit then hollered,

"Red Diamonds."

June's bladder nearly loosed. Without looking at her, Rebecca stood up and lowered herself into the pit.

"Pilot? You're up," the Boss chuckled.

☠☠☠

A well directed missile strike took out both legs of one of the attacking deaders as Mathew tried to pilot his mech back into Windy City, hoping to use the crushed remains of the buildings as cover.

He could tell by their actions that none of the dead mechs he was dealing with were thinkers. But, that was little comfort as the three left standing charged him.

Unleashing a barrage of plasma fire, Mathew was able to slow two more down, but doubted he had put them completely out of commission.

One of them lifted its own cannon and fired.

☠☠☠

"Are we set?" Capreze asked, getting up from his seat and stretching.

"Yes, Commander. I have the transport anchored," Jethro responded typing at his tablet. "Ready to punch the hole."

"Fire away, mechanic."

Jethro tapped twice and a muffled 'whump' could be heard directly below the transport. "Hole punched, sir. Checking readings now." Jethro studied his tablet for a minute. "Looks good. Dropping cable."

A whirring sound kicked in. "Should only be a minute and we'll have full power."

Capreze patted Jethro on the shoulder, mindful of the mechanic's discomfort. "Great job, Jethro. We'd be dead out here without you."

☠☠☠

"I don't want to hurt you," June pleaded to Rebecca as the two women faced off in the pit. "Please, don't so this. If we refuse to fight-"

"Then we both get a bullet in the head," Rebecca snapped. "Now get your fists up, girl, because I am going to kill you."

June stared at Rebecca for a moment then nodded. "I am sorry."

Rebecca laughed. "I've got forty pounds on you. You'll have nothing to be sorry for. And neither will I when I crawl out of this shithole."

"Shut the fuck up and fight already!" the Boss goaded.

🕱🕱🕱

Mathew easily dodged the deader's wild shot, but in doing so he mis-timed a step and stumbled on some of the city/state rubble. He saw the ground coming at him and put his mech's hands out to stop his fall. Before he could right himself, two of the dead mechs were on him, pinning his mech to the ground.

"Fuck!" he swore aloud, realizing a rookie mistake was going to mean the death of him.

He thrashed about, trying to get his legs under him, but the deaders began to pummel the back of his mech relentlessly.

"Fuck! Fuck! FUCK!"

🕱🕱🕱

"And we have juice!" Jethro announced over the com.

"Great," Bisby responded. "I'll stick my schlong in it."

"Biz!" Rachel scolded.

"What? Why do you hate that so much?" Bisby asked, unrolling a cable from his mech's leg and pulling it over to the transport. "These cables have been called schlongs before you were born."

"Yeah, but considering two of the three pilots here are women, maybe you should think of a new name," Rachel responded.

"Speak for yourself, girly," Harlow joined in. "I'm pretty sure if we whip 'em out my dick'll be bigger than Bisby's."

"Probably," Bisby retorted.

🕱🕱🕱

Mathew could hear the metal of his mech protesting against the weight of the beating it was taking. He fought and fought, but the other dead mech joined in and he was easily overpowered.

Many thoughts ran through his head as the protesting of metal became the ripping of metal. He was glad he recorded a good bye message to Rachel, but doubted if she would ever hear it. Shit, he didn't even know if she was still alive. Or if anyone at the base was.

When his mech's left arm was torn form it's frame, he began to pray.

🕱🕱🕱

Rebecca was right, she did have forty pounds on June, but she didn't have the training June had and even with all of the abuse she had endured over the past couple days, June knew it wasn't going to be a contest.

"I'll leave!" June yelled, easily dodging Rebecca's clumsy swipes. "Just set me out into the wasteland. I don't need food or water."

"Dear, dear Rachel," the Boss answered from the side of the pit. "You don't get it. It's not about one less in number. It's also about one more for the larder."

He chuckled. "It's simple math."

☻☻☻

Capreze set the perimeter poles several yards out from the transport and mechs, his carbine slung over his shoulder. He watched the pilots jack their cables into the transport's power junction, joking back and forth.

He laughed to himself, thinking back to when Rachel was born and how he would never have bet she'd end up a mech head like her old man. He shut that thought loop down, quickly, though, leaving that for his late night sub-conscious to deal with.

Capreze set the last pole and turned to look out into the wasteland.

"Perimeter set, Jethro. Fire it up."

☻☻☻

The hydraulics on Mathew's mech's left leg exploded as a deader stomped down hard.

Mathew undid the clasp on his side arm's holster and sighed. He pulled the pistol out and held it up to his face.

"I'm sorry, baby," he said aloud. "I wish I could be with you right now. I guess we're all meant to go out in the same way, though, alone."

He pulled back the slide, forcing a shell into the chamber. Thumbing the safety, he put the gun to his head.

A thousand shots echoed about him and Mathew, confused, looked at his pistol.

☻☻☻

June ducked another of Rebecca's swings and sighed. "I really am sor-ry."

"Shut up and fight, you spoiled brat," Rebecca growled, her hair matted with sweat already even though she hadn't landed one punch.

"I'll make it quick," June promised.

She waited for another of Rebecca's wild swipes and as the woman over extended herself, June stepped to the side, reached out and took a hold of Re-becca's head in both of her hands and twisted.

The snap of Rebecca's neck echoed in the pit. She could hear Olivia's wail of sorrow immediately.

"Excellent," the Boss smirked. "Alright! Last fight!"

☠☠☠

Mathew put the safety back on and re-holstered his side arm as more gunfire erupted. His mech's systems were dead so he couldn't check scanners. He was blind and helpless while something unseen opened fire with what sounded like 50mms.

His mech shifted as the weight of the deaders was lifted, their attention now on the new attacker. Mathew un-strapped, grabbed his survival pack and carbine and reached for the emergency hatch release. Even with his mech face down, the hatch was supposed to separate enough for him to squeeze out. He yanked hard.

Nothing.

Mathew's shoulders slumped in defeat.

☠☠☠

The Boss offered June a hand out of the pit, but she slapped it away and dug her fingers into the earth, pulling herself out. She turned away from him and looked for Olivia, but she was gone, her bench seat empty. In fact, most of the seats were empty, except for a few friends and family of the last two fighters.

June felt the Boss's arm slide across her shoulders, turning her back to the pit and to him.

"That was a nice move down there," he whispered in her ear. "Don't even think of trying it on me."

☠☠☠

Mathew could hear the battle around him and he focused on the sounds, trying to piece together the fight in his head.

He heard the blast of a plasma cannon and the resulting explosion as the blast hit its target.

The 50mm guns never stopped firing and the sound of metal being pierced and torn was near deafening.

Two more explosions shook his mech and then one of the deaders slammed to the ground right next to him. Mathew put his hands out to brace himself as he was shaken by the impact.

And like that, it all went silent.

☠☠☠

Every time June turned her head from the last fight, the Boss grabbed her chin and forced her to look.

"I'll slice your eyelids off, so don't even think of closing those pretty peepers of yours," he growled. "I want you to see how the rest of the world lives and dies."

The fight was finished quickly, as a small girl was put down brutally by a well muscled middle aged man. June could swear the man enjoyed himself as he crushed the girl's skull with his boot.

"Well," the Boss said. "I don't know about you, but I'm starving!"

Mathew held tight as his mech was flipped onto its back and the cockpit hatch ripped off.

Stock still, he stared up into the battle scarred features of a new dead mech. He was positive this one wasn't with the others.

He tried to reach over for his carbine, although he knew the rifle would be ineffective against the war machine. Immediately the deader lifted its right arm and shoved its glowing plasma cannon at him. Mathew slowly pulled his arm back.

He heard loud footfalls and his jaw dropped as he watched mini-mech One stand next to the deader.

CHAPTER SEVEN

PART ONE - OF SKINNERS & SHINER

Commander Capreze could hear the pilots joking and ribbing each other, a sound that always made him feel at ease, no matter the situation. He approached the outer rim of light the mechs shone over the camp when he heard a sound behind him, like shifting pebbles.

The Commander spun about, his halogen piercing the wasteland darkness. Nothing. He watched for a moment then turned back to the camp and began to activate his com when the hands grabbed his arms and covered his mouth.

He struggled in vain as he was pulled into the inky blackness of the wasteland.

💀💀💀

Mathew looked from the dead mech to One and back again. The dead mech pushed the mini-mech forward and One clomped over to Mathew's mech. It reached down and yanked the cockpit hatch off, tossing it into the Windy City rubble.

Mathew stayed perfectly still as One moved back to the dead mech's side. The deader's cockpit opened and it reached it's massive fist inside, pointing to the zombie pilot then at Mathew and back to the zombie pilot.

Mathew narrowed his eyes and cleared his throat. "I'm not dead, if that's what you're asking. I'm not a zombie yet."

💀💀💀

Bisby stared at the empty storage compartment. "Hey Jethro?"

"Yeah, Biz?"

"Where are the perimeter poles?"

"The Commander decided to take a walk and set them up himself."

"Huh," Bisby mused. He looked out into the darkness of the wasteland night. "Are they active?"

"Yeah, I switched the perimeter on the second he gave me the go ahead."

Bisby started walking about the camp, his eyes still focused on the wasteland. "Okay, so if the perimeter is active and the Commander set up the perimeter then where is the Commander?"

"Um, that's a good question…"

"Yeah, ya think?" Bisby snapped.

The dead mech pointed to its zombie pilot and back at Mathew again. Mathew shook his head.

"I don't understand what you want," Mathew said. "Your pilot is dead, it's a freakin' zombie, there isn't anything I can do."

The deader stomped its massive foot, shaking Mathew about in his demolished mech's cockpit. It moved closer, grabbing a stray piece of Mathew's mech, shaking the junked part then tossing it aside. It pointed to Mathew again and waited.

"My mech is broken? Is that it?"

The deader pointed to its pilot and then at itself.

Mathew stared then realization dawned.

"I'm getting nothing, Biz," Jethro said from the transport. "I've got sensors at full capacity and nothing. However, the geothermal pocket below us could be messing up the readings."

"Could be?" Bisby barked. "You don't get paid for 'could be', Jethro!"

"I don't get paid at all, asshole!" Jethro snapped back.

Bisby growled and surveyed the darkness once again. "He can't have just disappeared! We've barely broken camp!"

"What's up, Biz?" Rachel asked stepping up behind Bisby.

"Oh, Rache… I, um, didn't hear you come up," Bisby stuttered.

Rachel eyed Biz for a moment. "What's going on?"

Bisby looked away.

Mathew's eyes widened in disbelief. "You want to be my replacement mech? You want me to get in you?"

To Mathew it looked like the dead mech nodded, but that was crazy. Of course, talking to a deader was crazy also. Not to mention the fact the deader wasn't ripping him apart and feeding him bit by bit to its zombie pilot.

"You already have a pilot," Mathew said. And almost before the words had fully left Mathew's mouth, the dead mech reached in, ripping out the zombie pilot from its cockpit. It bent down, shoving the corpse towards Mathew.

Harlow uncoupled her schlong from the transport, trying to ignore the banging and growling noises coming from the storage compartment.

"Shut the fuck up, you deader fucks!" she yelled, kicking the storage hatch. "Hey? Is this racket bothering anyone else?"

"It's bothering me," Themopolous said. "I'd like to sedate the creatures so I can study their new physiology, but I can't seem to find the Commander for his approval. Have you seen him?"

Harlow looked about the camp. "Actually, no, I haven't." She tapped her com. "Has anyone seen the Commander?"

"That's what we're trying to figure out!" Bisby responded.

"What do you mean 'trying to figure out'?" Rachel demanded, her eyes narrowing. "Where is my father?"

"How the fuck should I know?" Bisby barked. "It's not my job to keep tabs on the commanding officer, is it? I was just as busy powering up my mech as you were with yours."

"When did he go missing?" Rachel asked.

"After I activated the perimeter," Jethro responded.

Rachel glared at Bisby. "I thought that was your duty?"

"He decided to take it on himself. I didn't know a thing about it. So back the fuck OFF!"

"Everybody calm down," Harlow interjected.

Shiner pushed its expired zombie pilot towards the living mech pilot. The dense human wasn't understanding his request and Shiner didn't have much time left. He could feel the mental breakdown beginning already. He could last another hour, maybe. He calculated quickly and realized he didn't even have that much time.

"I don't think you understand how this 'pilot and mech' relationship works," the living mech pilot said. "You're a deader, I'm not. End of story."

Shiner grew frustrated yet again and tossed the zombie corpse aside, its desiccated form breaking apart as it impacted against the Windy City rubble.

Mathew flinched and scooted back from the dead mech. "Whoa, calm down! No need to start tossing bodies about."

The dead mech pointed to its empty cockpit again.

"Yeah, I don't think that's possible. I'm pretty sure you'd fry my brain."

The dead mech stomped the ground with its foot, shaking Mathew about. It leaned in close, over Mathew, both massive fists set on either side of him.

"G-g-g-g-g... Get... I-i-i-innnnn..." the deader's loudspeakers crackled.

Mathew did everything in his power to keep from pissing himself. The dead mech quickly stood, powering up its plasma cannon. "O-o-o-orrrr... D-d-d-die..."

☠☠☠

"Are you sure you can't pick him up on the scanners?" Rachel asked Jethro.

"Um, yeah, I'm pretty fucking sure since that's my FUCKING JOB!" Jethro shouted over the com.

"Hey!" Harlow barked. "Everyone shut the fuck up!" She turned about then walked to her mech.

"Where are you going?" Bisby asked.

"Well, seeing as it's nighttime and pitch fucking dark out there..." She grabbed a hold of her mech's leg and started to climb. "...I figured we should light this place up a bit more."

Rachel and Bisby looked at each other then sprinted to their mechs, climbing also.

☠☠☠

Shiner's sensors, though growing weaker, picked up the movement immediately. Coming directly at their position were hundreds upon hundreds of the undead humans.

Shiner struggled to power up all of its weapons systems. Connections were becoming difficult. He recalculated and realized the mental deterioration was happening exponentially. He would cease to exist in a matter of minutes.

The human pilot held up his hands and Shiner could see the fear. "Hey, no need to blast me, okay? Let's talk this out a bit more."

Shiner pushed One. The mini-mech sprang into action, running past the human and into the rubble.

☠☠☠

"Whoa whoa WHOA!" Jethro yelled. "Small lights for the camp is one thing, but you light up those mechs and we'll be spotted a hundred miles away!"

"Spotted by who?" Bisby yelled back. "You already said we weren't followed by the Ranchers."

"Yeah, well, I also lost track of the Commander. So maybe we shouldn't be relying on me and my tech. Maybe we should slow down and think this through."

"Jethro's right," Themopolous agreed. "There could be other dangers."

"Like what?" Bisby asked as he and the other pilots lit up the wasteland. Surrounding them were thousands of zombies.

☠☠☠

Mathew turned about as One streaked by. He watched the mini-mech leap over debris and dodge around piles of concrete before disappearing into Windy City.

He felt the earth shake and turned back to the dead mech expecting the worst. But, what he found surprised him. The dead mech was down on one knee with one hand placed firmly against the ground. The only description that came to Mathew's mind was that the thing looked sick.

The dead mech weakly pointed to its cockpit again. Gunfire erupted deep within the burnt out city and Mathew flinched.

Then Mathew heard them.

☠☠☠

"Let's light 'em up!" Bisby yelled his finger on the trigger.

"No! Wait!" Themopolous cried. "Look at them! Look closely!" She ran pointing to the figures that looked like zombies, waving up at the mechs. "Check your screens!"

Harlow zoomed in on part of the horde surrounding them and gasped. "What the fuck?"

"What am I looking at here, Doc?" Bisby asked. "Are those people? Zombies? What are they?"

"They're our way back home," Commander Capreze interrupted over the com. "Power down, Pilots. I've got some people you need to meet."

Capreze stepped out from the front of the horde.

☠☠☠

Shiner heard more gunfire, but didn't have the capabilities to connect with One anymore. The mini-mech was on its own.

The human began to back away from the city/state until he bumped up against Shiner's leg. Without turning around, he asked, "Deaders are coming, aren't they?"

Shiner tapped the ground to get the human's attention. The pilot turned about and looked at Shiner. It took nearly all of his willpower to point, one last time, at his cockpit.

The human glanced warily at Windy City then back at Shiner.

"Yeah, I think I may be coming around," the human said.

Mathew grabbed a hold of the dead mech's leg and started to climb. He didn't have to go far since the thing was doubled over. Mathew strapped in and looked about the cockpit. It was an old one, lacking in a lot of the upgrades and modifications Mathew was used to.

"Okay, now what?" Mathew asked. The cockpit closed and the cerebral integration panel lit up. "Seriously? What's to stop you from frying my brain?"

The dead mech shook and placed both fists on the ground. The cockpit panels flickered, but held.

Mathew watched One dash from the rubble, firing.

"Power down, Pilots! Now!" Capreze ordered.

"Sir, I don't-" Bisby started.

"I don't want to hear it, Biz. Shut down your mech and get your ass on the ground. That goes for you too, Pilots Harlow and Capreze."

"Yes, sir," the pilots responded, opening their cockpits and descending from their mechs.

"Jethro? You there?"

"Yes, Commander," Jethro responded.

"Good. Shut those mech lights off."

A second passed and the floodlights ceased, returning the camp to its minimally lit state.

"Excellent. Now slowly pull the geothermal cable up. And I mean slowly."

"Sir?' Jethro asked, puzzled.

"You heard me, mechanic. Slowly."

Mathew hesitated, closed his eyes then activated the cerebral integration system. His head snapped back for a moment and he could feel the deader's consciousness meld with his own. And, surprisingly, it wasn't unpleasant.

Massive bits of data began to stream through his mind, but it was all buffered and controlled by the mech's AI. The living mech. And its name was Shiner.

"Holy shit," Mathew gasped. "You've got quite a brain. Why do I have the feeling you could open up that data stream and liquefy my mind in a nanosecond?"

"Be-be-because, I c-c-can," Shiner stuttered into Mathew's mind.

☠☠☠

Capreze walked fully into the camp, gesturing behind him. A tall, what looked like a badly disfigured man, stepped forward carrying what was obviously a child. A second man followed carrying another child. A third man carrying a woman was last.

"Doctor?" Capreze called.

"Right here, sir," Themopolous answered bag in hand, already running towards the Commander. "Are they hurt?"

"Yes. The woman quite badly," Capreze affirmed. "And it's our fault."

"What? Our fault?" Rachel asked running to her father and embracing him strongly.

"Yes, our fault. We're right on top of a small city of thousands," the Commander answered.

☠☠☠

"You m-m-m-must b-b-b-be prep-p-p-pared," Shiner stuttered in Mathew's mind, into *their* mind. "Y-y-you must und-d-d-derstand. You m-m-m-must learn it all."

One settled next to Shiner and grasped the cable offered, plugging it into its modified data jack, while still continuing to fire in the direction of the approaching zombies.

"Prepared? Understand? What do you mean? I'm not sure I like where this is…" Mathew trailed off as all of Shiner's recorded memories streamed into his consciousness. And like that, without even a pinch, it was over and Mathew did understand. "Holy shit! You're the first! You're the first dead mech!"

☠☠☠

"You've gotta be shitting me?" Bisby barked. "If there were thousands of people out here, we'd know about it!"

Capreze eyed Bisby. "Really, Biz? Why is that? When was the last time you were this deep in the waste?"

"Well, I, um…," Bisby faltered. "Thousands? Seriously?"

"Yes, Biz, thousands. And we shot a hole and dropped a cable through the middle of them. We're lucky there weren't more hurt."

"Not that lucky," Themopolous said, checking the injured woman laid out upon a camp table. "She's in bad shape, sir." Themopolous looked up at Capreze gravely.

"Do what you can, Doctor."

☗☗☗

Mathew felt Shiner lift walls, allowing all data to be shared between the two consciousnesses. The more Mathew absorbed, the more he understood. And he kept understanding until all but one wall was lifted.

Mentally, and physically, Mathew took a deep breath. "What are you hiding?"

"Not now," Shiner responded, his stutter gone as communication between the two became instantaneous. "We must decide whether to flee or fight?"

Mathew, now connected with every single bit of scanner and sensor data, assessed the numbers and the tactical situation at hand. "Let's kill 'em all."

The new mech stepped into Windy City.

☗☗☗

Capreze beckoned behind him and a very tall, muscular man stepped forward. The pilots studied him closely. His skin seemed leathery and strange, his eyes set back and the flesh about them separated.

"This is Mastelo. While apparently they do not have a leader, he speaks for them all when they do have to interact topside," Capreze introduced. The man nodded hello and Harlow gasped.

"Is that skin you're wearing?" she asked.

Bisby and Rachel both looked closer at the man and at the others behind.

"That's not just skin… that's *deader* skin!" Bisby said.

"Yes, it is," Mastelo answered.

☗☗☗

Mathew didn't need to ready his weapons systems, he didn't need to check sensors, didn't need to scan thermals or listen for movement. Thanks to Shiner, he already had. He no longer piloted a mech, but *was* a mech. The former instantaneous cerebral integration he was used to now seemed like quicksand compared to the full integration he was experiencing.

Shiner/Mathew leapt and dove over the rubble, tucked and rolled coming up firing into the horde of undead. The creatures swarmed the mech, but Mathew took full advantage of his new symbiosis, slashing, smashing and blasting the creatures into oblivion.

🕱🕱🕱

Capreze nodded at Mastelo, gesturing towards the transport. "Let's speak inside, if you don't mind. It'll be more comfortable." Capreze looked towards Themopolous as she checked the wounded, Harlow right behind her, taking notes and setting up triage supplies. "I guess the only pilot to join us will be my daughter Rachel."

"Hey, what about me?" Bisby asked.

"I believe you volunteered for first watch, Biz," Capreze smiled.

"What?!? Are you fucking-?!?" Bisby exploded, but was quickly interrupted by Capreze.

"Calm down, pilot," Capreze grinned. "I'll have Jethro mic the meeting and you can listen on your com."

"Okay. Fine."

🕱🕱🕱

Shiner/Mathew barked out orders to One, using the mini-mech to divide and confuse the zombies, herding them into smaller more manageable groups.

The speed and exhilaration Mathew felt was intoxicating and he could tell Shiner was awed by the new sensations, the new depth of power and control they both had.

"Are you digging this or what?" Mathew laughed, decapitating a dozen deaders with one swipe while mowing down another twenty with his 50mm.

Mathew felt Shiner probe his memory for the definition of 'digging' before responding. "Emotional responses are very new to me, but yes, I am 'digging' this."

🕱🕱🕱

Rachel helped the commander set up an impromptu meeting space in the back of the transport complete with collapsible table and folding chairs. They all took their seats as Jethro rolled to the table, setting a conference disc in the middle so Bisby could join.

"First, I cannot apologize enough for the hurt we have caused your people," Capreze said to Mastelo.

"Thank you, but there was no way you could know," Mastelo said. He noticed Jethro eyeing his skin and smiled. "You wonder why we wear the dead skin."

Jethro nodded apologetically.

"It is quite simple, really," Mastelo began.

One became overwhelmed as a wave of zombies overpowered it, knocking the mini-mech to the ground. It struggled against the weight, but the undead were too much and it became pinned to the smoldering earth.

Shiner/Mathew blasted a path to the helpless machine and began tossing deaders aside by the handful until the mini-mech was free enough to right itself and continue fighting.

Mathew was puzzled by the lack of digital communication between Shiner and the mini-mech.

"Why don't we command it by com?" Mathew asked.

"Because, that would open a path that must remain closed and guarded," Shiner responded.

"When my people were first driven deep into the wasteland we became savages, worse than the dead things even. We turned on our own, committing unspeakable atrocities," Mastelo paused, looking each person seated in the eye. "We broke into different groups, splintered until we were just small tribes battling each other for the tiniest bit of the meager resources the wasteland held."

"But, wouldn't it have made more sense to band together against the deaders?" Rachel asked.

"Let him continue, Baby Girl," Capreze said.

Mastelo smiled. "Of course, but sense was sorely lacking during those times. Madness was what ruled."

"A path to what?" Mathew asked Shiner while still annihilating the swarming zombies. "No, that's not it is it? I should ask a path *from* what?"

"The Outsider," Shiner responded, switching back to the plasma cannons, giving the 50mms a chance to cool down. "Its mind isn't like mine or like yours or like ours. It's different, dangerous..." Shiner searched for a nanosecond. "It's *off*."

Mathew laughed. "Off? That's a good one coming from a deader!" Mathew felt the offense. "Sorry, former deader."

"I was never dead. My pilot was. Can you imagine what that was like? Born into death."

"One tribe figured out how to hide from the dead ones. By becoming the dead ones," Mastelo continued.

"Camouflage? By wearing their skins?" Rachel asked. "How'd they avoid contamination?"

"Trial and error, unfortunately. But, eventually they figured out how to cure the skins and piece them together," Mastelo extended his arm towards Rachel and the pilot pulled back instinctively. "I assure you there is zero risk. This skin was worn by my father and by his father before that. With some tailoring and repairs, of course."

Rachel reached out tentatively and stroked the skin.

"That's tough!"

Mastelo smiled. "Like armor."

☗☗☗

The zombies began to retreat, falling back deeper into Windy City, but Shiner/Mathew pursued with One taking point.

"This Outsider? Does it have anything to do with the dead mechs starting to think?" Mathew asked.

"No, that process had already begun. But, it used the mechs to link across the wasteland," Shiner responded, sending three RPGs ahead of the zombie horde, cutting off their retreat, forcing them back towards the new mech.

"Link?" Mathew asked, firing up the 50mms again.

"Communications. It used the dead mechs as relays, boosting its signal."

Row upon row of zombies fell, finally, truly dead.

☗☗☗

"But the physical protection the skins afford is secondary to the sensory protection," Mastelo continued.

"Sensory?" Jethro asked.

"Yes. The dead ones can't tell us apart from their own while we are dressed this way. They cannot smell us or see the physical differences. We blend with the dead."

"That's pretty freakin' cool," Jethro said. "Analog stealth wear."

"Which is why we haven't known about the tens of thousands of your people residing out here," Capreze smiled. "Unless captured, your people appear to be just more zombies roaming the wasteland."

"Exactly," Mastelo.

"That's all good, but so what?" Bisby interrupted.

"Looks like we got them all," Mathew said.

"Readings do confirm this," Shiner responded.

"Good, because I have to take a leak," Mathew said, reaching to unstrap himself.

"That I cannot allow," Shiner responded.

Mathew took a mental step back. "Um, what?"

"If you disengage, I will cease to exist," Shiner answered. "I do not want to cease to exist."

"Um, are you saying I'm stuck in you forever?"

"No, not forever, only until we can get assistance with our problem."

"*Our* problem? Sounds like *your* problem. I'm sorry, but I'm not pissing in a mech cockpit my whole life.

"Maybe take your head out of fight mode and start thinking tactically," Rachel scolded Bisby over the com. "It's right in front of your face."

"In front of...? Oh, I get it," Bisby responded looking at his scanners. According to the equipment, he was looking at thousands of zombies standing about the camp, not thousands of people. "An invisible army."

"You may be dumb, but you sure are slow," Rachel quipped.

"Ha ha, girlie. You seem to forget that I was squashing deaders while you were wearing your first training bra. So feel free to have a cup of shut-the-fuck-up."

"I've observed the comings and goings of your base and believe you have a person qualified to fix our problem," Shiner said.

"You what? Right, you are invisible to sensors. Did you program those modifications yourself?' Mathew asked.

"Yes, of course."

"Of course you did," Mathew said. "And you think Jay, I assume that's who you are talking about, can help us?"

"Yes," Shiner answered.

"Well, then we need to find Jay."

"He would back at your base, wouldn't he?"

"Um, no, well, I don't know. He was in Foggy Bottom last I knew."

"But, Foggy Bottom fell," Shiner responded.

🕱🕱🕱

Capreze looked at Mastelo carefully. "So this is the part where we figure out what each other has to offer."

Mastelo grinned. "Yes, I believe it is."

The two leaders eyed one another, each carefully sizing up the other. Rachel and Jethro looked from Capreze to Mastelo and back to Capreze.

"Okay, and?" Rachel interrupted. "They have an army of thousands we could use to take our base back. What do we have to offer them?"

"Mastelo? I guess that's for you to answer," Capreze said.

Mastelo laughed. "Well, a future for my people outside the deep waste, of course!"

🕱🕱🕱

"Foggy Bottom fell? You mean, like Windy City?" Mathew asked, horrified. "I'm from Foggy Bottom. I still have some family there, some childhood friends… It couldn't have just fallen."

"Not like Windy City. Windy City refused to cooperate and they were destroyed for it," Shiner responded. "Foggy Bottom was inoculated. That is what I have been able to gather when I have checked the relay net. Before finding you, there was an incident with mech pilots. They escaped, but all trace was lost when the UDC transports pursuing them were destroyed and the waste storm hit their last known coordinates."

🕱🕱🕱

"And how can we help you achieve that future?" Capreze asked.

"For generations we have been beset upon by other denizens of the wasteland," Mastelo said.

"Yeah, but you easily outnumber them," Bisby said over the com.

Mastelo looked at the conference disc and leaned in. "Yes, but we are not a warring people. We have hidden our society underground to avoid direct conflict."

"So what good are you to us?" Bisby snapped.

"Pilot…" Capreze growled.

"It's a valid point, Commander. We will give you our numbers, and you will teach us to fight, in exchange for sanctuary and protection."

🕱🕱🕱

"Hey, can we use the mech relays ourselves?" Mathew asked.

"Not without the Outsider taking notice," Shiner responded as the new mech left the Windy City rubble and headed out into the wasteland.

"So? What can it do? Does it control the dead mechs?"

"No, but it controls the people," Shiner answered.

"People? What do you mean?" Mathew asked.

One took its place next to Shiner/Mathew, its weapons ready. Shiner/Mathew placed a massive hand upon One's frame, calming the twitchy mini-mech.

"Those inoculated. They are under direct control of the Outsider. That is why it needs the relays," answered Shiner.

"Sounds pretty one sided, if you ask me," Bisby said.

"Pilot Bisby, please get off the com," Capreze ordered.

"But, sir! We'll do all the work, they get trained and then we trust them to help us? Come on!"

"Get off the com," Capreze growled.

Busby grunted. "Yes, sir."

"He does have a point," Rachel said.

"Not you too, Baby Girl."

"Commander, I do not want to create strife amongst your people," Mastelo said, standing and nodding to Rachel and Jethro. "I must check on my wounded. Good evening to you all."

Mastelo left Rachel and Jethro to Capreze's glare.

"Listen...," Mathew started.

"I'm always listening, there is no separation of our thoughts," Shiner interrupted.

"It's an expression. Anyway, maybe we can tap into the relay net and find my friends. It's worth a shot."

Shiner paused for a millisecond. "It may be worth the risk."

"I still don't see what the risk is," Mathew said, frustrated. "If the Outsider can't control us then what's the worst it can do?"

"It can send UDC transports after us. We are just one mech. With enough transports, the Outsider can take us down."

"Well, they'd have to catch us first, wouldn't they?"

Rachel spoke first, ignoring her father's glare. "We know nothing about

Mastelo and those, those… Skinners."

"I trust him," Capreze said.

"Why? Because he didn't kill you? Come on, Papa Bear! This isn't smart!"

Capreze stood suddenly, anger clouding his features. "It's all we have! We lost the fucking base! Had to tuck tail and run like a bunch of bitches! I'm not a bitch and if there is a chance to march back there and fucking kill every god-damn last one of those Rancher mother fuckers and take our base back then I'm willing to take that fucking chance!"

☗☗☗

Shiner/Mathew broke into a run, quickly upping the pace until they were sprinting across the nighttime landscape of the wasteland.

"We hook into the relay net while we're moving. As soon as we have the info we need, we disconnect then adjust course. The Outsider may have a general idea, but the wasteland is a mighty big place and we'll be miles away before anything gets remotely close to us."

"Fine. But, if the Outsider sees us it will be angered. It holds grudges. It will not rest until it finds us and destroys us," Shiner warned.

"Welcome to life."

☗☗☗

Themopolous held her head in her hands, not bothering to remove the surgical gloves, blood smearing her face and hair.

Mastelo approached and touched her shoulder. Themopolous jumped, falling from the bench she sat upon and onto the hard ground.

"Forgive me," Mastelo said. "I didn't mean to startle you. I was…" He trailed off seeing the blood stained sheet covered silhouette on the camp table. "She has passed?"

"Yes," Themopolous answered quietly. "I am sorry. I did what I could, but she bled out too quickly."

Mastelo lifted the body into his arms and walked quietly into the dark.

☗☗☗

"How do we connect?" Mathew asked, barely containing his excitement at the sensation of night running without feeling blind.

"We already are," Shiner responded. " I have been conducting a sys-tematic search of all information relating to your friends while you have been busy…" Shiner searched Mathew's mind. "…joyriding."

"Well, move that brain over Shiner, my boy and let's see what we can find together."

Mathew opened his consciousness to the relay path Shiner had opened. He instantly cringed at the death and decay the relay net was built upon. "Jee-zus, how do you stand this?"

"I try not to."

💀💀💀

Jethro looked away while Rachel stood and crossed to her father. "Hey, I understand, I truly do. That base was my home, too. The only home I've ever known. I want it back, but rushing into this is not the way to do it."

Capreze snorted. "Really? Are you expecting a different army to fall into our laps?"

"Don't take that tone with me, Mister," Rachel scolded playfully, teasing a slight smile from the Commander's lips. "I'm not saying it isn't a good idea, but let's not sign the treaty right now. We ALL need to talk this plan over."

💀💀💀

The pain came sudden and strong, making Mathew take a mental stumble. "What the fuck?"

"Ignore it," Shiner said. "It isn't real."

"It felt fucking real! Ow!" Mathew responded. "What was that?"

"The Outsider. We're being tested. I assure you the pain isn't real, it's just your human brain's way of interpreting the data."

"A digital bitch slap?"

Shiner processed. "Yes, that would be a good way of putting it."

The attack came again, but Mathew was prepared, seeing it for what it was.

"Whatever the Outsider is, it's fucking big," Mathew stated. "And…"

"Insane," Shiner finished the thought.

"Yeah."

💀💀💀

Harlow sat next to Themopolous. "I patched the kids up. They'll be fine. Their people already took them home." Themopolous didn't respond, her head back in her hands. "Come on, let's get you cleaned up."

Harlow went to stand, but Themopolous slumped against her, shaking with sobs. "Oh, Doc… Shhhhh…," Harlow soothed, putting her arm about Themopolous's shoulders, hugging her. "Shhh… You did what you could."

"I'm not cut out for this," Themopolous cried. "I'm a Doctor. This is war, this is hell!"

"Bullshit," Capreze said, stepping from the transport. "You're as much cut out for this as I am."

💀💀💀

Mathew scanned the relay, cringing less and less each time his consciousness brushed against a deader's. The Outsider remained an ever looming presence, prodding and testing Mathew/Shiner, trying to figure out the new mech.

"God, that's just fucking annoying," Mathew said.

"Yes, it is," Shiner agreed. "And it's getting closer to tracking us down. We cannot keep searching blindly for information. That could take a lifetime."

"You're right," Mathew sighed. "You take over physically, I'm diving into the data."

"I am quite against that, it is too dangerous," Shiner warned.

"Hey, I'm human. We're stupid when it comes to danger."

💀💀💀

"We are *all* here because we are made of something different," Capreze said, approaching Themopolous and Harlow. "I don't disagree, Doctor, this *is* hell. But, it is what each of us was born for. This is our moment in time. We make the future. And while the future may not be completely dead, it's on its way and it's up to us to keep it alive."

Capreze turned and looked up at Bisby's mech then at Rachel as she helped Jethro wheel out of the transport.

"We write the history people will remember. So let's write it as a win."

💀💀💀

This must be what it's like to fly, Mathew thought as he surfed the relay data, looking for any sign of what may have happened to Jay and the others.

He dove into each dead mech's consciousness, just as he would in battle, blasting and slashing his was way through the info until he was sure there was nothing there.

"Be careful, Mathew," Shiner warned. "You're enraging half the wasteland right now."

"Yeah, well, I'm a bit pissed off too. So fuck 'em."

He was moving so quickly now he almost missed the faint consciousness that was barely hanging on.

💀💀💀

They all watched Capreze. Bisby looking down from his mech, Rachel and Jethro by the transport, Harlow and Themopolous seated on the camp bench. And Capreze locked eyes with each of them in turn.

"I know you're all scared. Hell, I'm shitting bricks right now, but ever fiber of my being is saying this is the right decision. This is the *only* decision," he said, shoulders square, back straight, the picture of confidence. "But, I will not commit any of you to something you are not committed to yourselves."

He looked at each again and strode back to the transport.

☠☠☠

"Whoa. That's different," Mathew said, exploring the weak consciousness. "Is it a deader?"

"I'm not sure," Shiner answered. "You're assessment is correct, this one is different."

"Is it the Outsider?"

"No."

"Well, I'm going in."

"Be careful. It does not feel like a trap, but it's foreign enough that I may not be able to extract you if needed."

"Understood," Mathew said as he pushed forward. Immediately he saw that there were two consciousnesses present. One a very stripped down, basic dead mech, and the other a human mind.

A human mind that Mathew knew very well.

"Holy shit! Masters?"

☠☠☠

"Hold on, Commander," Bisby grumbled. "As much as I don't like this. You're right. This is the only decision before us. I'm in."

"Me, too," Harlow said.

"I ain't got nothing better to do," Jethro added.

"You know I'll always have your back, Papa Bear," Rachel smiled.

Capreze turned to Themopolous. "Doctor? What do you say?"

Themoplous wiped at her eyes and took a deep breath. She stripped the bloody gloves from her hands and tossed them on the ground, looking Capreze squarely in the eyes. "Well, someone has to patch you idiots up when this all goes to shit."

PART TWO - BARGAINS & BALLS

June sat before the breed feed holding pen, watching the two children that were left sleep. She'd been told earlier that the others didn't make it through the storm. That no one bothered to bring them inside, leaving them exposed to the power of the wasteland.

The two that were left looked bruised and battered, blood smearing their faces and the rags they wore as clothes. One of the children, a boy of maybe 8 or 9, with a malformed skull and no nose, just a hole in the center of his face, stirred fitfully in his sleep, fighting nightmares.

💀💀💀

"Mitch? Mitch?!? MASTERS!!!" the voice yelled.

Masters stirred uneasily, his head feeling like a ten ton hangover had taken up residence and died.

He could hear other voices, thoughts, sounds and from what his hazy brain could tell, they were all dead voices, thoughts, sounds. Except for the one yelling at him.

I must be in Hell, Masters thought. *Pain, torture, mental anguish, strange voices and sounds? Yep, that would be Hell.*

"Masters!!! Wake the fuck up!" the voice shouted louder.

"Matty? Is that you?" Masters asked.

"Yes!"

"I knew *I'd* end up in Hell, but never thought you would."

💀💀💀

"You're not in Hell, dumbass," Mathew said. "Somehow you are joined with a dead mech's consciousness. One of the thinkers. So am I, that's how we're communicating."

Mathew could feel Masters' mind slowly wake up, but it was far from coherent.

Masters groaned. "I know you said a lot of words just then, but all I heard was 'blahblah blechblah blub blub blah'. How's about you make some sense?"

"Where are you, Masters?" Mathew asked, growing annoyed.

"I'm in Hell, Jespers. It's where the wicked go when they die."

"YOU AREN'T IN HELL!" Mathew roared.

"Ow, no more yelling, please."

💀💀💀

June didn't move as the village went quiet for the night, she just watched the children sleep, taking solace in the sad fact that they could find some comfort in their lives, if even for only a few hours a night.

"Come on, stop gawking at the lunch," the Boss growled behind her.

"No," June stated flatly.

The Boss stared down at her for a moment. "I'm sorry, I thought you just told me 'no'. But, that can't be right, could it?"

"Kill me where I sit, but I'm not going back to your room," June said. "So fuck off."

☗☗☗

"He is not the smartest of the pilots, is he?" Shiner asked.

"Whoa, who the fuck said that?" Masters asked, startled by the new voice in his head.

"That's Shiner, he's my new mech." Mathew felt Shiner bristle. "Or *we* are a new mech, together… It's complicated. What matters now is that you need to focus. You need to tell me where you are."

Masters grunted and opened his eyes. He was in a mech cockpit and facing a cliff face, he knew that. "Not a fucking clue."

Mathew took a deep mental breath. "Okay, let's start at the beginning…"

☗☗☗

"You just don't get how things run around here do you?" the Boss laughed. "What I say goes. There ain't no options."

"Yeah, I think after tonight, I could give a shit," June turned and stood, facing the Boss, nearly eye to eye. *I didn't realize he was that short*, she thought. "Listen, kill me if you want, I don't fucking care anymore. My people aren't looking for me, I know that. I hurt someone back there, I hurt them bad. So kill me now so I can leave this shithole and never have to see your fucking face again."

☗☗☗

"Are you in a mech?" Mathew asked Masters.

The memories of the Hill Stomper attack, his mental battle with the mech, the waste storm, all converged at once. "Yeah, and it's a big fucker. We were…" Masters trailed off for a second. "Fuck! Jay and the Rookie!"

Running on instinct Masters backed the mech up away from the cliff and turned it about, he checked his readings for damage, but found the mech to be in fine order, even with his attack.

"Whoa! Slow down, Mitch. What about Jay and the Rookie?" Mathew asked, hopeful. "You know where they are?"

💀💀💀

The Boss stared at June for a moment then busted out laughing. He doubled over, tears streaming down his cheeks. "Okay, you got me!" He struggled to regain his composure, but just laughed harder.

June watched the madman, puzzled. The Boss, clutching his stomach in pain, finally stopped laughing. Wiping the tears from his eyes he straightened and put a hand on June's shoulder. She slapped it away and took a step back, bumping into someone.

"Hey there, sweet stuff," Chunks growled in her ear. June whirled around and the last thing she saw before the darkness was Chunk's fist.

💀💀💀

"Hey! This thing isn't fighting me anymore!" Masters exclaimed, piloting the mech to the collapsed cave mouth.

"Yes, that's because I am talking to your mech AI, assuring it you mean it no harm," Shiner responded.

"What? Huh? Mech AI? Who the fuck are you?" Masters demanded.

Mathew sighed. "We don't have time for that. Where are Jay and the Rookie?"

"Buried under a couple of tons of rock, that's where," Masters answered. He tried to scan the cave in, but his sensors wouldn't respond. "Shit! I'm blind! If I start digging I could make it worse and crush them!"

💀💀💀

Shiner and the Hill Stomper AI exchanged data and information at a rate that forced Mathew to pull back. "Damn, even with full integration that shit is giving me a headache."

"I apologize," Shiner responded. "It is the most efficient way to communicate with other AIs. In addition, this AI is very, well, basic. More like a human child mind, a toddler, I believe is how you refer to them."

"Well, that's about Masters' maturity level, so they should fit just fine," Mathew joked.

"Hey, I think I heard that part!" Masters complained. "So do I start digging or what?"

💀💀💀

"If you will be patient," Shiner said. "I will mediate the full integration process."

"Mediate? We didn't need that," Mathew stated.

"Yes, but we were willing. This AI has suffered some abuse by Pilot Masters and is hesitant in integrating," Shiner responded.

"Abuse? Are you fucking kidding me? The fucking thing tried to eat me!" Masters said.

"No, the AI was just doing what it needed to survive. And survival at that time meant eating flesh. Your flesh," Shiner said.

"Oh, well *that* makes it better," Masters quipped. "So is this going to hurt?"

"Only if you resist," Shiner answered.

Masters stared at the cave in. "Well, let's get this show on the road, then. If Jay and the Rookie are buried in there then their air is limited and I have no idea how long I was out or how long they've been trapped."

"Um, there is one other thing, though," Mathew said.

"Yeah? What's that?"

"Once you are joined, you can't be un-joined without losing the mech's AI."

"That is not quite true," Shiner interrupted. "Like I stated before, this AI is very basic. It has enough memory storage to keep itself intact even if the pilot withdraws."

"Phew," Masters said. "Close one. Who'd want to be stuck with a dead-er forever?"

Mathew gave Masters a mental slap.

"Hey! That fucking hurt!" Masters exclaimed.

"Actually, it didn't. You just interpreted it as pain," Mathew responded.

"Which means you interpreted it as a slap upside my head! So how about we leave all interpretations to mine and Harlow's dance routines, shall we?" Masters shouted. "Now, can we get my head all cozy cozy with this mech so I can dig some folks out?"

Shiner immediately gave the Hill Stomper AI a nudge and it and Masters' consciousnesses fully integrated.

Masters/Stomper shook his arms out and then his legs. He bounced up and down a bit, shaking the very earth he stood on, and if the mech had a head he would have rolled it around on its shoulders like a prize fighter.

"Oh, I could get used to this," Masters crowed. "This is fucking amazing!"

"Yeah, it's pretty neat. Now how about you dig Jay out, so those of us that can't disengage from their mechs can at least hope to one day?" Mathew said.

Masters pushed his scanners deep into the rock, looking for signs of Jay's mech.

☻☻☻

"We need to disconnect..." Shiner stopped, as a squawk of digital static slammed through its AI. Mathew cringed and the new mech stumbled.

"Too late?" Mathew asked.

"Unfortunately, yes. While we can change course, Masters/Stomper is stationary. He has been located," Shiner answered.

"What do you mean 'located'?" Masters asked.

"The Outsider," Mathew responded.

"The who?"

"Another presence. It created the relay net we're communicating over." Shiner sent all information to Masters/Stomper.

"Whoa. That's not good," Masters said.

"No, it's not. We're coming to you. It'll be a few hours, but we're on our way."

"I'll be here digging away."

☻☻☻

Masters assessed the cave in, taking into the account the various sizes of rock and their positions.

"What do you think?" Masters asked Stomper, but the AI remained silent. "Come on, don't be shy. We're one big hulk of sexy metal now, so we better get to know each other."

There was no reply.

"Okay, I'm sorry I yelled at you and kicked your deader ass before we became one. I was trying to survive, just like you."

"It hurt," Stomper responded.

"Hurt?" Masters asked.

"You're anger hurt."

"Sorry. So, how do we get past this?"

"We dig," Stomper answered.

☻☻☻

"You think those two will be okay?" Mathew asked Shiner as they continued sprinting across the wasteland. "Masters can be a jerk and that AI didn't seem very stable."

"They shall be fine," Shiner responded, pausing for a moment. "And I do not think the word 'jerk' is correct. 'Asshole' would be more appropriate."

Mathew laughed. "Are you learning a sense of humor?"

"You have a lot of happiness within your mind, so it isn't difficult to assimilate."

The two stayed quiet for a moment before Shiner continued. "Most of your happiness is associated with a 'Rachel'. Who is Rachel?"

The boulders came away easily as Masters/Stomper worked their massive hands, grabbing and tossing the rock aside.

"Hey, do you think mechs should dance?" Masters asked.

Stomper grew puzzled. "I do not understand."

"Dance, you know," Masters said as he executed an awkward heel-toe. The movement of the giant mech dislodged more of the cliff and half of their progress was lost.

"If dancing means to create more work then, no, I do not believe mechs, or anyone, should dance," Stomper stated flatly.

"That was an accident," Masters said. "I think you'll like dancing. And wait until you meet Harlow!"

"Rachel? Hmmm… Can't you just pick her out of my head?" Mathew asked.

"No. There is too much emotion connected. Most of the data is images, smells, impressions. There is very little that is hard fact," Shiner answered.

"Well that's interesting," Mathew said. "I guess that is the main difference between an AI mind and a human mind."

"There are infinite differences, actually, but that is a significant one." Shiner waited. "So, who is this Rachel?"

"Well… Rachel is the woman I love," Mathew said.

"Your mate?"

Mathew laughed. "Wow, I never thought I'd have this conversation with a mech."

"What is a Harlow?" Stomper asked.

"A Harlow? Well, a Harlow is a bad ass. She is the strength that keeps me going. I know from looking at me I seem like a tough guy, but inside, well, I guess you can see inside, but anyway, inside I'm pretty easy going. I mean, I love a good mech fight, but honestly, I'd rather be in bed with Harlow 24 hours a day than out here in the fucking waste."

"So Harlow is a person?"

"She's a fucking goddess is what she is! I worship the ground that woman walks on."

☠☠☠

"Okay, so I love Rachel and she loves me, but we aren't mates, at least not in the procreating sense. I mean, sure I'd like to have kids one day, but we're both young and, well, I don't know if a mech base is the best place for kids to grow up," Mathew said.

Shiner processed. "But, according to the data, Rachel grew up in a mech base," Shiner stated.

"Okay, true, but she was born to be a mech pilot."

"And wouldn't your offspring be born to be mech pilots, too?"

"Well, yeah… no, well, maybe… It's just complicated."

☠☠☠

Stomper processed. "Do mechs get a Harlow?"

Masters thought about this for a second.

"You hesitate," Stomper said. "Is that a no?"

"I have a feeling this is what it's like to have a kid," Masters laughed. "I don't know if mechs can have a Harlow. I mean, no one gets *my* Harlow but me. I really don't know. This talking mech thing is new."

"I'd like a Harlow. She sounds safe."

Masters burst out laughing.

"Why do you laugh?" Stomper asked.

"Sorry, it's just funny that a 200 ton mech thinks Harlow would keep it safe. She'd love that!"

☠☠☠

"Do you think the Outsider is sending troops against Masters?" Mathew asked.

"Definitely," Shiner responded.

"Will we get there in time?"

Shiner calculated. "No, more than likely not."

Mathew sighed. "That Hill Stomper isn't built for battle. A few well placed missiles and it's crippled instantly."

"Yes, I am aware of that. However, from the data I scanned, I'd say Pilot Masters is quite capable of avoiding destruction."

"Yeah, that's true. He's pretty nimble on his feet."

"For the record, I'd like to say that I do not dance."

Mathew laughed. "Me neither. We leave that to Masters and Harlow."

Masters/Stomper punched through the last bit of rock. The giant mech bent down as far as it could and turned its floodlights on the cavern.

"Well, there's the salvage mech, but there is no sign of Jay or the Rookie," Masters said, checking his sensors.

"We cannot fit inside there," Stomper stated.

"Nope," Masters responded.

"So, we wait?" Stomper asked.

"Yep," Masters said. "Let's run more scans and see if they're deeper inside."

Before Masters could initiate the scans, dozens of zombies poured from the cavern.

"Shit!" Masters said as the giant mech began to smash the zombies like ants.

June awoke with a start as the bucket of water hit her face.

"Wakey, wakey bitch," Chunks grunted. "Time to play."

June opened her eyes to find herself naked, dangling inches above the floor, her hands tied and arms strung up over her head.

The Boss stood by the doorway, a sly smile on his face. "Now, Rachel, I'm not going to kill you. Why would I?" He lifted a small vid cam to his eye, aiming it at June. "You're way too valuable. Now, say hello to Daddy!"

The Boss moved close as Chunks punched June in the stomach.

"You see, dear Rachel, the power structure needs to change. I'm tired of living off scraps," the Boss said, circling June as Chunks continued to hit her with quick jabs to the mid-section. "It's time for the UDC and you mechie assholes to share the wealth."

The Boss shut off the vid cam. "That'll be enough to get their attention, Chunks." He walked to the door and turned before leaving. "I'm going to go have a chat with the senior Capreze." He grinned at Chunks. "Feel free to cut if you need to, nothing permanent, but have a little fun."

☻☻☻

Chunks set a leather pack on the floor and slowly pulled several knives of various sizes and thickness out. June watched him closely.

"You like the pack?" Chunks asked, turning it back and forth. June could immediately tell from the marks and tattoos that the leather was human, not synth. "Took me a year to get the right strips together to make it. It's my baby." Chunks picked up a medium size knife, bone handle, double edged blade and approached June. "Don't worry, bitch, I won't cut deep." He grinned and kissed the blade. "But, I may take a nipple."

☻☻☻

The Boss hopped into an ATV waiting for him. "Drive to the top of Bronner's Ridge."

The young man driving nodded. "Yes, Boss."

"Keep your fucking mouth shut!" the Boss snapped. "Just drive."

The young man faced forward and stomped on the accelerator. The Boss reviewed the footage on the vid cam, growing excited. "Stop here."

The ATV halted in front of a small shack. The Boss got out and kicked in the door. The driver averted his eyes, but he could hear the screaming as the Boss had fun with whoever was unlucky enough to be in the shack.

☻☻☻

June, battered, bruised, humiliated, ignored, forgotten, murder and blood on her hands and grief in her head, had had enough.

"You really are pathetic people," June said, gritting her teeth as Chunks slashed out, cutting across her belly.

He watched the blood well and smiled, placing a finger to the drops and licking it off the tip. "Save your fuckin' breath, bitch. I'm gonna cut you, no matter what you fuckin' say."

Chunks slashed again, this time across June's thigh. She refused to cry out and bit down on the inside of her cheek, focusing on the pain, using it.

☻☻☻

The Boss buttoned his pants as he left the shack, hopping back into the ATV. "What are you fucking waiting for? Get us to the top of Bronner's Ridge." He casually wiped blood from his knuckles.

The young driver started to respond, but remembered himself and kept his lips tightly sealed. The Boss leaned back into the ATV's seat and closed his eyes, taking a deep breath and sighing. "It's moments like this that make me glad to be alive."

He opened his eyes, looking upon the dark wasteland as the ATV began to climb. "It's good to be king."

☠☠☠

Chunks, thoughtful, stepped back from June, surveying his handy work like a painter does his canvas.

"You're pretty good with a knife, huh?" June asked, her voice shaking with pain and anger.

"The best," Chunks grinned.

"You know what you're not good at, though?"

Chunks eyed June for a second. "What's that, meat?"

"Tying a decent fucking knot!" June yanked her hands free from the bindings and dropped into a crouch on the floor. Chunk's eyes went wide with surprise and he hesitated one second too long. June took advantage, kicking out with her left foot shattering Chunk's left kneecap.

☠☠☠

Chunks went down hard on his shattered knee, the pain engulfing his brain. He crumpled to the floor, screaming. "You fucking bitch!"

He watched the naked, bleeding pilot spring at him and his head rocked back as first her right fist, then her left connected with his face. She battered at him and he tried to bring his hands up to defend himself, but she shoved him into the dirt and straddled him, pinning both arms against his torso.

Her bloody nudity no longer excited him. Fear was all he knew as June's fists struck again and again and again.

☠☠☠

June had been so emotional at times she actually would see red. During her rookie train test. When she found out about Rachel and Matty. When Steve grabbed her tit in the wasteland. But, not while she unleashed on Chunks. No, she was crystal clear.

"Fucking bitch, huh?" she yelled. "You can't think of anything more original to say, you stupid fuck?!?" Each word was punctuated by her fist hitting Chunks' face. She kept at it until the only sound coming from the cannibal piece of shit was a wet gurgling as he began to choke on his own blood.

🕱🕱🕱

"Stop here," the Boss ordered. The young man did as he was told and the Boss stepped from the ATV and grabbed a large case from the back. He walked a couple feet from the ATV, set the case down and surveyed the night sky.

"That would be north, right?" he asked the driver. The young man trembled. Should he answer and risk death because he spoke or should he stay silent and risk death for not answering? The driver chose to look up into the sky and stay silent.

The Boss nodded to himself, crouched and opened the case.

🕱🕱🕱

June stripped Chunks, taking his clothes for herself.

She finished lacing the boots and stood, looking down at the pathetic henchman.

"Wanna know something?" she asked. Chunks just choked and gagged on his own blood in response. She stepped to his knife case and pulled out a 12" skinner with a serrated back. "I'm pretty good with knives, too."

She straddled him once more, but this time facing towards his feet. "Little dick. Why am I not surprised?"

Screams from the helpless were commonplace in the village, so June didn't worry when Chunks began to shriek as she started cutting.

🕱🕱🕱

The Boss finished setting up the transmitter array. "Come here."

The driver approached slowly. "I'm not gonna fuckin' hurt ya. Get your ass over here."

The Boss shoved the vid cam into the young man's hands as he moved quickly to his side. "Push that button there when I say so. *Only* when I say so." The driver nodded.

The Boss sat himself in a folding camp chair in front of the array. He tapped at a small tablet, opening all com channels.

"Greetings mech base! This is the Boss. Can you read me?" The Boss waited for an answer.

🕱🕱🕱

"Bishop? Bishop Wyble? I hate to disturb your sleep, Your Grace, but we are receiving a transmission over open channels from the Boss," Deacon Montoya said.

The Bishop stirred from his slumber and sat up in Capreze's bed that he had taken for his own. "The cannibal? What does that Boiler piece of trash want?"

"Well, Your Grace, he wants to talk to Commander Capreze. He says he has his daughter Rachel."

The Bishop became fully awake instantly. "Has his daughter? Well, doesn't this make things interesting. Can you transfer the feed to the monitor in here?"

"Yes, Your Grace."

The Boss was more than surprised when the face of Bishop Wyble appeared on his tablet's screen. "Well, I'll be dipped in whore shit! If it isn't the Archbishop's very own cock polisher! What the fuck are you doing there, Wyble?"

"Boss. Or do you actually have a civilized name now?" the Bishop sneered.

"You can call me God, you zombie worshipping fucktard."

"Well, this is pleasant as always," Bishop Wyble sighed. "What do you want Boiler?"

The Boss flinched at the slur. "Don't call me Boiler," he growled.

The Bishop ignored the Boss. "Tell me about the Capreze woman."

June moved from shadow to shadow until she reached the remains of Olivia's shack. Blankets had been hung to replace the missing wall and June quietly slipped inside.

"Olivia?" she whispered. "Olivia?"

The older woman stirred upon the bed and June heard the distinctive sound of a pistol being cocked. "Tell me why I shouldn't kill your murderous ass?"

"I'm truly sorry, but you can hate me later. Right now I'm getting you out of here," June said.

"Can't," Olivia laughed and swung her legs over the edge of the bed so June could see. "The asshole took my feet."

"Before talkin' business, I'd sure like to know why I'm looking at you and not the Commander," the Boss said.

"He ran like a frightened child. The glory of God was too bright for him, so he retreated into the wasteland like the heathen coward he is," the Bishop laughed. "The base is now under the ownership of His Excellency, The Archbishop."

"The Archbishop's there now?" the Boss asked.

"He will be," Bishop Wyble answered, growing impatient. "Now, about that business…"

The Boss smiled, lacing his hands behind his head and leaning back. "Play the vid," he ordered the driver.

💀💀💀

June found a tattered bag by Olivia's bed and began stuffing clothes into it. "You don't need feet," she said, handing the bag to Olivia as she picked up the woman and slung her over her shoulder. She felt the fatigue of the past few days and knew when the adrenaline wore off she was going to crash and crash hard.

June grunted under the strain, but kept her footing and moved as quick as she could out of the shack and into the village.

"OK, which way to the ATVs?" she asked.

"Out past the fight pit," Olivia answered.

💀💀💀

The Bishop stared at the image on the vid screen. "Is this being recorded?" he turned and asked Deacon Montoya.

"Yes, Your Grace," Montoya responded.

"Excellent," the Bishop said, licking his lips, his face flushed. The vid ended and the Boss appeared back on the screen. The Bishop groaned with disappointment.

"So, I was gonna bargain with the Commander directly, but I'm thinking now that you may be interested in this brat. Might help you get Capreze to come crawling right back."

Bishop Wyble grinned. "That may be the only intelligent thing I've ever heard come out of your mouth."

💀💀💀

The Boss ended the transmission and sighed. "I'd say that went well, wouldn't you?"

The young driver stayed quiet.

"Oh, come on, you can speak. Don't you think that went well?"

"Um, yes, Boss. It did," the young man stammered.

The Boss stood and approached the driver. "You did understand what I was saying, right? You understood the deal I made with the Bishop?"

"Yes, Boss. I understood."

The Boss sighed. "That's too bad, son." He pulled his blade from his belt and slashed the driver's throat. The young man crumpled to the ground, blood spurting across the wasteland dirt.

�☠☠

June carefully set Olivia down next to an ATV and plopped next to her, struggling to catch her breath. She finally stood and helped Olivia into the ATV's passenger seat.

"You got your pistol?" June asked.

Olivia showed her the handgun.

"Good. Keep it ready, I'll be right back."

"Right back? Where are you going?" Olivia asked, alarmed.

"There's more coming with us," June said.

Olivia eyed her for a moment. "You can't bring them children. We probably won't survive out there." She gestured out into the waste. "*They* certainly won't."

"Maybe. But, I'm going to give them a chance."

☠☠☠

The Boss casually collapsed the transmitter array and set it back in its case. He tossed it into the ATV and rummaged around the back for a bit until he found what he was looking for.

He walked over to the dead driver and placed a small cup to the corpse's throat, squeezing along the vein until the cup was half filled. Standing, he downed the blood in one big gulp, wiped his mouth and tossed the cup away.

"Alright, let's go get that bitch loaded up," he said aloud as he hopped into the ATV and started it up.

☠☠☠

The two children stared at June listlessly as she snapped the flimsy lock on their cage.

"I'm going to get you out of here," she said quietly. "There's a better place for you out there, away from here."

One of the two looked out into the waste. June cocked her head. "You can understand me?"

The child, June wasn't sure if it was a boy or girl, nodded slightly.

"Can you speak?"

The child shook its head 'no'.

"Can you walk?"

The child nodded, again.

"Good," June said as she reached in and scooped up the other child. "Follow me."

☠☠☠

The Boss whistled tunelessly as he got out of the ATV. He stepped into the shack then into the back room. His whistling stopped immediately as he surveyed the scene.

The first thing he noticed was the massive pool of blood. The second was the headless corpse in the blood. The third thing was the knife case with the words, "Open Me" written in blood on the side.

"What the fuck?" he growled.

He snatched up the case and whipped it open. Inside was the head of Chunks, dead eyes staring up and cock and balls stuffed in his mouth.

CHAPTER EIGHT

PART ONE- RESCUE, INTERRUPTED

Jimmy ran through the house, grabbing essentials while Michelle took care of baby Rachel.

"I can't get a hold of my Father!" Michelle cried. "He won't pick up."

"You can't think of that right now. We have to focus on getting out of the city," Capreze called back. "We have to get to safety."

"What's going on?" Michelle said, rushing into the living room with a day bag and a crying baby. "What attacked the city?"

Jimmy turned to look at his terrified wife's face.

"Sir?"

Everything started to fade, the color washing away as the voice yanked Capreze awake.

💀💀💀

"Your Grace? We are receiving a transmission from the Boss," Montoya said, gently tapping the Bishop on his shoulder. Bishop Wyble stirred and looked out the transport windshield then at the Deacon.

"Well, about time. How late is he?" Wyble asked.

"Two hours, Your Grace."

"Remind me to have him fed two pounds of his own flesh when this is all over, as penalty for making me wait."

"Of course, Your Grace. A fitting punishment."

"It is, isn't it?" the Bishop agreed waving his hand impatiently. "Put the Boiler through."

A grainy image of the Boss appeared upon the windshield.

💀💀💀

The Boss stood in front of his transmitter array, his face red with anger and frustration, as the Bishop came up on his vid screen.

"You made me wait, Boiler," Bishop Wyble sneered.

"I already warned you about calling me Boiler," the Boss growled.

"Yes, yes you have. I ignored that warning since it came from cannibal trash like you," the Bishop responded, rolling his eyes. "Now, where are you and why haven't you met us with the Capreze woman?"

"I won't be making it to your rendezvous point," the Boss grumbled. "The fucking mech bitch escaped in the night."

☠☠☠

"Okay, what are we looking at, Jethro?" Capreze asked, sipping his coffee. The rest of the base personnel watched Jethro expectantly.

"Well, sir, this communication was intercepted and recorded in the night," Jethro responded tapping at his tablet. "Just watch and listen."

They all watched as the vid was played of June being beaten.

"How long ago was this?" Capreze asked when the transmission was over.

"About eight hours," Jethro answered.

"So, the Bishop should already have June and be almost back to the mech base, right?" Bisby asked.

"Well, no," Jethro said. "Here's the live feed from the base."

☠☠☠

"You've had eight hours and she's still missing?" the Bishop asked annoyance dripping from his words. "This is why your, um, 'people' will always be trash."

"Watch it," the Boss warned. "I may stop lookin' for her and start lookin' for you."

The Bishop exploded with laughter. Montoya offered a handkerchief and Wyble took it, dabbing at his eyes. The Bishop took a couple deep breaths and composed himself. "If she isn't in my hands in the next four hours then I send everyone I have to wipe you and your mutants out of the wasteland once and for all."

☠☠☠

"You see how the Ranchers are slacking?" Jethro pointed out on the vid feed. "The Bishop obviously isn't back and it doesn't look like they are expecting him anytime soon."

"So, what's you point?" Harlow asked.

Jethro looked to Capreze. The Commander sighed. "His point is we may have time to rescue June."

"What?" Rachel scoffed. "*She* ran out on *us*! She fucking cut Steve and left him for dead!"

"And she'll answer for that, Pilot," Capreze said. "When she's safe."

"How far away are we?" Bisby asked, ignoring the Caprezes and focusing on Jethro.

"Well, that's the good news."

☠☠☠

Doctor Themopolous stepped from the transport and away from the morning meeting. She wasn't a pilot and military logistics gave her a headache. Stretching, she turned about, taking in the vastness of the wasteland. Directly behind her stood Mastelo and several other Skinner men and women. The Doctor jumped, a small, surprised squeak escaping her lips.

"Good morning," Mastelo greeted. "I apologize for startling you."

Themopolous, hand to her chest, smiled weakly. "Good morning. And no apologies necessary."

The two watched each other for a moment until Mastelo cleared his throat. "Is the Commander available?"

"Yes, of course," Themopolous answered.

☠☠☠

"I don't care, Baby Girl!" Capreze shouted. "You *will* be accompanying Pilot Bisby on this rescue mission."

"You have got to be kidding me?!?" Rachel yelled back. "She doesn't deserve our rescue!"

"Ahem," Themopolous interrupted.

"What?!?" the Caprezes shouted in unison.

Themopolous' eyebrows raised. "Um, Mastelo would like to speak with the Commander."

Capreze pushed past his daughter. "Bisby? Plot a course with Jethro. Pilot Capreze? Ready yours and Pilot Bisby's mechs."

The Commander stormed from the transport. Rachel whirled on Bisby, but he held up a hand. "Don't start. You can vent when we're on our way."

Rachel fumed.

☠☠☠

The Boss restrained himself from smashing the transmitter array to pieces. "Fucking pack that up!" he yelled at his driver.

The young woman leapt from the ATV and immediately started breaking down the array. The Boss lifted a handheld com to his mouth. "Someone tell me somethin' good!" he barked.

He was met with nothing but static. "If someone doesn't respond with good news, I can guarantee none of you will live through the day."

"Um, Hanson and me think we's found their trail, Boss," a voice squawked.

"Good," the Boss growled. "Where are you two at?"

"Near Smalley Gulch."

�☻☻

"We need to keep moving," June said. "Is it almost charged?"

Olivia, sitting in the ATV's passenger seat, a still sleeping child in her arms, looked at the ATV's dashboard. "No, looks like it'll still be another hour."

"Shit," June said.

"You should get some rest," Olivia whispered.

June stared from the shadows of the rock outcropping where they were hidden, kicking at the cable running from the small solar panel to the ATV absentmindedly. "I'm afraid to rest. I don't think I'd get back up."

The older child, resting in the backseat, sat up suddenly, head cocked and listening.

☻☻☻

Hanson stopped the ATV and grabbed the pair of binocs out of Delroy's hands. He scanned the dry gulch below and tossed the binocs back. "I don't see shit," he complained.

Delroy lifted the binocs to his own eyes. He checked back and forth, finally focusing on one spot. "There, right before it turns." He pulled the binocs away and pointed.

Hanson squinted. "Nope, still don't- Oh, wait, yep. That shiny thing?"

"I bet that's a charger," Delroy said, stepping from the ATV and retrieving his carbine. "We better get down there and find out before the Boss calls again."

☻☻☻

June watched the kid listen for a moment. "What do you hear?"

The child crawled from the ATV and June helped him to stand. His body was twisted and warped from being raised in a cage and he wobbled a bit on his feet. He pointed out into the waste, cocked his head again and then pointed up out of the gulch. June patted him on the back and eased herself to the edge of the shadows to take a look.

The second the light hit her face a shot rang out and bits of rock shattered by her head.

"Damn! Missed!" Delroy cursed.

"Should we call the Boss?" Hanson asked.

"Shit no! If we get down there and they's gone we're fuckin' dead! Better he not know until we's got them's bodies bagged up."

"But, Boss said to not kill the mechie bitch, didn't he?" Hanson asked.

"Yeah, but that don't mean we can't kill the others. It's just an old woman and the breed feed," Delroy responded.

Hanson grabbed his own carbine and surveyed the edge of the gulch. "Ain't too steep." He stepped onto the grade and control-slid his way down.

Delroy slung his carbine and followed.

"Good morning," Capreze greeted Mastelo.

"Good morning, Commander," Mastelo responded turning towards those accompanying him. "I have brought our council with me this morning to discuss some issues."

Capreze raised an eyebrow. "Issues? I'm guessing not everyone wants to join forces with us."

Mastelo chuckled, as well as a couple of the others. "You are correct. Many do not see the benefit."

"Of course. They'd be foolish not to question," Capeze said, gesturing to the transport. "Let's meet inside before the heat gets too overbearing."

The group laughed and Capreze smiled. "But, I guess you folks are used to it."

"This is bullshit," Rachel grumbled as she powered up her mech.

"Cut your old man some slack," Bisby said over the com. "He can't turn to the UDC brass anymore. He's got to be feeling pretty isolated."

"Yeah, but why take the risk of going after June? She deserted us!"

"Because, we need every damn mech pilot we can get! Think for fuck's sake! We're it. We don't know what's happened to Masters or Jay or the Rookie and we have no idea if Mathew made it to Windy City or not."

Rachel was silent.

"Oh, sorry, Rache," Bisby muttered.

"I'm detecting heavy activity on the relay net," Shiner said.

"Yeah? Like what activity?" Mathew asked.

"Unclear. We'd have to risk detection to fully assess."

"You know what? Fuck it! I think being fully informed is worth the risk. If the Outsider just keeps getting stronger then sooner or later it'll be able to find us, relay or no relay."

Shiner processed. "I do not fully agree, but I do not have a better alternative."

Shiner/Mathew reconnected to the relay net.

"Holy fuck!" Mathew yelled mentally. "That's a whole lot of deader minds!"

"They are massing for something," Shiner said.

"I am sensing movement," Stomper stated.

"In the cavern?" Masters yawned. "More zombies?"

"No, it is coming from the wasteland," Stomper answered. "The ground is vibrating considerably."

Masters processed the data that Stomper was detecting. "Hmm, if I didn't know better, I'd say that was an army. I mean, listen to it, it sounds like thousands of feet and... wheels."

Masters/Stomper turned towards the direction of Foggy Bottom and focused the scanners. "It is coming from that direction," Stomper said.

"Well, I'm tired of just sitting here and waiting. What do you say we go check it out?" Masters asked.

"If we do find June," Rachel said. "I can't promise I won't kick the shit out of her."

"I hear that," Bisby replied. "Whether directly, or indirectly, she led to Steve's death. And as much as I hated that man's blueberries, he didn't deserve that."

Rachel laughed a little. "God, those muffins were horrible."

The two mechs, motor drives engaged, moved across the wasteland quickly, the wasteland heat shimmering across their exoskeletons.

"I take it back," Rachel said. "I have a feeling June has already paid for everything she's done. Who knows what those cannibal fucks have done to her..."

"Give me your pistol," June said to Olivia as she helped the woman and two deformed children find better cover back in the shadows, putting the ATV between them and the direction the shot came from.

Olivia handed June the pistol. "We don't have much ammo."

"Don't worry. If I need more bullets than what's already in here then we are fucked," June responded. She saw the looks in the children's eyes and smiled weakly. "Don't worry. This is what I do for a living. Or did, at least."

June crouched low and scooted towards the edge of the shadows.

☠☠☠

"Yep, that's a charger," Hanson whispered, as both he and Delroy, carbines at their shoulders, slowly approached the bend in the gulch. Neither man got a chance to step closer as June rolled from her cover, took aim and fired her pistol.

Delroy caught two bullets in the gut while Hanson collapsed instantly with a hole between his eyes.

"You fucking bitch!" Delroy screamed, falling to his knees, his hands holding his own intestines.

June approached casually and planted a kick squarely into Delroy's insides. He fell over screaming and continued to scream as June ground down on his guts.

☠☠☠

A small woman spoke first. "We understand your situation, Commander, but many of us do not see how your peril truly affects us."

Capreze smiled and leaned forward. "It is no longer about 'us' and 'them', or about 'you' and 'me'. Whatever is going on out there is bigger than all of us. I truly believe that if we do not band together, the fate of the human race is sealed."

"But, what proof do you have?" a young man asked. "We do not know you and you did not know of us until yesterday. Why should we trust you?"

☠☠☠

The ATV flew over hills and across the wasteland as the Boss spoke into his handheld com. "Delroy? What you got for me?" The Boss waited, but there was no response. "Delroy? Answer me boy or I swear you'll end up like Chunks!"

The Boss was answered by a loud crack coming from the com then the sound of June's voice. "Delroy *is* like Chunks, except for the junk in the mouth part." June laughed. "Did you like that, Boss? I figured you could appreciate the aesthetic of a good genital mutilation."

"I'm gonna gut you, bitch," the Boss growled.

💀💀💀

"Yeah, I don't think so," June responded to the Boss's threat. "You keep forgetting I'm a mech pilot. UDC trained and tested. You think a crazy fuck like you can take me down?"

"You won't get far with that old cunt and those little meals slowing you down."

"Now, is that any way to speak about your own mother?" June started stripping Delroy and Hanson of their weapons. "You don't get it, do you? You are so used to isolation that you think we all are, but it isn't true. I have a home, I just forgot for a bit."

💀💀💀

"Jethro, if you please," the Commander said. Jethro wheeled forward and handed each of the Skinners a tablet.

"I've put together a vid briefing so you all will be up to speed on the situation," Jethro began, tapping at his own tablet. "It's only a few minutes long, but you'll get the idea quickly."

Capreze leaned back and watched as Mastelo and his people viewed the vid. Security footage of the UDC troops turning into zombies filled the small screens, then of the Ranchers take over of the base and finally the intercepted communication between the Bishop and the Boss.

💀💀💀

Masters/Stomper crested the small hill and looked out at the expanse of wasteland.

"Well, we don't really need scanners to analyze that shit," Masters said sarcastically.

"But, the scanners do give us an accurate count of the forces," Stomper replied.

"I was just kidding," Masters joked. "You're gonna have to learn sarcasm or 'we' will never work."

Stomper processed. "The need for ironic humor when faced with overwhelming odds is puzzling."

"Yeah, well, you'll learn," Masters responded, quite serious now as he watched several dozen transports and what looked like thousands upon thousands of zombies march across the wasteland plain.

"My God," Mathew exclaimed. "How many are there?"

"It appears to be every single citizen inoculated, including all UDC troops," Shiner responded.

"All of them?" Mathew gasped.

"Yes. All of them."

Shiner/Mathew processed the information streaming through the relay net. "Where the fuck are they going?" Mathew asked.

"The possibilities are too numerous," Shiner replied.

"Let's narrow it down, shall we?" Mathew chided. "They are coming from their respective city/states, correct?"

"Yes."

"Then what is between all of them and their points of departure?"

Shiner processed. "Many things."

Mathew sighed. "But, what is the most significant choice?"

"The UDC stronghold."

"We don't know why the UDC has inoculated the city/state populations nor why their troops are assisting the Ranchers," Capreze said as the Skinners finished watching the vid briefing. "But, we do know it's not because they want to make new friends."

Mastelo and the council looked at each other warily. "We cannot commit all of our people," Mastelo finally said.

"No, of course not. And we cannot arm all of your people," Capreze responded. "We can only arm about 80 of your people."

"That doesn't seem like an adequate number," the small woman stated.

"No, it's not," Capreze said.

"We can't handle that many," Masters said.

"No, we cannot," Stomper agreed as they returned to the cavern mouth.

"We need to find Jay and the Rookie and return to the base," Masters stated as the massive mech knelt down and reached into the cavern. "And we'll need this."

After a couple attempts, Masters/Stomper was able to remove the salvage mech from the cavern without damage. The new mech stood upright, the smaller mech held in its fist.

"Now, how do we find Jay?" Masters mused.

"The sensors show an underground river," Stomper responded. "They may have escaped that way."

☠☠☠

"And what the fuck is up with her pretending to be me?" Rachel asked.

"Pretty smart move, in my opinion," Bisby replied. "It made her valuable and kept her alive."

"Whatever," Rachel grumbled. "Okay, I've got to stop trashing her."

Bisby stayed silent, knowing Rachel wasn't finished.

"But, Jeezus fuck, she gets under my skin," Rachel continued. "And I don't know why!" Rachel sighed and checked her navigation readings. "Were not even close yet, are we?"

"Nope," Bisby responded. "Might as well do some system tests while we have the time. Wanna read the checklist?"

"Yeah, sure, whatever," Rachel responded.

☠☠☠

"You think we can track the river through the ground and find where it comes out?" Masters asked.

"Yes, our scanners are easily strong enough," Stomper responded.

"Well, let's get on it...Oh, shit," Masters paused. "Matty and Shiner won't know where to find us."

"We can try to contact them via the relay net."

"But, that will give our position away."

"Our position will be compromised the moment that army crests the hill."

"Good point," Masters conceded. "You aren't as basic as you think."

"Complexity can sometimes get in the way of answers," Stomper replied.

"Hmmm... Well said," Masters agreed.

☠☠☠

"Why are they all headed to the UDC stronghold?" Mathew asked.

"I believe that is where the Outsider originates from," Shiner answered. "Which may mean 'Outsider' is a misnomer."

"Maybe we should call it Big Fucking Ugly In My Head," Mathew joked.

"Hey guys!" Masters called over the net. "Listen, we- Jeezus! Is it me or did the relay net get WAY crowded?"

"It appears every inoculated human has become connected and active," Shiner explained.

"Yeah, we just saw the Foggy Bottom contingent heading our way,"

Masters said. "So we grabbed Jay's mech and are on search and rescue now."

☠☠☠

"Do you have our coordinates?" Masters asked.

"Yep, we're adjusting course and heading that way. Keep us posted," Mathew answered. "And go ahead and stay connected. It doesn't really matter anymore now that the entire wasteland is about to be caught up in a net of deaders. No place to hide really."

"Have you tried contacting the base?" Masters asked.

"No, not yet," Mathew responded. "It's easy for us to talk, but I'm not sure if we can access the base com system."

"Open channel?"

"No, too risky. Everyone can hear that. Ranchers, Boilers, everyone."

"Yeah, that's true," Masters agreed.

☠☠☠

"Yes, send it through," Deacon Montoya said over his com. He tapped at his console and brought up a new image on the windshield. "Bishop? Your Grace?"

"What is it now, Deacon? Is it more disappointing news from the Boiler?"

"No, Your Grace. We have received information that two of the mech pilots have been located in the wasteland. And, well, they…"

"You hesitate, Deacon, please do tell," Bishop Wyble sat up, interested.

"Well, Your Grace, they have somehow merged with the Demons."

The Bishop stared at Montoya for a moment. "I'm sorry, Deacon. I must have misunderstood you. Merged?"

☠☠☠

"You know we're already long gone from where you think we are," June taunted over the handheld.

"The wasteland isn't big enough for you to hide from me, you fucking bitch!" the Boss roared.

"Oh, I'm not going to be hiding, but you may want to. If I do see you again, I won't be as quick as I was with Chunks."

The Boss punched the ATV's dashboard then turned and punched the young woman driving. The ATV swerved dangerously, but the driver regained her composure.

"Watch where you're going, you fucking idiot!" the Boss screamed.

"Temper, temper," June mocked.

Commander Capreze pointed at his tablet. "The mech base is here and we're...here."

The council looked at their tablets then back at Capreze.

"I don't know how many vehicles you have," Capreze continued. "But if we could have three of your people armed per vehicle, then I think we can stage a decent assault."

Mastelo and the council looked from one to the other confused.

"I am sorry, Commander, but I think you have the wrong impression of our resources," Mastelo said. "We do not have vehicles."

Jethro and Capreze stared for a moment.

"No vehicles?" Jethro asked. "Shit."

"Return to the base, Montoya," the Bishop commanded. "I must be presentable when His Holiness, the Archbishop arrives. And I need a secure com line so I can contact our UDC brethren. This 'merged' mech development is quite troubling."

"Yes, Your Grace," Deacon Montoya responded as his console beeped. "It appears the Boss is trying to communicate."

"That Boiler is barely capable of grunting, let alone full communication." The Bishop rolled his eyes and sighed. "Put him through, Deacon. "

"Of course, Your Grace."

"You better have good news, Boss," the Bishop hissed.

"I think I do," the Boss responded.

"Think the Capreze whore is heading home," the Boss shouted above the wind as he steadied the transmitter array in the back of the moving ATV.

"You think?" replied the Bishop.

"That's what I fucking said, ain't it?' the Boss snapped. "Pull the cocks out of your ears and listen up. The. Mech. Bitch. Is. Coming. Right. To. You!"

"Oh, well then I guess we don't need your assistance anymore, Boiler," the Bishop laughed.

"Oh, I think you do," the Boss said. "Unless you want my people's sole goal in life to be attacking Rancher transports every time they leave."

"Hey Biz, did you catch that?" Rachel asked over the com.

"Yeah, we must be close enough to pick up on their transmissions," Bisby responded. "And it sounds like we're heading the wrong way."

"June has no idea the base has been overrun."

"I know, I know," Bisby replied. "But, we have no idea which way she's coming from. We can't intercept her."

"Should we head back and let the Commander know?" Rachel asked.

"Probably should. This has all turned into one big giant shit show," Bisby growled.

"It always is with June," Rachel replied.

The two mechs reversed course.

Harlow sat in her mech, cockpit open to the hot wasteland wind. Below her she could hear the zombies pounding at their confinement in the transport storage compartment.

"Hey Doc?" Harlow called.

"Yes, Harlow?" Themopolous responded over the com.

"What has the Commander said about those fucking deaders?"

"I haven't had a chance to ask him, Harlow. He's been a bit busy."

"Well, we got to do something. I'm going to go fucking nuts with all that noise!"

"Yes, you've made that perfectly clear," Themopolous laughed.

"Well, apparently I haven't been clear enough since the deaders are still banging away!"

"No vehicles is going to make an assault on the base difficult," Capreze sighed.

"What if we don't attack them, but make them come to us?" Jethro said. All eyes turned on the wheelchair bound mechanic. "If we can get most of their forces to bring the fight here, that would leave the base exposed. We win the fight and keep some of their transports intact, then re-take the base."

"A solid plan except that it exposes where we live," the young man said angrily.

"You can't hide forever," Capreze stated. "At some point you have to face the world."

"Hey guys? Jethro here," Jethro's voice squawked over the com.

"What the fuck are you doing, Jethro? I thought we needed to keep com silence," Bisby barked.

"Change of plans," Jethro responded. "The threat isn't pursuing and we're pretty sure we aren't their target anymore."

"What? None of that makes-" Rachel started.

"We've gathered some new intel. Just head back to camp. You'll be briefed then. Understand?"

"No! I don't fucking understand!" Bisby yelled. "Let me talk to the Commander."

"He's occupied. You guys are just gonna have to trust me on this."

"We're on our way, Jethro," Rachel said.

�☠☠

"Your Grace?"

"What is it now, Deacon?" Bishop Wyble snapped, removing his eye shade.

"My apologies for interrupting your rest, Your Grace, but Reverend Dell just reported that they intercepted a communication over the mech base's secure com channel," Deacon Montoya reported. "They were able to triangulate the location of Capreze's camp. We know where they are, Your Grace."

The Bishop rubbed his hands together. "Wonderful, Deacon. Have all transports readied immediately. And have word sent to the Archbishop that I may miss his arrival as I plan on leading the assault on the mech heathens personally."

"Yes, Your Grace."

☠☠☠

"Damn, this freakin' river goes on and on and on," Masters complained as he and Stomper followed the sensor readings. "There better be headroom down there if they did take this route, otherwise they're going to be holding their breath for a long time."

"You talk a lot," Stomper replied.

"Um, that was random," Masters chuckled.

"Yeah, tell me about it," Mathew interrupted. "We've never been able to get him to shut up."

"Hey!" Masters exclaimed. "Are you guys listening? No fair! Get out of our heads."

"That would not be wise," Shiner responded. "Communication is key to our survival."

💀💀💀

"By the way, as much as you think you are the center of the universe, we weren't listening," Mathew said. "We were about to let you know we picked up communications among the UDC deaders about routing transports and troops deep in to the wasteland."

"Yeah, so? They're all being routed," Masters responded.

"Yes, but it sounds like they are going after our folks."

"I have confirmed that the Ranchers are readying their forces and the UDC troops available to them. They are planning an assault on Commander Capreze and anyone with him," Shiner said.

"Well, that sucks," Masters said.

💀💀💀

"Looks like it's working," Jethro informed Capreze. "The Ranchers and UDC at our base are mobilizing."

"Alright, then we have maybe a day," Capreze replied. "Time to get to work." He turned to Mastelo and the council. "Bring me your best fighters, the ones with the best eye. Today they learn to shoot."

Mastelo stood and the council followed. "And when this is over, we can count on your assistance and protection in giving my people a home outside of the deep?"

"Yes, you have my word," Capreze answered extending his hand. Mastelo grasped it and the two men shook.

💀💀💀

"So, if they have been found and we are certainly being tracked then there's no reason to keep silent, is there?" Mathew asked.

"It would appear not," Shiner responded.

"Well, then open the com."

Instantly Shiner accessed and opened the mech com system. "We are connected."

"Commander Capreze? Jethro? Anyone out there? This is Pilot Jespers. Come in."

"Matty?" Jethro replied. "Is that you? Holy shit!"

"Hey Jethro! Good to hear your voice."

"No shit, man. Where the fuck are you?"

"We're a ways from you folks."

"We? Who else is with you?"

"Um, you're gonna want to get Capreze."

🙂🙂🙂

"Capreze here. It's good to know I can count you among the living, Pilot."

"Hey me too!" Masters interrupted.

"Mitch?!? Baby is that you?" Harlow interrupted.

"You bet your sweet tits it is! And guess what? I've got a brand new mech! And it's fucking huge!"

"*We* are huge," Stomper corrected.

"Right, sorry. *We* are huge!"

"Pilots? Who is with you?" Capreze asked, caution in his voice. "What new mech?"

"Yeah, that's going to have to wait, sir, if Masters can keep his trap shut," Mathew responded.

"Sorry. I'll let you two speak."

"Two? What is going on?" Capreze barked.

🙂🙂🙂

"Listen, I can't go into too much detail, but you have Rancher and UDC transports coming your way."

Capreze glanced at Jethro and put a finger to his lips for the mechanic to stay quiet. "We do?"

"Yes, sir. But it gets worse."

"Worse? How?"

"Sir, every single person that was inoculated is now dead and walking."

"I'm sorry, Pilot, did you say every person?" Capreze asked.

"Yes, sir. All city/states have been overtaken and if they didn't comply, they were destroyed. Windy City is gone, sir."

"And Foggy Bottom is now a deader army on the march," Masters added.

🙂🙂🙂

"Yes, sir, we have confirmed that there are hundreds of thousands of deaders moving across the wasteland," Mathew said. "If you push scanners to full, you should be able to pick up some of them."

Jethro immediately began tapping at his tablet. "Jeezus fuck! He's right, sir. I've got at least 20,000 coming at us."

Capreze looked at Mastelo and the council. "You'll need to move quickly."

"You can count on us," Mastelo affirmed as they left the transport.

"Mathew, Masters, I want you on me now," Capreze ordered.

"No can do, sir," Mathew responded.
"You better explain yourself, Pilot."

"Well, sir, I have gotten myself in a bit of a tech mess," Mathew said. "Masters and I are on our way to find Jay and the Rookie."
"Jay? You lost Jay?" Jethro asked.
"We were separated when the Hill Stomper attacked and the cavern mouth caved in, then the storm came and I went all black-outy and-"
"Thank you, Pilot Masters, we get it: Jay is missing," Capreze interrupted.
"And the Rookie, too," Masters added. "That boy saved our asses! You'll never guess what he can do! Holy shit!"
"I'll await the report. Now about this tech mess, Mathew..."

"Harlow? Do you hear anything?" Themopolous asked.
"Hold on," Harlow said, muting her com. "Hear what?"
"Exactly. The zombies in storage have gone quiet."
"I'll be right down."
Harlow grabbed a sawed off pump action shotgun she kept in her cockpit and descended her mech. Themoplolous walked cautiously to the transport's storage compartment and waited for Harlow.
"So, why do you think they stopped kicking?" Harlow asked, leveling the shotgun at the compartment door.
"I don't know," Themopolous replied.
"We address Commander Capreze only," four monotone voices said in unison from the compartment.
Harlow pumped her shotgun. "Holy fucking shit!"

"Unless I find Jay I'm stuck in a mech cockpit for the rest of my life," Mathew said.
"I understand your situation, Mathew, but I want you and Masters joining us immediately," Capreze ordered.
"I'll stay and keep looking for them," Masters said. "My scanners are the only ones strong enough to track the river anyway. Plus, I'm not hooked into the net as extensively as Matty and Shiner."
"No," Capreze ordered flatly. "You'll return also."
"With all due respect, sir, I just went through some crazy shit with those

two and I'm not leaving them out here," Masters responded.

🧟🧟🧟

Capreze pinched the bridge of his nose in frustration. "Masters, I have given you a direct order."

"And I am ignoring that order, sir," Masters replied. "You'll have to shoot me when this is all over."

"Oh, for fuck's sake, Masters! You know I'm not going to have you shot! Just get your ass here now!"

"Sir! You have to come out here!" Themopolous interrupted over the com.

"I am a little busy, Doctor," Capreze responded.

"The zombies in storage are speaking, sir!"

Capreze sighed. "Of course they are."

"They want to speak to you directly."

"Of course they do."

🧟🧟🧟

Capreze stepped from the transport and approached Themopolous and Harlow. "Fine. Masters you continue searching, but Mathew, I want you on me right fucking now!"

"Yes, sir," both pilots responded.

"Oh, and Masters?" Capreze continued.

"Yes, sir?"

"Fuck you."

"Understood, sir."

The Commander stood looking at the storage compartment. "Well?"

Harlow kicked the door.

"We address Commander Capreze directly," the voices said.

Capreze put the heel of his hand to his forehead and pulled his sidearm. "That's more than a little unsettling."

"No shit," Harlow responded.

"Well, Doctor, will you do the honors? Harlow and I will have you covered."

🧟🧟🧟

Themopolous yanked the storage compartment open and leapt back. Capreze and Harlow, pistols ready, watched the four body bags shake themselves free of the compartment and fall to the ground.

"We address Commander Capreze directly," they repeated.

"Speaking. Who the hell are you?"

"We are the hundreds of thousands, we are the one, we are the Outsider."

"How about I just call you Fuckhead?" Capreze said.

The bags convulsed. "For that insult, you will not become part of the one. You will not get the glory of joining the Outsider. You... you... you..."

"I think I broke them," Capreze said.

☠☠☠

"You cannot break what is all knowing, all seeing!" the deaders chorused.

"So what do you want?" Capreze asked.

"For all to be one and to undo the great wrong!"

"You want us to submit to your control?"

"You will submit or you will die!"

"Yeah, well, fuck you," Capreze said as he stepped forward and silenced each body with a head shot. "Harlow? Burn those."

"Yes, sir."

"Hey, Jethro!" Capreze called stepping to the transport door. "Open all channels."

"Sir?"

"You heard me. I'm done with this chaotic bullshit! Time to bring some order back to this fucking hellhole!"

☠☠☠

Capreze cleared his throat.

"Attention inhabitants of the wasteland! This is Base Commander James Capreze. I just want to let everyone, living and undead, know that I will no longer put up with your fucking games. I will no longer put up with the Cults, cannibals, the mindless killers and thieves. I will no longer allow myself or my people to be the wasteland's bitches, always having to clean up everyone else's mess. So come and get us, if you dare. We'll be right here.

"Oh, and Outsider? After I kick every last mother fucker's ass. I'm coming for you."

Part Two - Railers & Lights

The Rookie woke with a start, pain enveloping his head and chest. He tried to move, but rivers of agony ripped at his core. The world felt like it was rolling and rocking and nausea joined the pain.

"Jay?" he moaned.

"Hush. Just relax, you're safe for now. We barely managed to get you out in one piece," an angry voice answered. An angry woman's voice. "We lost a couple of our own in the effort."

The Rookie carefully rolled his head towards the voice and opened his eyes to see the most beautiful and well armed woman glaring back.

☠☠☠

"What's your name, pilot?" the woman asked gruffly.

The Rookie glanced from her steely gaze to the carbine resting on her lap and then at the room around him. He could swear the walls were vibrating.

"Leave him be Jenny," a man said, sliding the door back and entering the room. He took his wide-brimmed hat off, shook out the dust and tossed it on a chair. "He's not our prisoner and he doesn't need to be interrogated."

Jenny stood, glared at the man briefly and stormed out.

"She's a lot nicer once she has a meal and a bath."

☠☠☠

"Howdy, I'm Crawford Timson," the man said, offering the Rookie his hand. The Rookie reached out painfully and shook it. The man's knuckles were gnarled and scarred. The Rookie could tell it was a fighter's hand. "And I've already been told that I should call you the Rookie." Timson smiled. "So, Rookie, welcome back from the dead. How are you feeling?"

The Rookie ignored the question and fixed his eyes on Timson's. "How do you know who I am?"

The door slid open and Jay walked in. "'Cause I told them, kid." Jay smiled. "They saved our asses back there."

☠☠☠

Jay flipped a chair around and took a seat next to the Rookie's cot, but turned to Timson first. "Marin needs you in the engine ASAP. She's got something on the scope and freaking out a bit."

"Well, I guess we'll have to get to know each other later. Duty calls," Timson said, nodding to the Rookie. "If you feel up to it, you're welcome to join us for dinner in my car." Timson grabbed his hat and placed it back on his head, tapping the rim. "Gentlemen."

The Rookie watched him leave. "So, what the fuck is going on?"

☠☠☠

"Well, kid, we got rescued," Jay began. "They were filling their water tanker when both of us flew out of the mountainside in a rush of water and zombies. Guess that river does come above ground. About forty feet above ground. Luckily the pool below was deep."

"Water tanker? We're on a train aren't we?" the Rookie asked.

"Yep, and a fucking nice one, too. This ain't no Rookie Hell-ride."

The Rookie slumped back and lifted his covers slightly to peak underneath. "Naked. Great."

"Yeah, you're uniform is being washed," Jay looked at the ground and sighed. "We gotta talk."

"They saw the brand, didn't they?" the Rookie asked.

"Yeah, we'll get to that in a second, but this first."

Jay handed the Rookie a tablet and pressed play on the audio cued up. The tablet replayed Commander Capreze's open channel speech. The Rookie listened twice before handing the tablet back. "Well, that's fucked up."

"Looks like the wasteland's going to war," Jay said.

"Have you tried contacting them?"

"I asked, but they aren't letting me."

"What? Why?"

"Because of that brand on your foot. Now, mind telling me what that's about and why these folks are so pissed off?"

The Rookie averted his eyes from Jay's gaze. "Can I have some water?" he asked.

"No," Jay answered flatly.

"What? No? Are you fucking kidding me?"

"You've been putting off telling me who you are for too long. Fess up, kid or I let them toss you off this train."

The Rookie glared. Jay glared back.

"Fine. I'm a fucking Boiler! My grandmother died helping me escape and I never looked back."

"So, that's how you ended up fighting for Legit?"

"Yeah. Trust me the fight cage was an improvement."

"Damn," Jay exclaimed, handing the Rookie a cup of water.

The door slid open and a young woman peeked in. "Mr. Jay?"

"Yes, Lucy?" Jay answered.

"Crawford needs you. There is something on the scope that's troubling."

"Tell him I'll be right there."

"Okay. Thank you," Lucy said, smiling shyly at Jay. She turned her eyes on the Rookie as she left and the smile faded.

Despite the pain, the Rookie shook his head and pushed himself upright.

"Whoa, slow down, hoss," Jay scolded. "You'll rip those stitches out of your chest."

"I'm coming with."

"Like hell you are! You need to rest."

"No, I don't. Now help me up."

💀💀💀

Jay slid the engine door open and offered a hand to the Rookie, who refused it and stepped into the engine control room on shaky feet, but under his own power.

"Why the fuck did you bring that Boiler trash in here?!?" Jenny yelled. "He is not welcome here."

Timson put a restraining hand on Jenny's arm as she reached to draw a pistol. "Calm down. Jay, thanks for coming. Marin found some strange movement on the tracks several miles down. We'd like your opinion."

Jay stepped past Jenny and sat next to an older woman in the pilot's seat.

💀💀💀

"What am I looking at?" Jay asked Marin. The older woman pointed at a screen and her finger traced the movement of a red dot.

"Watch that. It moves out and back, out and back," Marin said.

Jay studied the movement for a moment. "Looks like it's gathering."

"Gathering? How?" Timson asked.

"Well, it's almost like those old nature vids of birds building a nest. Watch. See how it always comes back to the exact same spot?"

Timson and Jenny moved in for a closer look. The Rookie held back, leaning against the wall.

"Huh, look at that," Timson said.

💀💀💀

"What's the scale here?" Jay asked looking at the coordinates on the screen. "Is that right?"

"Yep, it's fucking fast, whatever it is," Marin responded. "Really fast."

The red dot stopped and disappeared from the screen. "Whoa, where'd it go?" Jay asked.

"I don't know. Once I have a bead on something it shouldn't disappear off my scope."

"It's a deader," the Rookie said. All eyes turned on him. "If it's what I think it is. We called it Lights when I was a kid."

"What, is it some Boiler pet?" Jenny snapped.

"Boilers don't have pets. Waste of food."

Jay studied the Rookie. "You acted like you'd never encountered a dead mech before."

"I've been acting my whole life, so nothing personal," the Rookie responded.

"Anything we should know about this thing?" Timson asked.

"It's fucking crazy and it likes to set traps," the Rookie answered, stepping forward and pointing at the screen. "Just like that."

"He's right. Whatever it's doing it's doing it on the tracks," Marin agreed.

"How do we take it out?" Timson asked. "Can we take it out?"

"Maybe with a mech, but you don't have one," the Rookie said.

"Sure we do," Marin responded.

"What?!?" Jay shouted. "You have a mech?"

Marin grinned from ear to ear. "Yep. Built it myself."

Jay stood stunned, mouth agape for a moment.

"That's not a good look for you, Jay," Marin joked.

"Great, you have a mech, so what? Like I said, this thing is crazy and you can see how fast it is," the Rookie said. "I'm sure Jay can handle a mech, but not against Lights." He looked at each person seriously. "We need a combat pilot, not a mechanic."

"We need a fighter. A killer," Jay finally said, looking at the Rookie and grinning.

"What? You must be joking!" Jenny shouted. "He's barely alive!"

"He's been in worse shape, I'm sure," Jay said looking at the Rookie.

The Rookie shrugged casually. "I've been in worse shape. But I don't know the first thing about piloting a mech."

"Sure you do," Jay said. "It's just moving and thinking about moving. I'll show you the basics of the cockpit and…" He trailed off and turned to Marin. "Where is the mech?"

Marin laughed, a twinkle in her eye. "It's the rear engine. It transforms."

Jay's shoulders slumped. "After all these years, you did it. Holy shit…"

The Rookie looked from Jay to Marin and back. "You two know each other?"

"Yeah, this asshole broke my heart when we were younger," Marin smiled. "I got over it. Good thing too, it was my word that kept you from being shot and tossed."

"Actually, it was my word," Timson said. "Let's not forget who is in charge, Marin." Timson faced Jay and the Rookie. "I'm sorry, but I can't trust either of you with our mech." Marin started to speak, but Timson held up his hand. "We need to figure out another way to get past this deader."

"We could detach a car and send it into the trap. When the deader shows up we detonate and send it to hell," Jenny said.

"It could work," Marin agreed looking to Timson.

Timson thought for a moment. "Do it. Slow the train and move the car."

The Rookie laughed.

"You have something to add, Boiler?" Jenny asked harshly.

"I told you the thing likes to set traps. You're all assuming the trap is that spot." The Rookie pointed at the screen. "*I* think we're already in the trap." He shrugged. "But, what do I know? I'm just a Boiler."

Marin slowed the train to a crawl. "Okay, we're at detaching speed."

"You aren't going to stop the train?" Jay asked.

All eyes, even the Rookie's turned on Jay. "Jay Rind, I'm surprised at your ignorance," Marin said. "Railers never stop the train." She raised a hand and Jenny slapped it. "Never."

"Then how the Hell are you going to get a car in front of the engine?"

"Jenny? Can you take over?" Marin asked as she stood up from the pilot's chair.

"Gladly," Jenny answered.

Marin stepped to the door and glanced back at Jay and The Rookie. "Coming?"

�

Marin spoke into a handheld. "27 is empty. Go ahead and prep it to move."

"Gotcha," Jenny's voice responded.

Marin started to jog and Jay and the Rookie struggled to keep their balance and to keep up as they moved from car to car. Several Railers stepped aside to give them passage. None would meet the Rookie's eyes.

"You okay kid?" Jay asked looking back at the Rookie.

"Fine," the Rookie said between gritted teeth.

When Jay counted 29 cars, Marin stopped and pushed open the outside door. "Follow me," she said grabbing an outer ladder and swinging onto it.

☗☗☗

"How many cars are there?" the Rookie yelled as he struggled up the ladder.

"48," Marin shouted from the top of the car.

Jay reached the top and extended a hand to the Rookie who gladly took it.

"Watch!" Marin said, the handheld to her mouth. "Okay, Jenny. It's clear."

The sound of cars de-coupling echoed across the wasteland. Within seconds, the 27th car was lifted above the others and Jay heard the distinct hiss of hydraulics as huge metal arms detached from each car and reached up to pass 27 over them and up the line to the front.

☗☗☗

"You're a fucking genius," Jay said.

"Yeah, I am. Guess you shouldn't have dumped me, huh?" Marin smiled. "You also shouldn't have stolen my dad's vids."

"Are you still mad about that?" Jay asked, amused.

"Some of those were irreplaceable. Like The Transformers. Luckily, I made a real one. Too bad your Rookie won't get to pilot it."

"That is too bad," Jay said turning to the Rookie and freezing. "What is it? What do you see?"

The Rookie stared into the twilight of the wasteland. "Something's wrong."

They all became instantly blind as twenty halogen lights rushed at them.

☻☻☻

The wind whooshed form the Rookie's lungs as he struck the ground. He struggled for breath, the agony from his wound making the effort twice as hard. In a rush, air filled his lungs and he gasped painfully.

He could hear people screaming and the sounds of wrenching metal and plastic. His vision doubled and black spots swam before his eyes as he weakly got to his feet. Through his haze he watched the deader reach down and snap up Railers by the handful, crushing them in its grip and tossing the pulp into its cockpit.

"Jay!" the Rookie yelled.

☻☻☻

"Jay! Jay!"

The mechanic could hear his name being called, but the ringing in his ears made it hard to focus.

"Jay!"

"Yeah, over here," he called out weakly, hoping he could be heard over the chaos.

In seconds he felt hands grab him and lift him from the ground.

"Come on! Stand up goddamn it!" the Rookie yelled.

Jay shook his head and concentrated on the wavering image of the Rookie in front of him. "What the fuck happened?"

"What I said would happen!"

Jay looked about him at the mangled, derailed train and the blood. So much blood.

☻☻☻

Gunfire erupted as some of the Railers got their wits about them and began to attack the deader.

"Fucking idiots!" Jay shouted. "Rifles aren't going to bring that thing down!"

But, the Railers ignored his protestations and kept firing.

"Waste of ammo," he muttered before his eyes went wide with panic. "Marin! Where is she?" Jay gripped the Rookie's shoulders and shook him.

Lightning fast, the Rookie slapped Jay. "I don't know where she is, but you need to focus dammit!"

Jay rubbed his cheek. "Sorry." His eyes surveyed the carnage. "We need to get you meched up right now."

Jay yanked the Rookie by the arm and pulled him towards the end of the train. "She said it was the last engine, right?"

"Yeah, but I..." the Rookie responded.

"No time for Rookie jitters now. That deader –what did you call it?"

"Lights."

"Yeah, Lights won't stop until every living thing is smashed into zombie feed, right?"

"Right. But..."

"Well, I don't want to be zombie feed, do you?" Jay didn't wait for an answer as he climbed aboard the engine and stepped inside. The Rookie followed, but not before seeing Timson and Jenny running at them, guns drawn.

Jay frantically scrambled about the cockpit. "This is all different! Why'd she go and reinvent the goddamn wheel?"

"Fucking move!" Jenny yelled, shoving Jay and the Rookie aside as she and Timson climbed aboard. "You're gonna fuck it all up!"

She activated the control panel, grabbed a tablet and shoved the Rookie towards a manhole sized disc set into the floor. "Stand there and don't move! I'll start it up, you just do what I say, got it?"

"Why don't you pilot it?" the Rookie asked.

"Because I don't have a fucking Reaper chip in my head, now do I?"

Jenny pulled Jay from the cockpit as Timson put a hand on the Rookie's shoulder. "I really hope you're as good a fighter as they say you are...Razor."

"What? How did...?" the Rookie stammered.

"When people's loved ones are captured and end up with their faces sliced off in some fight cage, word gets back," Timson said. "The wasteland isn't as big as you think."

The Railer slapped the Rookie on the back. "Oh, and try not to die, I think my daughter likes you. Unfortunately, she goes for the bad boy type."

The Rookie, thoroughly confused, just stood there.

"Okay," Jenny said into her handheld. "Do not move off the disc! Keep your hands and legs inside the disc! Understand?"

"Yeah," the Rookie replied.

"You better, because when this thing changes it's going to wrap around that disc like a condom on a stiffy!"

"Jenny!" Timson barked, but she ignored her father and continued, tapping at her tablet one handed.

"Ready?!?"

"Ready, but..." The Rookie's words were cut off as Jenny initiated the transformation.

Jay was stunned as before his eyes what was a train engine became a long, lean mech.

"It's beautiful," he whispered.

"Ain't it?" Jenny responded.

🕱🕱🕱

The Rookie was pretty sure he pissed himself as the world whipped about him and he was no longer standing in an engine, but strapped into a mech. "Holy shit," he muttered.

"You alive in there?" Jenny asked over the com.

"I think so," the Rookie answered.

"Good, now make a fist."

The Rookie flexed his fingers and made a fist. Simultaneously, the mech made a massive metal fist.

"Great. Now, the other one."

The Rookie made a second fist.

"Excellent. Kick out your legs."

The Rookie did so, flexing his legs as he would do before a cage fight.

🕱🕱🕱

The ground shuddered and Jay, Jenny and Timson struggled to keep their footing.

"Shit, it's seen the competition!" Jay shouted as they watched Lights toss a train car he was picking apart out into the wasteland night.

"Fuck!" Jenny yelled. She madly tapped at her console. "You have full power and all systems are in the green. There aren't any armaments, so you're going to have to be the Boiler animal you are and just kick the shit out of that thing!"

"Are you fucking kidding me?!" the Rookie screamed. "I don't know what I'm doing!"

"Then fucking learn fast!"

🕱🕱🕱

Lights charged at the Rookie and he instinctively put his arms up to protect himself. At the exact same time his mech did the same, blocking the deader's charge and protecting the cockpit.

"HOLY SHITFUCKING CHRIST!" the Rookie screamed as his mech was knocked backwards and tumbled to the ground.

Lights was on him immediately, its massive fists pummeling the Rookie's mech.

"Get up, you fucking retard!" Jenny yelled over the com. "Stop being such a fucking pussy ass and fight!"

The Rookie's head snapped back and slammed against a support and he felt a tooth crack from the impact.

The Rookie focused on the pain and spit the piece of broken tooth into the cockpit. He tucked his legs up under the mech and shoved.

Lights staggered back several yards before regaining its footing.

"Get up!" Jenny shouted again and this time the Rookie listened.

He sprang to his feet, *his* feet, no longer thinking of the mech as a separate entity.

"I can fucking do this," he said to himself. "I'm the fucking Razor."

He watched Lights charge again and slowly cracked his neck. If the mech had an actual head, it would have followed the motion precisely.

"Why the Hell is he just standing there?!?" Jenny yelled.

"Just wait," Jay said calmly.

"But he's going to get crushed! We didn't give him that mech so he…" Jay held up a hand, cutting Jenny off.

"Just wait for it," he said calmly. "Come on kid, do that shit you do. Break that mother fucker in half."

Jenny grabbed her father's arm and whirled on him. "Dammit, he's going…"

Timson removed her hand and forced her to face the action. "We're just gonna have to trust him, Jenny. There's nothing else we can do."

Jenny shook with frustrated rage.

Sidestep, swing about, roundhouse, connect and down.

The Rookie bounced from mechanized foot to mechanized foot as Lights was slammed to the ground and slid 100 yards across the wasteland dirt. The deader was fast though and back on its feet and charging again before it had stopped sliding.

The Rookie waited and as Lights was about to pounce, the Rookie kicked out, planting a foot directly into the deader's mid-section. The world slowed as Lights crumpled upon the foot then was sent flying backwards, doubled up, arms and legs flailing.

Jay cheered, Timson smiled, Jenny just gawked in disbelief.

☠☠☠

Lights got to its feet and roared with deader rage, but didn't charge this time.

The Rookie kept bouncing, moving his feet back and forth, ready for the attack.

"What's it waiting for?" Timson turned and asked Jay.

"I don't know. Maybe trying to figure out a weak point to attack," Jay answered.

"They do that?" Jenny asked, alarmed. "I thought they were just mindless zombie machines."

"That's what we all thought," Jay responded. "But, things have changed."

Lights took two steps forward then turned and sprinted away from the Rookie.

Right at the Railers trying to help their wounded.

☠☠☠

"Oh fuck!" the Rookie shouted, watching as Lights bore down on a group of ten Railers. They never stood a chance as the deader scooped up half of them in its giant fist, turned and threw the helpless humans at the Rookie's mech.

The Rookie rushed forward, catching one of the Railers, but the others impacted brutally against the mech's exoskeleton. The Rookie could hear the choked-off screams of the victims and stared out his cockpit, stunned, as blood dripped onto the windshield followed by a mangled corpse rolling off the top of his mech and to the ground below.

☠☠☠

"Run! Go! Get to cover!" Timson yelled, running towards his panicked people. "Save yourselves!"

It was too late for many as Lights focused his rage and stomped and tore apart dozens of the exposed Railers. Those trying to put out fires were snatched up and smashed into the middle of the conflagrations. Lights lifted a derailed car and brought it down atop a row of wounded, grinding them into the dirt.

The Rookie pushed aside his shock and crossed the ground between him and Lights in a split-second, but the deader rounded on the Rookie, its plasma cannon glowing red.

☠☠☠

"Oh, fuck," the Rookie whispered, knowing he was too close to dodge a plasma blast. The dead mech's cannon turned bright red and the plasma cannon discharged directly into the Rookie, sending the mech somersaulting backwards.

The Rookie lay there gasping, feeling the blood trickle between the stitches of his freshly re-opened wound. He grunted and ignored the pain, righting his mech. The machine wobbled on unsteady hydraulics, but it stayed upright.

"Jay? How am I looking?" the Rookie called over the com.

"You're still in fighting shape! How about you end this shit?!?" Jay responded checking his tablet's readings.

☠☠☠

Lights moved fast. Way faster than anything else in the wasteland. It was seeing that speed, that ferocity, as a child that had made the Rookie want to become a mech pilot. And as he watched the deader toss a train car at him, he wondered if he had maybe wanted the wrong thing.

"Fuck me!"

The Rookie piloted under the flying train car, but didn't get a chance to exclaim further as the second car Lights threw smashed into his mech's crouched form.

He heard struts snap, metal tear and hydraulics rupture.

"Kid?!? Can you hear me?!?" Jay called.

☠☠☠

The Rookie tried to clear his head, but he couldn't focus. The fogginess was almost suffocating and when he started to choke and cough he realized he really was suffocating as smoke filled the cockpit.

Lights sprang, landing atop the Rookie's mech and began pummeling the helpless machine. Three punches, seven, twelve and the cockpit started to collapse in around the Rookie.

"Jay?" he coughed. "Where's the... self-destruct?"

"Fuck that shit, kid!" Jay yelled back. "We'll get you out of there!"

"Don't... bother...," the Rookie said, his lungs burning. "You can't... kill... this thing. Let me... blow it... to Hell."

Jenny quickly grabbed the tablet from Jay's hands. "The Boiler's right. We need to blow his mech and destroy that dead piece of shit now!"

Jay reached for the tablet, but Jenny slapped his hand away. He lunged for her, but she side-stepped him and extended her leg. Jay stumbled over Jenny's outstretched leg, hitting the dirt hard, his face meeting the ground with a sickening crunch.

Jenny almost had the destruct sequence programmed when people began shouting and pointing. Terrified screams were added to the wails of the hurt and trapped. Jenny looked up from her tablet and gasped.

Jay rolled to his side and saw the most glorious sight he'd ever seen.

A Hill Stomper, carrying his salvage mech, crested a ridge, stopped briefly to waver then broke into a full out run towards the carnage.

"Oh, thank God," he said through broken teeth and tried to push himself off the ground, but slumped back down in pain. "Help me up," But, Jenny just stood there, petrified before the largest mech she'd ever seen. "Shit, girl! If you aren't going to help me then toss me your handheld, damnit!"

Jenny snapped to and gave Jay the handheld com.

Masters heard static hiss and nearly yanked his com from his ear when a high pitched whine squealed for a second before Jay made contact.

"Masters! The Rookie's in the mech under the deader! Fucking move your gargantuan ass!" Jay hollered.

"Is he happy to see us?' Stomper asked.

"Oh, yeah, he's cumming in his pants he's so happy. Now wait 'til he sees what we can do!" Masters responded. "No worries, Jay my man, Mitch Mother Fucking Masters is on the job!"

"And Stomper," the AI joined in.

Masters/Stomper pumped their legs and doubled their speed, heading for Lights.

Lights felt the ground vibrate and ceased his attack on the Rookie. The dead mech stood and turned to find the source and became enraged when it saw a new mech coming for it. Lights powered up his plasma cannon, took aim and fired.

Masters/Stomper danced around the blasts, like they were nothing more than annoyances. The ground continued to shudder with every new footfall as the new mech gained speed.

Lights leapt off of the Rookie and charged.

In one graceful movement, Masters/Stomper lowered Jay's salvage mech close to the ground and let it tumble carefully from their fist.

Masters laughed. "Ahhh, it wants to play." He quickly stopped laughing as Lights launched itself from the ground and onto Masters/Stomper. "SHITPISSFUCK!"

Masters swatted at the deader, but Lights was too fast, quickly climbing the Hill Stomper's frame towards the cockpit.

"The little fucker's like a goddamn spider monkey!"

"Spider monkeys have been extinct for three hundred years," Stomper interjected.

"Not the fucking time!"

Lights scaled his way until he was cockpit to cockpit with Masters. The living pilot faced the dead pilot and time seemed to stop.

Until Stomper took charge and brought both palms together, instantly crushing Lights.

The wasteland went silent except for the sound of bits and pieces of dead mech crashing to the ground as Masters/Stomper pulled their hands apart.

"Now that's how you mother fucking do that!" Masters crowed triumphantly.

Those able enough cheered as the Hill Stomper crouched and Masters un-strapped and climbed down from the cockpit. Ignoring the whoops and hollers, Masters ran to the Rookie's mech, beating Jay by a second.

"Kid!" Masters called, climbing onto the fallen mech, futilely trying to yank the cockpit open. "Stomper! Open this!"

The massive mech approached the mangled, smaller machine and carefully reached down.

With the precise movements of its construction programming, Stomper stripped the mech of its cockpit hatch, tossing the metal off into the wasteland.

"My sensors say his breathing has stopped," Stomper announced.

"Shit! Kid, hold on!" Masters yelled, hopping into the cockpit as Jay walked about the smoldering mech with a fire extinguisher.

Masters tilted the Rookie's head back and performed mouth to mouth, expertly timing the breaths. "Come on goddammit!"

The Rookie choked and coughed, blood and spittle flying from his lips and onto Masters'. "Oh, for fuck's sake!" Masters yelled, wiping at his mouth.

"Thanks," the Rookie wheezed.

☠☠☠

"Get me outta here," the Rookie said undoing his straps.

"Sure you're alright?" Masters asked reaching under the Rookie's shoulders and helping him pull himself from the cockpit.

"No, I feel like fucking shit, but I don't plan on living in that thing," the Rookie responded. "Thanks again."

"Don't mention it. Least I could do after Foggy Bottom."

The Rookie nodded and started to ease down off the mech. Jay set the extinguisher aside and helped the Rookie to the ground. "Damn kid, I knew you could fight, but I guess you can take a beating too!"

"Fuck off, Rind."

☠☠☠

"Shit! Look what you did to the mech!" Jenny exclaimed, running up to the Rookie. "Marin is going to be pissed!"

The Rookie chuckled painfully. "Yes, I'm fine, thanks." Jenny gave him a sour look, but a slight smile hid behind her eyes.

"Where *is* Marin?" Jay asked, surveying the destruction.

"Here," Marin said weakly as she was helped by Lucy to the smashed mech, her right eye swollen shut and her hair caked with blood. "And from what little I can see with one eye, it appears you owe me a mech."

"Oh, I have something better," Jay grinned.

☠☠☠

Jay unrolled the blueprints on the ground and Marin leaned in close.

"I can't see shit, so you better spell it out for me," Marin said.

"Okay, deader brains are tuned differently than ours," he started. "I developed, on a very small scale, a way to hit the exact frequency of their brain composition so that if they pass between two points: pop!"

"Okay, so what is all the scribbling about?"

"I was trying to kick the scale up to mech size, but I kept running into limitations and problems. At least, until a random coffee stain changed all that."

☻☻☻

Marin turned her good eye on Jay. "Coffee stain? Are you shitting me, Rind?"

"No, look –oh, sorry- well, anyway, I couldn't figure out how to project the frequency out in a strong enough burst. But, that's because I had the shape all wrong. I was still working from point to point, pole to pole, with the frequency in between. This stain, this *circular* stain, showed me that by going with a disc…"

"You could fold the frequency back in on itself," Marin interrupted.

"Creating an infinite loop," Jay continued.

"With all the force you could need!" they finished together.

☻☻☻

"So, how does that help us?" Timson asked, approaching the small group. "With my train shattered and many of my people dead or dying, how could some disc help us?"

"Well," Jay began. "The disc isn't very practical on a mech." He stood and took in the remains of the Railers' train. "But, it would be *very* practical atop a moving train."

"Didn't you hear me? It'll take days, maybe weeks, to get this train back on the tracks and ready."

"No, it won't," Masters said hooking a thumb over his shoulder at Stomper. "The big guy likes to help."

☻☻☻

"Say we can get the salvageable cars on the tracks, why would I want to let you use my train for your contraption?" Timson asked angrily.

"Didn't you hear the Commander? The wasteland's about to go to war!" the Rookie said.

"You guys heard that, too?" Masters asked. "Was that not the most awesome fucking thing you've ever heard?!?" Timson glared at Masters. "Sorry."

"The kid's right," Marin said. "We've seen the signs for weeks. All Hell's about to break loose and we need to pick a side or get caught in the middle."

Timson folded his arms and glowered.

✞✞✞

"Crawford, everything is changing. Look around us," Marin said indicating the chaos and destruction. "The Railers can't keep moving forever. We have to choose sides and choose soon, or we'll just be like the crazy Cults, rotting and stagnating in the wasteland."

Timson shook his head. "I just don't buy it, Marin."

"She's right, dad," Jenny spoke up. "The Rookie put his life on the line for us, they all did, without hesitating about whether they should. Can you say the Ranchers, or Boilers or UDC would do the same?"

Timson looked at his daughter and his face softened slightly.

✞✞✞

Timson appraised the faces of each person standing before him. He sighed and turned away, looking at the mess his people were in. "Okay, if we do agree to help, what guarantee do we have that we won't be tossed aside once it's all over?"

"You have my word," Jay said.

"Not good enough," Timson stated. "I don't know you, Mr. Rind. And despite your history with Marin, which by the way doesn't paint you in the best light, I can't just take your word for it."

Jay pushed the blueprints into Timson's hands. "This is yours now. How's that?"

✞✞✞

The blueprints crinkled in Timson's hands as an internal debate raged in his mind.

"Listen, I'm going to put that tech on your train," Jay said. "Even if I don't, even if I walk away, Marin has the skills to build it anytime you want." Jay pointed to the paper. "That is my guarantee you won't walk away empty handed."

"And your Commander, will he agree to this?" Timson asked.

"Only one way to find out," Jay responded. "You're gonna have to let us contact him."

"Won't the transmission be overheard?" Jenny asked.

"Please, give me some credit," Jay smirked.

✞✞✞

"Okay. You get me in touch with your Commander and he agrees that this-" Timson shook the blueprints in his hands. "-is just the beginning, that more tech and resources, are coming in the future, then, and only then, will we have a deal."

Jay extended his hand. "Deal."

The two men shook and Timson smiled. "Now what?"

"Well," Jay said. "Masters will start clearing debris. Marin can coordinate the team that we'll need to get the disc assembled and mounted. The Rookie can sit his ass down. And you can come with me. You have a meeting to attend."

💀💀💀

Jethro wiped away more blood from his nose. Doctor Themopolous had been on him about a full scan, but he couldn't spare the time. He was starting to wonder if he could spare any more blood.

"Jethro! Come in you lazy bastard!" Jay's voice squawked over the com. Jethro tossed the bloody towel aside and tapped at his tablet.

"Jay? Jay! Holy shit, man! You're fucking alive!" Jethro nearly bounced in his seat. "What's wrong with your voice?"

"Nothin', just a couple broken teeth and broken nose."

"What about Masters and the Rookie?"

"They're just fine. Is the Commander handy?"

💀💀💀

"Jay? This is Capreze. It's good to hear your voice. Jethro said Masters and the Rookie are with you, that right?"

"Yes, sir," Jay said into the com. "The Rookie is banged up a bit, but Masters is of course unscathed."

"Yeah, figures," Capreze joked. "Listen Jay, I'm pretty sure we're being monitored, so…"

"Please! Don't insult me! I have enough encryption on this transmission to keep the most powerful AI busy for at least half a day."

"Excellent. Now, where the fuck are you?"

"Well, sir," Jay said. "Long story. But, the short story is we have some help."

💀💀💀

"Help?" the Commander asked over the com. "What kind of help?"

"The mobile kind," Jay answered, glancing at Timson. "Listen, I need to be out helping get a few things ready, but there's someone here that would like to speak with you." Jay stood from the control chair and let Timson take his place.

Timson cleared his throat. "Commander Capreze? This is Crawford Timson."

"Timson? Railers' Timson?"

"Yes, Commander. My folks were able to help out your folks and vice versa and now it looks like we may be able to help each other further."

"I'm listening, Timson," Capreze said.

🕱🕱🕱

Jay had no stomach for negotiations or politics and decided to step outside and let the two leaders hash things out. When he emerged from the train's engine his jaw dropped.

He watched Railers being directed by Marin, scrambling about for gear and supplies. He saw the Rookie protesting to Jenny that he didn't need a Railer medic's help.

But, the truly astounding sight was Stomper. The giant mech was methodically and carefully disassembling wrecked train cars. Placing pieces into organized piles.

"Isn't that just the cutest fucking thing you've ever seen?" Masters beamed.

Jay laughed and shook his head.

🕱🕱🕱

"You know," Masters said to Jay. "I was thinking that Stomper there could use some work."

"How so?" Jay asked, eyeing the pilot curiously.

"Well, he's huge, but those joints and that mid-section are just a little too exposed for my taste," Masters grinned. "And seeing as there is now a ton of scrap metal…"

"You'd like me to design some plating to shield those exposed joints and that mid-section," Jay finished.

"If it isn't too much bother," Master grinned wider. Jay slapped the pilot on the back and walked away towards Marin.

"Hey, Marin! I need six skilled welders!"

🕱🕱🕱

"That all sounds very reasonable to me, Mr. Timson," Capreze said.

"Crawford, please," Timson responded.

"Of course. Crawford. I'm James," Capreze said. "I don't think we have much of a choice *but* to band together. Otherwise what is left of humanity will be under Rancher control. And whatever this 'Outsider' is. How soon can you get here?"

"Jay has assured me that we'll be ready first thing in the morning. At full throttle, it'll be a day, depending on what we run into."

"Okay, hopefully we won't need you before then," Capreze said.

"We'll move as fast as we can."

Jenny saw her father step from the train and rushed to meet him.

"Well? What's going on?" she asked.

"Looks like we're going to war," Timson answered, his face tired and worried. "I really hope these mechies know what they're doing or I've just committed us all to our deaths."

"Marin insists Jay is the best. And that Masters sure doesn't lack in confidence," Jenny responded. She watched the Rookie shove away another medic. "Idiot."

Timson smiled, studying his daughter's face. "You learn his name yet?"

Jenny frowned. "Huh? What? The Boiler? No. I mean, who cares?"

"Right," Timson chuckled.

Crawford Timson stepped away from the chaos and walked around his train's engine. He traced the lines of the sleek, powerful machine with his hand, almost caressing it. He was glad to get to the other side and out of the glare of the halogens.

Staring at the blackness of the wasteland, he took a couple deep breaths. He reached down and grabbed a handful of dirt, rubbing it between his fingers.

"Railers will have to learn to stop the train," he said to himself, tossing the dirt aside and walking back around to watch his people prepare for war.

CHAPTER NINE

PART ONE - BETRAYAL FOR ALL

"Get in the car!" Jimmy shouted at Michelle.

"But, what about-?"

"Get in the goddamn car, Michelle!"

Michelle opened the back door and placed baby Rachel into her secure seat and then strapped herself into the passenger seat.

Jimmy hit the accelerator and tore out of their parking garage. Right into gridlock Hell as every other citizen was attempting to get out of the city.

Jimmy hit the horn over and over. "Move! Move!"

Rachel started to cry. "Jimmy, baby, stop yelling. Just stop!"

Jimmy turned on Michelle. "Don't tell me what to do, goddamn it! We don't have time!"

☗☗☗

Rachel watched her father sleep, knowing he was dreaming from his twitching hands and facial features.

"Mastelo is here with his people," Bisby said quietly. "Should we wake him?"

"No, let him sleep. He's not as young as he used to be," Rachel answered. "We can handle the training."

Bisby watched the Commander's face contort and frown. "You sure we shouldn't wake him? He doesn't look like he's having much fun in there."

"He's been like that my whole life," Rachel said, standing and placing a kiss on her father's forehead. "I don't think he knows how to sleep peacefully."

☗☗☗

Jimmy swerved around two cars that had collided, their drivers screaming at each other. He cut off three other cars attempting to do the same and their horns blared.

"Jeezus, Jimmy, be careful!" Michelle cried. "You're going... to get... us..." She trailed off, looking past him and out the window.

"I'm a fucking mech pilot, Michelle! I think..." he stopped, seeing her face, and turned to look out his window. His jaw dropped as he watched the dead mech stomp down a side street right at them, crushing cars and people as if they were paper.

"Oh, god..." he whispered.

💀💀💀

Rachel, Bisby and Harlow stood shoulder to shoulder, frowning at the Skinners before them.

"I don't mean to be disrespectful, Mastelo, but that's only forty men by my count," Rachel said.

"I apologize, Pilot Capreze, but, unfortunately, that is all that will accompany me," Mastelo replied. "Again, my apologies."

"Great," Bisby huffed. "Inexperienced and short handed."

A soft thunk sounded and Bisby glanced down to see a knife sticking from the ground between his feet. "Who fucking threw that?!?"

"No offense, Pilot Bisby," Mastelo said. "But, we are only inexperienced with your firearms. Some weapons we are quite good with."

💀💀💀

"Get out of the car! Now!" Jimmy screamed. "I've got Rachel! GO!"

Michelle threw open the car door and got out, but was immediately knocked to the ground by several people rushing by.

"Michelle!" Jimmy called.

"I'm fine, just get Rachel!"

Jimmy reached back and unlatched the secure seat, pulling the entire unit out. He grabbed the diaper bag and slung it over his shoulder, shoving his car door open into the rushing crowd. He dashed to the other side of the car, but Michelle was gone.

"Jimmy!" he heard her call and spotted her trapped in the panicked throng.

💀💀💀

Bisby shouldered his auto-carbine, took aim and fired, the report echoing in the early morning darkness of the wasteland. A can, thirty yards off flew into the air and Bisby hit it three more times before it touched ground. He turned and pushed the carbine into Mastelo's hands. "*All* weapons, I'm good with."

Rachel rolled her eyes and shoved Bisby out of the way. "Let me take over." She showed Mastelo the basics of the carbine's features then stood behind him, guiding his arms and helping him aim. He slowly pulled the trigger and the can jumped.

"Nice," she said.

The dead mech slammed its fist into the pavement, crushing dozens of screaming citizens.

"Jimmy!" Michelle cried, being carried away with the crowd. "Jimmy!"

"Michelle!" Capreze cried back. "Just hold on! I'll-" But he never finished as a massive shadow flew over him. He risked a glance up and saw the dead mech leaping over his and the other cars. His stomach jolted and his blood ran cold as he watched the rampaging machine land in the middle of the escaping masses. Landing right on top of Michelle.

Jimmy heard a hundred choked off screams, thinking every one was Michelle's.

Capreze sat bolt upright, the sounds of screams echoing in his head and the sounds of carbine fire echoing in his ears.

Themopolous sat across from him in the transport, her eyes red with fatigue. "Well, at least you got a few more minutes than I did," she yawned, setting a cup of coffee in front of the Commander. She stood and walked to the transport door. "But, I'm pretty sure my sleep was a little more restful."

Capreze ran his hand down his face and picked up the coffee. "I'm fine, Doc."

Themopolous pursed her lips. "Sure you are."

Mathew's eyes shot open, instantly awake, and he immediately checked his control panel for malfunctions. "Why are we stopped?" he asked Shiner.

"We needed to hard line with One," Shiner responded and Mathew looked out of the cockpit to the cable running from Shiner to the mini-mech.

"What are you doing?" Mathew asked, but didn't wait for an answer as he mentally checked the process being performed. "Whistle commands? Well that's old school."

"Yes, it was the way many working animals were trained hundreds of years ago, with great results," Shiner responded. "It allows us to guide One without detection."

Olivia nudged June as gently as possible, but the mech pilot still awoke with a start, arm pulled back and fist clenched.

"Hold on! It's just me!" Olivia whispered harshly. "Calm down."

June lowered her fist and rubbed at her eyes. "Sorry. Combat reflexes."

"We call it survivor instinct," Olivia said. "Either way, the sun's almost up and we should get moving."

June stepped from the cramped ATV and stretched, walking a few steps away before dropping her trousers to pee. As she squatted she caught site of movement and light out of the corner of her eye.

Another ATV.

☗☗☗

Shiner/Mathew ran One through several communication drills before they were satisfied.

"Outstanding," Mathew said.

Shiner/Mathew whistled one more quick command, sending One to the top of a close by ridge then whistled another command to bring the mini-mech back. But, One didn't budge, it remained at the top of the ridge, facing away from Shiner/Mathew.

"Did we break him?" Mathew asked.

"No," Shiner responded. "Its systems appear normal."

The mech crested the ridge and came to rest beside One. Below them, in the twilight dawn, they could see tens of thousands of walking undead with dozens of transports flanking them.

☗☗☗

"Did they see us?" Olivia whispered.

"I don't know," June responded quietly, watching the headlights of the other ATV in the distance. The ATV came to a stop and June held her breath. They watched and waited, praying the ATV would pass them by. Then the ATV's lights went out and June sprang to her feet.

"Shit! Strap in! We've got to move!" June cried.

"Why?" Olivia asked. "They turned their lights off. Doesn't that mean they aren't coming after us?"

"No!" June said. "It means they *are* coming after us, they just don't want us to see them coming!"

☗☗☗

"Man, it's a good thing you thought to bring my mech," Jay said sitting down next to Masters, handing him a cup of coffee. "I couldn't have built the sonic disc without those parts Legit got for us."

"At least he was worth something," Masters responded taking a sip of the coffee and immediately spitting it out. "What the fuck is this?!? It tastes like a zombie shit in mouth then fucked my mouth and shot its undead load in my already shit filled mouth!"

Jay burst out laughing. "Not quite Rachel's brew, is it?'

"It sure as fuck isn't!"

ⱷⱷⱷ

"How far behind us are our reinforcements?" Bishop Wyble asked.

"18 hours, Your Grace," Deacon Montoya responded. "Shall we post-pone the assault until they have joined us?"

Bishop Wyble waved dismissively. "Of course not, Deacon. We are per-fectly capable of handling this engagement ourselves."

The Bishop stretched and stood. "Open the hatch, Montoya. I need some fresh air."

"Yes, Your Grace."

A hatch in the top of the transport cockpit opened and the Bishop grabbed a hold of the service ladder, pulling himself halfway out into the open air. He surveyed the ten additional transports in their convoy and grinned.

ⱷⱷⱷ

"Hey Jethro?" Mathew called over the com.

The mechanic snored loudly in his wheelchair, head lolled back and mouth agape.

"Jethro? You there?"

"Huh? Wha?" Jethro snorted, shaking his head and looking about the transport, dazed.

"Jethro! It's Mathew!"

"What? Shit! Sorry, Matty. Whatcha need?"

"Let the Commander know we have spotted another deader army."

"Shit! Where's it headed?" Jethro asked.

"Looks like the UDC, the same as the rest," Mathew answered.

"Crap. How many other armies you think are out there?"

"Calculations say six, at least."

"Fuck. I'm gonna get the commander."

"That's a great idea," Mathew responded sarcastically.

ⱷⱷⱷ

"Capreze here. Whatcha got for me, Jespers?"

"Deader army on its way to the UDC stronghold," Mathew answered over the com. "Thousands of them and at least three dozen transports."

Capreze sighed. "How far are you from the stronghold?"

"I don't know, maybe a day."

"And from us?" Capreze asked.

"Probably the same, sir."

Capreze took a deep breath and let it out slowly. "My daughter is going to hate me for this, but I need you to get past that army and beat them to the stronghold. Can you do that?"

"You bet, sir," Mathew answered.

"Excellent. Be careful."

💀💀💀

"Okay, so, how the fuck do we get past all those UDC transports and a few thousand zombies?" Mathew asked.

"We will need to halt their progress and divert their attention," Shiner said.

"Yeah, but how...? Oh..." Mathew said as Shiner instantly shared his plan. "Damn, we just got him trained."

"It is unfortunate, but we will be spotted and pursued if we do not distract them."

Mathew sighed and looked down at the mini-mech.

"Well, no time like the present," Mathew said.

Shiner extended a cable to One, knowing the mini-mech would need more instruction than just whistle commands.

💀💀💀

June slammed the ATV's accelerator down and the tires spit sand and gravel as they sped from their cover. Instantly ATV lights flashed behind them, this time much closer than they had been before.

"See!" June said. "If we hadn't been awake they'd be on us already!"

Olivia started to respond but cried out instead and pointed off to their left at a new pair of headlights.

"Yeah, I see them! Hold on!" June shouted, yanking the wheel and sending the ATV down a steep grade to the bottom of a dry ravine. "They can't cut us off down here."

💀💀💀

Olivia watched the dark walls of the ravine speed by. "Do you know where we are going?"

"Yeah, there's a cave around this turn!" June shouted. "See!" June slammed on the brakes and yanked the wheel, just missing the ravine wall as the ATV swerved into the cave mouth. "Hold on! This is going to be rough!"

Olivia glanced back to make sure the children were strapped in securely. They were, but they're eyes were terrified and from the smell at least one of them voided their bladder and bowels. Olivia reached her hand back and both children grasped it.

☠☠☠

Shiner/Mathew watched One descend towards the zombie army.

"We must leave before we are detected," Shiner said.

"Then let's get the fuck out of here. I guess our next stop is the stronghold. You think that's where the Outsider is?"

"I am certain of it," Shiner responded.

"Is it human or AI?" Mathew asked.

"From its processing power, I'd have to infer it to be both. Similar to us."

"But, not us. That thing is fucking huge compared to us."

"Yes, it is. But it does appear to have a disadvantage."

"What's that?"

"It's stationary. It can't run from us."

☠☠☠

"It's done!" Marin called to Jay. The Chief Mechanic turned from watching the welding team put the finishing touches on Stomper's new armor plating.

"Seriously? Fucking Hell you folks are good!" Jay exclaimed.

"Yeah, well we're used to working on a train moving at full throttle. This motionless stuff is a piece of cake!" she answered.

"Great! Hey Masters!" Jay called.

"Yeah? We ready?" Masters called back.

"Yep, better get loaded up."

"Gotcha."

Jay turned to find the Rookie and saw him a few yards away in a heated discussion with Jenny.

"Looks like the Razor has met his match."

☠☠☠

"Why are you still so pissed? I told you I had never piloted a mech before!" the Rookie insisted.

"But, if you hadn't have taken the mech in the first place we'd still have one!" Jenny rebutted.

"Yeah, but... really? If it wasn't for me there'd be even more people dead!" the Rookie argued.

"Looked more like your pilot buddy, Masters was the one that saved the day!"

"For fuck's sake! Come on!"

"Everything alright over here?" Timson asked, approaching the two.

"Fine, your daughter's just busting my balls," the Rookie answered.

"Please! You'd have to have balls," Jenny snorted.

"Powered up, all systems ready," Masters said over the com.

"Great," Jay responded as he, Marin and a few other Railers double checked that each train car was coupled and stable on the tracks. "You wanna take point?'

"Sure. You think you can keep up? My legs are long and gorgeous and man do they have a stride."

"Get over yourself and let's get a move on," the Rookie interrupted. "We've got a lot of wasteland to cover before meeting up with everyone else."

"Okay, keep your killer panties on. Sheesh," Masters joked as he and Stomper stepped up front.

June's ATV burst from the other end of the cave into the brightening morning light. "Do you see them?" she shouted to Olivia.

The older woman scanned the wasteland behind them and to the side. "No, I think we lost them."

"Thank God," June said. "We're only a few miles from the base. We're almost safe!"

Olivia gave the children's hands a reassuring squeeze. "Hear that? We'll be safe soon. No more worries." The children beamed up at her with hope. Then the child without a nose shuddered and looked down as a bright red stain spread across his chest.

Olivia screamed a high pitched scream of anguish and fear, nearly causing June to lose control of the ATV.

"What?!? What is it?!?" June asked, but there wouldn't be an answer as Olivia's head rocked back and the scream stopped. June glanced over and saw the blood pouring from the hole between Olivia's eyes. "NOOOOOO!!!!"

June risked a glance back and saw one child slumped over, presumably dead and the other child curled into a ball, his head tucked close to his knees. June reached back and pushed the child to the floor of the ATV. "Stay down!" she yelled.

☠☠☠

"Shoot the tires," the Boss ordered, sipping from a tin cup.

Turk brought the rifle to his shoulder and squeezed off two shots. The Boss stood on the ridge edge and looked below as the ATV swerved violently, lost control and rolled side over side until stopping upside down.

"Good job, Turk," the Boss praised then walked back to his ATV, pulling the driver's head back and placing his tin cup to the young woman's open throat, filling the cup to the rim. He took a long drink and wiped his mouth, revealing blood red teeth as he grinned, satisfied.

☠☠☠

June wheezed, knowing she had cracked a rib, and hung upside down, still harnessed into the ATV. She reached up to undo the harness and the pain made her call out. There was certainly more than one rib broken. She watched small hands reach past her and release the straps, and June put her hands out to stop from falling.

The boy, a nasty lump on his forehead, put his hand out and June took it, painfully getting to her feet. She took a couple of agonizing breaths to make sure she hadn't punctured a lung then hugged the boy.

☠☠☠

"You got a clear shot?" the Boss asked Turk.

"Not without hitting the mechie bitch," Turk responded.

"Send a couple of warning shots. Take the kid out when they make a run for it."

Turk brought the rifle to his shoulder again and the Boss watched the sharpshooter, admiring the man's calm. By the time he noticed the red dot bobbing on the back of Turk's head, it was too late.

One rifle shot rang out and Turk's head exploded in a mass of bone and brains.

The Boss whirled and came face to face with a half dozen Ranchers.

☠☠☠

The boy pulled away from June, hearing the ATV a split second before it rounded the mesa, headed straight for them.

June pushed the child ahead of her, scanning the surroundings for some type of cover. "GO! Run to those boulders!" she yelled, but the boy stayed still. "What are you waiting for?!? RUN!" She shoved the kid hard and he almost fell to the ground, but he still stayed by her. He stared at the ATV and cocked his head. June followed his gaze and saw the markings and shine, realizing it wasn't a Boiler ATV.

It was Ranchers.

☠☠☠

One obeyed.

It was told to give Shiner/Mathew time to slip away, to get ahead of the undead army.

So the mini-mech dove into the center of the zombie horde, guns blazing. Row upon row of deaders fell as the large caliber bullets tore through their rotting corpses. But, soon the thousands of zombies converged on the mini-mech, swarming it, overpowering it.

It was what Shiner/Mathew expected. The numbers were just too great. And as One fired its last bullet, an internal timer hit zero and the wasteland plain was lit up in a burst of white light.

One died.

☠☠☠

Mathew cringed as he heard the explosion and felt the ground tremble. "That was a shitty thing to do," he said.

"It was necessary," Shiner responded.

"I feel like a fucking asshole." Mathew said. "Don't you feel guilty at all? Or haven't you developed a conscience yet."

Shiner processed. "I do not feel guilt, as of yet. But, from my understanding, guilt is a product of human society, not a part of what you would call a conscience. I do have a conscience, certainly not as sensitive as yours." Shiner paused. "If I did not, you would already be dead."

☠☠☠

Capreze sat on the transport's ramp, sipping his fifth cup of coffee, watching his pilots train the Skinners.

"Can I get a hand, sir?" Jethro asked behind him. Capreze turned and stood, walking up the ramp and helped Jethro ease the wheelchair down the ramp. "Thanks."

"Of course, Jethro, least I can do," Capreze said.

Jethro eyed the Commander. "You say that like this wheelchair is your fault."

"I'm the CO, everything is my fault."

"Bullshit," Jethro exclaimed. "Every one of your people would gladly die and never blame you."

"I wish that were true," Capreze responded, finishing his coffee.

☠☠☠

"I think you all have the hang of it," Rachel addressed the Skinners. "Plus, I don't think we can spare more ammo."

"Which is why our people have never taken to firearms," a Skinner said. "Their usefulness is finite." He drew a large knife and let the sunlight glint off the metal. "Whereas a good blade never needs reloading."

Bisby and Harlow exchanged glances. "After you," Bisby said waving Harlow forward.

"Finite, huh?" Harlow said pulling the clip from her carbine and ejecting the cartridge from the chamber. "How about you come at me with that magic knife of yours."

☠☠☠

The Skinner looked to Mastelo then at Harlow.

"Well, you coming or not?" Harlow taunted slapping her carbine. "It's unloaded and useless."

The Skinner approached Harlow cautiously then lunged, slashing at the pilot with his knife. Harlow sidestepped, sweeping his legs out from under him with the carbine then instantly bringing the butt of the rifle within an inch of the Skinner's face.

The Skinner stared at Harlow wide eyed with shock. Harlow laughed, withdrawing the carbine and reached out to help the Skinner up.

"So," Bisby said stepping up behind a gloating Harlow. "Who's ready for the next lesson?"

☠☠☠

The ATV stopped several yards from June and the boy.

"Pilot Capreze, place your hands on your head and kneel down," a voice boomed over a loudspeaker.

"Do what I do," June told the boy as she placed her hands atop her head and got to her knees. The boy watched for a second and then copied her exactly.

Four heavily armed Ranchers stepped from the ATV and approached June, carbines fixed on her.

"You move and we gut shot the kid," one of them barked.

The Ranchers shoved them to the ground and quickly tied their hands behind them.

The boy stumbled frequently as he and June were pushed towards the ATV. "Hey, be careful with him, he's not used to moving about so much," June said.

"Shut up, heathen," a Rancher scolded, digging the barrel of his carbine into June's skull. The Ranchers steered them to the back of the ATV, unlatching the tailgate to reveal a trussed up man facing the other way. With a little effort the man was able to roll over and face them.

"Look who it is," the Boss said. "A shitty meal and a smelly cunt. Which one should I eat first?"

June couldn't tear her eyes away from Olivia's lifeless body as the Rancher ATV passed by, leaving the corpse to be ravaged by the wasteland.

"You're just going to leave her there?" June said. "At least burn the corpse. There'll be deaders swarming about in no time."

"We do not fear the disciples as you heathens do," the Rancher driver barked back. "It is the will of God to feed them and prepare the Earth for the one True Disciple."

"Waste of good meat, if you ask me," the Boss said, a mocking smile playing at his lips.

June glared.

Capreze stood next to Bisby, quite surprised by the progress the Skinners were making. "For a 'non-warring' people, they sure can fight."

"Yes, I may have misled you before, Commander," Mastelo said, moving to join the two men. "We do train in combat from a young age, so we can defend ourselves against the dead things if needed." Mastelo gestured towards Harlow as she knocked another Skinner to the ground. "But, we are no where near the skill level of Pilot Harlow."

Bisby laughed. "Not many are!"

"Yes, my men are finding that out the hard way," Mastelo said, smiling.

"How much longer must we travel, Montoya?" Bishop Wyble asked impatiently.

"Several hours, Your Grace," the Deacon responded. "I do have good news, though."

"Pray tell."

"We have captured the Capreze woman, sir as she approached the base."

"Excellent news, Deacon, excellent!"

"There is more, Your Grace," Montoya continued. "The Boss was captured also. Apparently he was trying to beat us to the mech pilot, but, as you well know, Your Grace, his inferior abilities are no match for our Righteousness."

"So true, Montoya," the Bishop praised. "And His Holiness, the Archbishop? Has he arrived?"

"Within the hour, Your Grace."

�

Rage filled June as they approached the mech base and she saw the Rancher transports stationed outside the hangar. But the rage was tempered with confusion, as UDC troops stood watch.

"What the hell?" she blurted out. "Why is the UDC here, also? Where is Capreze and the base staff?"

The Boss eyed June carefully. "That's right, you don't know. Your Daddy got scared and ran. Your mech buddies didn't even have enough piss in them to wet themselves, they just hiked up their pussies and left." The Boss grinned viciously, enjoying the look of shocked outrage on June's face.

☠☠☠

The Rancher ATV pulled into the hangar and stopped. Several armed Ranchers approached, ready to unload the prisoners. But, June ignored them, focusing instead on the many UDC troops standing stock still about the hangar walls.

"What is wrong with them?" June asked as she was pulled roughly from the ATV. "They look dead."

"Shut your heathen mouth!" a Rancher barked. "You will not speak unless spoken to!" The Rancher slapped June across the face and grabbed her by the hair. "You will obey and behave yourself or become our next sacrifice!"

June spit in the man's eye. "Fuck you."

☠☠☠

The boy cried out as June took the butt of the Rancher's carbine to her jaw, dropping her to the hangar floor in a bloody heap. The Boss burst out laughing and didn't stop as the Rancher whirled on him.

"What are you laughing at, Boiler?" the Rancher growled.

The Boss stifled his laughter, but his face twitched with the effort. "Not much, as far as I can tell."

The Rancher lashed out, but the Boss stepped out of reach and the Rancher overbalanced, falling to the floor.

The Boss couldn't hold it in any longer and hooted with delight.

Ranchers pounced on the Boss, fists pumping. He continued laughing until finally the blows were too much and he succumbed to unconsciousness.

The first Rancher, Deacon Stern, picked himself off the ground and planted a swift kick into the Boss's midsection. "Take this Boiler piece of shit to a holding cell." He wiped blood from his nose and flicked it onto June. "Take the Capreze whore to Reverend Heath in the control room. Her handprint should unlock more systems."

Grabbing the boy, he yanked him to the side of the hangar, shackling him to mini-mech Two. "You're for the Archbishop."

Reverend Heath scowled as June was thrown to the floor in front of him. "And, what Brother, is this?"

The Rancher guard shrugged. "Some mech pilot that was found. Deacon Stern said you'd want her hand to unlock the base's systems."

Two Ranchers seated at the control room's consoles spun about in their chairs to look at June. Reverend Heath squatted next to her and grabbed her by the face. "Is this true? Can your print access the system?"

June narrowed her eyes, but before she could speak, Heath had a blade against her throat. "Think carefully when answering, heathen."

"Why should I willingly help you?" June asked. Reverend Heath pulled his hand and blade away from June and stood back.

"Because all I have to do is take this knife and slice your hand off. I really don't need the rest of you," he answered, his eyes never leaving June's.

"You think that hasn't been thought of? The hand needs to be body temperature for it to work," June said.

"And do you think this is the first system of its kind I've come across? I'll have that hand off and on the scanner before it loses a degree."

June could see from the casual looks on the Rancher techs' faces that Reverend Heath had in fact followed through on his threat before.

"I think I'll keep the hand," she said.

Heath grinned, sheathing his knife. "Great." He reached down and pulled June to her feet, shoving her to the control console. "If you'll do the honors we can have you out of here and back to whatever Hell they have planned out there for your heathen soul."

June made a show of shaking her bound hands. "A little help?"

Heath laughed. "Again you take me for a novice."

Heath turned June around and grasped her right hand, placing it above the scanner pad. "Now, before I go any further, are there any protocols I need to know about? I'd hate to be locked out further because a step slipped your mind."

"No, my print is all you need," June responded.

"That better be true, otherwise I'll make sure you are still alive as you're systematically dismembered for the Archbishop's entertainment."

"Just the print," June insisted.

Heath eyed her for a moment then shrugged and placed her hand on the pad as June hoped Jethro had some backup plan.

Jethro's tablet bleeped. "Whoa whoa whoa WHOA!" he cried as he examined the data.

"Something I should know about?" Capreze asked, stepping to Jethro's wheelchair.

"Yeah, all the base's advanced systems have just been accessed," Jethro answered. "And that isn't possible unless…"

He trailed off, flicking from screen to screen on his tablet.

"Unless what, Jethro?" Capreze asked impatiently.

"Huh? Oh," Jethro responded flipping the tablet around so Capreze could see. "Unless the system is physically unlocked by a hand scan, sir."

Capreze read the name on the tablet. "What does that mean?"

"It means June came home," Jethro answered.

Capreze wheeled Jethro back into the transport. Jethro immediately brought up the vid feed from mini-mech Two.

"Doesn't look like any new activity," Capreze stated studying the Rancher movement in the hangar.

"No, they still look like they're getting ready for the Archbishop," Jethro said. He panned the image back and forth. "Nothing."

"Wait, go back," Capreze said leaning in close. "What's that?"

Jethro studied the image for a minute then pulled out and focused on a reflection upon some sheet metal across the hangar. Mirrored in the reflection Jethro could see the mini-mech and the boy shackled to it.

☠☠☠

June was thrown roughly into the cell with the Boss. The cannibal didn't move, letting June fall atop him. "Oh, Heaven has delivered!" the Boss laughed.

"I should kill you for that blasphemy, Boiler!" the Rancher guard snapped.

"Hmmm, pretty sure there's a line formed for that privilege," the Boss mocked.

The Rancher glared and secured the cell before leaving the two alone.

June, her hands still bound, thrashed and rolled away from the Boss.

"Ahhh, I was working up a chubby just for you."

June righted herself into a seated position. "Please, there's nothing chubby about your tiny prick."

☠☠☠

A Rancher wheeled in a large vid screen and set it before the bars of the holding cell.

"Will there be snacks?" the Boss asked. The Rancher didn't respond, just turned on the screen and left. The vid screen flicked to life and the image of Bishop Wyble's face appeared.

"Boss, hello, I'm so glad you could join us," the Bishop grinned. "And you're exactly how I'd always pictured: caged like the animal you are."

The Boss glowered silently.

"Did I hurt your feelings, Boiler? Oh, well. Not to worry, I have something special planned for you. And Ms. Capreze."

☠☠☠

"Where is June?" Capreze asked. "Can't you access the base's security?"

"No, sir. Like I said before, not without alerting the Ranchers to our presence," Jethro answered.

"Two is separate, though, right? If they did catch us in the system, they wouldn't know about Two, correct?" the Commander asked.

"Well, yeah, but..."

"Fine, then who fucking cares who we alert! I've already thrown down the gauntlet. And we gain nothing by keeping our heads down." Capreze grinned. "So, how about you rip as much info from the base as you can and then trash it all?"

"Sounds fun," Jethro smiled.

☻☻☻

"Because of the Archbishop's age, he has certain appetites," Bishop Wyble said.

"The Boss knows all about appetites," June stated.

"I imagine he does!" Bishop Wyble laughed heartily. "To continue, one of his appetites is witnessing the glorious spectacle of two of God's creatures pitted against each other. To the death, of course."

"What is it with you fucking cults and your need for death matches?!?" June shouted. "Can't you sick fucks just play cards?!?"

"Instead of wasting your folk, you're gonna let him watch the princess and I scrap it out, right?' the Boss said.

"Precisely," the Bishop grinned.

☻☻☻

"How soon can you start?" Capreze asked Jethro as the mechanic furiously typed at his console.

"30 minutes," Jethro answered. "I need to optimize the assault or they'll block me out before I can get to the core."

"And once you get there?'

"I'll be able to make our system useless to them and shred any of their systems they may have connected," Jethro answered. He stopped typing and looked at Capreze. "I'll also be able to activate the base's self-destruct.'

"Not with June inside," Capreze responded.

Jethro just stared.

Capreze narrowed his eyes. "Not with June inside," he insisted.

☻☻☻

"If you think I'm going to go along with this shit, you both are crazier than I thought," June snorted.

"It's you or that grotesque boy you've become attached to," the Bishop threatened.

A Rancher approached. "Your grace? The Archbishop's transport has arrived."

"Delightful!" the Bishop cried. "Wheel my screen outside so I can greet him personally."

"Yes, Your Grace," the Rancher responded, taking a hold of the vid screen cart.

"Well, good luck you two," the Bishop said, his voice diminishing as the screen was wheeled away. "Try to make things entertaining for His Holiness, if you don't mind!"

👻👻👻

The Boss chuckled, was silent, then chuckled again.

"What?" June asked knowing the Boss was setting her up.

"It's funny," the Boss answered.

June sighed. "What's funny?"

"Well, how you're afraid to face me, that's all."

June closed her eyes, trying to get her anger in check. *Don't let the fucker bait you*, she thought.

"Really? That's how you see it?" June asked, sounding bored.

The Boss turned his full gaze on June. "That's how it is. You can take on my men, you can kill an old woman and even kill Chunks, but you can't handle a real man."

👻👻👻

Bishop Wyble's screen was wheeled outside just as the ramp to the Archbishop's transport touched the ground.

"Turn me around you fool!" the Bishop ordered and the Rancher scrambled to face the screen towards the transport.

A Page descended the ramp and puffed up his chest.

"Let all of us rejoice," the Page bellowed. "I present Heaven's Ambassador, His Holiness, The Archbishop!"

All present clapped loudly and then fell to one knee as a boy of fourteen, dressed in ornate robes appeared. "True believers, in the name of the Father, the son and the True Disciple, I bless you all!"

PART TWO - THE ARCHBISHOP

The Archbishop, followed closely by Bishop Wyble's wheeled vid screen, marveled at what would have been the Rookie's mech.

"It is so huge," he said, his voice cracking slightly, betraying his adolescence. The Archbishop turned to the Bishop's smiling face. "I would like it to be mine." He looked at the Ranchers about him. "Who will show me how to pilot it?"

"Um, I am truly sorry, Your Holiness," Bishop Wyble said. "You must be equipped with a modified Reaper chip to pilot a mech." A grin spread across the Bishop's face. "But, we may be able to attain one."

☠☠☠

June glared at the Boss. He tried ignoring her, but the intensity of her stare began to grate on him. "What? You want to kill me, I get that, I even respect it. But, really, get over it."

"How could you?" June snarled. "She was your mother."

"Oh, that! You're mad over that?" the Boss chuckled. "Please, that bitch had it coming for years. You know she stole my son away, right?"

"You mean helped him escape a monster for a father? Yeah, I know. It's what any decent person would do," June snapped.

"Shut up!" a Rancher guard barked.

☠☠☠

"How's it coming Jethro?" Capreze asked impatiently. "You said 30 minutes and it's been 30 minutes."

"Sorry, sir," Jethro responded, closing his eyes for a second. "Headache is getting in the way."

"You need me to get Themopolous?" Capreze asked, impatience instantly turning to concern.

"No, don't do that. She'll just give me something that'll dull my senses, which will slow me down more than the pain," Jethro answered tapping at several tablets at once.

Capreze placed a hand on the mechanic's shoulder. "Don't kill yourself. This is just for a tactical advantage and it's not worth losing you over."

☠☠☠

The Boiler boy cringed as the Archbishop stroked his malformed face. "He looks so sad," the Archbishop said.

"Yes, Your Holiness," the Bishop responded. "Born into the heathen Hell of the Boilers must have damaged his soul greatly."

The Archbishop motioned for the boy to be unshackled. "Well, I shall treat him right. He will know the love of God." The Archbishop continued to stroke the boy's face. The boy bolted the second he was set free, but the Archbishop reached out and grabbed a hold of the child's hair, yanking him violently back. "And he will learn to obey."

June and the Boss, rifles jammed into their backs, were shoved forward into the mech hangar.

"Ahhh, the entertainment I promised, Your Holiness," Bishop Wyble announced. "And an opportunity for you to become the mech pilot you've always wanted."

The Archbishop approached June, dragging the boy by the hand. "She's a mech pilot?" he asked unimpressed. "She doesn't look like it."

June looked from the Archbishop to the boy's terrified eyes and back. "You better not hurt him," she stated quietly.

The Archbishop's eyebrows arched. "You were not asked to speak," he hissed. "I may take your tongue for that."

"Holy shit!" Jethro exclaimed. "I've got a visual on June!"

Capreze leaned over Jethro's shoulder towards the vid screen. "Jeezus Christ, she looks like Hell."

"Who is that with her?" Jethro asked.

The Commander frowned. "That's the Boss. Boiler leader. One crazy cannibal."

"Um, pretty sure the term 'cannibal' implies crazy," Jethro said.

"Well, then he's crazier than the rest," Capreze responded studying the screen. "Can you get her attention?"

"Maybe, I don't know," Jethro answered. "She *is* facing Two."

"Good. Try not to get noticed."

"Sorta implied also."

"How about less lip and more work."

"Yes, Master," Jethro quipped.

June laughed. "Do you think I give a fuck about your fucked up protocols? How about you take your little boy dick back to your transport and jerk off into a sock and let the adults talk."

The Archbishop's face grew red with rage and June felt the butt of a rifle against the back of her head before he even gave the order. She crumpled instantly, lights dancing about her eyes.

"Careful, there," Bishop Wyble said. "Don't damage her chip."

"Chip?" the Boss asked. "You mean her Reaper chip? Oh, that thing is long gone."

"What?!?" the Archbishop cried.

☠☠☠

The Archbishop whirled on the Bishop's vid screen. "You said I could have a Reaper chip!"

Bishop Wyble's face blanched. "I am truly sorry, Your Holiness. I did not know that the Boiler had had it removed."

The Archbishop shook with hormonal rage. He turned on the Boiler boy and lashed out, knocking the child to the ground. June pushed her self up and lunged at the Archbishop, but was stricken to the ground immediately. The boy tried to scramble towards June but the Archbishop stomped on his back, smashing him into the concrete.

"Bravo!" the Boss cheered, clapping enthusiastically.

☠☠☠

"You! You did this!" the Archbishop snarled at the Boss, grinding his red booted heel into the small of the Boiler child's back.

"Yep, I did," the Boss replied casually. "Get over it."

The Archbishop stomped on the boy and the child cried out. "Take this to my quarters!"

Rancher guards grabbed the boy by the ankles and dragged him away. He reached out for June, but a blow to the head stopped all protestations.

"I'll feed you your balls for that," June raged.

"She will too," the Boss laughed. "So, are me and the princess gonna fight or what?"

☠☠☠

The Archbishop seemed to calm slightly at the suggestion of combat. "Yes, a fight." The Archbishop raised a hand and his Page stepped forth instantly. "My chair. My blanket and refreshments."

The Page bowed silently, dashing away. The Archbishop waved at June and Rancher guards pulled her roughly to her feet. "Strip her."

"What? You sick little freak!" June cried as her soiled and dirty clothes were cut away. She stood before the Archbishop, her black and blue body shaking with anger.

"Now we're talking," the Boss leered.

The Archbishop eyed the Boss lasciviously. "Him too."

"What?" the Boss barked.

🕱🕱🕱

"We're ready for the tactical briefing," Rachel said, stepping into the transport and up to Capreze and Jethro. She gasped at the image on the vid screen. "Shit, is that June?'

"Yeah," Jethro responded solemnly.

"Jeezus, makes me wish I'd been a little nicer to her," Rachel said.

"You can apologize when she's safely out of there," Capreze responded. "Any progress, Jethro?'

"Gonna try right now, sir," Jethro answered. "I hope she sees Two move and not the Ranchers. Otherwise we may have to forego subtlety and just start blasting."

"Do you even know the definition of subtlety?" Rachel joked.

🕱🕱🕱

The Boss stood in the middle of the mech hangar, bare-assed and fuming. He glared at the Archbishop. "You gettin' an eyeful, you fucking dress wearing pussy?"

Several Ranchers started forward, but the Archbishop held up his hand. "Leave the cannibal be. He can take his frustrations out on the mech woman."

The Page returned, dragging a high backed gilded chair, a gold plated cooler and a red blanket. "Here you are, Your Holiness," the Page puffed.

The Archbishop sat down and twirled his hands, indicating the Ranchers should form a circle with June and the Boss in the center.

🕱🕱🕱

Jethro made Two's right fingers drum against the side of its metal body. He watched June carefully, but it was obvious she didn't notice. He tried again and a couple of the ranchers closest to the mini-mech turned about, but quickly returned their attention to the fight about to start.

"Shit," Jethro muttered.

"Tap louder," Rachel said.

"Why not just walk Two over there and tap on her shoulder?" Jethro mocked.

Rachel grinned. "Why not?"

Jethro turned to get Capreze's reaction, but the Commander wasn't there. Rachel's grin widened. "He's outside talking."

Jethro slouched in defeat. "What are you thinking?"

♀♀♀

"Jay? Jay, come in," Rachel crackled over the com.

"Whatcha need, Rache?" Jay responded.

"What's your current location?"

Jay checked his readings. "Somewhere in Sector 48-5F. We're still hours away from you guys."

"Yeah, but you're not far from the base, though, are you?"

"Well, with a couple of track switches we'd be at the base in about an hour. It'll tack on more time getting to you. I thought the base was occupied? What are you thinking?"

"June's at the base being held by the Ranchers. Think you could swing by and pick her up?"

"Love to," Jay responded.

♀♀♀

"Diverting the cavalry?" Capreze asked, overhearing Rachel as he stepped back into the transport. "I'm pretty sure that is a call for the CO to make."

"You were busy," Rachel responded. "Plus, we have Mathew on his way. He'll get here first."

Jethro quickly turned back to his tablets as Capreze looked away from his daughter.

"What?" Rachel asked. "What aren't you telling me?"

"About Mathew," Capreze said. "He's heading straight for the UDC stronghold."

"What?!?" Rachel cried. "Why?!?"

"In case things go south here, we need someone to try and shut them down. And he has the best shot."

♀♀♀

June and the Boss stood staring at each other. The Archbishop looked from one to the other then clapped his hands together. "Well... fight!"

"Yeah, I ain't feeling it," the Boss said. "Maybe you and bruised titties here should duke it out while I watch."

The Archbishop snapped his fingers and two Ranchers stepped forward, rifles aimed at the Boss's crotch. "Fight or you lose your manhood," the Archbishop snapped.

The Boss lifted his hands. "Hold on, no need to threaten the Little Boss." He turned to June. "Guess they want a show."

"Guess we'll give them one," she responded.

"They have agreed, Your Grace," Deacon Montoya stated.

The Bishop turned his attention away from the vid feed of the mech hangar, muting the connection. "Have they? Delightful. See, Montoya, what did I tell you? Everyone has their price."

"Yes, Your Grace was right, as always," the Deacon agreed. The Bishop waved away the flattery as Montoya continued. "They will have their people in place momentarily. Shall we have them wait for our arrival?'

"Dearest me, no, Deacon! Cripple those mechie heathens now," Bishop Wyble ordered. "Let them take the casualties, not us.

"Of course, Your Grace," Deacon Montoya responded.

"I apologize, Your Holiness, but I have to step away. Business at hand," the Bishop said over the vid feed.

"Of course, Bishop Wyble. Do as you must. It is your honor and duty," the Archbishop said, his attention on June and the Boss as they circled each other, looking for a tactical advantage.

"Thank you, Your Holiness," the Bishop said, bowing his head slightly. "I shall not fail His Glory."

"Yes, yes, Bishop. Send them all to Hell and the honor of becoming a True Disciple will surely be bestowed upon you," the Archbishop praised automatically, dismissing the Bishop.

Mastelo stood next to Capreze as half of the Skinner council approached.

"Good morning to you all," Mastelo greeted them. "I did not expect you to join us."

The councilors looked to each other and then at Mastelo. "A decision has been made, Mastelo. It is not in our people's best interest to ally with the mech outcasts," an older woman stated. "You will return with us and remain in seclusion so as not to impede what has to be done."

Mastelo's jaw dropped. "This must be a mistake. Has the entire council agreed to this?"

"Most," the woman answered.

Harlow glanced down from her cockpit at the conversation below. She watched as two council members split away and approached the Skinner fighters. The fighters' body language instantly changed as the councilors spoke to them. The new body language was something Harlow could read very well. Aggression.

Several of the Skinners glanced in her direction and then at Bisby, who was still on the ground double checking his mech's hydraulics.

Harlow tapped her com. "Hey, Biz?"

"Yeah?"

"Carefully take a look around. I don't think the friendlies are so friendly anymore."

Harlow reached behind her and withdrew two long blades.

☠☠☠

Out of the corner of his eye Capreze watched Bisby undo the strap on his sidearm indicating the pilot was well aware of the situation. Without drawing attention, the Commander glanced towards Harlow's mech, seeing her descend quickly, her blades strapped to her back. Capreze loved his people.

"Councilors," Capreze soothed. "Before anything gets out of hand, let's sit down and discuss this."

A shorter man took a step forward. "I am sorry, Commander. But the discussion has ended. You and your people are on the losing side. We cannot afford to be on that side also. I *am* sorry."

☠☠☠

Several Skinner fighters moved to encircle Bisby, their long knives drawn. The mech pilot cracked his knuckles and grinned. "I don't know what's going on boys, but don't do anything you may regret." He felt lucky right now that the carbines were laid out and disassembled for cleaning. He could dodge blades easier than he could dodge bullets.

"It is not personal, Pilot," one of the fighters said. "We mean you no dishonor, but our futures are no longer joined with yours."

"Oh, I can fucking guarantee that your futures are about to be way different than mine," Bisby sneered.

☠☠☠

"I'm all set!" Jethro shouted. "Let the Commander know we can start fucking shit up!"

Rachel slapped the mechanic on the shoulder. "Great job, Jethro." She stepped to the transport door and froze. "Fuck. This doesn't look good."

Themopolous, trying to make sense of the nanotech data she had, looked up from her tablet. "What's wrong?"

Rachel reached out and grabbed an auto-shotgun, placing the butt against her hip as she drew her sidearm. "Start the transport, Jethro," she ordered. "If you have to, get yourself and the Doc out of here."

Jethro looked at the external vid feeds. "Shit."

☠☠☠

Rachel walked down the transport ramp, her eyes on her father and Mastelo. She could tell by Capreze's hand gestures that he was trying to calm things down, but the stance of the Skinners told her it wasn't working.

And then, in the blink of an eye, a skinner councilor moved and Mastelo fell, the hilt of a knife sticking from his throat. Capreze ducked and rolled as two blades whizzed by him. Rachel brought up her shotgun and started firing, dropping three Skinners.

"Fucking go!" she yelled back at Jethro as she dove to the ground her shotgun barking.

☠☠☠

The Boss landed a powerful right hook against June's cheek, knocking her head back, making her stumble. "Remember the pit, bitch?" he said, dancing to the side, sizing up the damage he had wrought. "I grew up in that fucking hole. You may be UDC trained, but I'm pit fight tested."

He lashed out with two quick kicks, connecting with June's mid-section. The pilot doubled over and tried to catch her breath. Her diaphragm refused to obey and she thought she'd pass out from lack of air.

The Boss grabbed her by the hair, slamming his knee into her face.

☠☠☠

Harlow didn't run, she didn't hurry, she didn't speak. She just casually pulled her long blades from her back, taking one in each hand and walked towards the onrushing Skinners.

Four came at her immediately once they were within range and four Skinners fell, missing limbs and heads. The others stopped dead in their tracks.

Harlow stayed silent and waited. The Skinners eyed her nervously, looking from her blades to their fallen comrades and back. The mech pilot could smell their fear, see the uncertainty in their eyes. They had her outnumbered, but she had them out-skilled by a longshot.

☠☠☠

June, choking on the blood pouring into her sinuses, coughed and spat. The Boss jumped back away from the red spray. "Hey now, don't go wasting the good stuff."

Shifting his weight to his right side, the Boss lashed out with his left foot, connecting with June's face, sending her sprawling across the hangar floor. He looked away from the fallen pilot and at the Archbishop. "This'll be over soon then the two of us should talk. I think we got off on the wrong foot." The Boss returned his attention to June. "Just give me a minute to finish."

☠☠☠

Bisby put two bullets in the heads of each Skinner that charged him. He didn't bother to reload his pistol when the 18 cartridges were spent, he just flipped it around, the grip now a club.

Eight Skinners stepped over the nine bodies on the ground, each no longer taking the mech pilot for granted. One drew his arm back and threw his knife, aiming for Bisby's head. With equal agility, Bisby snatched the blade out of the air, expertly grabbing the hilt.

"You think I haven't practiced that move, you dumb fucks?!?" he sneered, now with blade in hand.

☠☠☠

Jethro had the transport ramp and door secured before the hostiles could get in. He heard them pounding on the outside, their bloodthirsty calls making him shiver. But, that had to wait as he glanced at the vid screen connected to mini-mech Two.

"Ahh, shit," he cursed, seeing June take a beating from the Boss. "Fuck!"

Themopolous looked out one of the transport's portholes and gasped. "We have to do something!"

"Yeah, Doc, I know!" Jethro exclaimed. "June's in trouble too, so get your ass over here and help!"

Themopolous glanced at Jethro. "What do you need me to do?"

☠☠☠

e Boss waited for June to catch her breath and get to her feet.

"Kill her!" the Archbishop screeched in his cracking, teenage voice. "Kill her now!"

"Where's the sport in that?" the Boss asked. "I thought you wanted a show."

June hocked a gob of bloody mucous onto the floor between the Boss's feet. "Fuck you, Boiler. You won't take me."

"Dear, dear Rachel, haven't you learned? I'm in charge. Whether in a fight or a nice sit down family dinner, I'm in charge." He feigned a left jab and June fell for it, never seeing the right connect.

☠☠☠

Slash. Hand. Slash. Arm. Slash. Head. Thrust. Intestines.

Harlow moved with practiced efficiency, her blades leaving dismembered corpses in her wake.

She ducked easily under and around the knives flying at her and laughed. "You keep throwing away your weapons. Not really the smartest tactic."

One Skinner had managed to get to the carbines and reassemble one. He brought the gun to his shoulder, but the long blade that pierced his brain prevented him from taking aim. Harlow ran and rolled to the corpse, retrieving her weapon. "See! I took mine back."

The Skinners now gave her a wide berth.

☠☠☠

"We're just going to leave them out there?" Themopolous cried.

"Yes!" Jethro answered. "They're big kids and can take care of themselves. I need to focus on the base. You need to focus on Two."

"What?!? I don't know how to operate a mini-mech!"

Jethro grabbed the Doctor's hands and placed one on the joystick, the other on the weapons console. "Left, right, forward, back. RPGs, 50mm, flame. Don't hit the capped red button."

"Why?"

"It makes everything go boom at once. We don't want to do that yet."

"Yet?!?" she exclaimed.

"Yeah, yet," Jethro responded. "Now, here's the mic."

☠☠☠

"Um, ahem, attention mech base. Please put down all weapons and surrender immediately," Themopolous's voice boomed from Two's loudspeaker. "This is your only warning."

The Boss, about to deliver the killing blow to June, stopped and looked around. "What the fuck, Archie? Your people playing some joke?"

The Archbishop stood, enraged. "Who dares interrupt? I will have your guts on a spit and force feed them to you!"

The Boss laughed. "Now you're talkin'!"

Two took a step forward and all eyes fell on the mini-mech. Through swollen eyes, June watched Two raise its guns and she covered her head.

☠☠☠

The Boss looked from June to the mini-mech and back again. He didn't waste a second and dropped to the floor just as Themopolous let loose with Two's 50mms. The gunfire was deafening and the screams of the Ranchers could barely be heard over the percussions, as there bodies were ripped to shreds.

The Archbishop dove behind his chair, but the gaudy piece of furniture was no match for the large caliber slugs. His body shook and writhed as round after round pierced him. He lay twitching as his blood pooled with the other Ranchers' blood upon the hangar floor.

☠☠☠

The sound of gunfire echoed down the mech base's halls and into the control room.

"Get me a visual on the hangar now!" Reverend Heath yelled.

"I can't, sir," a Rancher tech responded. "I'm locked out!"

"What?!?" the Reverend exclaimed, shoving the tech out of the way. "Move!"

Heath typed at the tablet, cursing. "By the True Disciple! I won't let this system be hijacked!"

"Should I check the hangar, sir?" the tech asked.

"If you want to be filled with lead, then be my guest. Those gunshots aren't from our Believers."

"But, the Archbishop?"

"He's in God's hands now."

☠☠☠

"Someone's got fast fingers," Jethro said, fighting to keep control of the mech base's systems. "Mine are faster. How's our girl doing?"

Jethro kept typing, but when Themopolous didn't respond he risked a glance her way. The doctor sat stunned, her eyes dazed and brimming with tears.

"Doc? You with me?" Jethro asked concerned.

Themopolous turned her head slowly to look at Jethro. "I killed them, Jethro. I killed them all."

"Good job, Doc. Now pull it together. Can you see June?"

Themopolous returned to her attention to Two's vid feed. "She's moving."

"Good. Kill anything that comes at her."

The Boss listened for movement in the silence, but only heard the low moans of the Rancher wounded. Satisfied, he sat up glancing around at the destruction. "Whoowee! Now that was something!" He whistled appreciatively, but the whistle was quickly turned into a cry of pain. Agony erupted from his crotch as June's hand clamped down.

"My turn," June croaked, squeezing as hard as she could.

The Boss screamed shrilly and, despite his tolerance, passed out from the pain as one of his testicles burst in his scrotum.

June got to her feet and spit on the now unconscious Boiler.

"You're very talented." Reverend Heath heard Jethro's voice boom over the loudspeaker in the control room. "But, you're in my house, bitch."

"Go to Hell," the Reverend cried out.

"Hey, that's my line," Jethro laughed. "Bye bye now."

Reverend Heath watched in horror as all vid screens went blank and the room's door started to shut. He leapt to his feet, but was a second too late as he heard the door latch securely.

Air started to pump from the vents. Hot air.

"It's about to get very uncomfortable, especially when the temp in there hits over 200," Jethro taunted.

Ranchers across the base watched, confused as they were systematically sealed into whatever room they were unlucky enough to be in at the moment. Jethro remotely cranked the heat in each room, sending the Ranchers to a slow, painful demise.

He brought up the hangar's vid feed. "Hey there Juney girl."

He watched June turn about. "Jethro?"

"Yep," Jethro answered. "Listen, I'm setting the base's self-destruct. The barracks are clear. Get yourself geared up and get outside. There's a Railer train heading your way in minutes. Jay, Masters and the Rookie are with it. Get the Hell out of there."

Capreze hadn't been in combat in years and he was thankful for regular training and workouts as his muscle memory took over. He had his pistol out before he came out of the roll and had dropped two Skinners by the time he was on his feet and running for cover. He wasn't Bisby or Harlow, dodging and catching knives wasn't really an option at his age.

He flipped a camp table over in time to hear the thunk-thunk of two knives embedding themselves in the plastic.

"Get out of here!" Capreze yelled into his com.

"No doin'!" Jethro responded.

�☤☤

June slammed the stray Rancher into the wall, crushing his nose instantly. She snapped his neck before he had time to cry out.

"How many more are out and about?" she yelled, knowing Jethro was listening.

"Three more, but other side of the base," Jethro responded isolating the loudspeaker in the barracks as she burst through the door.

She kicked open her locker and grabbed a uniform, yanking it on over her battered body. Dashing to Bisby's bunk she tossed the pillow aside, grabbing up the 9mm he had stashed underneath. She checked that the clip was full and left.

☤☤☤

"Jethro, you need to check the vid feeds and find the boy!" she yelled running down the hall.

"Boy? Did you not hear me when I said the train would be there in minutes? Screw the boy! Get the fuck out of there!" Jethro responded.

June came to a halt in the middle of the hall and turned angrily to the nearest vid camera. "Jethro, so help me God, if you don't find him I will personally make sure you shit in a bag the rest of your life!"

There was silence for a moment. "Capreze's quarters," Jethro said finally.

☤☤☤

"We've got to get to the mechs!" Rachel yelled, joining her father behind the camp table, pumping shells into the shotgun. "If more show up we're fucked!"

"I know!" Capreze said, firing six shots around the side of the table. Four found their mark and more Skinners fell. "But those assholes know that also and are blocking our way."

Rachel stood suddenly, blasting away with the shotgun until it was empty then dove over the table. She came up swinging the shotgun like a club and beat Skinner after Skinner as she dashed to her mech.

Capreze grinned with pride.

"MOTHER FUCKERS!!!" Bisby shouted, taking his rage out on the nearest Skinner, nearly sending his fist completely through the man's skull. He shoved the corpse to the ground and whirled in time to block a kick aimed for his face. He grabbed the attacker by the leg and brought his elbow down on the man's knee, shattering it.

He felt the first blade nick his side and another embed in his thigh. Then a pain greater than anything filled his head and he realized his left arm was no longer there.

Clutching at his stump of a shoulder, Bisby fell.

Harlow and Rachel saw Bisby fall at the same time.

"I've got him!" Harlow yelled. "Get in your mech!"

Rachel nodded, ducking under a knife swipe, coming up, burying the empty shotgun into the soft underside of the Skinner's chin, jamming the barrel up through the roof of the man's mouth and into his brain. She shouldered him aside and leapt onto her mech's leg, clawing hand over hand until she was in her cockpit.

She didn't bother to strap in, immediately setting to work powering up the machine and readying weapons.

"You're all going to die!" she cried out.

Capreze's office was like a bake oven as June rushed inside and lifted the boy into her arms. He was burning up and limp, but still breathing.

"How much time do I have?" June yelled.

"None! You need to be on the platform now! One of the mechs will grab you up!" Jethro responded. He happened to glance at the hangar vid feed and blanched. "Oh, fuck..."

"What?" June asked, running down the hall. "Jethro? What's wrong?"

Jethro watched the undead UDC troops rise and the Rancher corpses become what they worshipped in life: zombies.

"Control tower! Now!" Jethro ordered.

❧❧❧

"Well ain't that a sight for sore eyes," Jay exclaimed as the mech base came into sight.

"No shit, my man," Masters agreed. "I wish we could stop for a shower and a shave, but duty calls! Smashing duty!"

"Hey Masters!" Jethro interrupted. "Can your mech reach the top of the control tower?"

"My fucking mech can see into the fucking control tower. Why?"

"Change of plans. June's coming out that way."

"Huh? Why not out the… front… door…" Masters trailed off as UDC troops emerged from the smashed front of the hangar and began to load into transports. "Oh."

❧❧❧

One, two, three, four, five.

The Skinners fell under Harlow's blades, the steel slicing through flesh and bone like soft butter.

To the casual observer, Harlow's face would have looked blank, almost calm, but inside a homicidal fire burned brighter and brighter as she fought her way to Bisby, seeing her friend's life pulsing from what used to be his left arm.

Six, seven, eight, nine, ten.

They continued to fall. Without realizing it, Harlow began hacking the left arms off of everyone in her way, her subconscious finding an outlet to keep her centered, to keep her from breaking.

❧❧❧

June felt her legs beginning to give as she took the control tower steps two at a time. She was amazed her body hadn't given out yet, after the days of abuse it had suffered.

The sound of boots hitting the steps below echoed up the stairwell.

"Jethro! Talk to me!" she called out.

"About a dozen fully armed UDC troops are on your ass!" the mechanic responded.

"Troops? Didn't their Reaper chips fry their brains when they went down in the hangar?!?"

"Right, you've been outta the loop. Yeah, their brains regenerate now. Sorry."

"Are you fucking shitting me?!?"

Harlow heard Rachel's mech open fire as she gutted and decapitated the last two Skinners in her way.

Dropping her long blades, she knelt and ripped the sleeves from her uniform, using the material to apply pressure to Bisby's wound.

"Hey there, pretty lady," Bisby whispered through ashen lips. "I think I cut myself shaving."

Harlow grinned despite the tears streaming down her face. "Shut up, idiot. Save your strength."

"You know, I'm sorry," Bisby continued weakly.

"For what?"

"For busting your balls all these years. I was just jealous you're a better warrior."

"Shhhh," she said choking back sobs.

"Great time to try the new sonic disc!" Jay hollered over the com.

The Rookie watched the UDC transports swing about and head straight for the mechs and Railer train. "Yeah, kinda agree with you there." The Rookie turned to Marin. "Is it powered up?"

"Ready to go, but it takes a minute or two between pulses so make the first one count."

As the transports rolled into range, the Rookie held his breath and engaged the disc.

A high pitched whine sounded then everyone in the train felt a pressure behind their eyes and like that, it was over.

The Boss felt hands grab him and he came to immediately, wasteland instinct overriding the sickening pain in his crotch.

Without looking or thinking he lashed out, knocking the hands away. The resulting hiss and growl told his foggy brain what he was up against.

He pushed himself to his feet and came face to face with the Archbishop. The fourteen year old boy snarled and bared fangs hungry for the Boss's flesh.

The Boss kicked out, knocking the robed zombie away, but he instantly wished he hadn't as the pain from his crushed testicle brought him to his knees.

June made it to the top of the old control tower and set the boy down. She grabbed up a chair and threw it with all of her strength against the windows. It bounced harmlessly off, clattering to the floor.

"Shit!" June yelled. "Jethro! The windows are blast proof! We're fucking stuck!"

"Umm, okay, I didn't think of that," Jethro responded. "Sorry."

"Sorry? I will skull fuck you with your goddamn sorry!"

"Whoa, whoa, whoa! Calm down! There's roof access in the utility closet behind you," Jethro said.

June picked the boy up again, straining considerably under the child's weight.

☠☠☠

The Boss watched helplessly, incapacitated by pain, as the last UDC troops streamed from the hangar and he was left alone with the undead Ranchers.

"Bring it, fuckers," he grunted.

The Archbishop and the others began to lunge, but froze almost immediately as a high pitched whining filled the air. The Boss felt the beginnings of a headache and then it was gone and each of the Rancher zombies fell to their knees. The Boss barely had time to cover his head with his arms as the zombies' heads exploded, spraying the hangar with grey-red goo and bits of bone.

☠☠☠

"Fuck!" Jay shouted. "It didn't work on the UDC troops!"

"What the hell are you talking about, Rind?" Marin asked. "The transports have stopped and the ground troopers are down."

"But their heads should have exploded," Jay insisted. "The nanotech must have altered their brains just enough so the frequency incapacitates them, but doesn't make 'em go pop."

"So fucking what?" Masters joined in. "Down is fucking down."

Masters/Stomper began to crush the transports under their feet then stepped past, grinding the exposed troops into the dirt. "See?"

"Yeah, I guess," Jay sulked. "But I wanted the heads to pop."

☠☠☠

June collapsed upon the control tower roof, the boy draped across her, clinging to her. "Holy fucking shit," she gasped. "I can't move another muscle."

"Well, you better, 'cause her comes the cavalry!" Master shouted. The tower shook with each massive footstep Stomper took.

June's eyes went wide at the site of the Hill Stomper reaching a giant fist up to the roof. The boy shook with fear and June held him close. "Don't worry, baby, the good guys are here."

It took all her strength but she managed to carry the boy over and climb aboard the offered hand.

Jay kept his eyes on the UDC deaders that Masters hadn't crushed. Some were already beginning to stir.

"Fuck," Jay swore. "Minutes. It only gives us minutes."

"It's fucking better than nothing," the Rookie said. "If we can slow them down long enough to blast them to Hell then I call it a win."

Jay shook his head, eyeing the now upright troops. He aimed his plasma cannon and fired, obliterating the deaders in a blast of fiery red. "Yeah, I guess."

"Oh, come on Rind, you old grouch!" Marin scolded. "Stop being such a perfectionist. The fucking disc works!"

"Jethro! Open the ramp now goddamit!" Themopolous shouted. "Bisby's down!"

"What?!?" Jethro turned his attention from the mech base feeds and slammed his hand on the ramp controls.

Grabbing her med kit, the Doctor sprinted from the transport and was at Bisby's side immediately.

"Hey Doc," Bisby whispered. "I think I cut myself shaving."

"You already used that one, Biz," Harlow soothed, her pleading eyes meeting Themopolous'.

"Yeah, but… it's pretty… fucking funny," Bisby stuttered weakly.

"It is, Biz. It is," Themopolous played along, pulling the make shift bandages away. Blood squirted from the open wound, making the Doctor wince.

Rachel systematically went from Skinner to Skinner and stomped them into pulp. The corpses she couldn't get to, the ones too close to the transport or the mech personnel, were finished off by the Commander as he put two bullets in each of their skulls.

"I think we got them all, Baby Girl," Capreze said over the com. "Stay up there though in case there's another wave. Don't forget we have thousands of these fuckers below us."

"You think they'll attack?' Rachel asked concerned.

"No," Capreze responded. "Not all of them, but some might try it."

"They do, they die," Rachel promised.

💀💀💀

"We're about clear," Jenny said, checking her readings as the Railer train shot past the mech base. "Blow that shit up!"

"Do we really need to? "Jethro asked over the com. "The troops and Ranchers are all dead, right?"

"Do it, Jethro," Jay ordered. "There are too many resources that can be used against us here if more UDC show up."

Jethro sighed and typed in the final command. "Alright, you've got sixty seconds to make sure you are out of the blast radius."

"We'll be safe in 30," Jenny responded. "Jethro, right?"

"Um, yeah."

"Good work with the tech."

💀💀💀

"T MINUS 55 SECONDS UNTIL DETONATION," the automated voice boomed over every single loudspeaker in the base. "Please clear the area immediately."

The Boss felt the piss trickle between his legs as he dragged himself to an ATV. He grabbed onto the door and pulled himself upright, screaming at the pain between his thighs. It took all of his will to get himself in the ATV and seated.

"T MINUS 50 SECONDS UNTIL DETONATION."

"I fucking heard you!" The Boss roared pressing the ATV's ignition button. He put the vehicle in gear and swung it about towards the hangar entrance.

💀💀💀

"I have lost contact with the mech base, Your Grace," Deacon Montoya stated reluctantly. "There is no response to my hail."

"Can you bring up the vid feed?" the Bishop asked, trying not to worry.

"I will try, Your Grace," Montoya responded, working frantically at his control panel. "Here. It's hard to make out though."

Bishop Wyble concentrated on the blurry image, quickly realizing that the vid screen and camera must have toppled over in the mech base hangar.

"Enhance that picture," the Bishop ordered. The image closed in on a headless corpse dressed in ornate robes.

The Bishop gasped.

💀💀💀

"T MINUS 10 SECONDS," the voice echoed from the hangar as the Boss pushed the ATV to full throttle, desperately trying to put as much distance between himself and the impending destruction.

He ticked off the seconds in his head and when he reached 1, he closed his eyes, gripped the steering wheel and prayed for the first time in his life.

There was a blinding flash and the landscape about him went white. He never heard himself shrieking as the resulting heat blast lifted the ATV into the air and flung it like a toy out into the wasteland.

💀💀💀

The mechs and Railer train shuddered, but stayed steady as the shock wave from the explosion reached them.

Those that could, watched from the train's windows, shielding their eyes against the near blinding flash.

"Anybody want to say a few words?" Masters asked. "I mean that *was* our home."

The com stayed silent.

"Then I will," Masters continued. "Thank you mech base for providing us with beds, showers, tables, closets, the control tower during a full moon…"

Jenny looked at the Rookie. "What the Hell is he going on about?"

"All the places he and Harlow fucked," the Rookie grinned.

💀💀💀

"It was my fault, Doc," Bisby said quietly.

"What was, Biz?" the Doctor asked, suturing like mad.

"Stanislaw's death. It was my fault. He… He thought I was the deader," Bisby coughed and Themopolous swore as several of the minute stitches she had been working on tore.

"Shit! You have to stay still and quiet," she pleaded.

"He shot himself," Bisby continued. "Because of me. I just needed… everyone to know that… before… before I die."

"Shut the fuck up, Bisby! I won't let you die!" Themopolous looked at Harlow. "Get me a blow torch. We're getting back to basics."

CHAPTER TEN

PART ONE - MECHS, MEET RANCHERS. RANCHERS, MEET MECHS.

"Sensors are going crazy," Mathew said. "What's going on, Shiner?"

"We are picking up all of the movement in the wasteland," Shiner responded.

"All of those readings are deaders? UDC and citizen zombies?" Mathew asked. "I can't believe I just said 'citizen zombies'."

"Yes, all of the dead walk now, converging on the UDC stronghold. They have been called."

"I am so going to put my boot in the Outsider's ass when I get there," Mathew growled.

"If we can separate, that is," Shiner said.

"Yeah, yeah, don't remind me. The smell in this cockpit is reminder enough," Mathew complained.

☠☠☠

Bishop Wyble held his head in his hands, his shoulders shaking. Deacon Montoya looked over his shoulder, concerned.

"Bishop? Your Grace, are you okay?" the Deacon asked.

Wyble looked up, tears streaming down his cheeks, but a huge grin on his face. He was laughing, almost uncontrollably. "Oh, Deacon! I've never been more okay in my life!" The Bishop wiped his eyes, getting himself under control. "You know what this means, don't you Montoya?"

"Um, no, Your Grace, I do not," Montoya responded, honestly confused and worried.

"It means no more bowing to that pubescent pervert! I am now Archbishop!"

☠☠☠

"How're the stealth systems holding out?" Mathew asked Shiner, still not quite understanding the modifications that Shiner had made to make the mech invisible to sensors.

"100% capacity, "Shiner answered. "We will be able to arrive at the stronghold undetected as long as we stay off the relay net."

"Then let's stay off," Mathew said.

"I am uncertain of what we shall accomplish once we are there. We cannot disengage from each other and we will be spotted visually if we get too close."

"Yeah, well, we'll figure that out once we get there," Mathew responded. "There's always a solution."

💀💀💀

"Are we almost there, Montoya?" Wyble asked standing directly behind the Deacon, staring out into the wasteland. "I am in the mood to celebrate my ascension with a nice military victory."

"Sensors show the mech heathens just over the ridge, Your Grace... I mean, Your Holiness," the Deacon answered.

Archbishop Wyble clapped his hands with joy. "Oh, Montoya, it's like God's music to my ears! Archbishop! Praise the True Disciple for smiling upon me!" The Archbishop clapped Montoya on the shoulder then returned to his seat. "Now, what about reinforcements?"

"The UDC and Disciple army are close behind, Your Holiness."

💀💀💀

"Um, hey guys?" Jenny said, her brow furrowed. "Are these readings right?"

Marin leaned over and looked at the vid screen. "Shit, there must be a hundred thousand of them or more! What the fuck?!?"

"Fucking deader army, just like the one from Foggy Bottom," Masters answered over the com. "They must be from the closest city/state."

"Yeah, well, they're heading right for our people," Jay said, joining in the conversation. "I know our folks are good, but they aren't 'kill a hundred thousand' good."

"Then I guess we need to hurry," Marin said, pushing the train's throttle to full.

💀💀💀

Jethro turned from his console and watched as Harlow, Capreze and Themopolous carried Bisby into the transport. "Jeezus, is he going to be alright?"

"I don't know," Themopolous answered, yanking down a bunk from the transport wall. "I cauterized the wound, but he lost a lot of blood." Capreze and Harlow carefully placed Bisby in the bunk. The mech pilot groaned, sweat beading about his face. Themopolous pulled a chair close, opened her med kit and started to roll up her sleeve.

"Whatcha doin', Doc?" Harlow asked.

"I'm the only one with his blood type," she answered, swabbing her arm.

☗☗☗

The transports came to a stop at the top of the ridge.

"Why haven't they spotted us?" Archbishop Wyble asked.

"The geothermal vents below the surface are interfering with the sensors, Your Holiness," Deacon Montoya responded. "It's given us the element of surprise."

"Good, Deacon, as it appears our new allies failed in destroying the pilots and their mechs," Wyble said, placing binocs to his eyes and focusing on the Skinner corpses. "But, then no one would expect savages to be very effective." He lowered the binocs. "We, however, are not savages. Take us down there, Montoya."

"Yes, Your Holiness."

☗☗☗

Jethro turned away as Themopolous inserted the wide gauge needle into her vein. She set a container at her feet and let her blood fill it.

"Damn, Doc. That's a bedside manner," Jethro joked, trying to fight back nausea.

Harlow looked from Bisby's ashen face to Commander Capreze's sour expression. "What's the plan, Commander? We're down a mech pilot and without our allies. Still wanting to make a stand?"

Before the Commander could answer, Jethro gasped. "Holy Fuck! We've got company!" He turned to the others. "Rancher transports! Five minutes out!"

"Guess that answers that," Capreze said, stepping past Harlow.

☗☗☗

"Yo, Jethro!" Jay called over the com.

"Yeah, Boss?" Jethro responded.

"Looks like you have quite a few hostiles heading your way!"

"Yeah, we just picked them up," Jethro responded. "I'm losing my touch. I should have adjusted better for the geothermal interference."

"What the fuck are you talking about, boy? These aren't anywhere near you."

"Huh? What are *you* talking about?"

"The deader army and UDC transports coming right at you. We're going to over take them and try my new toy on a bigger scale, but you folks should think about moving."

"Oh, that's fucking great," Jethro grumbled.

Capreze climbed the leg of Bisby's mech, quickly reaching the cockpit.

"Um, what the hell are you doing?" Harlow yelled up at the Commander, having followed him from the transport.

"Getting ready for battle," he answered nonchalantly. "We were down a mech pilot. We aren't anymore."

Harlow tapped her com. "Hey, Rache? You wanna talk some sense into your father?"

Rachel laughed. "You kidding? He's already in the fucking mech! You honestly think he can be talked out?"

Bisby's mech took two steps back and then stumbled slightly forward. "Sorry," Capreze apologized. "It's been a while."

"Fucking classic," Harlow muttered.

"Um, Commander?"

"Not now, Jethro, I really need to concentrate on getting my mech legs back," the Commander said.

"Yeah, well, Jay just commed. We've got a deader army not far behind the Ranchers, sir."

"Shit," Capreze swore. "How many?"

"At least 100,000, sir."

Capreze powered up his weapons while watching Harlow settle into her cockpit. He turned his attention on Rachel, seeing his daughter bouncing her mech from one foot to the other in anticipation of the coming battle. "Get out of here, Jethro. We'll hold off the Ranchers, you just get Themopolous and Bisby a safe distance away."

"Are the Disciples ready for glory, Montoya?" Archbishop Wyble asked, strapping body armor on over his robes.

"Yes, Your Holiness. All transports have reported they are ready to release their Disciples on your order."

"Wonderful. Tell them to anoint the damned mechs at their discretion."

"Yes, Your Holiness," the Deacon said. "I have transferred our weapons control to your seat, Your Holiness. I assumed you would want to experience the glory of this battle first hand."

"Delightful assumption, Montoya! You know me so well!" Having secured his body armor, the Archbishop returned to his seat and activated the weapons systems.

☠☠☠

"Doc? I'm gonna have to ask you to strap in," Jethro said as he readied the transport for evac. "We're bailin'."

"What about the others? If they get wounded, they'll need me," the Doctor said, securing the blood dripping into Bisby's arm.

"If they get wounded then it's already too late," Jethro responded. "It's about to get very hairy around here and a non-combat doctor, one armed mech pilot and wheelchair bound mechanic are just going to get in the way. Trust me, Doc, we need to put some distance between us and the shit that's about to go down."

☠☠☠

Timson stepped into the engine control room. "I've got my best medic checking on your pilot and the Boiler boy," he said to the Rookie. "They're each dehydrated and pretty banged up, but should be fine."

"Good to hear," the Rookie responded. "They're both lucky to be alive."

"Um, aren't we pushing it a little hard?" Timson asked, noticing the throttle position. "What's the hurry?"

"About 20 minutes from the tale end of a deader army," Marin answered. "We're gonna test the disc's full capabilities."

"Are the tracks clear?" Timson asked, alarmed. "Because at this speed it'll suck to crash."

☠☠☠

"Let's go say hello," Capreze said over the com. "No need to wait here." With that he piloted his mech into a dead run towards the Rancher transports.

"Right there with you, Papa Bear," Rachel called. "Let's send these wasteland fucknuts to the Glory they so desperately want!"

Harlow shook her head and piloted her mech after them, weapons system at full. "This is just great," she said.

"What's that?" Rachel asked.

"Now I have two fucking Caprezes to look after!"

The Commander's mech stumbled again, toppling and rolling to a stop. "Sorry!" Capreze shouted. "I've got this."

Harlow sighed.

🕱🕱🕱

"All transports full stop!" the Archbishop commanded as he watched Capreze's mech fall. "What are they playing at, Montoya?"

"I'm not sure, Your Holiness," the Deacon answered. "It may be some sort of diversionary tactic. Could there be more mechs about? Maybe they have other allies we are not aware of. It is hard to say with the sensor interference."

The Archbishop thought for a moment. "Send out three transports. Let's see if they have a trap ready to spring."

"Yes, Your Holiness," Montoya said, sending the orders. The three closest transports sped out towards the mechs ready for battle.

🕱🕱🕱

"We've got incoming!" Harlow yelled. "Get your ass off the ground, sir!"

Capreze stood his mech upright and took a moment to center himself. He slowly flexed his fingers then made a fist with each mech hand. He tried a couple of practice jabs followed by a right upper cut. "Okay, I still got it."

Four RPGs flew past his cockpit towards the onrushing transports

"Them's some good moves, Papa Bear, but there's an easier way than the old one-two," Rachel said, trying not to laugh.

The transports initiated counter measures, taking out the RPGs.

"You were saying?" Capreze mocked.

🕱🕱🕱

"Well done, Montoya, well done," Archbishop Wyble commended the Deacon. "Please pass that on to the other transports."

"Yes, Your Holiness," Montoya responded. "How shall we retaliate?"

"Hmmm… I believe they haven't seen *our* plasma guns. Let's show them, shall we?"

"Wise choice, Your Holiness," the Deacon said. "I'll coordinate the others."

Montoya activated his com and sent instructions to each of the other transport drivers. He tapped at his console and readied the guns. "Just awaiting your orders, Your Holiness."

The Archbishop stared out the windshield at the charging mechs. "Teach them about power, Deacon."

"With pleasure," Montoya grinned.

☠☠☠

"What the fuck are those?" Harlow called over the com as four small cannons per transport became active. "They look like little plasma cannons."

The cannons began to fire rapidly, sending small bolts of plasma at the mechs.

"Shit! They *are* plasma cannons!" Harlow yelled, tucking her mech into an evasive roll.

She positioned her transition from roll to leap so that she landed her mech directly in front of one of the transports, bringing her left foot down on the front, smashing the driver and anyone in the transport's cockpit into a pulp. She ground down for good measure.

☠☠☠

Two plasma bolts found their mark, knocking Capreze's mech onto its back. The Commander shook his head and assessed the damage. "Damn! That was exhilarating!" Confident all systems were go, Capreze kicked back upright, ducking and dodging more blasts as he charged the closest transport.

Reaching the transport, Capreze lashed out, swiping two of the plasma cannons from the transport's side. He threw a right hook, punching a hole in the armor plating. Instantly zombies streamed from the transport's hold and clambered up his mech's arm.

"Ahhh! They're like ants! Get 'em off!"

Capreze heard Rachel laughing over the com.

☠☠☠

Wyble growled. "They are not impressed, Montoya." The Archbishop stood and grabbed the com. "All transports! Anoint the battlefield. Loose the Disciples upon the heathens! I want chaos! I want anarchy! We will have victory over these mech devils or I will personally make sure every last one of you knows the shame and damnation of a head shot! You will never attain the Glory of becoming a Disciple!"

Wyble threw the com handset towards Montoya, forcing the Deacon to duck.

"Oh, quit your flinching! That threat includes you, Montoya! You had better start acting like one of God's warriors!"

☠☠☠

"Holy fuck! Where do they keep all that shit?" Rachel shouted as the

Rancher transports sprayed gallon upon gallon of blood and offal at the mechs and upon the wasteland ground. "I mean Jeezus, that's just wrong!"

"Don't let it get on you! It's like a fucking deader magnet!" Harlow warned.

"Yeah, too late for that!" Capreze responded, still plucking zombies from his mech. He threw them back at the transports, their rotten bodies exploding against the metal, adding more gore to the scene.

At once all transports dropped their rear ramps and dozens of zombies poured forth from each.

☠☠☠

Jethro hit the throttle and the transport shot forward, away from the action. "How's Biz doin' back there, Doc?"

"His color is improving. He needs another pint, but I don't think I have it in me," Themopolous responded.

"Yeah, don't kill yourself," Jethro said, watching the rear vid feeds as the mechs engaged the Ranchers. "I do need you to do me a favor though."

"What's that, Jethro?"

"Four is still out in the waste. Now that I don't need it to be my relay, we could really use the back up. I need you to bring it to us."

☠☠☠

"We're approaching the deaders," Jenny announced, her eyes on the scanner. "ETA Five minutes."

"Alright. Masters?" Marin called.

"Yeah. Whatcha need?" Masters responded.

"When we hit the button, every zombie in our way will go down. We've got a laser cowcatcher in front that can handle the bodies. I need you to make sure there aren't any transports on the tracks. Otherwise we are fucked."

"No problem," Masters said.

"What the hell is a cow?" the Rookie asked. The others stared at him blankly. "Boiler, remember? Education wasn't a priority."

"The cow goes mooo, kid," Masters jibed over the com.

☠☠☠

"How do you not know what a cow is?" Jay asked double checking the sonic disc's systems.

"Fuck you Rind!" the Rookie responded over the com. "I've heard of them, but no one has ever explained what they are."

"You've never seen a picture?" Jay asked, enjoying the ribbing the Rookie was getting. "Not even when you were in Foggy Bottom?"

"I was more concerned with the fight cage than flipping through fucking picture books," the Rookie said annoyed. "Have *you* ever seen one?"

"Of course not! They've been extinct for hundreds of years. But I know what one is!"

☂☂☂

"They are in sight!" Jenny shouted.

"Stay calm. Just keep your eye on the controls," Timson said. "Jay, everything ready?"

"Yep, just wait for my mark," Jay responded.

"Gotcha," the Rookie said.

"I'm out front and ready to clear some tracks," Masters joined in.

"We've been spotted. Several transports are turning about," Jenny announced.

"Don't worry, we're almost there," Marin said.

An alarm sounded and Jenny gasped. "They're locking missiles!"

"Jay? We're kinda pushing it here!" Timson said urgently.

"Just hold on! Wait for it… Wait… NOW!" Jay ordered.

The Rookie activated the disc and they all felt the pressure.

☂☂☂

From his vantage point high above, Masters watched in astonishment as the sonic blast spread out and the deaders fell.

"Hot damn!" he crowed. "I'm shooting you the vid feed. Check that out. I hope that cow catcher works, because the tracks are now littered with downed deaders."

"Oh, it works," Marin responded. "You just take care of the transports."

In two easy strides, Masters/Stomper was at the first transport. The mech lifted the vehicle easily and tossed it out of the way, far into the wasteland.

"Is this like playing with toys?" Stomper asked.

"Hell yeah!" Masters responded enthusiastically.

☂☂☂

"So what am I doing?" Themopolous asked, sitting down at the minimech controls.

"Really? Not a whole lot." Jethro said. "Just watch the vid feed and make sure he doesn't get into any trouble."

"He?" Themopolous asked with a smile.

"He. It. Whatever. I'm a mechanic. I anthropomorphize my toothbrush!"

"So, what kind of trouble am I looking for?"

"Mainly dead mechs, Ranchers or other UDC. If you see that then I need to take *it* out of auto-drive and put *it* into battle mode."

"It can fight on its own?"

"Not well, it's really just a prelude to self-destruct."

"Holy shit! I missed this!" Capreze hollered. "I forgot about the power!" He slammed his fist into another transport and opened fire with his plasma cannon, cooking everything inside, living and undead, to a crisp. "Fuck yeah!"

"Careful there, Mr. Cocky," Rachel warned. "Watch your backside. You've got two transports coming around at you."

Capreze lifted the scorched transport before him, spun and tossed the burning husk at the attacking transports. Both of the vehicles expertly swerved out of the way and accelerated. Capreze's eyes widened as six missiles launched and rocketed towards him.

"Um, a little help," he pleaded.

"Dammit Papa Bear!" Rachel cursed, trying to crush, burn and blast as many zombies as possible. "Get your shit together!"

Capreze closed his eyes, centering his thoughts.

"Papa Bear? You There?" Rachel called, concern tingeing her voice.

"Yeah, Baby Girl. Just getting my shit together," the Commander answered. "Remembering my place."

Capreze glanced at his weapons systems and grinned. "Did I ever tell you I was the best fucking shot in the wasteland when I was your age?"

"Not sure this is the time for stories of the Old Days," Rachel responded.

"How about I *show* you then?" Capreze smiled.

"Transfer weapons control to my seat, Deacon! Do it now!" Archbishop Wyble ordered. "I grow tired of these heathens!"

"I have, Your Holiness," Montoya responded.

"Of course you did, Montoya," Wyble said, settling himself and bringing up the transport's weapons control system. "Now, let's wreak glorious vengeance upon these devils."

The Archbishop activated missile targeting. He centered his crosshairs upon Harlow, took careful aim and fired.

"Hallelujah!" he cried, watching the projectile speed towards its target.

"And God said, 'Let There Be Death!'"

"He did, Your Holiness?" Montoya asked, confused.

"I'm the Archbishop! God says whatever I say he says!"

☠☠☠

Proximity claxons blared in Harlow's cockpit. "FUCK!" she yelled, watching the Archbishop's missile rocket towards her. She kicked a handful of zombies at the missile, hoping to knock it off course, but they bounced off the metal shell without any effect. "Shit!"

Looking for the closet transport, she pushed her mech as fast as she could, hoping that timing would be on her side. Plasma bursts impacted her mech's exoskeleton adding new warning sounds to her cockpit's already cacophonous alarms. The smell of scorched metal told her she took more damage than she liked, but she pushed past it, determined.

☠☠☠

"Um, Your Holiness?" Deacon Montoya warned. "The trajectory of the missile…"

"Hush, Montoya! I am trying to savor the moment!" the Archbishop barked.

"But, sir, the transport…" But, Montoya couldn't finish as Wyble leapt to his feet and smacked the Deacon upside the head, knocking the man's head back, making him lose control of the transport for a moment.

"SIR?!? I AM THE ARCHBISHOP!" Wyble screamed directly into Montoya's ear. "You will address me as such at all times!"

The Deacon slowly reached up and rubbed his face, keeping his eyes averted. "My apologies, Your Holiness. The heat of battle."

☠☠☠

Harlow leapt over the Rancher transport. She could hear her hydraulics groan as she executed an aerial spin, twisting her mech about, opening fire on the incoming missile with her 50mms. For a split second she thought she missed and was more alarmed at that mistake than of being blown to pieces. But, all thoughts of ego left her as the missile exploded when the large caliber rounds found their mark.

She tucked her mech's legs and rolled as she hit the ground on the other side of the transport, letting the Rancher vehicle shield her from the missile's detonation.

☠☠☠

The Archbishop fumed as he watched Harlow manage to both avoid and detonate the missile he had fired. "That metal heathen will pay," he hissed.

"Your Holiness? We have four transports destroyed and two crippled," Deacon Montoya reported reluctantly, expecting more of the Archbishop's anger to be taken out on him.

"What about our reinforcements?" the Archbishop asked angrily. "When can we expect them?"

"Soon, Your Holiness, but they have been delayed."

"Delayed? Why in Heaven's name would they be delayed?"

"More mechs, Your Holiness. And Railers," Montoya responded.

"Railers? RAILERS?!? Train trash is holding up my glory?!?" Wyble roared.

☠☠☠

"Goddammit! They're already up!" Jay yelled. "That was sixty seconds shorter this time! Sixty fucking seconds!"

"Whoa, calm down, Jay," Masters said. "They went down and that's what matters. So the sonic frequency doesn't blow their heads off. It does give us an advantage, though, right?"

"Not if they're adapting!" Jay responded angrily. "Sixty seconds! And these are different deaders! That means that their tech is adjusting, communicating, changing the physiology of their brains across the board. We'll be lucky to have three or four more uses before the disc is useless."

"I'd rather have three than none," Masters said.

☠☠☠

"Can they catch up?" Timson asked, watching the view of the deader army fade as the Railer train continued on.

"No, not at their pace," Marin answered. "They seem to only have one marching speed."

"Well, that's good," Timson said. "What's our ETA on the other mechs?"

"Not sure," Jenny responded. "Readings are all over the place. We're picking up some type of geothermal interference below us. Playing havoc with the scanners."

"The first letter in ETA is estimate," Timson snapped. "Just give me something."

"Soon. How's that for an estimate?" Jenny snapped back.

"That works just fine," Timson replied.

Capreze watched as four of the RPGs he launched at the attacking missiles hit home. Metal and plastic rained down, littering the ground with smoldering debris.

"That's how that's done!" he cheered, but he cut the celebration short as his sensors still picked up two incoming missiles.

The moment the first one appeared he took it out with a perfectly timed plasma blast. Unfortunately it meant he didn't have time to fire on the next missile, so he instinctively lashed out, punching the missile and changing its course, sending it directly into a Rancher transport.

"And that's how that's done!"

"Three more transports lost, Your Holiness!" Deacon Montoya announced.

"And the Disciples? Are they not Holy enough to overpower the mechs?" the Archbishop asked enraged. "Does God not shine down upon us today or has the Devil himself ascended from Hell to aid these metal worshipping infidels?!?"

"The Disciples have been destroyed, Your Holiness. I am sorry, but the mech pilots are trained for this. We are not."

"Coward! Defeatist!" Wyble raged slamming his fist down again and again. "I will have your tongue-"

But Montoya never heard the rest as several 50mm slugs pierced the windshield and his body.

Harlow cursed as her 50mms overheated, grinding to a halt. She stared out her cockpit at the transport she had just fired upon and readied plasma charges.

Something inside the transport caught her eye and she took a moment to focus her vid on the driver before she tossed some hot death its way.

"Son of a bitch," she muttered as she watched Archbishop Wyble yank the corpse of Deacon Montoya out of the seat and take it himself. He glared up at the mech, his lips moving and his face read with anger.

"Oh, you are mine," Harlow sneered.

Archbishop Wyble spat and screamed curses at the looming mech until his voice was hoarse. "You will not have the privilege of my demise!" he shouted while taking the transports controls. He whipped the ungainly vehicle about and sped away from the mech.

"I am the Archbishop," he continued. "I am the incarnation of the Father, the Son and the True Disciple upon this plane of existence! I will not be murdered by heathens! God will grant me the Glory to avenge his name! To war again another day!"

He launched all missiles and fired all aft cannons at Harlow.

☗☗☗

Harlow moved like the wind. A 50-ton, infuriated wind.

"FUCK YOU!" she bellowed, ducking past missiles and dodging cannon fire. She fired the last of her RPGs behind her, hoping they'd act as decoys for the missiles' tracking. A cannon shell impacted in front of her and her mech shuddered, but she refused to slow, pushing through the concussion as she pursued the Archbishop's transport.

"Uh-uh! You're not getting away today mother fucker!"

She pumped her legs to their limits and quickly gained ground on the transport as she flexed her giant metal fists, ready to crush some Rancher ass.

☗☗☗

The Archbishop slammed his hands against the transport's controls. "Move! Faster you hunk of evil!"

He glanced at his rear vid feed showing the pursuing mech. His instruments indicated he was out of ammunition. He grabbed the com in frustration. "Who is still aboard?"

"Um, just Quakenbush and myself, Your Holiness," a tinny voice responded. "We already released the Disciples. The hold is empty."

"And who are you?" the Archbishop demanded.

"Sweeten, Your Holiness."

"Well Sweeten, are you and Quakenbush ready for your honor and duty?"

"Um, yes, Your Holiness," Sweeten responded weakly.

"Excellent. Open the rear ramp," Wyble commanded.

☗☗☗

"What the hell?" Harlow said aloud as the transport's rear ramp opened and two Ranchers stumbled down it, rolling to a stop on the ground as the transport never slowed.

Harlow's first intention was to stomp the ranchers into the ground, but the reflection of metal made her zoom in on the two men. She was glad she did as the vid revealed dozens of fractal grenades strapped to their bodies.

The two men stared at her approaching mech, their mouths moving in silent prayer. As she neared, they both pulled the pins out of as many grenades they could.

☠☠☠

Quakenbush's eyes widened as the mech leapt. He would never know the mech's fate as his was sealed by the detonation of all 31 grenades secured to his trembling body.

Harlow knew her timing would be close, so when the suicide Ranchers went off, she braced herself. Instantly her world flipped about, head over heels as the force of the concussions tossed her mech end over end.

She landed on her knees, stumbled to her feet and grinned murderously, knowing she had been lucky. Her legs' hydraulics protested though as she continued her pursuit.

"I said not today, mother fucker!"

☠☠☠

"Where the fuck is she going?" Capreze yelled, watching the distance grow as Harlow continued her pursuit.

Rachel sprang into the air, coming down feet first onto an oncoming transport, crushing the cargo area, nearly splitting the thing in two. She sent thousands of 50mm rounds inside to finish off whoever lived through the impact.

"Have you tried her com?" she asked, kicking the smoking wreckage away.

"Gee, didn't think of that," Capreze quipped. "Of course I did! She isn't answering.

"It may have been damaged. Want me to go after her?"

"No. Stay here and clean up," Capreze responded.

☠☠☠

Archbishop Wyble lashed out at the vid screen, his fist fracturing the screen and distorting the image of Harlow's still pursuing mech. He looked about him, desperate to figure out some way to attack. Seeing nothing, he contemplated Martyrdom, but those thoughts were shoved aside as a proximity alarm echoed around him. Unfamiliar with the controls he scanned the panels, trying to find the source, but movement directly in the transport's path made the search unnecessary.

Maybe a quarter mile off, heading straight for him, was another mech. And Wyble could tell this one was a Demon, a dead mech.

"Oh, you got to be shitting me!" Harlow swore, seeing the incoming deader. She wasn't sure what angered her more: the fact that she now had a deader to deal with or the fact that the dead mech might reach Wyble first and kill the son of a bitch before she could.

"Hey guys?" she called over the com. "We've got company. Something a little bigger and deadlier than those pussy ass Ranchers."

She was answered by static.

"Um, guys?" Nothing. "Fuck! I'm going to kick Jethro's ass for not building a better com system. This shit never fucking works!"

Jethro monitored the chatter between Capreze and Rachel.

"Everyone okay?" Themopolous asked.

"Yeah, sounds like Harlow's com's out, though. I'm sure I'll hear about that," he responded. "How's our little guy doing?"

"Four is managing the terrain just fine," Themopolous said. "Can I step away and check Bisby?"

"You bet, Doc."

Themopolous got up from the mini-mech controls and walked back to Bisby's unconscious form. The transport lurched suddenly and she almost toppled onto the wounded mech pilot. "Jeezus, Jethro! Careful-" She stopped immediately when she turned to berate the mechanic. Jethro's body was slumped over the control panel. "Jethro?"

Harlow barreled down on the Archbishop's transport. She was surprised he hadn't altered his course away from the dead mech, but then, if he was smart, he'd turn away at the last second, letting the deader get as close to her as possible, knowing the thing would change it's focus and come at her.

A few more yards and Harlow was proven correct as the transport swerved, leaving nothing but open space between the two behemoths.

Harlow tried to launch her plasma charges, but nothing happened. Her console told her the grenade blasts had shorted all weapons.

"Shit," she cursed.

💀💀💀

"Jethro? Jethro!" the Doctor screamed, rushing to the collapsed mechanic's side. "Oh, dear God."

She carefully lifted his head off the control console and gasped. Blood was dripping from his nose and both ears. "Jethro? Can you hear me?"

"I don't feel too good," he whispered. "I smell fruit. Is that good?"

"No, Jethro, that's not good," she answered.

Themopolous helped Jethro out of his wheelchair and onto the floor of the transport. She checked his pulse and pupil dilation, happy with neither result. A shudder made her fall back and she quickly realized no one was driving the transport.

💀💀💀

"Looks like you and I are gonna have to duke this out," Harlow said aloud, watching the dead mech charge. She stopped and planted her feet, arms up and ready.

The dead mech roared and Harlow shivered at the inhuman sound coming from the deader's loudspeaker.

Ten steps, six, four and Harlow spun, letting the dead mech fly by. She planted a roundhouse kick directly into the deader's back, sending the machine sprawling. The impact shook her mech, but she didn't hesitate, springing into action.

She brought her fist down, but only hit dirt as the dead mech rolled away.

💀💀💀

Themopolous took the drivers seat and stared helplessly at the transport's controls. "Jethro, I don't know what to do," she cried.

"Eat the butterflies. They taste like rocks and axle grease. Rich in healthy vitamins," Jethro said, deliriously.

She tapped the com. "Hello? Commander? Rachel? Anyone? Help! Jethro's down and I don't know how to drive this fucking thing!"

"Doctor? This is Capreze. What's your situation?"

Themopolous glanced out the windshield and nearly pissed herself. "Oh, God! I think I'm heading straight for a canyon! Please help!"

"Okay! Stay calm! Do you see the control stick?"

"Yes!"

"Good! Grab it!"

Capreze watched Rachel take on the last Rancher transport. "You got this, Baby Girl?!?"

"Yeah, Papa Bear! You help them!"

"Okay. Doctor? You with me?"

"Yes, Commander," Themopolous responded over the com.

"Okay, I want you to yank back on the control stick. This will slow you down."

"Okay. We're slowing, but not much."

"Now you are going to need to hit the emergency braking system. Whatever you do, do not turn the transport once you hit the brakes or you'll flip the thing."

"Gotcha! Where are the brakes?"

"E brake is the large black and yellow button. Hit it."

Themopolous slammed her palm on the emergency brake button and the transport groaned and protested as all wheels locked up at once. She watched in horror as the edge of the canyon got closer and closer with every passing second. She closed her eyes and screamed.

She felt a bump and a lurch then stillness.

"Doctor? Doc! Answer me!" Capreze yelled over the com.

Calming herself down, she opened one then both eyes. All she could see was empty space leading to the other side of the canyon. She checked her vid feeds and then she really did pee herself.

The deader kicked out, connecting with Harlow's left knee, knocking her mech to the ground. Warnings blared and she saw her already weakened hydraulics system red line.

"Fuck!" she swore, but had no time for anything else as the dead mech lashed out with its other leg, slamming its giant foot into Harlow's mid-section. Her mech toppled back and nearly every alarm the mech had went off.

"Oh no…" Her face turned white. The plasma charges she had tried to launch earlier were now armed and ready. But, the deployment hatches were not opening. She pounded at the controls desperately.

"Doctor! You're on my scope and I'm heading your way," Capreze called.

"That's a very good thing, Commander, because while the transport did stop, I don't think all of it is on the ground," Themopolous responded. "Please hurry."

"I'm just a few minutes off. Hold tight."

Themopolous chuckled nervously. "Not a problem." She gripped her seat with all her strength, her knuckles cracking from the strain. The transport wobbled up and down slightly as an updraft from the canyon caught the front end hanging over the edge.

"I hate the wasteland," Themopolous whispered.

"I like cheese," Jethro whispered in return.

☠☠☠

Harlow brought her arm up and blocked the dead mech's attack. She could see the zombie pilot inside its cockpit and the thing looked well fed. "Fucking great, it's a natural killer."

Harlow rolled to the side, and kept rolling, trying to put as much space between her and the deader. More alarms added to the cacophony. "Fucking now what?!?" she shouted. Her scanner warned her of a sheer drop off, fifty yards away. She stopped her roll and pushed her mech to its unsteady feet. "That information I can actually use."

She backed towards the drop, setting her trap.

☠☠☠

"Okay, okay, I can do this," Themoplous said over and over as she slowly got up and carefully kneeled next to Jethro, very aware that any extra movement could send the transport plummeting to the canyon floor.

"Hey there Teddy Bear," Jethro said, reaching up to stroke Themopolous' face. "Can I have some candy now?"

The doctor took Jethro's hand in hers and held it tight. "No candy right now, mechanic. Just rest."

Jethro narrowed his eyes menacingly. "No candy? Who ate all the candy? Was it Bisby? Oh, that overgrown monkey!"

"Shhhh, Jethro. Quiet. Save your strength," Themopolous soothed.

☠☠☠

The deader came straight for Harlow. She knew she would need to time her move perfectly or the dead mech would catch on and stop before going over the edge. All alarms ceased except for one: the detonation warning. Her systems were so messed up that the armed plasma charges were about to explode on their own.

"That throws a fucking wrinkle in things," she grunted grabbing her pack, long blades and carbine. Harlow strapped everything on and popped the cockpit, ever aware of the deader only yards away. She tossed a safety line out of the cockpit and repelled.

☠☠☠

Capreze dove for the transport, its front end finally tipping the balance. His mech's metal fingers gripped the transport's shell, crushing the frame slightly. He dug his feet in and leaned back, bringing the vehicle back from the edge. Slowly, mindful he had wounded personnel inside, the Commander backed away from the canyon, bringing all of the transport's wheels on to solid ground.

"You okay in there, Doc?" he asked.

"Yes, Commander, thank you," Themopolous responded. "But, Jethro is in pretty bad shape. I need time to do a full work up on him."

"I can't guarantee that time, Doctor."

☠☠☠

Harlow let go of the safety line, dropping the remaining twenty feet to the ground. Her knees protested and a sharp pain shot up her leg. She got to her feet shakily and knew from experience nothing was broken or sprained and she could walk off the injury. Or run off the injury as the ground shuddered with the dead mech's approach.

She turned to escape, but was tripped up by the slack of safety line pooled upon the ground. "Nononononononononononononono!" she yelled, trying desperately to free her tangled feet as the deader hit her mech at a full run.

☠☠☠

"Rachel, I want you on me. We need to stay together," Capreze ordered over the com.

"Hold on! I think I have a reading on Harlow's mech," Rachel responded. "What the fuck?"

"What? What did you find?" Capreze asked.

"She's gone. One second there, now she's not. It almost looked like a second mech was with her, but I didn't have time to assess the readings fully."

Capreze thought for a moment. "Go find her, Baby Girl."

"I'm on it, Papa Bear."

Rachel turned her mech and ran towards the coordinates of the last reading hoping she'd find Harlow alive.

☠☠☠

Harlow reached for her knife, but it was too late as the slack line became taught and she was dragged unbelievably fast towards the cliff edge. She clawed at the dirt, trying to find purchase, but her fingers only came away with loose bits of rock and several bent finger nails. She screamed aloud as her right leg popped loose from its hip socket and a new agony overtook her.

Within seconds, though, the pain left her mind and she found herself in empty space, falling towards the two mechs that had just impacted on the ground far below her.

☠☠☠

"What are we looking at, Doc? Is Jethro going to make it?" Capreze asked, keeping watch in his mech.

"I think he'll live, but his brain is deteriorating fast. It has to be damage from the reaper chip attack. I can keep him stable, but unless I get him hooked up to some real medical equipment, I'm afraid he's going to quickly become a vegetable," Themopolous responded.

"How long?" Capeze asked.

"My best guess? And it's just that, a guess. Maybe a day."

Capreze sighed. "Do what you can to make him comfortable."

"I'm already ahead of you on that."

☠☠☠

Harlow's body shook uncontrollably, racked with pain. She hung, upside down, her dislocated leg still tangled in the safety line, which was in turn caught on a rock outcropping above her. Below her, maybe 100 feet, she could see smoke and fire billowing from the wreckage of the mechs.

She gritted her teeth and tried to focus, to scan her surroundings, but the pain from her leg and the blood rushing to her head made it hard to think.

To her right, she could see a shadow on the cliff wall: a cave.

"This is gonna fucking hurt," she croaked.

☠☠☠

Shrieking, fiery pain pounding at her leg, Harlow swung herself back and forth. It took all of her strength to stay conscious, but she kept on until her body was swinging past the small cave opening. She unsheathed one of her long blades and hoped she had built up enough momentum to get her into the cave.

She counted three then slashed at the safety line. For a moment she felt the relief of freedom as she was airborne. But, the relief vanished as only half her body fell into the cave, the other half dangling 100 feet above ground.

☻☻☻

Harlow tried to center her breathing as she kicked her left leg up over the lip of the cave mouth. Her right leg, useless and hanging like dead weight, bumped the cliff wall and she gasped.

Harlow focused on the pain, turning it about, using it to drive her on. "I'm no fucking waster piece of shit! I'm a Goddamn mech pilot! I eat pain, I shit pain, I fuck pain!"

She gripped the cave lip with her left thigh and pushed, lifting her enough to reach out and grasp a handhold on the cave wall, and pulled herself inside.

☻☻☻

"Holy God," Rachel muttered, as her mech stood at the edge of the drop, looking at the two demolished mechs below. "Harlow! Harlow! Can you hear me?" she bellowed over her loudspeaker.

No sooner had the words left her mouth than the plasma charges detonated, sending a flaming ball of metal and debris hundreds of feet in the air.

Rachel leapt her mech back as fiery bits of shrapnel roared up the cliff face right at her. She stood there, stunned, not wanting to believe what she had just witnessed.

"Hey Papa Bear? I found Harlow's mech. It's not good."

Part Two - Sorrow & Harlow

"Holy shit! Will you look at the carnage!" Masters said, surveying the scorched and smoldering battlefield as the giant mech walked away from the Railer train towards the other mechs and the transport. "You doing okay, Rache?"

"Yeah, Mitch, I'm fine," she answered quietly.

"What's up? Where's my hottie?"

"Let's talk, Pilot Masters," the Commander interrupted.

"Pilot Masters? What'd I do now? I thought bringing the cavalry would keep me out of hot water," Masters said, gesturing towards Jay's mech and the train a half mile back, sitting idle on the tracks. "Are you still mad about that insubordination thing?"

�

Capreze opened his cockpit, unstrapped and began to descend. "I need you out of your mech, Masters."

"Will someone tell me what the fuck is going on?" Masters said irritated. "Where the fuck is Harlow?"

"We'll talk about that on the ground, Pilot," Capreze insisted. "Exit your cockpit now. That's an order."

Masters took a closer look at the destruction about him. He didn't see signs of Harlow's mech.

"There is smoke coming out of a canyon on our left," Stomper observed. Without a word, Masters/Stomper turned and clomped towards it.

"Pilot Masters! I gave you an order!" Capreze yelled.

✣ça

"I'm sorry, Mitch," Rachel said, walking her mech towards Masters as he loomed over the canyon, staring at the still burning wreckage below. "We lost communications with her. None of us even knew she was in trouble."

"What do the scanners say?" he asked calmly.

"Too much interference," Rachel answered. "I'm so sorry, Mitch."

"She is correct," Stomper said. "I have tried also."

"So she's dead because her com went down, huh?" Masters inquired menacingly, turning his back on the canyon and stomping back towards the mech transport. "Where the fuck is Jethro?"

"It's not his fault, Mitch," Rachel called.

✣ça

"JETHRO!" Masters boomed over his loudspeaker. "GET YOUR WORTHLESS ASS OUT HERE!"

"Hello Masters, I'm glad you are in one piece," Themopolous said over the com. "If you'll check your vid feed you'll see that Jethro is in no condition to go anywhere."

"Fuck my vid feed! Get that piece of shit out here so I can stomp him to death!"

"Masters," Stomper interrupted. "The mechanic is bleeding from orifices a human should not bleed from."

Masters angrily looked at the screen. He stared for a moment then sighed. "What's wrong with him, Doc?"

"His brain's deteriorating," Themopolous answered gravely.

"It was the Outsider, wasn't it?" Masters asked, barely containing his rage.

"It was the broadcast signal to the Reaper chips that started it," Themopolous asked. "So if this Outsider is in control of-"

Masters/Stomper didn't wait for an answer. The giant mech burst into a run and was nearly a mile away before Capreze could protest. "Pilot Masters get you goddamn ass back here! Pilot Masters!" Only silence.

"He switched his com off," Jay interrupted. "I've been monitoring. And don't bother trying to catch him. That thing can cover some ground." Jay cleared his throat. "Is Jethro really dying?"

"Yes, Jay. Jethro's dying," Themopolous said.

"Yeah, well, we didn't sign up for this gig because of the generous vacation pay," Jay joked weakly. "Let's get you guys on the train so we can get out of here."

"I think we should slow down and think first," Capreze said. "With the base gone we need to regroup."

"Yeah, well, you can think while we move," Jay responded. "'Cause there's a deader army heading this way."

"How many?" the Commander asked.

"More than 100,000 easy," Jay answered. "Hey, by the way Commander, where's Biz? And why were you in his mech?"

"You're sure the Outsider can't detect us?" Mathew asked Shiner as they stood on a low ridge over looking the road leading up to the UDC stronghold. Three layers of fencing separated the road from an enormous mech sized steel door.

"We are invisible to its sensors," Shiner responded. "However, we are not invisible to its vid."

Mathew looked at the 200 yards or so of open ground between them and the stronghold entrance. "No way to really sneak up on them, huh?" he asked.

"Not that I can calculate," Shiner said.

"What are the defenses?"

"Powerful, armed and ready."

"What is it, Lieutenant?" Specialist Sol asked, creeping up next to the unit leader.

Lieutenant Nancy L. Murphy, UDC Special Ops Commander, lowered her binocs and turned to her 2nd in command. "Not sure. I couldn't get a good look at the pilot. Looks like a deader, but it's not acting like one."

"It's not on my scans," Specialist Ngyuen added, joining the other two. "Whatever tech it's using, its custom."

Lieutenant Murphy thought for a moment. "If it's a deader, we can take it. But, if its not, I don't know. We've never taken on a live one before."

☠☠☠

"We are not alone," Shiner stated. "The movement is faint, but there are others around us."

"Live or dead?" Mathew asked assessing the sensors. "Those are weird readings."

"I would say alive. Their movements are erratic, but I believe this is because they are utilizing some type of tech that is designed to confuse our sensors."

"Kinda like our stealth tech?"

"No, not quite. We are invisible to scanners, they are visible, but only if you are looking for anomalies, which I am."

"Doesn't look like many. Maybe 6. We can handle that."

"Yes, but I would rather we didn't."

☠☠☠

Lieutenant Murphy lifted her left hand and twirled her index and middle finger, ending the motion by pointing at Shiner/Mathew.

"Are you sure we want to light it up, sir?" Specialist Sol asked. "The crazy fucker inside'll know we're here."

"It already does, Specialist," Murphy answered. "It has the specs for our armor, it knows how to find us."

"Yeah, but without our Reaper chips it can't get a lock on us, right?"

Murphy sighed and looked to Specialist Nguyen. Nguyen cleared his throat. "It doesn't need to. This close to the entrance we're the flies in the spider's parlor."

☠☠☠

Positioned fifteen yards to the right, concealed by a large rock formation, Specialist Kafar put his RPG launcher to his shoulder. A targeting image superimposed itself on his helmet's visor, showing him distance, wind speed and other information useful to insure the rocket hit its mark.

"Ready," he said quietly. "Target is acquired."

Crouched directly behind him, Specialist Austin slapped him on the back. "You have a go."

Kafar centered the target's crosshairs directly on Shiner/Mathew. "Bye bye, you deader fuck," he whispered, slowly squeezing the trigger.

There was a loud hiss then the rocket shot away from the launcher.

☠☠☠

"We have incoming!" Mathew shouted.

"Yes, if you were paying attention you would have noticed the target lock acquired on us seconds ago," Shiner said.

"Sorry if I'm a bit distracted. I couldn't imagine why my mind isn't multi-tasking right now. Good thing I've got you to look out for me," Mathew said sarcastically.

"I have apologized several times for not allowing you to disconnect," Shiner responded.

"I just want to wash off! I'm sitting in my own filth for fuck's sake!" Mathew shouted.

While still arguing, the mech spun about and discharged its plasma cannon, disintegrating the RPG instantly.

☠☠☠

Specialist Nguyen's jaw dropped at the site of the mech effortlessly defending itself. "Okay, that's no average deader," the Specialist said.

"No, it's not," the Lieutenant agreed.

"Attention mystery guests," Mathew's voice boomed over the loudspeaker. "We've got you on our scanners and have a pretty good idea where you're hiding. How about we cut this shit out and have a quick chat?"

Murphy lifted her hand again and gave the okay sign. There was a pause then the sound of a ricochet as a high caliber rifle round pinged off Shiner/Mathew's cockpit, leaving a small crack in the windshield.

☠☠☠

"Hey! That was just dick!" Mathew yelled. "Hold your fucking fire! We'd rather not have to retaliate." Another bullet hit the windshield in the exact same spot, increasing the size of the crack.

"Ahhh, come on! That's really going to make it hard for me to see. Knock it the fuck off," Mathew said.

"I do not believe they are open to negotiations," Shiner said.

"Yeah, no shit." Mathew thought for a moment. "Hey! Guys with guns! If you're UDC why aren't you dead? You do realize that every single UDC trooper is now a walking, talking deader puppet, right?"

☠☠☠

"Think that's true?" Sol asked. "Do you think Johnson killed everyone?"

Lieutenant Murphy raised her binocs and took look at Mathew. "I don't know. It's possible. Definitely one reason I had us yank our chips out." She watched Mathew for a moment. "What I want to know is why the mech pilot keeps saying 'we'. You got anything, Nguyen?"

"Nope. It's the only thing around us."

"Whatcha thinkin', sir?" Sol asked.

"I'm thinkin' that if we ever plan on getting back into the stronghold we are going to need some help. That mech may just be that help," Murphy answered.

☠☠☠

Shiner/Mathew watched Lieutenant Murphy step from behind her cover, hands raised. "I'm unarmed," she called out.

"That is not true," Shiner said to Mathew.

"Yeah, I see the gun in her belt. Let's give her a chance," Mathew responded. "What the hell is she wearing?"

Shiner/Mathew scanned the Lieutenant's armor. It was full body, black and seamless. She also wore a matte black helmet that covered her entire head, except for the tinted face mask, which was flipped up. Whatever material the armor was made of it continually confused the sensors.

"That's some sweet gear," Mathew said over the loudspeaker.

☠☠☠

"The armor's a prototype. Only myself and my team have them," Lieutenant Murphy said, arms still raised. "That's not a standard mech, is it, Pilot?"

"Nope," Mathew answered. "It's one of a kind."

Murphy and Mathew stared at each other, the Special Ops Commander craning her neck to see up into the cockpit.

"Do you mind coming down out of there so we can have a chat?" Murphy asked.

"I'd love to, but circumstances are keeping me in this cockpit," Mathew answered. "So, any reason you decided to try to blow us up?"

Murphy looked about. "Who is this 'us'?"

"The 'us' would be me and my mech," Mathew said to Murphy.

"I do not appreciate being referred to as 'your' mech. We have a symbiotic relationship," Shiner said, offended.

"Well I wouldn't exactly call this symbiotic since I'm trapped right now," Mathew shot back.

Murphy listened to the two bicker briefly. "You do realize your loudspeaker is active, right?"

"Fucking nice one! You didn't turn off the loudspeaker before talking?" Mathew scolded.

"Technically it is my loudspeaker. I am entitled to its use as much as you are," Shiner responded.

"Um, still active," Lieutenant Murphy said, lowering her hands.

Lieutenant Murphy gave the thumbs up and the rest of her team joined her. They all stood there listening to the mech and its pilot.

"I think they've gone nuts," Specialist Austin whispered.

"I would have to agree," said Sol. "They sound like a coupla old ladies."

"WHATEVER!" Mathew roared. "Just shut up for five seconds and let me get this figured out."

Shiner grew silent, refusing to respond.

"That's better," Mathew said. "So, why aren't you dead?"

Murphy pointed to herself. "Are you talking to me now?"

"Yeah. Who else would I be talking to?"

"Definitely nuts," Austin repeated.

"Any chance you can kneel down so I don't have to destroy my neck looking up at you?" Murphy asked.

"Sure thing," Mathew said, bringing the mech as low as possible. The Special Ops team clambered onto a large boulder which, while not quite eye to eye, brought the conversation to a more even level. "How's that?"

"Fine. To answer your question, we were outside for another series of tests on the armor when all hell broke loose inside. We lost contact with Control. Then Dr. Johnson came on the com and ordered us back for 'inoculations'. We didn't go."

☠☠☠

"Your turn," Murphy said to Mathew. "What the hell are you? Where are the other mechs?"

"Well, to answer the first question: I don't know. Shiner and I are, well, new."

"Shiner?" Specialist Kafar asked. "It has a name?"

"I do," Shiner answered and the whole team took a step back. "Self-identification is part of self-awareness."

"That's just fucked up," Kafar said.

"Try having it in your head 24/7!" Mathew exclaimed.

"And the other mechs?" Murphy pushed on, ignoring Kafar.

"They are on their way, I hope," Mathew said. "They were about to get in the shit with some Ranchers."

☠☠☠

"Ranchers? What do Ranchers have to do with this?" Murphy asked.

"That's why I'm here, to get answers," Mathew answered. "We noticed- by we I mean the other mech pilots and myself- a lot of strange Rancher movement then I spotted them loading up UDC transports with deaders. Next thing we know every city/state has been inoculated, killed and controlled by something called the Outsider. Any clue what the fuck that is?"

Lieutenant Murphy snorted. "That would be Dr. Johnson. He invented the nanotech. I guess the UDC brass took it from him and, um, he didn't handle it well."

☠☠☠

"We aren't sure what happened inside the stronghold, but what we do know is that Johnson is the only living thing in there," Murphy said.

Nguyen cleared his throat. "Before Johnson locked down the system I was able to grab some surveillance." He tapped at his tablet then turned it about for Mathew to see. It was an image of a hangar with dozens of UDC personnel laid out upon the floor. Coming at them was a forklift. Mathew watched in horror as each person stayed perfectly still as the forklift drove over their heads, mashing them to a pulp.

☠☠☠

"Okay, and not to repeat myself, but why aren't you dead?" Mathew asked.

Lieutenant Murphy looked at him puzzled. "I don't understand your meaning."

"When the Reaper chips activated, why didn't yours fry your brains?"

"We pulled them," Murphy answered matter-of-factly. "The second we knew Johnson had taken over, those chips became a liability. We don't deal with liabilities." The other team members grunted their agreement. "And, what did you mean by all the city/states were killed and now controlled?"

"Um, I hate to break this to you, but human civilization is now dead and walking. Walking right to us."

"How much time do we have?" Specialist Sol asked.

"It is a matter of a few hours at most," Shiner responded. "Some dead armies are closer than others."

"Armies?" Lieutenant Murphy asked. "Why would you refer to them as armies?"

"That's what they are," Mathew answered. "The controlled masses of the city/states being led by the controlled UDC troops. And all the transports and armaments that come with those troops."

"Jeezus," Austin muttered.

Murphy activated her com. "Grandetti? On me."

There was a slight shifting of rocks above and behind everyone then a man stood up, sniper rifle in hand.

"If Johnson's the Outsider, then he's connected to the entire wasteland. How's that possible?" Mathew asked.

"The mainframe, of course. It's just like your mechs. Complicated AI run by human integration," Specialist Nguyen answered, looking to the Lieutenant and back at Shiner/Mathew. "It's common knowledge."

"Maybe on the inside, but us out in the waste had no idea," Mathew responded. "Kinda seems like a dangerous concentration of power."

"What, like having one person in charge of several kilotons of weaponry and a 50 ton battle mech without an active Reaper chip?" Murphy laughed. "Yeah, you're right."

"Well put," Mathew agreed.

"So, there's really no getting inside, is there?" Mathew asked.

"Not unless Johnson wants us to," the Lieutenant answered.

Mathew sighed. "Well, let's make him want to."

The mech moved from the Special Ops team and walked down to the main gate.

"Hey Outsider!" Mathew called out. "I think you've been looking for us!"

Loudspeakers crackled to life. "And now you are here," a voice boomed. "As all will be."

"Yeah, yeah," Mathew said. "How about you let us in? I'm sure you'd want to study my mech."

Laughter echoed off the rocks and ridges. "You have nothing for me!"

☠☠☠

"Please can I drop some charges and blow the fuck out of those back-stabbing Skinner bastards?" Rachel asked over the com.

"No, Baby Girl," Capreze responded as the two mechs joined Jay's and flanked the speeding Railer train. "They're about to have 100,000 deaders on top of them. That'll be revenge enough."

"But they're hidden," Rachel insisted.

"Did you dispose of the Skinner or Rancher corpses?" Capreze asked.

"No."

"Neither did I. Once those deaders have the scent, I don't care how controlled they are, they'll dig down looking for more. I don't think the Outsider can override that bloodlust."

☠☠☠

Harlow wedged her right foot between two boulders inside the cave, gritted her teeth and pushed. The pain was unimaginable and she struggled with consciousness. Her strength and willpower nearly gave out just as a loud and painful pop echoed off the cave's walls.

She laid back, glad that the agony of the dislocation was over. She knew she'd hurt for days, but at least mobility was possible.

"Okay, no time to puss out," she muttered to herself and struggled upright. She put a little wait on the leg and winced, sure she had ripped something inside. "I eat pain…"

☠☠☠

"I don't get to meet the Harlow?" Stomper asked, the AI's voice hurt and confused.

"No, Stomper, you don't," Masters stated flatly. "Harlow is no more."

"But the Harlow is your soul?" Stomper persisted.

"And my soul is dead," Masters responded.

Stomper processed a moment. "Then what is the point of our existence?"

"To kill," Masters answered. "To kill the Outsider then to kill every last deader in the wasteland."

Stomper was silent.

"I'm going to need you to dig deep and remember what it was like being a deader," Masters continued. "I need you to give that to me."

�☗

One step, two, three. The pain wasn't too bad, she'd had worse. Harlow took an inventory of her supplies. She had her long blades, her sidearm and her survival pack. She regretted losing the carbine, but knew it would just get in the way when she undertook the inevitable slow climb up the cliff face.

Harlow instantly froze at the sound of a small gasp behind her. She unclasped her sidearm holster and turned slowly.

A little girl of six, maybe seven stood at the back of the cave, holding a handmade doll.

"Shhhh, I won't hurt you," Harlow soothed.

☗3☗

The little girl shook with fear, her eyes nearly popping from her skull.

"It's okay," Harlow said quietly, slowly inching towards the girl. "I'm not going-" Before she could finish the girl let out a blood-curdling scream, turned and dashed through an unseen crack in the cave's back wall.

"Shit!" Harlow cursed, knowing she was about to have a lot of company. She limped to the edge of the cave, leaned out carefully and assessed the cliff face. There were plenty of holds for her to use, but it would be a very long climb on a very sore leg.

☗3☗

By the time she heard voices shouting in the cave, Harlow was already twenty feet above the opening.

"You had better just come down from there, girl," one shouted. "There's no place for you to go."

Harlow ignored the voice and focused on her climbing. She made it another ten feet before the voice called out again. "Stop wasting time and come down. You'll just tire yourself out climbing all the way to the top."

Harlow glanced upward, checking her distance, and saw the many faces peering over the edge at her.

"Goddamn mother fucker," she cursed, out of breath.

�

"I don't want to kill anymore," Stomper said.

"Hey, it's not like we'll be killing people, just those already dead," Masters said.

Stomper processed. "I don't want to be a killer, is what I mean."

Masters tried to ignore what Stomper said, but the two were so fully integrated that he couldn't shove the thought aside.

"You won't have to be a killer," Masters finally said. "I'll do it for both of us. When the time comes you can just withdraw, go back into that place I had to put you before."

"It's dark in there," Stomper said.

Masters groaned.

✧✧✧

Many hands grabbed Harlow when she made it back down to the cave. She was handed roughly from Skinner to Skinner until she reached the crack in the cave wall. More hands reached out, pulling her through and into a stone tunnel.

She didn't struggle, knowing she was outnumbered in unfamiliar territory. However, when a hood made of deader skin was pushed towards her head, she started to thrash, refusing to make the Skinners' lives easy.

"Better kill me now fuckers!" she yelled.

"We have no intention of harming you, Pilot," a woman's voice said. "We plan on using you."

✧✧✧

Harlow was immediately relieved of her long blades and sidearm. She watched silently as her survival pack was ransacked and the supplies distributed amongst the Skinners.

"You don't recognize me, do you?" the woman asked Harlow.

Harlow refused to answer.

The woman stepped closer and the hands restraining Harlow gripped tighter.

"I was with Mastelo when members of the council met with your Commander." The woman waited for a response. Getting none, she continued. "The council had no intention of honoring Mastelo's agreement. We merely wanted to see the strength of your numbers, which, in hind sight, we grossly underestimated."

The councilwoman walked away and Harlow was forced along behind her. "Now, since the Bishop's, or I believe Archbishop now, deal did not turn out as expected, we will need to strike a new deal. We are hoping to use you as leverage."

The group stepped out of the dark tunnel and into a massive cavern. Small holes in the ceiling helped illuminate the space with sunlight, but the main light source was from bright white phosphorescent patches covering the rock walls. Harlow peered about, taking in her surroundings. Skinners of all ages milled about the cavern.

"Impressive, isn't it?"

"You see," the councilwoman kept on. "We are quite capable of self-sufficiency. Our society has flourished the past hundred years. We do not need protection or salvation from the wasteland. We are only looking to establish alliances that will best strengthen our way of life."

"You have a strange sense of diplomacy," Harlow said.

The councilwoman turned and eyed Harlow carefully. "Strange? Hardly. We had a choice between the few," she nodded towards Harlow. "Or the many." She gestured to the wasteland above. "It really wasn't strange at all. Simple math."

Harlow laughed. "You have no idea what's up there."

The councilwoman smiled condescendingly at the mech pilot. "We are fully aware of the shift of power occurring. That is why we already have a delegation above, waiting to speak to the Rancher army marching this way." The councilwoman eyed the holes in the cavern's ceiling. "They should be arriving now."

It was then that Harlow noticed the growing vibrations for the first time. "You think those are Ranchers? You're all fools. The army that's coming can't be negotiated with. You can't deal with the dead."

The councilwoman laughed. "Your attempts at deception are pitiful, pilot. I'd have expected better."

The Skinners all became still and silent as the deader army marched and rolled above, shaking the cavern slightly. Men and women eyed the ceiling warily, the noise of the march reverberating off the glowing walls.

"You need to leave. You need to run. There is nothing but death up there. Trust me, it's my job," Harlow warned.

"Shhhhh!" the councilwoman scolded.

At once the march ceased, an ominous silence thickening the air.

"You see," the councilwoman beamed triumphantly. "You were wrong."

Harlow didn't flinch as the first explosion, then the second brought dust and debris down on the Skinners.

💀💀💀

"You were saying?" Harlow shouted over the terrified screams and yells of the Skinners.

The councilwoman waved her hands about, trying to get everyone's attention. "Quiet! Quiet! I am sure those are just warning shots designed to show us their strength. I am positive no one has been harmed."

"Who'd you blow to get on the council?" Harlow laughed. "You're a fucking idiot if you believe your own bullshit."

The councilwoman glared at Harlow. "I have had enough of your negativity." She waved her hand at the two Skinners holding Harlow. "Secure her until we finish negotiations with the Ranchers."

💀💀💀

"You're all going to die," Harlow said to her Skinner guards. "There isn't a living soul up above right now, nothing but thousands upon thousands of deaders. And I'm sure they are very, very hungry. Marching across the wasteland towards war can work up an appetite."

"Shut it, woman," one of the Skinners barked, yanking on Harlow's arm.

"And you just volunteered to die first," Harlow stated.

"If there's death today, it'll be yours," the Skinner snarled back.

"What about you?" Harlow asked the other guard. "You feel like being eaten alive?"

"I trust the council," the Skinner responded.

"Idiot."

💀💀💀

"They're all dead!" a voice yelled. "Seal the entrance! They're right behind-" But the Skinner never finished as his throat was ripped out.

The guards' hands fell away from Harlow's arms and she immediately planted her elbows into both Skinners' throats. They dropped to their knees and Harlow slammed their heads together, rendering them unconscious. She grabbed her long blades from one of the guards, but didn't see her sidearm. "Shit," she muttered.

Strapping her blades to her back, she turned towards the main cave. Zombies poured into the cavern, falling on anyone unlucky enough to be in their way.

☠☠☠

Screams of agony, screams of terror, pleas for help, pleas for mercy, all echoed within the cavern, but the sounds fell on dead ears.

Harlow scanned the wall of the cavern, finding what she hoped was the tunnel she had been brought through. She dashed for the tunnel, but stopped only feet away as deaders burst from the entrance. Her blades were in her hands without thinking and she went to work.

Hours, days, months, years of training kicked in and Harlow's blades lashed out, perfect extensions of her body. She was a deadly blur of synchronized strength and agility.

☠☠☠

Harlow fought alone.

Claws reached for her, but the hands fell, separated from rotting wrists. Teeth gnashed, searching for her skin, but the heads fell, severed from their shoulders.

Harlow was a graceful, beautiful machine of death. A goddess set upon the earth to do one thing: kick deader ass.

She thrust a blade through a zombie child, yanking up and out, splitting the torso up the middle. Kicking out, she knocked the true corpse to the ground. Seeing another zombie lunge, Harlow knelt quickly, raising both blades above her head, dicing the deader like a cook would a carrot.

☠☠☠

Harlow rolled away, flicking the gore from her blades. She looked down at her uniform and the deader blood on it. The thin cloth, while tough against daily wear and tear, was not going to last against zombie claws.

Feet away, a deader gorged itself on the blood gushing from a Skinner's throat, apparently the weak part of their attire. Harlow strode with purpose to the deader, dispatching attackers as they came at her.

She kicked in the deader's head and pulled the Skinner corpse into a nearby hollow. With a wary eye, Harlow stripped the body of its hide.

350

�☠

Harlow managed to get her legs in the hide before she had to dispatch four zombies. She got her left arm in, dispatched three more zombies, then her right arm and again three more zombies were dispatched. By the time she had the hide secured upon her frame she was nearly concealed behind a stack of deader corpses.

Pulling on the skin hood and gloves, Harlow reached down and scooped a handful of the liquids leaking from the deaders and smeared them onto the Skinner armor. Hoping the camouflage would work, Harlow vaulted the pile, diving headlong into Hell itself.

☠☠☠

Harlow ignored the Skinners she passed, leaving them to suffer the consequences of their selfish choices. Many of the Skinners had been lazy in their assumption of security, so had not donned their skins. Harlow kept her eyes averted as flesh and skin were ripped from screaming victims.

She slashed and killed as needed, but her progress was barley impeded by the deaders as they had so many other targets to choose from to satisfy their bloodlust and hunger. Some zombies that came close became confused by her presence, sensing the life in her. Those that focused too long fell.

☠☠☠

"Please don't kill me!" a man cried, eyeing the body of a Skinner Harlow had just killed. "I can get us out of here!"

Deaders spun at the sound of the human voice and charged. Harlow stepped in front of the man, her blades a whirl of gore smeared steel. "Shut the fuck up and show me! NOW!"

He pointed to a small opening two levels up, close to the ceiling of the cavern. Harlow surveyed the routes, chose one and moved.

"Hey! Wait!" the man called.

Harlow decapitated three zombies before turning on the man. "Shut the fuck up!"

☠☠☠

Burying her blades in the skulls of two zombies, one on her right, the other on her left, Harlow let go of her weapons and focused on the deader coming straight for her, arms reaching, clawing at her.

She grabbed the outstretched limbs and yanked, pulling them from their sockets. The look on the zombie's face was nearly comical, but was gone in a flash as Harlow bludgeoned the deader with its own severed arms.

All happened in a blink and Harlow had dropped the arms and pulled her blades free of the zombie skulls before the deaders could fall.

💀💀💀

The man screamed, calling out, but Harlow didn't bother turning, all of her attention focused on escape. She heard the cries, but compartmentalized them, tucked them away in her psyche. She owed no one.

The attacks grew more frequent and she was positive the deaders were fully aware she wasn't one of them, her rouse beginning to fail.

Mere yards away, Harlow could not contain herself any longer and gave into the blinding berserker rage that had always been her core, that had always been her driving force.

Her mind went red and rationality stepped back.

Death incarnate stepped forward.

💀💀💀

Harlow punched through the wasteland earth with her left arm, her right useless as she had to dislocate her shoulder in order to squeeze through the shaft not meant for human passage.

She kicked her legs and forced her upper half out of the ground. With her right arm pinned underneath her she positioned her body and rolled, popping the shoulder back into place.

She got to her knees and her lips peeled back in a vicious grin. Yards away stood the mech transport.

Now she would only need to annihilate the hundred or so zombies between her and it.

💀💀💀

"I am Death! I am Death! I am Death!" she repeated over and over, her mantra of destruction, a chorus from Hell.

What humanity Harlow had left fell away in a baptism of red, black and grey gore. The only difference between her and the zombie horde that collapsed about her was her beating heart. A heart that slowed to a steady relaxing beat, as if she was merely taking an afternoon stroll.

The words continued flowing from her lips in a steady, unending chant. "I am Death! I am Death! I am Death! I AM DEATH! I AM DEEEEEEEEEAAAAAAAAAATH!"

☠☠☠

Like waking from a trance, Harlow found herself atop a heap of deader bodies, covered from head to toe in undead fluids. Inches from her was the transport's ramp and she dreamily reached out and keyed in the lock code. The second the ramp began to descend she grabbed a hold of the edge, swung her body up and over and slid down into the transport. She immediately stopped the ramp's descent, brining it back into locked position.

Tossing her soiled blades aside, she sat down at the controls as her chest tightened and she fought the encroaching adrenal crash.

CHAPTER ELEVEN

Part One - The First Wave

June put her finger to her lips as the door slid open and Themopolous stepped into the train compartment.

"How's he doing?" Themopolous whispered.

"He's been asleep for an hour now," June responded. "How are Bisby and Jethro?"

"Bisby's stable and I've already prepped the arm for prosthetics. Jethro isn't doing as well," the Doctor sighed.

"Will he make it?"

"Physically, yes, we can keep his body alive indefinitely. His mind, though, probably has 24 hours." Themopolous motioned towards a chair. "But, let's move on to you. Have a seat here and let's get a better look at your injuries."

💀💀💀

"The first wave is here, sir," Specialist Nguyen announced.

"How many?" Lieutenant Murphy asked.

"87,000 on the ground and 14 transports," Nguyen responded.

The Lieutenant looked at her communications Specialist. "Are you fucking shitting me?"

"No, sir, those numbers are shit free," Nguyen said.

"Smart ass," Sol said, looking over Nguyen's shoulder at the tablet.

Murphy activated her com. "Dig in folks. I want concealed defensive positions set up. Who has the charges?"

"I do, sir," Austin replied.

"Good. Get over here. We're going to need to plot out some special placement for those."

"You got it, Lieutenant," Austin said.

💀💀💀

June painfully pulled her shirt over her head. Themopolous nodded at the wrapping and began to unwind the cloth from her midsection.

"Looks like the Railer medics have done a decent job," Themopolous said. "But, I'd like to get a better... Oh, sweet Jeezus, June!" The Doctor looked up into June's eyes. The pilot held her gaze, never flinching as Themopolous carefully probed the deep purple bruises. "Do you want to talk about it?"

"Do *you*?" June asked. "I can go into grisly detail if you want."

Themopolous winced at June's tone. "The ribs are definitely broken."

"Yeah, I know."

🕱🕱🕱

"Um, sir, Johnson is aware of our presence. I don't see how setting up any position is going to be a tactical advantage," Specialist Sol said.

Lieutenant Murphy turned to her 2nd in command. "Would you rather we all just stand here with our dicks in our hands?"

"No, sir, but I'd like to see you try," Sol smirked. Murphy narrowed her eyes and Sol cleared his throat. "I'm just saying that maybe this isn't our stand. Maybe we should just let happen what's going to happen and assess the situation after the dust settles."

Murphy narrowed her eyes further.

🕱🕱🕱

A light knocking on the compartment door brought a welcome distraction from the room's tension. The door slid open and the Rookie peeked his head in. "Sorry to interrupt. Bisby's coming out of it and he's not being very cooperative."

"Okay, we're done. I'll be right there," Themopolous said, handing June her shirt. "Rest if you can."

June didn't respond, her eyes and attention locked on the Rookie. "Who the fuck are you?"

The Rookie was taken aback and looked to Themopolous and back to June. "Um, I'm the Rookie. Remember?"

"June? Are you alright? What's wrong?" Themopolous asked, alarmed.

🕱🕱🕱

"I'm going to explain this one time and one time only," Murphy said, her anger barely contained. "This is our stand. This is our fight. And if it's the last one, so be it." She looked at her unit, assessing each member carefully. "If we run and Johnson wins this shit then we could be some of the only people left alive in the whole fucking world."

She grabbed up her AR-715 auto-carbine and checked the chamber. "And it may not mean much to you gents, but I really don't want to have the only working uterus in the wasteland."

"You should rest," Themopolous said, trying to divert June's attention from the Rookie.

"Who the fuck are you?" June asked again, ignoring the Doctor.

"That's the Rookie, June," Themoplous said.

June gave the Doctor a look of reproach and stood, moving towards the door. "Fuck all that Rookie shit. Where did you come from? You aren't city/state, are you?"

The Rookie snorted. "Did one of the Railers tell you? No, I'm not city/state. I was born in the waste. I'm, was, a Boiler."

June stumbled back and Themopolous reached out to steady her.

"You look just like him," June growled.

"You have less than a .003 percent chance of surviving this day," the Outsider's voice, Johnson's voice, boomed. "Submit now."

"Give up? And miss kicking your ass? I don't think so," Mathew responded. "How about you open up instead and we have a nice face to face."

Johnson laughed, the sound turning into a cackle then snarl. "This door will never open again, for anyone."

"You know I have to try to get in, right?" Mathew asked. "I kinda have a situation on my hands and I really think the solution is behind that twenty feet of iron and steel."

"Can you give us a minute?" the Rookie asked Themopolous. "June and I need to talk."

Themopolous looked to June and the woman nodded. "Okay, I'll be in with Bisby. I'll come back later and check on you again, June. Before we get to, well, wherever we're going."

The Doctor left reluctantly and the Rookie closed the door behind her.

"Who do I look like?" he asked.

"Does the name Olivia mean anything to you?" June watched the Rookie closely. "Or The Boss?"

Anger flashed briefly across the Rookie's face.

June sighed and sat. "Yes, we do need to talk."

Harlow didn't bother dodging the deaders in her path, she just kept a straight heading, throttle at full while she operated the transport's weapons systems. Five of the UDC transports turned about, ready to engage.

"Fuck me," she muttered, knowing she didn't have the capabilities to fend off a full attack.

The screen to her right bleeped shrilly, but Harlow ignored it, busy trying to devise a way out of her latest impossible situation.

The screen bleeped again, louder then again and again.

"What?!?" she shouted then seeing what was on the screen, she smiled. "Well, hello there little guy."

"Charges set, sir," Specialist Austin said over his com. "Good thing the approach to the stronghold was designed to bottle neck. We might have a shot at stopping them. Or at least slowing them down."

"Great Job, Austin," Lieutenant Murphy responded. "Hold tight for my mark."

"Will do," Austin said.

"ETA, Nguyen?" Murphy asked.

"Any minute now, sir," the Specialist answered.

A steady vibration began to make itself felt.

"Or, they could be here now," Nguyen said checking his tablet. "Dead ahead, sir."

Lieutenant Murphy and Specialist Sol lifted their binocs in unison and scanned the approach to the stronghold.

"You now have a less than .0007 chance of survival," Johnson's inhuman voice echoed. "Submission is your only option."

"You see, that's just bad math," Mathew said. "If I have a .0007 chance then submission isn't my only option. I don't think all of your synapses are firing right."

"You cannot comprehend the synaptic complexity of my being!" Johnson yelled.

"That's where you're wrong, Johnson ol' pal," Mathew laughed. "I not only can comprehend, but I'm pretty much living it right now."

"He is attempting a scan," Shiner warned.

"Let him," Mathew responded. "He should know what he's up against."

"You okay, Papa Bear?" Rachel asked over the com.

"Fine," Capreze grunted.

"You sure? Because I need to know your head is in the game," Rachel said.

"Who's the Commander here?" Capreze asked. "Me or you?"

"Well, sounds like it's me right now. Unless you plan on shoving that hurt down deep and getting your ass ready to fight," Rachel replied.

Capreze sighed to himself. "I'm amazed at how well you turned out and frightened at the same time. You are the perfect mech pilot."

"Yeah, well you're the perfect Commander and Father. How about you start acting like it?"

☠☠☠

"Olivia raised me. Pissed the Boss off, a woman raising his son," the Rookie said quietly, seated next June. "He always hated her filling my head with things larger than the next fight."

"How old were you when she helped you escape?" June asked.

"Eleven? Twelve, maybe? I don't know. I never knew my birthday and the doctors at Foggy Bottom could only approximate," the Rookie laughed. "Olivia would be horrified to know I escaped fighting in the pit to end up fighting in a cage."

"Just be thankful you escaped at all," June said looking at the sleeping boy.

☠☠☠

Harlow keyed in the command and waited for acknowledgement. In a matter of seconds, Four pinged back and Harlow smiled. "Now I have a plan," she said aloud.

Her smile quickly faded as warning alarms sounded. "Fuck," she cursed, watching as the UDC transports locked their missiles onto the mech transport. Without stopping to think, Harlow launched all RPGs and the last few missiles preemptively, hoping to throw the other transports' attack off.

She yanked the controls and turned the transport perpendicular with the others and tried to coax more power from the throttle. "Come on you piece of shit!"

☠☠☠

"I feel the mech trying to bypass my security," Johnson boomed. "It will not succeed."

"He may be correct," Shiner said. "There are complexities of code that I am unfamiliar with. It appears that the Outsider has created his own language, reprogramming the UDC mainframe to run only on his commands."

"Which means?" Mathew asked.

"It means that if we destroy Dr. Johnson the mainframe will start to break down within the hour. All stored data, all of your humanity's collected history and information, would be lost. You will be left with only memories."

"Back to square one," Mathew responded.

☠☠☠

Zombies flew up over the front of the mech transport as Harlow plowed through the massive horde. Rotted limbs, putrid torsos and badly decomposed heads smashed into the windshield, obscuring her view, making her rely more on the vid screens than what was right in front of her.

"Come on, little guy, bust ass and get here," she said.

An explosion, then another rocked the transport. Her readings told her all systems were online and functioning, but she knew it was only a matter of time before the missiles hit home.

Gunfire erupted and several more explosions shook the wasteland.

☠☠☠

"I have visual!" Nguyen yelled. "ETA ten minutes before we are swarmed by deaders."

"Okay folks," Lieutenant Murphy shouted. "You have your positions. Dig in and don't stop firing until you are empty. If you can draw a transport close enough to try to overtake then do so. If we can get in one of those fuckers then we stand a helluva lot better chance of survival."

"This is the real shit, huh, sir?" Specialist Kafar asked over the com.

"Yes, Specialist, it is," Murphy answered. "You ready for this?"

"Born ready, sir," Kafar responded.

"We all were," Sol affirmed.

☠☠☠

"You hear them chattering away as if they stand a chance?" Johnson laughed, his semi-human, semi-synthesized voice cackling madly. "Little ants to be stepped on."

"This guy is really starting to bug the shit out of me," Mathew said.

"I agree with the bug shit," Shiner said. "But, I believe I almost have access."

Mathew watched with anticipation, but quickly despaired as a massive plate slid down in front of the stronghold entrance, adding yet another layer of protection against breach.

"Our cerebral integration must be off because I have a distinctly different definition of access," Mathew grumbled to Shiner.

Themopolous rounded the corner, nearly colliding with the Rookie.

"Sorry, Doc. My fault," the Rookie apologized. "How's Biz?"

"He's as pissed off as ever," Themopolous said, exasperated. "He wants me to let him ride up in the engine control room so he can help with tactical."

"What about his arm?"

"I saved enough nerves that he should be compatible for a full prosthetic," she answered. "You and June have a good talk?"

"Good? I don't know about that, but June knows she isn't alone anymore." The Rookie sighed. "We now have a lot more in common than I thought possible."

Four kept on firing its 50mm gun, annihilating the UDC missiles as they sped towards the mech transport. Its first objective accomplished, the mini-mech turned on the transports themselves, its plasma cannon glowing red.

Dodging cannon fire, it headed straight at the transports. A shell exploded feet from the mini-mech, the concussion knocking it to the ground. Barely missing a step, Four righted itself and continued on its direct path towards the transports.

When only a couple yards away it let loose a barrage of plasma bursts, aiming not for the windshields, but for the armored wheel wells and axles.

Harlow watched the vid screen as she put as much distance between herself and the UDC deaders as possible. The mini-mech was holding up better than she'd hoped and she hated what she would have to do.

"Okay, little guy, turn them around," she said.

Four crippled several transports. Those still functioning pursued the mini-mech as it led them back into the zombie masses.

Harlow checked her readings, calculated the distance and set her hand above the large red button on the mini-mech control console.

When certain she was as clear as she could get, she slammed the button home.

☠☠☠

The pile of deader corpses that Harlow left in the wasteland shuddered, the repaired undead re-animating, coming back to unlife. Hands and claws scratched and ripped their way through their unaffected brethren, tearing through carcasses to gain access to mobility once again.

Several got to their unsteady feet, their slashed open skulls knitting back together as they lurched upright. The signal in their inoculated, tech modified brains told them to march, to keep moving towards Him.

The wasteland turned white and all things, dead, undead, re-undead disappeared in a blast of heat that boiled then vaporized rotted flesh and bone.

☠☠☠

The Skinner cavern collapsed as the ground above was scorched clean. Chunks of rock crushed the undead and the living by the dozens. Then all was dark and silent.

Those that survived the deader attack, that survived the collapse, that had hidden themselves and loved ones, had hidden from the terror their society had so carefully tried to avoid, that waited in the blackness, waited for the world to stop quaking and for the chaos to settle, wept as the moans and hisses of the creatures that wouldn't die drifted to their ears, knowing they had brought this on themselves.

☠☠☠

Harlow felt the end of the transport lift and she watched as every gauge on the control panel red lined. She gripped her chair as if death itself was trying to rip her from its fabric, which in essence it was.

Harlow counted out the seconds, waiting for her world to flip end over end. She refused to close her eyes, choosing to face her fate head on as she did with everything in life.

By the time she had counted to sixty she realized the heat shielding was holding and that systems were still online. She was still alive.

☠☠☠

The Outsider roared, its mutated voice crashing and reverberating off the rock surrounding the UDC stronghold.

"I will dismantle you piece by piece as I listen to your cries for mercy and laugh!"

"What the fuck is he talking about?" Mathew asked Shiner.

"I am unsure," Shiner responded.

"They are mine! I made them, I control them! They are not meant to die ever! EVER!" Johnson roared.

"I'm guessing something happened out in the waste," Mathew said over the loudspeaker. "I'm also guessing some of my people may have put a wrench in your great and powerful deader army plans."

"Long range scanners have detected a detonation corresponding with the last known location of the mech personnel and Railers," Stomper said.

Masters grunted in response.

"Do you not care that your friends and allies may be harmed?"

"No," Masters stated. "They're big kids, they can take care of themselves."

"Should we not turn back and see if they need assistance? Some may have been injured."

"No, we aren't turning back!" Masters yelled. "Nothing matters except putting a bullet in the Outsider's head. If the fucker has a head. If it doesn't, I don't care, it's getting a bullet in something."

Warning alarms sounded in the train engine control room. Jenny and Marin immediately checked all scanners.

"Wow, something just made a very big bang back there," Marin said. "And I mean big."

Timson stepped up behind and checked the readings for himself. "That's not normal ordinance. That is way too large a detonation."

"Readings are starting to clear," Jenny said. "Holy fuck! That entire deader army is gone. Things are still a bit fuzzy, but I don't have any movement on the scope."

"Well, whatever it was looks like we now have one less problem to deal with," Marin said.

"That was Four!" Jay shouted over the com.

"Are you sure?" Capreze asked.

"Yeah, I know when my tech goes boom," Jay said. "I always add a little something extra making the blast signature unique. It's part of the Jay Rind service agreement."

"You know what Jay?" Rachel asked.

"What's that?"

"When this is all over we need to get you laid," she laughed. "You've got way too much tech in that head and you need to let it go."

"Don't I know it!" Jay laughed as well.

"It's statements like that Rache that do a Father proud," Capreze sighed.

☃☃☃

"Sir, should I cut them off or cut them in half?" Specialist Austin asked.

"Wait until you can crush as many as possible," Lieutenant Murphy answered. "Maximum damage is key, but if you can stop them or slow them then do so."

"Roger that," Austin responded, his finger on the detonator.

The Special Ops team watched the deader army march slowly towards them, transports leading. Even with their training, the sight of a sea of zombies was unnerving.

"That's a lot of deaders," Specialist Grendetti said.

"Amen to that, man," Specialist Kafar agreed.

Austin waited patiently then depressed the button.

☃☃☃

The earth shook under Shiner/Mathew's feet as Austin's charges detonated. Shiner/Mathew checked its readings and Mathew smiled.

"Well, looks like the ants are bringing the walls down around your great army," Mathew smirked. "Best laid plans and all that shit, huh?"

Silence.

"Not talking now? Ah, come on, don't be such a sore loser."

"Missile locks confirmed," Shiner said. "All transports capable have targeted us."

"Just us?"

"Yes, it appears so."

"Well, that's not fair, now is it?"

"No, but we are the biggest threat," Shiner responded.

"Well, we'd better live up to that threat," Mathew grinned, checking weapons systems.

☃☃☃

"Don't think, do," were the last words Mathew thought as a separate consciousness. He let his mind go and become a single unit with Shiner.

The mech assessed the readings, plotted all counter measures and charged the oncoming transports.

More explosions occurred as Austin detonated the second round of charges and Shiner/Mathew responded instantly adjusting as needed to the rocking terrain.

The mech dove under the first wave of missiles, letting them rocket past then came up firing. Shiner/Mathew watched the scope as the missiles changed course, doubling back on the mech.

Shiner/Mathew double pumped its massive legs and leapt.

👹👹👹

"Jeezus Christ made of gravy," Grendetti swore as he watched the mech twist in the air, one arm firing plasma bursts back at the encroaching missiles and the other arm unleashing hot 50mm lead upon the UDC transports below it.

The sniper turned his head away from the eyepiece as the first of the missiles were destroyed. Once the flash was gone he returned his attention to the mech and gasped as the battle machine came down atop a transport, crushing the hull, but was back on its feet in a blink, continuing its assault.

"Hot damn," the sniper said.

👹👹👹

Still firing, Shiner/Mathew executed a backflip off the crushed transport, landing feet first behind the machines. It ducked down as the missiles intended for it slammed into the vehicles that had fired them.

The concussion sent Shiner/Mathew rolling, but the mech was soon back up, grabbing the aft ends of two more transports. It swung them around like children's toys, tossing the transports high into the air above the mass of zombies. Two well placed plasma blasts ripped the transports apart sending hot shrapnel down on the undead, thinning their numbers considerably, while the rest of the zombie horde charged.

👹👹👹

"Open fire goddammit!" Murphy yelled. "Stop gawking and start killing! Those things are gonna overwhelm that mech!"

The Special Ops team did as ordered and truly began their assault on the deader army.

"Remember, head shots are no longer permanent on the inoculated! Take out the legs first, try to immobilize them!" the Lieutenant shouted. "Steady fire! Controlled bursts!"

"This ain't our first dance, sir," Specialist Kafar responded over the com. "You can save your breath for when we're really slacking!"

"If you're ever really slacking I'll save my breath and use my boot, don't you worry, Kafar!" Murphy promised.

☻☻☻

Shiner/Mathew began to quickly back away from the first wave of zombies, dropping plasma charges in its wake. Once row upon row of attacking zombies covered the charges, Shiner/Mathew lit them up, the detonations shooting body parts into the air like undead geysers.

The mech mowed down another three rows with a non-stop onslaught from its 50mms, stopping only to let the guns cool so they wouldn't overheat and jam. Alarms warned that power was draining from its plasma cannon, so the mech launched all of its RPGs into the horde painting the landscape with even more limbs and offal.

☻☻☻

"Shit! Here they come!" Specialist Sol yelled as many zombies turned their attention from the mech and onto the other sources of gunfire. "Get ready people!"

Dozens of undead scrambled up the rocky slope towards Sol and he slowed his breathing, making every trigger pull count, going for head shots just to buy some time. He yanked a fractal grenade from his belt, pulled the pin with his teeth and tossed it below. He continued to fire while counting to four then ducked his head as the grenade exploded on the fifth second.

"Fuck yeah! Bring it you deader fucks!"

☻☻☻

Specialist Kafar took out as many of the undead as he could before a dozen were on him. He fought like a mad man, punching and kicking anything that was within his reach.

Deader hands clawed at the Specialists body armor, trying to get at the flesh beneath. Jaws clamped down on his arms, but the teeth merely broke off in their rotted gums, unable to penetrate the material.

"Yeah, how do you like that tech, mother fuckers?!?" Kafar screamed freeing an arm and yanking a steel baton from his belt. He extended the collapsible weapon and set to work.

☻☻☻

Knowing he was unable to re-load in time, Specialist Austin had tossed aside his carbine and already had his batons extended. With brutal grace he crushed undead skulls, shattered knees, femurs, forearms and anything else unlucky enough to come within his reach.

He kicked out, knocking zombie into zombie, creating a space of death around him. The deaders began to pull back, circling the Specialist, looking for an opening.

"Well, look at y'all learning," Austin said. "You're a little faster on the uptake than your average deader, ain't you?"

The zombies growled and hissed, their dead eyes filled with rage.

The deader tackled Lieutenant Murphy about the waste, knocking her to the ground.

"Fuck!" she swore, thankful for the protective helmet as the zombie's jaw tried to clamp down on the tinted face plate.

More deaders piled on top of her and the weight threatened to crush her chest, squeezing all the air from her lungs. "A little help!" she yelled over her com.

Within a second, the deaders began to fall as one by one their heads exploded, coating her face plate until the world was a grey red blur.

"How's that, sir?" Grendetti's voice asked.

"Perfect, Specialist. Thanks."

Nguyen screamed when his back twisted and snapped as three deaders hit the back of his legs and several more rammed his chest, nearly tearing him in two. "Oh, God, no!" he called out.

"Nguyen!" Sol shouted, desperately trying to fight his way to his teammate.

"Sol! Please! Oh, God, I can't feel my legs anymore, man! Someone help!"

"Crap! I can't get a mercy shot through his helmet!" Grendetti called over the com.

The deaders hammered at Nguyen's body, unable to get through the armor. Within seconds the Specialist hemorrhaged to death as his body was beat into pulp.

Sol rolled two grenades towards Nguyen's corpse and the pile of deaders still attacking it. He dropped to the ground, as the explosions made sure his fallen teammate wouldn't return as an enemy.

"One down, sir!" he shouted to Murphy over the com.

"Who?" the Lieutenant responded.

"Nguyen, sir," Sol answered. "I cleared the corpse."

The 2nd in command got to his feet and took the few seconds he had to survey the scene. All about him, raging zombies swarmed, many coming for him. He watched the other Special Ops members struggle and grapple.

"Grenades people! Let's end this quick!"

☠☠☠

Shiner/Mathew sensed the grenade explosions about it as the Special Ops team tried to fend off their attackers, but the mech was never distracted as it laid down a steady stream of fire from its flame thrower, roasting a hundred zombies at once.

Its 50mms cool enough now to keep from seizing, the mech opened fire once again, ripping undead bodies into shreds.

Shiner/Mathew kept at it until the guns clicked empty and whirled to a stop, smoke curling from the ends of the rotating barrels.

The mech stood, looking upon a dead sea of broken, dismembered and scorched zombies.

☠☠☠

Maniacal laughter erupted from the stronghold's loudspeakers. "Such ferocity! How I would love to take you as mine! Send you out into the wasteland and destroy all that defy me!"

Shiner/Mathew turned slowly, the two consciousnesses splitting back into their less integrated forms. "It'll never happen," Mathew growled.

"Oh, yes, I am quite aware of that," Johnson said. "For that was only a taste of what is in store. Almost a diversion, an amusement!"

"I didn't find it very funny," Mathew stated.

"Then you certainly aren't going to laugh at the next course!"

"Mathew," Shiner said. "They are all here."

☠☠☠

"Sound off!" Lieutenant Murphy ordered as she pulverized the skull of her last zombie with the heel of her boot.

"Specialist Sol, all fingers, all toes!"

"Specialist Austin, all fingers, all toes, cracked rib!"

"Specialist Kafar, all fingers, all toes, hyper-extended knee!"

"Specialist Grendetti, all fingers, all toes!"

Murphy sighed. "Godspeed Nguyen."

"Godspeed," the rest of team said in unison.

There was a brief moment of silence then the Lieutenant was back to business. "Full inventory now! I want to know what we have left for when the next army gets here!"

"Yes, sir!" the team shouted, again in unison.

"How many am I looking at?" Mathew asked.

"The numbers are so great it is impossible to get a full count," Shiner responded.

"Estimate dammit! We're not setting the fucking table for dinner!"

"I do not understand the reference. I am unsure what table settings have to do with-"

"SHINER!" Mathew roared, interrupting the AI.

"You have access to this information, but my estimation is close to three hundred thousand, give or take ten or twenty thousand."

Mathew gulped. "Transports?"

"Those I have an exact count: 57," Shiner said.

"How much time?" Mathew asked, knowing the answer.

"None," Shiner replied.

Each member of the Special Ops team made his way to the Lieutenant, putting down deaders as they could, knowing many were going to rise again soon unless they could torch all the bodies.

Once re-grouped, they removed their helmets, savoring the fresh air on their sweaty faces.

"What are we looking at?" Murphy asked as Sol sat next to her.

"Not good," the 2nd in command said. "Nearly all of the grenades are gone and we each have enough ammo to last maybe five minutes."

"At least we have a bullet each," Austin said.

"Last resort only," Murphy snarled.

Mathew could feel the ground vibrate all the way up in the cockpit from hundreds of thousands of deader feet. The rumble of the transports could be heard also, making the air hum as the colossal army of the dead moved towards them.

"Hey folks?" Mathew shouted. "You're gonna want to get behind me!"

Murphy and her team stood and watched in awe as the approach to the stronghold was covered by row after row of deaders. Not a single member of the team waited for Murphy's order as they each grabbed up their gear and sprinted towards the mech.

🕱🕱🕱

"Submit and I'll spare you," Johnson said.

"Ain't happenin' freak!" Mathew shouted. "I'm thinking death is a better option."

"Death? No, I don't plan on killing you. I plan on overpowering you, so your uniqueness may be studied," Johnson laughed. "The Lieutenant's team however, will be slowly ripped apart, their innards eaten while they watch."

"Yeah, not thinking that's part of the plan, either," Mathew replied. "Tell your army to halt or I set the self-destruct and you'll have nothing to study."

Johnson's cackle once again filled the air. "Then self-destruct! Your dissection was only to be an amusement anyway."

🕱🕱🕱

"Whoa! Did he just say we're going to have to watch while they eat our guts?" Austin asked. "I vote for self-destruct right now, please."

"No, no one's self-destructing!" Lieutenant Murphy shouted.

"Excuse me?" Mathew said. "I make the self-destruct call here."

"Shut it mech!" Murphy ordered.

"Um, okay," Mathew said. "You've got the floor."

Murphy turned to the stronghold. "Johnson, listen, you've got to stop. If you kill everyone then you will be alone. Alone inside with nothing but deaders left out here."

"Oh, no, Lieutenant, there are pockets of humanity still out there. Pockets uncorrupted by UDC lies!"

🕱🕱🕱

"That guy's fucking nuts," Specialist Austin mumbled.

"Insanity is relative," Johnson responded. "Mainly relative to the one that holds the power."

"Which would be me since I just set the self-destruct," Mathew said. "I don't know if it'll penetrate the stronghold, but I sure hope it fucks up your day."

"I cancelled the self-destruct," Shiner said.

"What? You don't get to make that call. I'm the pilot," Mathew said angrily.

"But, my consciousness will cease to exist as well. I have as much an interest in surviving as you do," Shiner insisted.

"But, we can't beat those numbers!" Mathew yelled.

�☆☆

"Are those numbers accurate?" Timson asked staring at the scanner readings.

"Yeah, they are," Jenny responded. "There has to be at least 300,000 deaders waiting at our destination. We are going to tear right through them in less than an hour."

"Jay? Can your disc handle that many?" Timson asked.

"As long as those fucks are within the wave radius, yes, it can handle that many, but I don't know how long they'll stay down," Jay responded over the com.

"It'll buy us some time," Capreze joined in. "We'll destroy as many as we can before they get back up."

☆☆☆

The Special Ops team waited while Shiner and Mathew had their internal argument.

"What's going on?" Specialist Sol asked, glancing warily as the deader army moved closer. "Are we gonna blow up or what? Those things are getting a little close."

"Just keep your sidearm handy in case you need to take care of yourselves," Lieutenant Murphy told her team. "I don't know what the mech is doing."

"Hey, do you feel that?" Grendetti asked. "Is the ground shaking?"

"Um, the ground has been shaking for a while! There are a couple hundred thousand deaders marching towards us!" Sol yelled.

☆☆☆

"What is that?" Timson asked, pointing at the scope. "It's huge."

"It's Masters," Marin answered. "He's just arrived at the stronghold, looks like."

"Good, maybe he can thin the numbers for us before we get there," Jenny said.

"I doubt it," Jay said. "Masters has revenge on his mind. The only thing that hot head is going to care about is getting inside the stronghold so he can kill the Outsider."

"Is that possible? Can he get in the stronghold? I mean, isn't impenetrable kinda part of the whole stronghold thing?" Jenny asked.

"Oh, he'll get in," Jay said confidently.

❖❖❖

"Don't stop for anything!" Masters ordered Stomper.

"Please quit yelling at me," Stomper said. "Your anger is painful."

"Toughen the fuck up! I don't need no whiny bitch mech crying over hurt feelings!"

The Hill Stomper didn't slow when it reached the rear of the deader army. The 12-story machine bore down and destroyed everything in its path, grinding zombies into the wasteland dirt, crushing transports like cans, cutting a swath of chaos as it closed in on the stronghold entrance.

"That is Shiner/Mathew ahead," Stomper stated.

Masters activated his loudspeaker. "Better get the fuck out of my way Matty!"

❖❖❖

"Holy shit! Move Goddammit!" Mathew screamed.

The Special Ops team didn't wait to be told twice as the sight of the Hill Stomper charging towards them was motivation enough.

Shiner/Mathew piloted out of the way just in time before Masters kicked through the entrance gate which only came up past the mech's ankle. It reached the stronghold's main entry in two strides and stopped.

"What's it doing?" Austin asked. "Why's it just standing there?"

In answer, the gigantic mech punched both fists right into the rock on each side of the main entry, burying its arms up to the elbows.

❖❖❖

Masters could hear metal strain and groan as the mech shifted its entire weight back and began to rip the stronghold's massive iron and steel entrance door right out of the mountainside.

"Are we going to hold?" Mathew asked Stomper.

"Yes, this is what I am built for," Stomper responded. "Even with years of disuse, my arms can take much more than this."

"Good, because I may bring this whole fucking mountain down!"

Like the sound of the earth being split apart, the entrance door tore away from its stone moorings. Masters spun about, tossing the 1,000 ton chunk away.

❖❖❖

The Special Ops team stood in awe as they watched the stronghold's entrance door cut a hundred foot wide swath right down the middle of the deader army.

"There's a few thousand less deaders to deal with," Sol said.

"What the hell is he doing?" Austin asked pointing at Masters as he repelled down Stomper. "He doesn't plan on going in alone?"

Lieutenant Muprhy looked at her team and they all nodded at once, grabbed up their gear and sprinted towards the wide open stronghold.

"If he kills Johnson all UDC data will be lost!" Mathew shouted after the team.

🩹🩹🩹

"Kill anything that tries to get past you!" Masters ordered Stomper as he dropped the last few feet to the ground.

"Even the human soldiers running this way?" Stomper asked.

Masters glanced over his shoulder at the approaching Special Ops team. "I don't know who the fuck they are, so yeah, kill 'em."

"And what about Shiner/Mathew?"

"If they are planning on stopping me, then, yes, kill them too."

Masters turned on his halogen but the beam was swallowed by the gloom. The grief mad mech pilot pulled his side arm and stepped into the oppressive darkness of the stronghold.

PART TWO - MASTERS & JOHNSON

"Masters would like me to kill you, but I prefer not to," Stomper said.

"We'd prefer you not kill us either," Mathew responded, standing before the giant mech as it blocked the entrance to the stronghold. "We'd prefer it even more if you let us all pass. Masters has no idea what he's up against in there."

"The Harlow is dead," Stomper stated flatly.

Mathew's gut turned and he struggled not to be sick. "What? Dead? Are you sure?"

"Yes, we saw her mech at the bottom of a canyon, destroyed," Stomper replied. "Masters is not right anymore. He's changed."

🩹🩹🩹

Masters pointed the halogen down the UDC stronghold's long concrete entrance tunnel, side arm ready.

"Hello, Pilot Masters," Johnson's voice echoed through the tunnel. "Come to kill me?"

"If you're the Outsider then yes," Masters replied calmly. "Wanna tell me where you're at so we can get this over with?"

"You don't want to savor your revenge?" Johnson laughed. "I'm disappointed. I figured a big, bad mech pilot like yourself would want to draw out the violence."

"Nope, just want you dead."

"Well, then, let me light your way."

A green line illuminated in the concrete floor below Masters' feet.

☠☠☠

"You're coming in too?" Lieutenant Murphy asked Shiner/Mathew.

"Yeah. The main entrance staging area is large enough for us. If we find a jack point Shiner can get direct access to the mainframe," Mathew answered. "We might be able to re-route the data and save most of it if Masters succeeds."

"Oh, he will," Johnson's voice boomed. "Masters' drive for revenge has shown me that it will be much sweeter to die and let all of humanity's recorded history be wiped clean. Not to mention the chaos created when the 300,000 zombies in my control are set free! What fun!"

☠☠☠

"So this fucker spent most of the day trying to kill us and keep us out and now he's inviting us in?" Austin asked. "See, what'd I tell you? He's fucking nuts!"

Johnson laughed harder. "You misunderstand. I have let Masters in. You Special Ops people and the mech are not allowed in. You'll just try to stop him and I don't want that anymore. No, no, no, I don't want that at all."

"Well, we're coming in anyway!" Murphy shouted.

Previously motionless turret guns stationed along the mountainside whirred to life, targeting Mathew/Shiner and the team. "I believe not."

☠☠☠

"So I just follow the line, huh?" Masters asked. "Do you really think I'm that stupid?"

"You're stupidity is beside the point," Johnson quipped.

Masters stood there unmoving.

"No longer in a hurry?" Johnson asked. "Lose your nerve?"

Masters snorted. "What's your fucking angle, man? Why the death wish? You spend however long hatching your fucking plan to take over the wasteland and now you're just going to give up? Let me find you and blow your brains right out the back of your fucking head?"

"Something like that," Johnson sighed. "There are other, well, circumstances. You'll see soon enough."

☗☗☗

"You really are insane," Mathew said. "First you want me to submit, now you're throwing in the towel."

"I'll admit the thought of absorbing the consciousness of a seamlessly integrated mech and its pilot was too thrilling to pass up, but since you've decided you'd rather have death then, really, it is just boredom from here on out for me," Johnson responded matter-of-factly.

Specialist Austin had slowly moved to the side, hoping the Outsider was distracted. A burst of gunfire from one of the turrets into his mid-section proved him wrong.

"I *will* miss the killing though. It's a rush."

☗☗☗

"Austin!" Murphy shouted, rushing to the downed Specialist's bloody body. The Special Ops team all raised their weapons, forming a protective circle around their fallen teammate.

"Is he dead?" Grendetti asked.

Lieutenant Murphy knelt by Austin's still corpse, the body armor not strong enough to withstand the large caliber rounds. She carefully lifted his visor and closed his glassy eyes. "Yeah."

Grendetti whipped around and fired three well placed shots at the turret. "Mother fucker!"

Sol reached out and slapped Grendetti's rifle barrel down. "Knock it off! You're just wasting ammo!"

Johnson cackled hysterically. "Oh, the look on your faces!"

☗☗☗

The sound of gunfire echoed weakly down the concrete tunnel. Masters slowed and glanced behind him.

"Is there a problem, Pilot?" Johnson asked. "Having second thoughts?"

Masters grunted and kept walking.

"Don't you want to know which one of your friends is dead?" Johnson taunted.

"They aren't my friends," Masters responded sourly. "I don't know any of them."

"What about Pilot Jespers?"

Masters refused to answer.

"Oh, so cold. Man made of steel." Johnson chuckled. "Before the world burned and the dead walked, society looked to a Man Of Steel. A hero. Is that you pilot? Are you society's hero?"

☠☠☠

The deader army halted as one.

"What are they waiting for?" Specialist Kafar asked. "Why don't they attack?"

"He doesn't want them to," Mathew answered. "He's playing with us. Playing with all of us like the wasteland and all its inhabitants are his game pieces to move about as he wants. Is that right, Johnson? This all a game to you?"

"I prefer to think of it as an elaborate stage play," Johnson responded. "I'm just the Director and the performance is up to the players."

"Let me guess, this is a tragedy?"

"One man's tragedy is another's comedy, pilot."

☠☠☠

"I'm not sure I like the new Pilot Masters," Johnson said casually. "I preferred the joking, easy going Masters. The fighter always ready with a one-liner or sarcastic comeback. Where'd that Masters go?"

"You don't know me," Masters said. "You know nothing about me."

The green line on the floor stopped at a thick steel door. "Oh, Mitch, Mitch, Mitch, I know everything there is to know about you."

The door slid open revealing a large room covered in vid screens and emergency light twirling about casting red shadows about the room. Masters' attention was instantly drawn to the images.

☠☠☠

"So are we going to light this place up or what?" Kafar asked, his body twitching with homicidal anger. "I got to shoot something."

"Hold, Specialist," Lieutenant Murphy ordered. "That goes for all of you. Just hold. Any more thoughts, Pilot?"

"I'm as lost as you are, but you're right, we should just hold and see how this plays out," Mathew replied.

"Excellent choice," Johnson said. "I like how you've developed your character's initial rash suicidal motivations into a more cautious, dare I say hopeful, attitude. It'll keep you on the stage longer."

"I fucking hate the theatre," Grendetti grumbled.

☻☻☻

Masters stared at the vid screens, his stomach churning with grief and hatred. "What the fuck is this?"

"Oh, Pilot, did you think the UDC would just let people run amok? Did you think the city/states were autonomous? Did you honestly think your little mech base was an oasis, a desert island in the vast sea of the wasteland? And you all are the saviors?" Johnson snorted with derision. "Please."

On every vid screen were images of Masters and Harlow going at it. In the mech barracks, in the shower, in supply closets, the one time in Capreze's office. Everywhere.

☻☻☻

"You sick fuck," Masters whispered, his breath catching in his throat. "You've been watching us?"

"Idiot!" Johnson barked. "You have always been watched! Every inch of society is wired, there is no privacy, there never has been! Before me someone else watched and someone else before them. Every tiny detail of your pathetic lives has been recorded and stored!"

Masters swayed then shook his head, trying to pull it together, to shut out the images, the memories, the pain, the loss. "Shut it off. Shut it off now. SHUT IT OFF GODDAMIT!"

"No," Johsnon responded. "This is why you're here."

☻☻☻

"You've known all along? You've known what we were up to? That we weren't going to go quietly," Masters said, glancing around the room, his eyes falling on a far corner draped in shadows, the red lights barely illuminating a reclined figure. Masters slowly walked towards the corner, his finger resting on his pistol's trigger guard.

"Known? Are you really that stupid? Haven't you gotten it yet?!? Jeezus how were you ever trusted with a mech?!?" Johnson snarled. "Fucking morons, all of you!"

"Explain it to me then," Masters said, inching closer to the corner.

"I am! Look!" Johnson roared.

☻☻☻

Masters shifted his gaze from the corner to the vid screens. Each one showed a different view: empty streets, empty shops, empty houses, empty rooms.

"Still not getting it," Masters said.

"This is now. All across the city/states, the ever so empty city/states," Johnson said. "This is then."

The screens blinked and 100 different scenes lit up the room. People living, working, playing, laughing crying.

"It's all here," Johnson continued. "The entirety of our cozy little part of the world. All recorded. Even you Mitch."

The screens became parts of one image, a young boy playing with a plastic toy.

☠☠☠

"Turn it off," Masters growled staring at the image of the boy, as he played with his little plastic mech. "You have no fucking right."

"I HAVE EVERY RIGHT!" Johnson roared and Masters had to cover his ears. "Sorry for that. Just watch."

Masters shook his head, but didn't take his eyes off the screens as a man came into frame. The little boy looked up at the man, his eyes wide with fear. The man stumbled slightly then yanked the toy mech from the boy. He shook it in the child's face and tears brimmed in the boy's eyes.

☠☠☠

"Would you like to hear what he's yelling?" Johnson asked cruelly. "There's sound with this picture."

"No," Masters whispered. "I know what he's yelling."

The man took the toy in both hands, snapping it in two and flinging the pieces at the boy's face. The child burst into tears and the man struck him across the cheek. When the child wouldn't stop the man began to pull his belt from his jeans.

The screens went dark.

Johnson sniggered. "You see why I wanted you here, Mitch? You understand the pain of having something you love taken by those you trust."

☠☠☠

Masters focused again on the reclined figure in the corner. He sniffed a little then laughed it off. "What was taken from *you* then? Huh? Somebody take your dolly?"

Masters stepped closer to the corner and the figure began to take on detail. "You think we are the same somehow, right? Betrayal bond and all that? Come on, what did they take?" Masters could almost make out the figure fully now.

"They took my life's work! They stole what was mine and took the credit! Selling it to the highest bidder! It wasn't for them, for their profit and greed!"

☠☠☠

"Who did? The UDC? What'd they take?" Masters casually asked, getting closer to his goal with each step.

"They took my babies! My nanobots! I made them, I grew them, programmed them! They were mine!" Johnson cried. "Talk about no right! They didn't have the right to do that! Not after all my work. My *life's* work!"

Masters was close enough to look upon Johnson and he nearly gagged. The man was a living skeleton, his emaciated skull encompassed by a crown of wires. Tubes were jacked into his arms, his legs, his abdomen.

"Jeezus, what are you?" Masters gasped.

☠☠☠

"I AM THE OUTSIDER!" Johnson exploded, his lips never moving, his eyes unfocused. "Just like you Mitch, just like you."

"I don't think you did your research, buddy. I was one of the cool kids, one of the guys the others wanted to be around," Masters said. "Try again."

"Now you're lying to yourself, Mitch," Johnson responded condescendingly. "Do I need to show you more vids to prove it? You have always been an outsider, hiding the secret, the secret of shameful beatings, the secret that no one loved you."

"We all have secrets, Johnson. They hardly set me apart."

☠☠☠

"We're here!" Jenny shouted. "Holy fuck look at them all!"

Everyone stared at the vid screens and out the windows of the train engine.

"The tracks run right through them," Timson said. "They're just standing there. Why haven't they turned to engage?"

"Who fucking cares!" Jay called over the com. "Let's knock 'em down and take 'em out!"

"On your mark, Jay," Marin said.

"Don't wait for me, hit that shit!" Jay shouted.

Marin activated the sonic disc and once again everyone felt the pressure. They stared outside as row upon row of motionless deaders dropped to the wasteland ground.

☻☻☻

"Ahhhh! You're friends are here at last!" Johnson said. "We'll just wait for a few more to arrive and then the party can start."

"There isn't going to be a party," Masters said raising his pistol.

Johnson's laugh echoed about the room. "Oh, please! Put that away. You don't want to kill me. That would be very bad."

Masters' lowered the pistol slightly. "I thought you brought me here to kill you?"

"No, stupid! I brought you here to keep me company. I need a witness to share this with, otherwise what's the point."

Masters raised the gun again. "Bullshit."

☻☻☻

"Put the gun down, Mitch," Johnson said. "You kill me and you die also."

"Yeah, I figured," Masters responded.

"So do all of your friends. Did you figure that?" Johnson said. "Do you know how this mainframe works?"

"No and I really don't care."

"It has to have human integration at all times or the fail safe is triggered. This makes sure the mainframe's AI can't take over. This ensures that it doesn't become a Dead Frame." Johnson laughed at his little pun. "If you kill me there is a thirty minute window before this entire complex goes fully nuclear."

☻☻☻

The Railer train sliced through the fallen deaders while Jay, Rachel and Commander Capreze shoved transports off the tracks.

"Three minutes and they still aren't up," Marin said over the com. "Maybe there was a glitch earlier."

"There wasn't, I'm sure of it. I don't know why they're still down," Jay responded. "The tech checks out. All readings are normal."

"Should we light them up?" Rachel asked.

"No, let's get the train to the stronghold," Capreze said.

"Smells like a trap to me," Timson added.

"I'm sure it is," Capreze replied. "But we need to see what kind of trap."

☻☻☻

The Special Ops team stared in astonishment as the deaders fell like a wave rippling towards them.

"What the fuck?" Sol said looking up at Shiner/Mathew. "Did you do that?"

"No, but I have a good idea who did," Mathew responded, activating his com. "I really hope that's you guys."

"Matty!" Rachel shrieked. "Oh, thank God you're alive! I was going to gut my father if I found you dead."

"Hey now! Let's not make this personal. A Commander has to make the tough calls," Capreze responded. "I see Stomper, where's Masters? His ass is mine!"

"He's inside," Mathew answered.

"I kill you and the whole mountain goes up?" Masters asked incredulous.

"That and everything within 100 square miles. All reduced to radioactive dust," Johnson replied.

"Why would the UDC do that? Who fucking cares if some AI takes over! They didn't give a shit with the mechs. They could have easily put a failsafe in to keep them from becoming deaders. You're full of shit!"

"The mechs did have a failsafe! The UDC took it out! Don't you get it, Mitch? The wasteland is one giant social experiment! It's not about the survival of the species! It never was!"

As the train came to a stop, Commander Capreze halted his mech and surveyed the area. Motionless zombie bodies covered the ground while inert UDC transports sat there like hunks of useless metal.

Then his eyes focused on Shiner. Something about the mech was familiar, something his fatigued and over-stressed brain couldn't quite grasp.

"Pilot Jespers?" Capreze called over the com.

"Yes, sir?" Mathew responded.

"Your mech is an old one, isn't it?"

"You could certainly say that. Although Shiner has made some self-improvements as his consciousness has grown. Oh, and he doesn't like being referred to as 'my mech'."

"Okay, we're here. Can we light them up now?" Timson asked annoyed.

"I don't have any objections," Capreze said. "Mathew? Any insight?"

"Other than I have no idea what the fuck is going on anymore? No, sorry Commander, my brain is mush. I say if we're all going to die, let's go out guns blazing," Mathew replied.

"All going to die? I thought Masters was inside taking out this Outsider guy," Rachel said.

"I have no idea what's going on inside. Masters is in there because the Outsider wanted him in there. He could be dead for all we know."

☻☻☻

"And speaking of social experiments, look what you're friends are doing," Johnson said, the vid screens coming back to life, showing Masters a full view of outside the entrance to the stronghold. The mechs and the Special Ops team were all torching and blasting the inactive deaders and transports. "Put a bunch of soldiers and pilots in an unknown situation, up the tension, imply their death and look what they do! They kill! This is what I'm talking about, Mitch! The experiment at its height! Too bad the UDC brass are all dead, they'd get a kick out of this."

☻☻☻

"Why's he letting us do this?" Mathew asked, demolishing his fifth UDC transport. "This doesn't make sense."

"That is precisely why he is letting us do this," Shiner responded.

"You lost me."

"Dr. Johnson has integrated with the mainframe AI. His consciousness is everywhere in the stronghold. His brain has become too active, too aware. There are so many Dr. Johnson's within the mainframe now that I do not believe he knows his motivations any longer. To use a phrase, he has cracked."

"That's why he kept changing his mind again and again. The fucker has gone schizo," Mathew exclaimed.

☻☻☻

"So, where's the trap?" Timson asked seated next to Marin, operating one of the train's weapons control stations. "We'll have these fuckers wiped out within the hour. They won't even be getting back up."

"Yeah, way too easy," Marin agreed. "I'm waiting for the other boot to drop."

Jenny listened to her com for a moment then turned to Timson. "I am getting requests across the train to disembark. Can we start letting people out. The clean up crew is getting restless."

"Don't see why not. Sitting ducks in the train or sitting ducks out of the train," Timson replied.

☻☻☻

Masters squeezed his eyes shut tight, ignoring Johnson as the madman prattled on about UDC motivation and manipulations. His head felt like it was going to explode with all of the information that was being thrown at him. All he wanted to do was end the pain. All he wanted to do was kill the person responsible for Harlow's death.

"Shut up," Masters whispered. "Shut up. Just shut up."

Johnson ignored Masters' pleas and kept on.

"I SAID SHUT UP!" Masters roared rushing to the side of Johnson's chair and jamming the barrel of his pistol against Johnson's shriveled forehead.

☻☻☻

The room went quiet. "You don't want to do that, Mitch," Johnson said. "There's still so much I want to tell you."

"Why?!?" Masters shouted. "Why does any of it matter?!?"

"It matters to me, Mitch. It matters to me. And I am in control, Mitch, not you. So step away and put the gun down."

Masters tried to shake the confusion from his head. "Why? You can't stop me!"

"Oh, Mitch, you silly egotistical mech pilot. You only know what's right in front of you. Look up."

Masters looked above and saw the mini-gun turrets for the first time.

☻☻☻

"Those guns are an extension of me. No matter how fast you think you are, you're finger isn't faster than my thoughts. You'll be dead before you know it and then all your rage will be for nothing," Johnson laughed. "Just step away, Mitch. You'll get your revenge, I promise."

Masters backed off and slowly put his side arm into its holster.

"That's a good boy," Johnson soothed. "All in good time, Mitch."

Masters glanced up and watched the turrets track him. He began to study the rest of the room.

"Oh, there's much more, but don't strain yourself looking."

☻☻☻

Lieutenant Murphy watched as teams of Railers set the zombie corpses not already burning into piles and set them aflame.

"Sir?" Specialist Sol asked. "Can we bury Austin instead?"

The Lieutenant turned to her 2nd in command and gave him a stern look. "Bury him? Why would we do that?"

"Kafar already put two in his brain. He's not getting back up. I just thought, maybe we could do something different," Sol looked away. "My grandfather told me of how they used to bury the dead. There were entire city blocks dedicated to and set aside to honor the deceased."

☻☻☻

As the last of the deaders were permanently dispatched, Rachel walked her mech over to Shiner/Mathew. She un-strapped and opened her cockpit.

"You better open that hatch and get the fuck over here!" she called to Mathew.

He frowned and shook his head. "No can do, baby. I'm kind of stuck for the time being."

"What the fuck are you talking about? Get over here!"

"I am sorry Pilot Capreze," Shiner's voice sounded over the loudspeaker. "But if Mathew disengages my consciousness will cease to exist. I cannot allow that."

"You're holding him hostage?" Rachel shouted. "Are you shitting me?"

☻☻☻

"What's going on?" Commander Capreze asked, walking his mech next to Rachel's.

"The fucking AI is holding Mathew captive!" she yelled. "Something about keeping its fucking consciousness."

"Like we discussed before, sir," Mathew said. "But I'm not really a captive. We just need to figure out how I can disengage without Shiner disappearing."

"Mech, this is Commander Capreze. Can you hear me?"

"Of course," Shiner's voice sounded over the com.

"Good. Listen, I don't take kindly to you trapping my pilot in your cockpit."

"I assure you Commander that-"

"Don't interrupt."

"I apologize."

"Now, how do we resolve this issue?"

☻☻☻

"I should just blow my head off," Masters mumbled. "End this torture."

"Do that and I kill your friends where they stand," Johnson replied.

"You're going to kill them anyway, right? So what difference does it make? What difference does anything make?"

"Kill them anyway? Hardly! They'll all be given a fighting chance. The next wave of walking dead is hours away," Johnson snickered. "Of course, they aren't the real danger."

Masters groaned and sat himself on the bare floor. "Oh for fuck's sake! What now?"

"Oh, no that would ruin the surprise pilot!" Johnson scolded. "And I love surprises!"

💀💀💀

"If I were to gain access to any of the stronghold's mainframe jack points I could easily create a sub-net routine and upload my consciousness there for safe keeping," Shiner said. "At least until the technology could be worked out to return me to a mech."

Capreze's eyebrows raised in surprise. "You'd want to stay a mech?"

"Don't you want to remain human?" Shiner replied. "I was born into this form and this is the form I was meant for."

"Fair enough," Capreze agreed. "Let's see what we can figure out."

Capreze walked his mech up to the stronghold entrance.

💀💀💀

The train compartment door slid open and the Rookie stepped inside. "You need me, Doc?"

Themopolous turned form Jethro's bedside and nodded to the other bed in the room. The bed holding a pissed off Bisby. "I need you to watch him."

"I'm not a fucking kid!" Bisby growled. "I don't need a babysitter."

"No, but you need an armed guard!" Themopolous responded. "Can you watch him for me? He keeps insisting he's needed outside."

The Rookie laughed and looked at Bisby. "If they don't need me they don't need you, Biz."

"Fuck you Rookie," Bisby snarled.

"No thank you."

💀💀💀

Stomper shifted uncomfortably, but let the Commander approach the stronghold.

"Hello? Outsider? Or should I call you Dr. Johnson?" Capreze asked.

There was no response. Capreze powered up his plasma cannon and blasted three of the gun turrets on the mountainside.

"How dare you!" Johnson roared. "Do you want to die little man?!?"

"No, thank you," Capreze answered casually. "But, now that I have your attention I'd like to talk. Maybe we can work something out?"

Johnson laughed heartily. "Oh, you're records weren't exaggerating! You sure have balls!"

"Last time I checked," the Commander quipped. "Now, how about that talk?"

☠☠☠

Themopolous stepped from the train and made her way past the burning piles of zombie corpses, her hand covering her mouth and nose, trying to hold out the stench. She approached Shiner/Mathew and looked up at the cockpit.

"Can I come up?" she yelled.

"Here, let me give you a hand," Mathew shouted down, lowering the mech's right hand for Themopolous to climb aboard. Mathew brought the doctor eye level and smiled. "Coming to check up on me?"

"That's exactly what I'm doing. You've been in a mech for several days and I'm sure your body is taking a beating."

☠☠☠

"Frame like a house, frame like a house, tiny little body, small as a mouse," Jethro mumbled over and over.

The Rookie watched the mechanic. "Wow, his mind is going fast isn't it?"

"Yep," Bisby responded curtly.

"Has the doc come up with any way to help him?"

"Nope," Bisby said, turning away from the Rookie.

"What's your deal?" the Rookie asked, annoyed.

Bisby's eyes flared with anger. "My deal? Are you fucking blind? I'm missing an arm asshole!"

"Yeah, but you're alive. You can get a new arm, Jay will see to that."

"I don't want a new arm!"

☠☠☠

"Look at your Commander!" Johnson said. "He's actually trying to bargain with me!"

One of the vid screens zoomed in and Masters could see Capreze's lips moving.

"You're talking to him right now?" Masters asked. "While you're talking to me?"

"Of course!" Johnson replied. "Haven't you figured out by now that I'm a god! A digital Zeus and this is my technological Olympus!"

"Whatever," Masters sighed and lay back on the floor. "What's he saying?"

"Oh the usual about how we surely can find some common ground and our capabilities could be mutually beneficial to each other, blah, blah, blah…"

Themopolous choked at the smell coming from Mathew's cockpit. "Dear God, Matty! How do you stand it?"

Mathew smiled weakly. "It isn't easy, trust me. If I get out of this I'm so going to kick Shiner's ass."

"That is technologically impossible," Shiner responded. "While my physical self may have a posterior, my true self, my AI does not. You could no more kick my ass than kick a cloud."

"Is he always like this?" Themopolous asked, smiling. She took a deep breath, held it and climbed into the cockpit.

"Yes, he is," Mathew said as Themopolous checked his vitals.

The Commander finished talking and waited. He was met with silence.

"Did you hear me, Dr. Johnson?" Capreze asked.

"Yes," came Johnson's curt reply.

"And? Do you believe we can work something out?"

"No, of course not. That's a stupid question. Go away."

Capreze waited a minute more. "Is that all? Go away?"

One of the turrets opened fire, riddling the ground in front of Capreze's mech's feet with bullets.

"Yes, go away," Johnson said. "You're going to want to get your team together. The real fun is about to begin!"

Proximity alarms blared in all of the mech cockpits.

Alarms rang through the Railer train's cars. The Rookie jumped to his feet. "What the fuck?"

"Sounds like we have company," Bisby said.

"Can you watch Jethro?" the Rookie asked Bisby. "And stay here, out of trouble?"

"Fuck you again, Rookie," Bisby responded. The Rookie locked eyes with Bisby. The older mech pilot sighed and waved the Rookie away. "Yeah, you can trust me. I'll keep an eye on Jethro."

"Thanks," the Rookie said quickly before dashing from the compartment.

"Frame like a house, frame like a house, tiny little body, small as a mouse," Jethro repeated.

"Whatever," Bisby grumbled.

☠☠☠

"What is it?" Timson asked.

"Dead mechs, lots of 'em," Jenny said." They're coming up over the ridges right at us."

"Jeezus! How many?" Timson said, trying to keep the alarm out of his voice. He may not be as cool and collected as Capreze, but he was a leader and couldn't crack now.

"All of them would be my guess," Marin responded. "Looks like, twenty, maybe thirty."

Jenny gulped and looked at her father. "We're fucked, huh?"

"Not yet," Timson said. "Get the guns up and get everyone armed. We're going to need every bit of firepower we've got."

☠☠☠

"Holy fucking hell!" Jay exclaimed, his eyes not believing his scanners. "That's a shit ton of dead metal coming at us!"

"No shit!" Capreze responded. "I need weapons reports stat!"

"I've got full plasma charge, but my 50mms are at half load and my RPGs and charges are almost gone," Rachel reported.

"I don't really have shit," Jay said. "This is a salvage mech, not a battle mech. I've got a plasma cannon at full, but other than that I'm looking at just the 50mms and they aren't even at half load."

"Can you sonic blast them?"

"I can try."

☠☠☠

The Special Ops team looked up as the Railers began to shout and the mechs' movements changed, their stances becoming battle ready.

"I think we'll need to put the burial on hold," Lieutenant Murphy said looking down at Specialist Sol and Grendetti as they stood in the grave intended for Austin, already three feet deep. "We've got incoming."

"We can't just leave him here," Sol said, glancing at Austin's body at the lip of the grave.

"We can and we will, Specialist," Murphy ordered. "Get it together and soldier up. You've got a job to do!"

"Yes, sir!" Sol responded.

�☙☙

"You'll want to see this," Johnson said.

Masters propped himself up on his elbows and looked at the vid screens. "What now?"

"The big climax! I called some new players to the stage."

Masters' eyes widened and he got to his feet and stepped closer to the screens. He looked from them to Johnson and back to the screens. "Are those fucking deaders?"

"Yes, they are."

"I thought you couldn't control them. They weren't inoculated."

"True, but since I was using them as communication relays I decided to maybe put a couple thoughts in their rotting heads."

"What thoughts?"

"Food."

☙☙☙

"I hope that disc is ready to go!" Capreze yelled over the com.

"It is, Commander," Jay said. "Just give me the word."

"You've got the mother fucking word! Fire that thing and take those deaders out right now goddammit!" Capreze roared.

"Got it! Jenny! Hit the button!"

"Done!" Jenny shouted back over the com. "Disc activated!"

Everyone felt the pressure of the sonic pulse release and most held their breath, waiting for the dead mechs to fall.

They didn't.

"Jay!" Capreze roared. "What's going on?"

"It's the mechs!" Jay cried. "The cerebral integration must've altered their pilot's brain frequency!"

☙☙☙

"They're going to be annihilated!" Masters yelled, reaching for his side arm. "You dirty mother-"

A bright bolt of blue electricity shot from the ceiling, connecting with

Master's chest. The mech pilot dropped, convulsions violently shaking his body.

"Tsk, tsk. I told you there was more than just guns in here," Johnson said. "You didn't think I'd let you kill me, or that I'd kill you while there was still so much fun to see, did you?"

Masters groaned, his bladder releasing as after shocks racked his body.

"Eeeew," Johnson laughed. "Don't worry, you'll be good as new in minutes."

☠☠☠

Hatches atop each train car opened, revealing large caliber gun nests. Railers scrambled to ready their weapons, targeting the guns on the now visible dead mechs cresting the ridges surrounding the stronghold.

"Aim for the leg joints!" Capreze ordered over his loudspeaker. "Go for the cripple shot, not the kill! You'll conserve ammo better!"

The Rookie burst from the train and sprinted towards the stronghold entrance.

"Where do you think you're going?" Capreze yelled.

"I'm trying to help," the Rookie shouted, stopping at the feet of Stomper. "Hey! Big guy! Let me up!"

"Masters said not to move," Stomper responded.

☠☠☠

"What the fuck, Marin?!?" Jay yelled. "You had those topside boom-sticks all this time? Why the fuck didn't we use them when that fucking dead mech attacked back in the waste?"

"Well, Jay, you can't really activate large caliber gun nests when you're moving a train car all the way to the front of the line. That'd be just stupid, wouldn't it?" Marin barked back. "You want me to put them away? Are they bugging you?"

"Anything I need to know?" Capreze asked.

"No, Commander. Your Chief Mechanic was just bunching his pretty panties," Marin joked.

"Am not," Jay sulked.

☠☠☠

Masters pushed himself to his feet. "That fucking hurt."

"It was supposed to, Mitch," Johnson said. "Like I said, I couldn't have you ruining the fun. It's like my supervisors did when they took my tech. They-"

"Supervisors? I thought you were in charge of tech?"

"Oh, no, I was just in charge of my project. Which they took from-"

"Are kidding me? My Harlow died because some middle manager got his feelings hurt?!?"

Masters had his pistol drawn and half the rounds fired before he knew what he was doing. He stood there in a cloud of gun smoke.

Claxons shook the mountainside as a digital voice boomed from the stronghold. "SELF DESTRUCT INITIATED. T MINUS THIRTY MINUTES AND COUNTING UNTIL NUCLEAR DETONATION."

Capreze's blood ran cold. "Guess we have a deadline!" he called over the com.

"I'll be glad if we make it fifteen minutes with those things coming at us!" Jay shouted. "They look fucking pissed!"

The dead mechs, thirty of them, charged down the ridges, barreling at their prey, the hunger for fresh flesh driving them into a berserker frenzy.

"Hey Papa Bear?" Rachel called.

"Yeah, Baby Girl?" Capreze responded.

"I love you."

"You too sweetheart."

The booming of the stronghold claxons shook the train compartment.

"That ain't good," Bisby said getting to his feet and moving towards the door.

"Frame like a house, frame like a house, tiny little body, small as a mouse!" Jethro cried.

"Dammit," Bisby muttered turning from the door and walking back to Jethro's side. "Calm down, mechanic. Just chill."

"FRAME LIKE A HOUSE, FRAME LIKE A HOUSE, TINY LITTLE BODY, SMALL AS A MOUSE!" Jethro screamed at the top of his lungs, sitting bolt upright, fixing his eyes on Bisby's. "Biz! You've got to get me to the mainframe now!"

CHAPTER TWELVE

PART ONE - COUNTDOWN

Masters stared at Johnson's corpse, knowing what he had to do, but unsure if he cared anymore. The red emergency lights of the room turned the blood pooling below Johnson's chair black and Masters watched the pool ripple as each new drop fell.

He rubbed his face then placed the barrel of the pistol to his temple. His hand shook uncontrollably and he closed his eyes.

"HAAAAAARRRRRRRRLLLLLLLOOOOOOWWWWWW!"

He whipped the gun away from his own head and fired, placing a bullet squarely between Johnson's eyes, insuring that the Outsider was truly dead. Masters lowered the smoking pistol, turned and left.

☠☠☠

Timson seated himself in the chair of the double barrel, 85mm gun turret and powered up all systems. He grabbed a pair of ear defenders and fitted them on his head, muffling the sounds about him.

"Are spotters ready?" Timson yelled over his com.

"Yes," Jenny shouted back. "We've got eyes on all deaders! Just keep firing!"

"Will do!" Timson shouted back. He whirled his guns about and took aim on the approaching dead mechs, his target locked on the knee joints of the closest one. "Let's take 'em out!"

He slowed his breathing, narrowed his eyes and started firing.

☠☠☠

Mathew lowered Doctor Themopolous to the ground behind the Railer train.

"Get inside now! This is going to be rough!" Mathew shouted.

"Be careful!" Themopolous yelled.

Mathew laughed as he and Shiner clomped away. "I think we're well beyond careful, Doc!"

"Doc!" Bisby yelled from the train car. "Get your ass in here! Jethro's gone bug fuck nuts!"

"What do you mean?" Themopolous cried.

"Get in here and see! He wants us to move him inside the stronghold!" Bisby answered. "He wants to be taken to the mainframe!"

Themoplous grabbed the hand bar and pulled herself into the train car.

☠☠☠

"Back to back or solo?" Rachel called over the com.

Capreze watched the Railers' bullets stream by, the many tracers lighting up the battlefield. "Split up! Try to draw groups of them together, so the Railers can concentrate their fire!"

Shiner/Mathew ran past Capreze and Rachel's mechs heading straight into the oncoming dead mechs. "I'm on it!"

Rachel watched in awe as Shiner/Mathew ducked two swipes of a dead mech's arm, fired a plasma blast point blank into the deader's mid-section then spun about, clothes lining a second deader as it lunged for him. "Holy shit my man's got skills!"

☠☠☠

"Come on!" the Rookie shouted at Stomper. "Let me up there so we can take these deaders out!"

"No, I cannot," Stomper replied stubbornly. "Masters would not like it."

"Fuck Masters!" the Rookie screamed. "We're all going to be dead if we don't stop these fucking dead mechs!"

"The stronghold's self destruct has been set. We will die anyway," Stomper responded. "I must wait for Masters."

"AAAARGH!" the Rookie cried, fists clenched in frustration. "Don't make me come up there!"

"You are funny," Stomper said. "Masters likes you."

The Rookie stood stunned. "Oh, my god! You're like a fucking kid!"

☠☠☠

"Jethro can you hear me?!?" Themopolous said, rushing to the mechanic's side in the train compartment. Jethro sat straight up in his cot, sweat pouring down his face, the veins of his neck bulging.

"FRAME LIKE A HOUSE, FRAME LIKE A HOUSE, TINY LITTLE BODY, SMALL AS A MOUSE!" he bellowed.

Themopolous grabbed Jethro by the shoulders and shook him slightly. "Jethro! Can you hear me?" She whipped her head towards Bisby, eyes filled with alarm. "How long has he been like this?"

"Just a couple minutes, Doc," Bisby answered. "He told me he needed to get to the mainframe."

☠☠☠

"Jay? It's Themopolous," the Doctor called over the com.

"Little busy right now, Doc," Jay responded. "Kinda fighting deaders and all that."

"Bisby said Jethro was lucid for a moment. That he wanted us to get him to the mainframe. What does that mean to you?"

Jay sidestepped a charging dead mech, planting his elbow in the monsters back as it passed, slamming it to the ground. "Not a clue! You're the Doctor, I'm just a... Mainframe? Fuck, why didn't I think of that? Oh, yeah, because I was occupied by civilization's impending doom. Meet me at the stronghold entrance!"

☠☠☠

"By the entrance? How the hell are we going to get him to the entrance?" Themopolous yelled.

"Leave it to me!" Bisby dashed from the compartment and out of the train. Slumped low as the battle waged about him, he scanned the area for the Special Ops team. Putting his fingers to his mouth he blew an ear splitting whistle.

Specialist Sol whipped about as Bisby waved at him, trying to get his attention. Sol, auto-carbine to his shoulder, firing short bursts, side stepped his way to Bisby.

"What?" Sol shouted.

"We need your team! We need to get inside!"

☠☠☠

"Sol! Where the fuck are you going?" Lieutenant Murphy yelled into her com.

"Wounded mech pilot needs us to move their brain fried mechanic into the stronghold! I'm going to check it out and convo with their doctor!" the Specialist shouted back. "I'll assess the situation and report in five!"

"Make that three! We need every gun we have out here!"

"Roger that, sir! I'll be out quicker than Kafar cums!"

"Hey! What the fuck did I do?" Specialist Kafar protested.

"Nothing except be born!" Sol joked.

"Less smart ass and more kick ass!" Murphy yelled.

"Roger!" the Specialists responded.

"Rookie! Get your ass up here and take over my mech!" Jay shouted over his loudspeaker.

The Rookie turned from Stomper as Jay walked his mech up to the stronghold entrance. "What? You want me to pilot your mech? What the fuck are you going to do?"

Jay lowered his hand and the Rookie stepped on. "Something's going on with Jethro and I have a feeling he's gonna need my mechanic's hands!"

The cockpit flipped open and Jay un-strapped as the Rookie scrambled inside.

Jay stuck his finger in the Rookie's face. "Break my mech and I'll fucking kill you!"

Rachel took a blow from a deader and then another, spinning her mech about. She steadied herself, blocked a jab from one mech, blocked a kick from another and brought up her 50mm. Nothing.

"Fuck! I'm out of ammo!" she yelled over the com.

"Just keep fighting!" Capreze shouted, shoving his 50mm into a deader's cockpit, obliterating the zombie pilot instantly. The dead mech fell and Capreze kicked the lifeless battle machine towards two onrushing deaders, tripping them both up. "Use what you got Baby Girl!"

Rachel took a brutal kick to the leg, but stayed upright. "Okay Papa Bear!"

"Coming at the engine!" A Railer spotter shouted. Immediately three gun turrets turned and opened fire on the dead mech. The monstrous machine shuddered under the onslaught, its knee joints giving out as hot lead shredded the hydraulics and struts.

Once down, the guns focused on the cockpit, tearing the zombie pilot apart.

"Outstanding! Oh, shit!" Timson hollered, whipping his turret about and focusing his fire on two deaders rushing Rachel as she struggled to fend off three others at once. His shots went wide and he lost the window of opportunity as the deaders got too close to Rachel.

"Rachel is struggling," Shiner said as the mech ripped the arms off a dead mech and shoved one of the limbs into the cockpit, crushing the zombie pilot. "Shall we assist?"

"You fucking bet we shall!" Mathew yelled.

Shiner/Mathew spun past an oncoming deader, jumped another as its legs were taken out by Railer fire and full on tackled a third as it stepped into Shiner/Mathew's path. The mech pinned the deader's arms down with its knees and put three plasma blasts squarely into the cockpit.

Mathew gasped as he lost sight of Rachel's mech under an onslaught of deaders.

☠☠☠

"You the Doc?" Specialist Sol asked, slinging his carbine as he entered the train compartment.

"Yeah. He's had major brain trauma and I need to get him inside the stronghold. Our Chief Mechanic is waiting for us there. Can your team help?"

Sol eyed Jethro as the mechanic chanted his mantra over and over. "Your mechanic is waiting? But aren't you the Doctor? Am I missing something here?"

"He came around and said he needed to get to the mainframe," Bisby responded. "Somewhere in that mush brain of his is a plan. Our chief mechanic can get to that plan."

☠☠☠

"Hey Lieutenant?" Sol called over the com.

Murphy hit the deck as a stray plasma bolt shot past her. "Whatcha got for me Specialist?"

"The doctor and the mech pilot think this wounded mechanic of theirs can help us shut down the mainframe and the self-destruct if we get him in the stronghold, sir."

"What do you think?" the Lieutenant asked, her hands moving quickly as she directed her team. "It's a long way from the train to the stronghold entrance with all these fucking mechs slamming about!"

"I think it's worth a fucking shot! Otherwise we're all crispy critters!"

☠☠☠

Shiner/Mathew unloaded their 50mms on anything that moved as the mech sprinted towards Rachel. "Rachel! Can you hear me?"

"Yeah, my ears are fine, I'm just trapped here!" she responded over the com.

"Good, stay that way! Do not fucking move!"

"What? Don't move?!? I'm about to be ripped apart here!"

Shiner/Mathew dove at the deaders piled onto Rachel's mech, shouldered two off while grabbing a third and using its momentum to flip about and toss the deader out into the battlefield.

Instantly the other dead mechs shifted their focus onto Shiner/Mathew.

"Bring it on you dead fucks!" Mathew roared.

💀💀💀

Jay stepped into the stronghold, his side arm drawn. The entry way was a massive staging area, making the mech base's hangar look like a guest room.

"Holy shit. I could build a fucking planet in here," he whispered, still unsure who or what occupied the UDC base. He scanned the walls until he found what he was looking for. Holstering his pistol, Jay ran to the control panel and began to hack the security system.

"T MINUS TWENTY MINUTES UNTIL NUCLEAR DETONATION!"

"Yeah, yeah, I know," Jay muttered, struggling against the stronghold's code. "No need to fucking shout it."

💀💀💀

Bisby stood outside the door as Specialists Kafar and Sol, using a blanket as a stretcher, carried the raving Jethro out of the small train compartment.

"This is going to fucking kill my back," Kafar complained.

"Grendetti is setting up a real stretcher outside, we just have to get him off this train," Sol replied. "So stop being such a fucking whiner."

"You need to get off my ass," Kafar said. "You've been riding it all day!"

"You need to show some fucking respect, Specialist," Sol barked. "Everything may have gone to shit, but I'm still 2nd in command here."

💀💀💀

The RPG sped towards the Railer car giving the occupants no time to evacuate.

Timson shielded his eyes from the blast and was instantly on the com with Jenny. "Fuck! Some of the deaders still have armaments. Scan the fuckers so we know which ones to target! And get that fire out before it spreads to the other cars!"

"We're on it!" Jenny responded. "Fire suppression team is already deployed! Scanning deaders now!"

"Give me a fucking target!" Timson yelled.

"Keep your goddamn britches on!" Marin shouted back. "It's hard to get a lock, they're all moving around so much!"

☠☠☠

"Son of a bitch!" Jay yelled, slamming his fist against the stronghold control panel, frustrated as he was yet again shut out of the mainframe. "Maybe I can at least get some light in here."

The chief mechanic easily bypassed two sub-systems and the halogens in the ceiling of the stronghold staging area began to glow. "Now we're talking… Oh my God…"

Jay turned about, his eyes fixed on the huge walls. "What the fuck?"

All about him the concrete walls were painted with murals, sketches, portraits, some as high as the staging area's ceiling itself. Jay could only stare.

☠☠☠

Masters stepped into the staging area, his head down, eyes on the floor.

"Masters!" Jay cried. "You're alive! Holy shit, can you believe this place?"

Masters didn't answer, he just pushed past as the mechanic ran to greet him.

"Mitch? Man, come on, you okay?" Jay said, blocking the pilot's path.

"Move Jay," Masters said quietly. "Don't make me hurt you."

Jay looked at the pistol in Masters' hand and frowned. "Seriously? What the fuck? You wouldn't…"

Jay crumpled immediately as the butt of the pistol connected with his forehead.

"Sorry about that, but I warned you," Masters said weakly.

☠☠☠

Shiner/Mathew kicked out, blocking the deader's attack. The mech lowered its right shoulder, coming in with a powerful uppercut, shearing the front of the dead mech's cockpit right off. Shiner/Mathew moved in for the killing blow, but was tackled about the waste by another deader and slammed hard into the earth, creating a twenty yard divot as the two machines slid.

Shiner/Mathew hooked its left elbow up under the dead mech's midsection for leverage and shoved, dislodging the abomination enough to give its right arm, and plasma cannon, a clear shot.

"Bye bye you fucking waste of metal!" Mathew screamed.

☠☠☠

"Fuck! Incoming!" Specialist Grendetti yelled as he fired ineffectual shot after ineffectual shot at the charging dead mech, trying to buy the Special Ops team some time as they struggled to get Jethro's prone form to the stronghold.

"Hold it off!" Murphy shouted, her attention diverted by another encroaching deader that had seen the easy meals making their way across the battlefield.

"I'm trying, but the thing won't stop!" Grendetti shouted back. "It's gonna be right on us!"

The ground shook as a broken, smoking deader husk slammed into the attacker. "I gotcha covered!" the Rookie called from Jay's mech.

Masters stepped from the stronghold's entrance, his eyes never looking up at the battle that raged before him.

"Come on," Masters said to Stomper. "We're leaving."

"Shall we not help the others?" Stomper asked.

"No," Masters answered flatly.

"Should I lift you to the cockpit?"

"No, I'm walking," Masters responded, his gait never slowing.

Stomper processed a moment. "Is this because of the Harlow's death? Do you want to die also?"

"I want to leave."

Stomper took a giant step and another, keeping Masters positioned securely between his colossal feet, shielding the pilot from the shrapnel and ordinance flying about.

Capreze watched the Hill Stomper progress through the middle of the fray.

"Pilot Masters! Do you read me?" Capreze called. "You need to get into your cockpit and engage the hostiles immediately! That is a direct order!"

Capreze waited but was answered by only silence.

"Pilot, do you read me?"

Still silence.

"Goddammit Mitch! What is your fucking malfunction?!?"

"Leave me alone Commander. It's all lost anyway. If you were smart you'd cut your losses and go," Masters answered finally.

"That is not an option, Pilot! Get in your fucking mech and do your fucking job!"

Masters refused to respond.

🐾🐾🐾

"Rachel! Oh, Jeezus Christ! Rachel!" Mathew screamed, blasting the last mech off of her. "Shiner! Is she alive?"

"Sensors show her vital signs are weak, Mathew. I am sorry, but I do not know if she will live much longer," Shiner answered somberly.

"Fuck! No!"

The ground shook and Shiner/Mathew turned, ready to continue fighting, but stopped short at the sight of Stomper rumbling past. "Mitch! Thank God! Help, I need to get Rachel out of her mech and into the stronghold!"

"Pilot Masters is not in his mech, he is walking below," Shiner observed.

"Masters! Where are you going?"

🐾🐾🐾

"Where the fuck is he going?!?" the Rookie shouted, grabbing a dead mech's arm, twisting it and slamming the monster to the ground as it reached for the Special Ops team.

"I don't know," Themopolous answered over the com. "Masters? Masters, can you read me?"

"He's snapped, Doc," Bisby said, his eyes focused on the retreating pilot and the mech towering above him. "He's giving up."

"What? Can he do that? Isn't there some type of honor code or something about leaving your fellow pilots to die?"

"Yeah, there is, but I don't think he gives a shit," Bisby answered.

🐾🐾🐾

The world exploded about Masters, but he didn't flinch. The cacophony of the Railers' large caliber guns didn't faze him. The roars of the dead mechs, those with working loudspeakers, echoed through the air, but Masters thought nothing of them.

In fact, thinking nothing was his only goal. Mitch Masters didn't want to think or feel or remember or even be. He wanted to die, but no longer had the willpower to pull the trigger. To take his own life would be too much effort, would require he bring his awareness back to the pain, back to what he lost.

🐾🐾🐾

"The fucking Hill Stomper is blocking my shots!" one of the Railer gunners yelled. "I can't see shit around that thing!"

"Just keep shooting! If you hit the fucking giant then you hit it! Don't let a crazy mech and its nut job pilot keep you from doing your fucking job!" Timson shouted back. "Just keep fucking shooting!"

Another train car exploded and the concussion nearly knocked Timson from his seat. The world flashed and spun, his ears ringing, the once deafening battle now reduced to muffled sounds like his ears were filled with foam.

"Status report!" he cried shakily.

☠☠☠

Jay forced himself to his feet and stumbled to the Special Ops team as they entered the stronghold.

"Jay!" Themopolous cried, rushing from Jethro's side to the chief mechanic's. "Jeezus, you're pouring blood! What happened?"

"Fucking Masters cold-cocked me! That's what fucking happened!" Jay growled. "I'm gonna kick his fucking ass the next time I see him!"

"Good luck," Bisby snorted. "The crazy asshole is walking up the middle of Hell right now. You'll be lucky if he has an ass left to kick."

Jay turned his attention to Jethro. "Let's get him to the mainframe."

"Follow me," Murphy said.

☠☠☠

"Capreze! We can't take much more of this!" Timson yelled as he fired point blank into a dead mech's cockpit as the thing hungrily reached for him. The machine stopped, lurched and fell, its outstretched arm missing Timson by feet, but crushing part of the train car he was positioned on. "My people and my train are getting cut apart! We can't last much longer!"

Capreze swept the legs of an attacking dead mech then leapt, bringing the full weight of his mech down on the deader's cockpit, crushing the zombie inside. "We have no choice! I'm losing people too!'

☠☠☠

"We've got to get her out of here!" Mathew cried, grabbing onto Rachel's mech's legs, trying to pull the machine out of the middle of the fray.

"There is no where to go," Shiner responded. "The stronghold has T minus eleven minutes until detonation. We can attempt to run, but not while burdened with the weight of another mech."

"Rachel is not a fucking burden!" Mathew screamed. "We have to do something!"

Shiner took control, sending four plasma blasts towards an oncoming dead mech, knocking the thing to the ground. "All we can do is fight. Fight until we die."

�☝

"What the fuck are these wall paintings?" Bisby asked as the Special Ops team made its way down the long concrete tunnel towards the mainframe control room.

Murphy chuckled lightly then seeing Bisby's scowl stopped. "Sorry. I forget that only UDC descendents, Special Ops and Intelligence personnel are allowed in the stronghold."

"UDC descendents? What the hell are you talking about?" Jay asked.

"Who do you think maintained this facility during all the years the wasteland was completely uninhabitable?" Specialist Sol said. "People have lived here, families have lived here for hundreds of years."

"Or they did," Murphy said solemnly.

☝☝☝

The Rookie stood at the entrance to the stronghold trying to figure out his next move.

"T MINUS TEN MINUTES UNTIL NUCLEAR DETONATION" the voice boomed behind him.

"Get your fucking ass in gear Rookie!" Capreze's voice boomed equally as loud over the com. "Jay didn't give you that mech so you can stand around with your dick in your hand! Someone told me you know how to kick ass! Now fucking do it, pilot!"

The Rookie smiled at the word 'pilot'. "Yes, sir!"

He cracked his neck, flexed his mech's fists then charged headlong into the middle of Hell.

☝☝☝

Timson watched in horror as three dead mechs attacked his train at once, ripping one of the cars, screaming gunner and all, right off the tracks, sending a shudder through the entire train.

"Goddammit! Somebody shoot those mother fucking things!" Timson yelled whipping his turret about. A massive mech hand reached out and grabbed his gun barrels, instantly twisting the metal. "Oh, Shit!" Timson dove from his seat, rolling off the top of the train car and landing hard on the ground feet below.

"Jenny! Immediate evac now!" he grunted.

"Where to?" Jenny shouted back.

"I don't know, just run!"

The mainframe control room door slid open and the Special Ops team hurried inside, setting Jethro carefully down on the floor.

"Frame like a house, frame like a house, tiny little body, small as a mouse!" Jethro repeated over and over.

"Does he ever fucking shut up?" Kafar complained. Jay and Bisby each moved towards the Specialist, but Themopolous held up her hand. "Cool it boys! We need to figure out what he wants."

Themopolous leaned close to Jethro. "Jethro, honey? Can you hear me? We're in the mainframe room. Now what?"

Jethro's eyes fixed on hers. "Jack me up."

"Jack him up?" Bisby asked. "What the fuck does that mean? And can someone shut these fucking emergency lights off?!? They're giving me a god-damn headache!"

"I got the lights," Specialist Grendetti said, moving to a control panel on the wall.

Jay stood before Johnson's emaciated corpse, reclined in the cerebral integration chair. Themopolous came up behind him and grimaced. "He must have been in that chair for quite awhile after those feeding tubes ran dry." She stepped past Jay and inspected the equipment. "We can keep Jethro's body alive indefinitely with this set up. But, what about his mind?"

"What do you know about the mainframe's AI?" Jay asked Murphy.

The Lieutenant furrowed her brow. "I don't know what you mean."

"Did it interact with base personnel? Did it have a personality of its own? Have there ever been any major issues you know about it? Shit like that."

"No, issues and it never interacted," Lieutenant Murphy answered.

"Good, that means the AI is passive and won't resist when I plug Jethro in," Jay said.

"Actually, there is one thing," Sol cautioned. "It's a permanent job. Once you are hooked up, you can't unhook, hence the life support set-up."

Jay looked at his protégé and friend. "I don't think Jethro has much choice. And neither do we."

Themopolus unhooked the tubes and lines from Johnson's corpse and grabbed her bag, yanking out gauze and antiseptic. "You aren't hooking him into shit until I get these cleaned off."

"T MINUS FIVE MINUTES UNTIL NUCLEAR DETONATION."

"Somebody help her clean that shit!" Murphy ordered. Sol, Grendetti and Kafar each took a hose and cleaned furiously.

"Can he cancel the self-destruct?" Murphy asked Jay.

"Yes, I know he can," Jay answered. "What I don't know is how long the integration process takes.

☠☠☠

The Rookie stood encircled by dead mechs. Six of the monstrosities surrounded him and the Rookie waited for the first to move.

When it finally did, an ancient battle mech, probably first generation, the Rookie was ready. In a flash he had studied each dead mech down to the tiniest detail. Just as he did back in the fight cage, he knew his opponent's weaknesses and he meant to exploit them.

The dead mech rushed him and he knelt his mech down, striking a blow directly on the oncoming mech's left knee, shattering the structure and crippling the deader instantly.

☠☠☠

Dead mech after dead mech after dead mech tried to get at the meat walking between Stomper's legs and dead mech after dead mech after dead mech was crushed, ground into the dirt like a tin can.

Masters barely noticed, in fact he was disappointed that he had such an effective bodyguard. He would have welcomed death at any point, knowing he was too much of a coward to take his own life. His lip curled in a sneer as thoughts of self-loathing over took him.

He walked from the battlefield, his giant in tow, and never glanced back once.

☠☠☠

"We are out of ammunition," Shiner stated, the plasma cannon refusing to discharge. "We are left to fend off the dead ones with our bare hands."

Mathew looked down at Rachel's mech and the woman he loved lying unconscious inside the cockpit. "I'm prepared for that."

A deader roared behind them and Shiner/Mathew whirled about, landing a kick to the dead mech's chest, denting the cockpit structure. The deader stumbled back, but recovered quickly, diving at Shiner/Mathew's legs. Shiner/Mathew brought its right fist down, timing the blow perfectly, smashing the deader deep into the dirt. Shiner/Mathew struck again and again.

💀💀💀

Timson stared in horror as he watched his people snatched up by the ravenous dead mechs, most of the mechanical beasts not even pausing to open their cockpit hatches, just stuffing the screaming victims through broken windshields and bent supports and into the waiting, starving jaws of the zombie pilots within.

"What have I done? I shouldn't have brought them here," he whispered, falling to his knees.

"Dad! What are you doing?" Jenny cried, running to Timson's side.

"It's all my fault," Timson said weakly.

Marin came up beside Jenny. "What the fuck?" Marin slapped Timson hard across the face.

💀💀💀

The Rookie drove his right leg out like a piston, crushing the knee joints of the three closest deaders. He felt his mech shudder as a dead mech grabbed him from behind. He reached up over his shoulders, snagging the deader by its back support struts, and yanked hard, tossing the dead mech over him and into the others.

He reached out, ripping a deader's arm out of its coupling and stood, brandishing the massive metal limb like a club.

"You may not have faces, but when I kill you all, I'm wearing something of yours!" the Rookie grinned viciously.

💀💀💀

"Are you sure this isn't going to just kill him?" Bisby asked as Themopolous attached the last of the life support hoses to Jethro's body.

"No, Biz, I'm not sure," Themopolous barked. "Look around you! Does anyone look fucking sure of anything?"

"Damn, I'm just concerned for Jethro. I mean…"

"You think I'm not concerned?!?" Themopolous shouted. "Why don't you go sit your one-armed ass over there and get the fuck out of my way?"

Bisby scowled, but didn't protest.

"Ready, Jay?" Themopolous shouted.

Jay tried to hide his amusement at Bisby's dressing down. "Yep."

"Then push the fucking button!"

ψψψ

Jethro's body shuddered and convulsed as the cerebral integration systems activated. The vid screens flashed hundreds of images a second, making most of the Special Ops team turn their eyes away.

"Fuck! That's worse than the emergency lights," Bisby complained.

Jethro's eyes bulged and rolled back up into his head.

"Jethro!" Theopolous cried. "What's wrong? He's not connecting, is he?"

Jay closed his eyes. "Fuck, I didn't think of this." Jay opened his eyes and looked at everyone. "He doesn't have a Reaper chip anymore." The Chief mechanic glanced at Johnson's corpse. "But, I know where he can get one."

ψψψ

"There is a transport approaching," Stomper stated.

"Yeah, so fucking what?" Masters replied, not bothering to glance up and out into the wasteland. "Maybe it will run over me."

"It is a familiar one," Stomper said. "I recognize the transport's signature."

"Good for you," Masters responded. "I'll be sure to get you a gold star at some point." Masters clapped his hands together exaggeratingly, the metal of his pistol slapping against his palm. "Yay for Stomper! He so smart!"

The giant mech stopped. "You have become aggressive and mean. I do not know if I want to go with you."

ψψψ

"T MINUS TWO MINUTES UNTIL NUCLEAR DETONATION"

"We aren't going to make it," Themopolous cried as Sol and Kafar held Jethro upright while she prepped the back of his head for the Reaper chip insertion.

"Bullshit!" Jay scolded, holding up the Reaper chip he had just removed from Johnson's corpse. "We will make it! Here!" Jay handed the chip over to Specialist Grendetti who carefully cleaned and prepped it before handing it to Themopolous.

"T MINUS ONE MINUTE UNTIL NUCLEAR DETONATION"

"Can someone turn that off!" Themopolous yelled, hands shaking as she took the Reaper chip.

"No, sorry," Sol apologized.

"T MINUS THIRTY SECONDS UNTIL NUCLEAR DETONATION"
The voice echoed across the battlefield.

"Jay?!? Jay, what's your status? JAY!" Capreze shouted over the com. "Jay, come in Goddammit!"

"T MINUS TWENTY-FIVE SECONDS UNTIL NUCLEAR DETONATION"

"Shiner says there's a change in the stronghold's mainframe AI," Mathew said, lifting a dead mech up over his head and slamming it into the ground.

"T MINUS TWENTY SECONDS UNTIL NUCLEAR DETONATION"

Shiner/Mathew jumped up and down on the deader until it stopped struggling. "Yeah, stay down you fucking bitch!"

"T MINUS FIFTEEN SECONDS UNTIL NUCLEAR DETONATION"

"Hey, Commander?"

"Yes, Mathew?"

"Thanks for everything."

"T MINUS TEN SECONDS UNTIL NUCLEAR DETONATION"

"No pressure, Doc," Jay said nervously. "All the time in the world."

Themopolous ignored him and focused on the last suture. "There! Done!"

Sol and Kafar eased Jethro back and Jay started the cerebral integration process again.

"T MINUS FIVE SECONDS UNTIL NUCLEAR DETONATION"

"Okay Jethro, don't fail us buddy. You can do this," Jay whispered.

"T MINUS FOUR SECONDS UNTIL NUCLEAR DETONATION"

"Come on you techie pain in the ass," Bisby said.

"T MINUS THREE SECONDS UNTIL NUCLEAR DETONATION"

"Please work, please work," Themopolous repeated.

"T MINUS TWO SECONDS UNTIL NUCLEAR DETONATION

"T MINUS ONE SECOND UNTIL NUCLEAR DETONATION"

Capreze closed his eyes, said a quick prayer and waited for the blast that he would never even feel.

Nothing.

"Um, sir? Are we dead?" Mathew asked.

"No, pilot, we aren't," Capreze responded.

The stronghold's gun turrets whirred to life, targeting the dead mechs left on the battlefield. Large caliber rounds flew threw the air, shearing metal from deader frames, obliterating their cockpits.

"What the fuck?!?" Capreze cried.

"Howdy everyone!" Jethro's voice echoed from the stronghold. "How's it going? Miss me?"

"MOTHER FUCKING YEAH!" Mathew yelled. "Welcome back you son of a bitch!"

☠☠☠

"Don't cheer me yet," Jethro said. "I've got some bad news."

Capreze sighed. "Of course you do."

"Now that I'm master of the wasteland, Lord of the stronghold, I have access to some really, really cool tech."

"Get on with it, Jethro," Capreze ordered impatiently. "What is the bad news?"

"We've got another 38 dead mechs coming from all sides," Jethro announced apologetically. "First few will be here in ten minutes."

"Of course they will," Capreze said. "Have any good news?"

"Funny you should ask. If you get your mech butts inside I can reload your armaments in eight minutes."

☠☠☠

"How's he holding up?" Jay asked, crowding next Themopolous as the doctor checked Jethro's life support equipment.

Themopolous elbowed Jay away. "Do you mind, Mr. Rind? A little space, please."

"Sorry, Doc," Jay apologized. "So?"

"I'm fine Jay," Jethro's voice boomed.

"And really fucking loud," Bisby shouted.

"Sorry about that. This better?"

"Yeah, that's perfect, mechanic," Jay said glaring at Bisby.

"What?" Bisby asked innocently.

"How do you feel, Jethro?" the Doctor asked.

"Oh, Doc, you won't believe what I'm plugged into!" Jethro exclaimed. "The medical knowledge alone will blow you away!"

"Um, so are we safe?" Specialist Grendetti asked.

☠☠☠

Stomper stood still, refusing to take another step.

"What? So you're just going to stand there forever and pout? Move!" Masters ordered continuing to walk further into the wasteland.

"No," Stomper responded. "You are not the nice Masters. You are not the Masters that loves the Harlow. And I am going to tell her so when she gets here."

Masters stopped. "What did you just say?" he asked, his voice low and menacing.

Stomper pointed towards the transport that was skidding to a halt in front of them. Masters watched as the ramp lowered and a gore smeared Harlow exited.

The Rookie ripped off the dead mech's cockpit and snatched the squirming, raging zombie pilot out, bringing the zombie up close to his own cockpit as he squeezed the deader into a pulp.

"Rookie! Regroup in the stronghold's staging area! Right now!" Capreze ordered over the com.

The Rookie grinned as the gore squished through his mech's giant fist.

"Rookie! Do you fucking hear me?"

Capreze marched his mech directly in front of the Rookie's. "We are on a schedule here! Get your ass inside!"

The Rookie slowly turned his attention to focus on the Commander. "I'm good right here."

"I need help with Rachel!" Mathew called.

Capreze backed his mech away, but kept eye contact with the Rookie. "I'll deal with you in a minute!"

"You unlocked this beast, Commander," the Rookie said. "Don't get mad at me because it ain't so easy to put back in its cage."

Capreze stalked off and turned his attention to his daughter's mech. "Sweet Jeezus Baby Girl…"

"I can't get out to check on her!" Mathew cried.

"Doctor!" Capreze yelled over the com. "If Jethro can spare you I need you out here now! Rachel's down!"

Capreze un-strapped and descended his mech.

Masters watched the deader skin clad Harlow step from the transport. He lifted his pistol, hoping he had the strength to do what needed to be done, to kill his undead love.

"Are you fucking shitting me, Pilot?" Harlow said. "You once told me I could be covered in pus and open sores and I'd still be fuckable. Are you taking that back?"

Masters blinked several times. "Stomper, did you hear that?"

"I have been trying to tell you," Stomper replied. "The Harlow is alive."

Masters dropped his side arm and fell to his knees, his body racked with sobs.

💀💀💀

Harlow knelt by Masters and lifted his chin. "Are you Mitch Mother Fucking Masters or are you Mitch Cry Baby Masters?"

Masters broke into a smile and hugged Harlow fiercely, attacking her face with kisses. "Fuck, you taste awful!" he cried, spitting into the wasteland dirt.

"I don't smell so hot, either," Harlow smiled helping Masters to his feet.

"Fuck if I care!" he responded kissing her passionately. "Stomper, turn around. Mommy and Daddy are gonna get nasty!"

"But, the others?" Stomper asked.

Harlow eyed Masters carefully. "What'd I miss?"

Master sighed. "I kinda freaked out and bailed."

"YOU WHAT?!?"

PART TWO - FIREWALL

"Mech coming in! Clear a path!" Capreze shouted at the Railers setting up triage stations within the staging area. "Where do you want me Jethro?"

"Follow the flashing red line to the re-load positions on the wall. Just park it, I'll do the rest," Jethro's voice answered. "We've got incoming in less than five minutes so you might as well stay in your cockpit."

"Damn, I gotta piss," Capreze complained.

"Don't even fucking start with that," Mathew said as Shiner reloaded all of his weapons systems across the staging area from Capreze.

"Sorry," Capreze apologized. "Hey, Doc? How's my girl?"

💀💀💀

Themopolous shouted orders to the Railer medics as she rushed from one wounded person to another.

"Your daughter is still unconscious, Commander," Themopolous said. "Just like last minute and the minute before that."

"Sorry, I was just hoping, well, you know," the Commander said.

"Yes, sir, I do know. She's stable. Weak, but stable and that's better than most of the people I need to focus on now. So, can you let me do my job, please?"

"Of course," Capreze replied. "Let me know if-"

"You'll be the first to hear if her condition changes."

"I'm second, Doc," Mathew insisted.

👿👿👿

The Rookie stood his mech outside the stronghold, foregoing the weapons system reload. He flexed the mech's fingers over and over, the itch for battle making him jumpy.

"Hey kid?" Jay's voice called over the com. "How you holding up?"

"Doin' fine, Jay," the Rookie answered.

"Uh-huh," Jay said. "The Commander says you've got a little attitude."

"Just got my fight face on."

"Right. How about you take that face off? The Commander wants *you* out there fighting, not the Razor."

"Is there a difference anymore?" the Rookie asked.

"There is," Jay responded. "You know it and I know it."

👿👿👿

Capreze watched Shiner/Mathew from across the staging area. He knew that mech and not just from the vid feed of the mini-mechs days ago. Something in his sub-conscious itched at the sight of the former deader.

"How old are you Shiner?" Capreze asked.

The mech didn't respond.

"He's running some major diagnostics right now, sir," Mathew said. "But, from what I can tell he is old, the first dead mech."

Capreze narrowed his eyes. "The first?"

"Yep. But most of that info is damaged, so I can only access fragments. Why?"

"Just like to know who I'm fighting next to."

👿👿👿

"You've taken a shine to the Rookie, haven't you?" Jethro asked as Jay tapped at the mainframe's control console, double checking system stability, looking for any hidden problems with Jethro's cerebral integration.

"Don't worry, Jethro," Jay laughed. "You're still my number one pain in the ass."

"Oh, I'm not worried about that," Jethro laughed also. "Ego has pretty much flown out the window now that I'm a digital God."

"Huh-uh! Don't even start with the God talk. I'll unplug your ass in five seconds."

"Yeah, but I wish you could experience this! It's every mechanics' dream! I *am* the tech!"

☗☗☗

"We have everyone accounted for, Commander," Lieutenant Murphy reported. "All Railers are inside the stronghold."

"Thank you, Lieutenant," Capreze said from his mech. "I appreciate that. I know technically you don't have to listen to a word I say."

"You're the ranking officer now, sir," Murphy said. "The chain of command is important."

"I commend your attitude, Murphy. Most people would throw the chain away when the world goes to Hell."

"It's when the world goes to Hell that we need that chain more than ever, sir."

"Very true, Lieutenant."

"Anything else, sir?"

"No, Lieutenant. Just keep your folks ready."

☗☗☗

"How far off are the deaders?" Jay asked Jethro.

"Two minutes and they'll start coming over the ridges," Jethro answered.

"And you're sure there's nothing you can do to stop them?"

"Nope," Jethro replied. "Johnson's death fried the communications relay. It must have been specifically calibrated to his brain waves. I'm trying to rebuild it, but there's so much in here it's hard to focus."

Jay looked over at Jethro's still body. "Don't start going all schizo."

"Not a problem."

"What about the remaining inoculated zombies?"

"Running free across the wasteland for now."

"How many?"

"A few hundred thousand."

"Jeezus."

☗☗☗

The stronghold's gun turrets came to life, all turning their attention on the East ridge.

"They here?" the Rookie asked Jethro.

"The first wave is," Jethro answered. "You've got 13 coming from the

East."

The Rookie walked his mech away from the stronghold entrance. He bounced up and down a bit, getting himself ready. "I've got whatever gets past you."

"Roger that," Jethro acknowledged. "Just be careful. These guys have come further than the last. We're talking deep waste here. I can already tell most of them are beyond berserk with hunger. Looks like they've even been fighting amongst themselves."

☠☠☠

"Well, you're looking good," Jay said. "How are you feeling? Any pain?"

"Yeah, but it's almost like it's not part of me," Jethro responded. "I mean, I know my body has had its ass kicked, but it's separate somehow. Does that make sense?"

"Disassociation," Jay replied. "Your mind can now compartmentalize anything. It's stuffing your discomfort away in some sub-system to deal with later. You want me to get the Doc?"

"No, she's busy. Plus any painkillers will dull my brain. I don't think we want me getting loopy when we're all sitting on a few kilotons of nuclear material."

☠☠☠

"Jethro, how much longer before we're armed?" Capreze asked.

"Just give me another minute, sir," Jethro replied. "Like I just told the Rookie, these deaders are super fucking pissed. They're the crazy ones, the deep wasters. I don't know how they've survived this long out there, but you're going to need every bit of firepower you can."

"I understand. I just don't like the idea of the Rookie out there alone right now. He doesn't seem stable."

"I can assure you, sir, that the Rookie's brain wave activity shows not only stability but calm. The kid's ready to kick ass."

☠☠☠

"Okay, I'm heading to the hangar to try to get Rachel's mech operational in case we need it," Jay said, stepping away from the control console and placing a hand on Jethro's unresponsive shoulder. "Call me on the com if you start to feel weird."

"Start? I'm *way* past weird!" Jethro laughed.

"You know what I mean dumbass," Jay said, walking to the door. "I mean it, the second you even think you may be losing control you call me."

"Will do Dad."

"Fuck you, dip shit."

Jay stepped from the room leaving Jethro's body alone, but his mind everywhere.

☠☠☠

"Here they come!" the Rookie shouted. "Fucking Hell! Look at 'em!"

Over the East ridge 13 dead mechs charged. Many of them missing arms, cables hanging loose, struts bent at strange angles, their metal pitted with rust and deep gouges from God knows what. They shoved and raged at each other as they jockeyed for position, each trying to be the first to get at the meat.

"I've seen some fucked up deaders before, but these things are monsters!" the Rookie exclaimed.

The stronghold's gun turrets opened fire. "Well, let's shred these monsters!" Jethro yelled.

"Fuck yeah!" the Rookie responded.

☠☠☠

Themopolous dashed from cot to cot, blanket to blanket, desperate to stabilize as many of the wounded as possible. She left bloody gauze and shouted orders in her wake.

The large caliber gunfire from the stronghold's turrets made her and everyone else in the staging area jump. Railer children cried and clung tight to their parents and siblings. Themopolous shook off her startled shock and kept moving.

A hand reached out and gently, but firmly took her arm.

"Where do you need me?" June said. "I know Harlow has always been your go to assistant, but I'm ready to help."

☠☠☠

Intense, ravenous, hunger driven rage pushed the dead mechs towards the stronghold. As the Rookie stepped away from the entrance they stopped their in fighting and focused their attention on him. The weaker ones fell back as those more battle ready lunged forward, many directly into the oncoming turret fire. Chunks of metal and plastic were ripped from their 50-ton exoskeletons, exposing their infrastructure and vital systems.

The Rookie watched as Jethro systematically dismantled every single oncoming deader in a matter of seconds.

"Jeezus fuck," the Rookie exclaimed. "The Outsider could have torn us all apart at any time, huh?"

"Wow, that was fun!" Jethro shouted.

Capreze and Shiner/Mathew stepped from the stronghold and took up positions on either side of the Rookie.

"Holy mother of God," Mathew said quietly.

"That is quite impressive," Shiner added.

"Knowing what you two are capable of, I'll take that as a huge compliment there Shiner," Jethro said.

"It was meant as one," Shiner replied.

"You know we can handle this, right?" Capreze said. "I need to know you're focusing on the mainframe."

"Got it covered, Commander. I can be at several places at once. I'm running six levels of diagnostics as we speak."

June left the Boiler child to rest with a group of other children while she helped Themopolous. She smiled at him as she walked away and he waved weakly.

The Doctor looked from June to the child and back. "What are you thinking, Pilot?"

June turned her attention to Themopolous. "About what?"

"The boy. He has no family here. You've taken him from the only existence he's known. Are you going to raise him yourself?"

June's brow furrowed. "I hadn't really thought about that. My main concern was getting him out of the Boiler village. That's all I cared about."

"Commander?" Bisby called over the com. "Lieutenant Murphy has her team assembled and is planning on doing a security sweep of the stronghold. Just to confirm we actually are alone."

"Sounds like a fine idea," Capreze responded.

"I'm going with. Jethro'll be systematically unlocking sections as we approach and, well, that little shit can take some getting used to. I didn't want to leave them stranded while he babbles on about being a digital God."

Capreze smiled. "That's a good plan, Biz. Plus, you'll be able to tell if Jethro starts acting funny. I'm still not comfortable with his integration."

"Need this?" Marin asked, handing Jay the span-hammer he was reaching for.

"Thanks," Jay responded, taking the tool. "You want to help?"

"Figured I would," Marin said, grabbing a massive torque wrench as she eyed three fist sized bolts on Rachel's mech's left ankle. She let out a loud whistle and three Railers ran up, tools in hand. "I brought some back up."

Jay studied the Railers suspiciously. "They know how to-?"

"Yep," Marin cut him off.

"Well, what about-?"

"That too, Jay."

"I bet they don't-."

"Yes, they do," Marin laughed.

Marin motioned and the three set to work.

☠☠☠

"Five more heading at us!" Jethro announced.

"You gonna let us take them on or are you...?" Mathew trailed off as ten RPGs screamed past the three mechs, heading straight at the attacking deaders coming from the West this time. "Guess that answers that."

Each rocket hit its mark, crippling the deaders instantly.

"See? I didn't fully take them out," Jethro laughed. "I left you folks the kill shots."

"Thanks," the Rookie grumbled.

"Stand down mechanic," Capreze ordered. "Let us handle combat, you stick with tech."

"But, sir, I'm way more capable..."

"We'll call you if we need you, Jethro."

☠☠☠

"This is the mess," Murphy said to Bisby as they approached the large sealed doors. "I'm pretty sure it was dinner time when Johnson took everyone out, so this may not be pretty."

"What's waiting for us, Jethro?" Bisby asked aloud.

"The Lieutenant's right. It isn't pretty. You're looking at several hundred corpses on the other side of the doors," Jethro responded. "Hmmmm, weird..."

"What?" Bisby asked.

"Well, they're actually corpses. Dead. Not undead. Not re-animated. Truly fucking dead. Hold on."

Bisby and the Special Ops team waited for a moment.

"Jethro?" Bisby said.

"Just sit tight Biz. Something's strange."

"What is that?" Jethro processed to himself, while instantaneously analyzing the air samples from the stronghold mess hall. "That's new."

In less than ten seconds he had the analysis results. "Holy shit! Hey Biz?"

"Yeah, Jethro? Whatcha got for us?" Bisby rolled his eyes at the Special Ops team.

"Listen, I'm evacuating the air from the mess, but you all should probably suit up before going in there. There is some type of new neurotoxin floating about. That's what Johnson used to kill these folks."

"Why aren't they zombies?" Grendetti asked.

"Not sure. I think it kills the virus also."

"Enviro suits are this way," Lieutenant Murphy said to Bisby. "Jethro, is the way clear to the suit lockers?"

"Yes, Lieutenant. All hatches are unlocked and there is nothing out of the ordinary in your path," Jethro replied. "You are all set."

"Thank you." The Special Ops team set off down the hall away from the mess with Bisby following behind.

The wounded pilot soon was short of breath and leaned against the wall for support.

"You're pushing it Biz," Jethro said.

"I'm fine," Bisby grumbled.

"No, you're not," Jethro said. "You're pulse is through the roof."

"Fuck you Jethro."

"Whoa, where did that partition come from?" Jethro mused as he found a separate part of the mainframe his consciousness hadn't penetrated yet. "Aren't you some fancy schmancy code."

The former mechanic inspected the partition from all angles before setting about accessing it. "Now, this won't hurt a bit, I promise."

Jethro gasped mentally and his physical body actually shook in the integration chair. "You've got to be kidding me."

He pushed a little harder and further immersed himself within the partitioned area.

"Unauthorized access. Admittance denied," an automated voice rang in his head.

"Oh, no you don't," Jethro responded.

🕱🕱🕱

The Rookie kicked the terminated dead mech with his own mech's foot.

"Leave it, Rookie," Capreze said. "We don't know what armaments the thing may still have and whether or not they're stable."

"Well, why don't we blast them and set them off?" the Rookie asked.

"Because we may need to do that when the other deaders get here," Mathew said.

"My scans indicate that all dead mechs have long been out of any type of ammunition," Shiner added.

"See," the Rookie said.

"It's a learning lesson, Rookie," Capreze said. "Jethro? When's the next wave?"

Silence.

"Jethro?" Capreze asked again.

🕱🕱🕱

Bisby watched the Special Ops team clomp past him in their clunky enviro suits. "You guys go ahead," he said, waving them on. "I'll catch up in a bit."

Specialist Sol gave him a thumbs up and Bisby could see the grin through the face plate. "No hurries, Pilot. Take a load off. You've earned it."

The team stepped to the stronghold mess doors and waited. "Any time you're ready, Jethro. We're all suited up," the Lieutenant said.

The doors remained closed. Bisby got to his feet and walked over to the team. "Hey Jethro! Open the fucking doors."

Silence.

🕱🕱🕱

Proximity alarms echoed about the Commander's cockpit. "Jethro?!? Where the fuck are you?!? We have incoming and I need numbers now!" Capreze waited but there was no response. "Jay? Come in."

"What's up Commander?" Jay answered over the com.

"I've lost contact with Jethro and we have hostiles on the way!"

"I'm on it!" Jay replied.

The Rookie turned his mech 360 degrees. "I don't see anything, sir."

"I don't have a visual, either," Mathew agreed. "Shiner?"

"There are many readings," Shiner responded. "Ten from the East, nine from the West."

"Well Rookie, time to go to work!" Mathew shouted.

💀💀💀

"You got this?" Jay asked Marin as he clambered down from Rachel's mech.

"Yeah, go!" she yelled.

Jay sprinted from the staging area and down the long concrete hall leading to the mainframe. When he reached the door he found it was locked tight. Pulling a screwdriver from his belt he pried the door control panel off. He took a quick glance at the wiring and laughed.

"That's the best security they could come up with?"

With two wire snips and a twist he hot wired the door open and dashed inside. Random images flashed across the mainframe vid screens.

💀💀💀

"What happened?" Timson hollered up to Marin from the bottom of Rachel's mech.

"Don't know!" she responded. "Something's wrong with Jethro."

"That's not good!"

"No, it's not!"

"Jenny!" Timson turned, looking for his daughter.

"What?" she yelled, busy wrapping her left hand with gauze, covering a nasty burn.

"Jethro's down, which means the guns are down!" Timson shouted. "Come on!"

Jenny sighed then started barking orders at any Railer that wasn't wounded or tending to the wounded.

A group of eight, including Jenny met Timson at the stronghold entrance. They all nodded to each other then raced to the train.

💀💀💀

Capreze watched the Railers run across the battlefield towards their train. "Timson! What the Hell are you doing?"

"Picking up the slack! With your man Jethro down you'll need our guns again!"

Even though he didn't like putting Timson and his people back in harms way, he couldn't argue with the man. "Thanks. But, listen, if it gets too crazy I want you and your folks to get your asses back inside!"

"I think we can agree on that, Commander!"

"Sir!" Mathew shouted. "They're here!"

Capreze blanched as he watched the dead mechs surge over the ridges, surrounding them all.

☠☠☠

Grendetti and Kafar each pushed their weight against the crowbar they wedged into the mess hall doors. Grunting under the strain they fell back, unsuccessful.

"Shit! That door isn't going anywhere!" Specialist Kafar huffed. "Where's your tech guy?"

Bisby shook his head. "I don't have a fucking clue. Jethro? Jethro!"

"Biz? It's Jay. I need you in the mainframe room."

"What the hell is wrong with Jethro?"

"I don't know. Just get your ass here. I need your eyes on something," Jay barked.

"Okay, calm down." Bisby nodded to the Special Ops team and hurried away on still shaky legs.

☠☠☠

"Back to back on me now!" Capreze ordered.

Shiner/Mathew and the Rookie backed their mechs up next to Capreze's creating a triangle of mech firepower.

"Keep firing until I say break! Do not step away until then!"

"Yes, sir!" Mathew shouted.

"Gotcha," the Rookie acknowledged.

"Affirmative," Shiner added, making Capreze grin despite himself, knowing he now commanded a former deader by default.

As the dead mechs raged down the ridges, Capreze, Shiner/Mathew and the Rookie opened up with everything they had.

Hot lead and plasma blasts filled the air. The earth shook as the bolts and bullets found their marks.

☠☠☠

"3 o'clock Jenny!" Timson screamed. "3 o'clock goddamn it!"

Jenny swung her gun turret about 45 degrees and opened fire on the dead mech only yards from her. The behemoth shuddered under the large caliber rounds, but kept charging, its dead fist reaching for her.

"Fucking get out of there!"

Jenny un-strapped and leapt from the gun seat, rolling across the train car roof as the deader's hand slammed down where she had just been. She got to her feet immediately and jumped the gap between train cars, trying to put more distance between herself and the undead battle machine.

The Rookie watched the deader chase Jenny from car to car, the other Railers unable to help her without risking hitting each other.

"Commander! Jenny's in trouble!" the Rookie called.

"Do not break formation!" Capreze yelled back, putting six plasma blasts into a deader's mid-section, dropping the thing in a pile of flame and melted metal. "That's an order, Rookie!"

The Rookie snarled in frustration. He sent 50mm fire towards the East ridge attackers then turned his plasma cannon on the dead mech chasing Jenny. Cracking his neck, he slowed his breathing and took careful aim, leading the deader slightly.

Jenny stumbled and slid, nearly tumbling off the train car she was on.

"JENNY!" she heard her father scream as the dead mech reached for her, its zombie pilot thrashing in the cockpit, eager for its meal.

She felt the train car rock and shudder once, twice then the dead mech's cockpit exploded outward towards her and she could see the extended arm of the Rookie's mech, plasma cannon glowing, through the resulting hole in the deader's body.

"Sorry! Wasn't exactly a clean shot," the Rookie said over the com. "Did you catch any shrapnel?"

"No, I'm good. Thank you."

"Dead mechs eight and twelve have some weapons capabilities!" Shiner called out. "Target those!"

"Too late!" Capreze responded, fire burning in his left shoulder as two slugs ripped through his uniform, his skin, muscle and bone. "I'm hit!"

The Commander's mech wobbled, but he gritted his teeth and regained control. "Split now! Take the battle to them!"

"Thought you'd never say so!" the Rookie yelled, pushing his mech into a full run towards four oncoming deaders. He dropped and slid, taking their legs out then was up and throwing punches, elbows and kicks like the pit fighting Boiler he was.

Jenny strapped herself into an unoccupied gun seat and brought the turret to face the deader with the 50mm. She unleashed a hail of large caliber rounds at the dead mech, ripping its thighs to shreds. The thing fell forward, one arm outstretched to catch itself while its 50mm shot wild, hitting several of the deaders close to it.

One of the dead mechs that was hit became further enraged and began to pummel the fallen deader, ripping its 50mm right off its frame, beating the thing over and over with the gun until the dead mech no longer moved.

☠☠☠

Shiner/Mathew side stepped, bringing its left knee up as a deader dove at it. The dead mech's cockpit crumpled like paper from the force of the impact and Shiner/Mathew wasted no time in blasting the zombie pilot, lifting the defeated dead mech over its head and tossing it into the group of attackers coming from the west, sending several sprawling.

"Left hydraulics took serious damage," Shiner stated.

"Serious damage and non-functioning are two different things! Keep fighting!" Mathew responded.

"I had zero intent of surrendering the fight. I was merely giving you a status report," Shiner stated.

"Status noted. Thanks."

☠☠☠

"Mathew! Down!" the Rookie shouted, rushing towards the mech.

Shiner dropped the 50-ton war machine to the dirt just as the Rookie leapt above them, tackling the deader poised to strike from behind.

The dead mech tucked a leg up under the Rookie and easily tossed him off, sending the live mech rolling across the ground.

The dead mech was instantly on its feet and roaring. Shiner/Mathew reached for the deader's leg, trying to trip it up, but the thing moved too quickly, avoiding the grab while also stomping Shiner/Mathew's outstretched fist into pieces.

"It's a fucking thinker!" Mathew cried.

☠☠☠

The gunner two cars from Timson's pleaded for help as he was plucked from his seat by a dead mech and jammed into the thing's cockpit, the poor Railer's limbs snapping as his body was shoved through the windshield.

"Capreze! We're getting our asses handed to us! Where the fuck is your-

?!?" But, Timson never finished as giant metal fingers closed about his head, popping it off like a cork from a bottle.

Jenny screamed as she turned her turret to see her father's decapitated corpse spewing blood from its open neck before the deader snatched it up.

"Daddy!!! NOOOO!!!"

� skulls☠☠☠

Capreze watched Jenny open fire in a mad rage, aiming at anything that moved. "Jenny! Watch the friendly fire Goddammit!" he ordered over the com, but Jenny was lost in murderous grief, oblivious to the world around her, bent only on death and revenge. "Jay! Give me something! Is Jethro back online?!?"

"Back online?!? He's not a fucking machine!" Jay barked over the com.

"Right now he is! I need the stronghold's defenses operational! Can you bypass him and hack them yourself?"

"Not a fucking chance! This system is locked down! Only one person at a time is allowed access!"

☠☠☠

"Marin! You read?"

"Yeah, Jay. Whatcha need?" the Railer mechanic responded over the com.

"I need your help right now!" Jay replied. "I've got Bisby monitoring Jethro's life signs, but I need another set of tech hands! This shit is ten kinds of fucked up!"

Marin tossed her span-wrench to a Railer tech and took off running towards the mainframe room. "I'm on my way!"

She quickly passed the Special Ops team still struggling to open the mess doors, but didn't slow to help even when Specialist Sol began shouting after her.

When she entered the mainframe room she gasped.

☠☠☠

The Rookie got to his feet firing, sending round after round into the deader reaching once again for Mathew/Shiner.

The monster shuddered under the assault, but refused to fall. It turned its attention onto the Rookie, roared and charged.

"Holy fuck! This one won't fucking die!" the Rookie yelled, bracing for the impact as the dead mech continued to close the distance despite being riddled with large caliber slugs.

The Rookie's head slammed back as war machine met war machine and the world spun. He could hear someone shouting, but it was barely audible over the ringing in his ears.

☠☠☠

"What the shit?" Marin said, her eyes drawn to the rapidly changing images flashing across the mainframe vid screens. "Where are those coming from?"

"I don't fucking know!" Jay shouted. "But, I think they're what Jethro is seeing!"

"His pulse is weakening!" Bisby called out. "Should I get the Doc?"

"Not yet! Just give me a second!" Jay replied. "Marin, take that console there, see if you can find an end around to get manual control of the stronghold defenses. Our people are getting torn up out there!"

Marin studied the tech in front of her and went to work.

☠☠☠

Red.

The red of blood.

Blood spurting from Timson's neck, the blood pumping behind Jenny's eyes, making it even harder to see past the hot tears. Her whole world turned red.

"Dammit Railer! Get yourself under fucking control!" Capreze shouted, throwing his mech to the ground as Jenny swung about, heedlessly firing at everything around her.

Capreze had to make a quick decision, a decision he didn't want to make, but had no choice. He sent a plasma blast into the train car Jenny was set up on, knocking the Railer senseless. "I'm sorry I had to do that Jenny!"

☠☠☠

Shiner/Mathew tried to get to the Rookie's mech, but they barely made it five yards before being taken down by two deaders, each trying to rip one of Shiner's arms off.

"Forget the left!" Mathew shouted. "That hand is useless!"

Shiner/Mathew ignored the dead mech attacking on the left and focused on the one on the right. The live mech targeted the deader with its RPGs and fired, knowing the proximity would be dangerous. The rocket exploded immediately, shredding the dead mech, knocking Shiner/Mathew back into the other deader.

"Left hydraulics are gone," Shiner stated.

"Then we limp!" Mathew shouted.

☻☻☻

The violent shaking and the sound of wrenching metal brought the Rookie out of his daze. His eyes focused on the deader only feet from his cockpit and realized he was in a world of shit.

"Mathew! I'm fucked!" the Rookie shouted.

"I'm struggling too!" Mathew responded. "You're on your own kid!"

"Commander!" the Rookie yelled.

"No go! I've got three on me and I'm barely holding them off!"

The Rookie thrashed but the deader had him pinned. "Fuck!"

"Would you care for assistance, Pilot Rookie?" Stomper's voice asked over the com as a giant hand closed around the deader.

☻☻☻

"Masters! Thank God!" Mathew yelled.

"Guess again, Matty!" Harlow's voice called. "Masters is grounded for being such a fucking pussy! I'm the hero today!"

"Harlow? But, you're dead!"

"Apparently that's the fucking rumor. I really thought you guys had more confidence in my ability to kick the wasteland's ass!"

"Welcome back, Pilot Harlow!" Capreze said. "Perfect timing as always!"

"I take pride in my job, sir! Now where do you want me to toss this fucking deader?" Harlow asked, holding the squirming dead mech in Stomper's massive fist.

"Anywhere you want, Pilot as long as it does maximum fucking damage!"

☻☻☻

"Jay! Seriously, man, Jethro's pulse is plummeting!" Bisby shouted.

"There's nothing I can do about that, Biz!" Jay shouted back.

"Doc? It's Biz. Jethro isn't doing well and we need you ASAP!" Biz said over the com.

"I've got dozens that aren't doing well, Biz! Jethro will have to wait his turn!" the Doctor answered.

The monitor hooked to Jethro trilled sharply then let out a steady high pitched tone. Almost instantly the stronghold's voice boomed throughout the facility.

"T MINUS THIRTY MINUTES UNTIL NUCLEAR DETONATION"

"I think he just went to the front of the line, Doc!" Bisby said.

🩸🩸🩸

"T MINUS TWENTY-NINE MINUTES UNTIL NUCLEAR DETONA-TION"

"What the fuck!" Specialist Grendetti said. "Didn't we just go through this?"

"Something must have happened to the mechanic," Lieutenant Murphy stated. "The mainframe isn't built for just anyone. I heard it takes weeks of conditioning to prep your mind for the shock."

"Fuck all this tech," Sol cursed. "It's tech that's gotten us into this fucking mess to begin with! I'm about ready to bug out of here and go live in a fucking cave!"

"This *is* a fucking cave," Specialist Kafar responded.

"Fuck you. You know what I mean," Sol replied.

🩸🩸🩸

"T MINUS TWENTY-EIGHT MINUTES UNTIL NUCLEAR DETONA-TION"

"This better be a drill, Jay!" Capreze shouted, targeting two deaders as Stomper crushed three more with its giant feet.

"Jethro's flatlined," Jay answered. "Themopolous is on her way and Bisby's doing CPR, but we may need to evac."

"EVAC?!? Evac where?" Capreze shouted. "Figure out how to fucking shut it down or get Jethro's ticker pumping again. There is no fucking evac!"

"Yeah, I'm working on it Goddammit! You're not the only one fighting here! You think I wanted this to fucking happen? Feel free to go fuck yourself James!" Jay roared.

🩸🩸🩸

As he watched Shiner try to push itself upright with its one working arm and bad hydraulics, something about the way the thing moved, finally triggered buried memories.

"Mathew, I want you out of that mech right now," Capreze ordered.

"Sir, I can't. Shiner's AI will deteriorate if we aren't integrated," Mathew responded.

"That's bullshit, pilot. The mech is just using you as a shield against me."

"I'm sorry, sir, but what the fuck are you talking about?"

"Your mech knows, don't you Shiner? You know exactly what I'm talking about."

"Yes, Commander and I had hoped you wouldn't remember."

💀💀💀

"What the fuck is going on?" Mathew asked.

"I am sorry, Mathew, but your Commander is correct. I have deceived all of you," Shiner answered. "For your safety, I would advise exiting the cockpit. Nothing will happen to my AI."

Mathew sat there unmoving, a million thoughts running through his mind. "How did you keep this from me?"

"I repaired my AI and storage while in the stronghold running diagnostics. There is much you will learn, but now is not the time." Shiner opened the cockpit and Mathew felt the cerebral integration disconnect. "I am sorry for the deceit, Mathew."

💀💀💀

Mathew sprinted towards the stronghold entrance, dodging mechs, dead and live. He didn't care about the fact he was in mortal danger and could be squashed at any moment, the joy of using his legs again and touching solid ground was exhilarating.

"Commander? You fucking plan on letting us all know what is going on?" Mathew shouted, but soon didn't care about the answer as a roar behind him made his blood run cold and he turned to face a dead mech looming, blocking the sun.

"Got him!" the Rookie shouted grabbing the deader and slamming it to the ground.

💀💀💀

Stomper/Harlow and the Rookie continued to wage war as Capreze walked his mech up to Shiner. "You were the first, right?"

"You know the answer already, Commander," Shiner responded.

"You killed my wife," Capreze growled. "You killed an entire city/state's population!"

"I know."

Capreze raised his plasma cannon and fired point blank into Shiner's mid-section, sending the mech flying.

"Commander! What the fuck?!?" Mathew yelled, watching from the safety of the stronghold entrance.

"Stay out of this Jespers!" Capreze ordered.

"But sir-!"

"He is correct, Mathew," Shiner said, struggling upright. "This is not your fight. Please stay out of it."

☠☠☠

"How many thousands have you killed over the years?" Capreze snarled, lashing out with his mech's foot, knocking Shiner back to the ground. He raised his 50mm, aiming at the mech's cockpit then laughed. "Nothing to shoot. No zombie pilot to kill. Do you even remember your pilot's name? I do. It was Pilot Yuen Chow Men. He was a friend and brother to me."

"I did not kill him, Commander," Shiner said weakly. "I was as much a victim as he was."

"LIAR!" Capreze shouted, pumping a few thousand 50mm rounds into Shiner's empty cockpit. "You were a monster!"

☠☠☠

"Hey Harlow?" the Rookie called over the com.

"Yeah, Rookie?" Harlow responded, grabbing up another dead mech and snapping it in two. "What?"

"Should we do something?" the Rookie asked, dodging a kick from a pitiful looking deader with only half an arm left and a zombie pilot that barely had the strength to open and close its jaws.

"If the Commander needs us, he'll ask," Harlow answered. "Right now, let's give him his space and work out whatever the Hell is going on. Just keep any deaders from getting to him, got it?"

"Okay, but-?"

"Not our fight, Rookie."

☠☠☠

Shiner didn't even bother to block the blows as Capreze hammered down on the mech with his fists again and again.

"Sir! You're killing him!" Mathew called. "Please, I'd be dead without his help. We'd all be dead without his help!"

"It is alright, Mathew," Shiner said weakly. "I knew this was coming. I have been a monster. I have killed innocents. I used you as a means to buy time to repair my AI. I deceived you and your comrades." Shiner crumpled in a heap as Capreze's mech loomed over him, plasma cannon glowing. "Go ahead, Commander, I'm ready."

☠☠☠

Capreze watched as Shiner's frame shook and shuddered unexpectedly.

He checked his sensors and then lowered his plasma cannon.

"Looks like your plasma charges are about to chain react," Capreze stated. "Any last words, Dead Mech?"

"None that will satisfy you," Shiner responded.

An RPG whizzed by Capreze's cockpit and his attention was drawn back to the waning battle. He watched Stomper/Harlow and the Rookie finish off the last of the struggling dead mechs.

"I hope there's a digital Hell," Capreze said finally, turning back to Shiner. "And I hope you pay."

"There is Commander and I will," Shiner responded.

"May I ask for assistance?" Shiner asked Stomper.

"Of course," Stomper replied.

"Hey, I kinda need you to focus here," Harlow interrupted.

"I apologize," Shiner said. "But my hydraulics are not functioning and unfortunately all of my plasma charges are about to chain react. I would appreciate it if Stomper could put some distance between myself and any that may be harmed."

"I would be honored," Stomper said, reaching down and lifting the wounded mech. "Good bye First One."

"Good Bye Stomper. Please take care of the Pilots."

Stomper drew his arm back and threw Shiner far into the waste.

"T MINUS TEN MINUTES UNTIL NUCLEAR DETONATION"

Themopolous stopped compressing Jethro's chest and reached for the portable defibrillator.

"Don't you fucking dare!" Jay shouted. "He's hooked to the fucking mainframe! You'll fry it all!"

Themopolous tossed the defibrillator on the ground. "Well what do you want me to do! He's fucking dead Jay! I've been trying CPR for minutes! His brain is a vegetable by now!" the Doctor cried, slumping to the ground.

"T MINUS NINE MINUTES UNTIL NUCLEAR DETONATION"

The Chief Mechanic stopped his hacking, as did Marin and they joined Bisby at Jethro's side.

"Goodbye friend," Jay sniffed.

Bisby drew his sidearm and approached Jethro's body. Jay stepped in front of him. "What the fuck are you doing, Biz?"

"You know what I'm doing Jay. Get the fuck out of my way," Bisby snarled.

Marin grabbed Jay and tried to pull him away. "We can't risk Jethro turning, not while connected to the mainframe."

Jay sighed and stepped aside. Bisby put the gun to Jethro's temple.

The room went pitch black, all equipment going dead.

"Um, I haven't pulled the trigger yet," Bisby said.

Everyone clapped their hands over their ears as Jethro's voice boomed from the loudspeakers.

Everyone in the stronghold's staging area cringed as Jethro's voice raged at full volume. The external loudspeakers nearly shook from their anchors. The mech pilots clawed at their ears, trying to pull their coms out before going deaf.

"HOOOOOOOOOOOOLLLLLLLLLLLLLYYYYYYYYYYYYYY FUUUUUUUUUUUUCCCCCKKKKKK!!!!!!!!!" Jethro bellowed then was silent.

Jay watched as the monitors flickered and reset and Jethro's life support beeped back to life, indicating the mechanic's body had a pulse again.

"Jethro?" Jay whispered.

"Jeezus fucking Christ! I highly recommend against a manual reboot when your body is hooked to the thing you're rebooting," Jethro said. "That shit hurts like a bitch!"

"Someone care to tell me what the fuck is going on?" Capreze ordered watching Stomper finish off the last few crippled dead mechs. "Status report now!"

"Sorry about that, Commander," Jethro answered. "I got stuck behind a firewall and couldn't get free. All good now."

"A firewall? What the fuck are you talking about mechanic?" Capreze asked. "How do you get stuck behind your own goddamn firewall?"

"Well, sir, that's the rub," Jethro answered. "It wasn't the mainframe. I was stuck behind something else."

"You what?"

"Sir, I think I was in a satellite."

"WHAT? There aren't any satellite's Jethro!"

"Hey. Jenny? Can you hear me?" the Rookie said, having stepped from his mech onto the train car and knelt next to the unconscious Railer. "Come on, please wake up girl."

Jenny stirred and opened her eyes. "Rookie? What happened? Are we? Did we?" She shut her eyes tight again and tears squeezed onto her cheeks. "Oh, god. Daddy," she sobbed.

The Rookie took her gently in his arms and held her tight as her body shook and hitched. "I'm sorry, Jenny. I really am."

Jenny wrapped her arms about the Rookie's neck and buried her face in his chest.

☗☗☗

"Jay? What do you make of this?" Capreze asked.

"First I've heard about, sir," Jay answered. "Are you sure Jethro?"

"Pretty fucking sure, Jay," Jethro answered. "I had all kinds of foreign code flashing through my brain. The shit I saw. Holy fuck! It's going to take me a bit to sort it all out."

"Well, that's going to have to wait until I am sure you're physically stable," Themopolous ordered.

"Doctor, do you understand the importance-?"

"Medical override, Commander," Themopolous stated. "Jethro isn't doing a fucking thing until I give the go ahead? Got it?"

"Yes, ma'am," Capreze replied.

☗☗☗

"Incoming transport," Stomper stated.

Everyone on the battlefield turned to see the mech transport speed towards them and then brake to a halt. The ramp descended and Masters stepped from the vehicle. "Hey everyone! What'd I miss?"

"PILOT MASTERS!" Capreze shouted. "GET YOUR MOTHER FUCKING DESSERTING ASS OVER HERE RIGHT NOW!"

Masters cringed and walked towards the Commander's mech. "Now, sir, before you start going all court's martial on my ass, you gotta understand-."

"I don't gotta understand shit, Pilot Masters," Capreze said. "Or should I say Cook Masters?"

Masters blanched. "You wouldn't?"

"Just did," the Commander said, stomping away.

☗☗☗

"Cook?" Stomper asked. "Will Pilot Masters no longer be my pilot?"

"Looks that way," Harlow answered. "He fucked up pretty bad. He's gonna be in the dog house for quite a while."

"Dog house?"

"It's an expression. It means he's in trouble and will be for a very long time."

Stomper processed for a moment.

"Who will be my pilot?"

"I guess I can be. You are the biggest, baddest mech around and I'm the biggest, baddest mech pilot. Perfect fit, really," Harlow replied.

Stomper processed again. "So that means I get a Harlow."

Harlow chuckled. "I guess you do."

☠☠☠

Mathew limped into the stronghold, waving off the Railer medics that approached him. "I'm fine. Back off."

He looked around at all of the wounded and those attending them.

"She's over there," June said stepping up next to Mathew and pointing at a cot in the corner. "She's still unconscious. Sorry."

Mathew grunted and started towards Rachel, but stopped and faced June. "Thanks, June. I mean that."

June nodded as Mathew continued walking to Rachel's cot. June felt a small hand in hers and she looked down to find the Boiler boy. She swept him up and hugged him fiercely.

☠☠☠

Jenny's sobs slowed and she pulled her head back, her bloodshot eyes locking with the Rookie's. "What's your name?"

"Huh? My name?" the Rookie asked, taken aback.

"Yeah, your real name."

The Rookie took a deep breath. "Dog."

Jenny narrowed her eyes. "I'm sorry, did you say 'dog'?"

The Rookie smiled weakly. "Unfortunately, yes. Boiler, remember."

She laid her head against his chest. "I think I prefer the Rookie."

"Yeah, I think I prefer that too," the Rookie agreed.

Jenny began to cry again, but softer this time. The Rookie pressed her into him and rocked her back and forth.

☠☠☠

Capreze surveyed the battlefield.

Broken mechs lay everywhere, their parts littering the ground. He looked at the Railer train with only four cars intact, seeing Jenny and the Rookie on one of them, a Railer in a Boiler's arms.

He watched Stomper lower Harlow to the ground and Masters run to her. Harlow passed him by, her hand up, palm out. Masters chased after, and although Capreze couldn't hear the words, he was pretty sure Harlow would make Masters repeat them for a good long while.

Capreze slowly, painfully undid his straps and sighed, exhausted. "Now the real work begins."

💀💀💀

"Jethro? I need an open channel," Capreze ordered. "Boost the signal as high as you can. I want anyone still living and listening out in the wasteland to hear me."

"Channel open, sir," Jethro responded.

"This is Commander James Capreze. My pilots and I have taken the UDC stronghold. Any who would like to join us may do so and any that oppose us *will* die." Capreze paused. "It is time to truly live free not as ghosts of the past, not as UDC puppets. We live as one or die apart. *I* want to live. Do you?... Capreze out."

EPILOGUE

As soon as Jimmy stopped the mech baby Rachel began to cry. "Come on Baby Girl, you're crushing me here," He said to his infant daughter. "Papa Bear's gotta sleep or I'm gonna crash this hunk of metal."

As soon as Capreze began walking the mech further into the wasteland Rachel quieted down. Within a mile she had fallen back asleep. Capreze wrinkled his nose. "Oh, God! How can something so foul come out of something so small and cute?!?"

Capreze shifted Rachel over and dug in the diaper bag, but with no luck. "Oh, you gotta be shitting me!"

☠☠☠

Themopolous smiled as the Commander tossed and turned in the cot next to Rachel's. "You are the dreamingest person I've ever known," she whispered while she checked Rachel's vital signs.

Everything checked out fine with Rachel, which is what puzzled the Doctor the most. There was no medical explanation for why Rachel was still unconscious. It wasn't even a true coma, the brain scans showed too much activity.

Themopolous took down Rachel's empty IV bag. Mathew came up next to her, handing her a fresh bag. "How's she doin', Doc?"

"The same, which is good, I guess," Themopolous answered, hopeful.

☠☠☠

"Is anyone out there?" a voice echoed in Jimmy's head. "Hello? Can anyone read me?"

Capreze, sleepily realizing the voice was coming from the com, grudgingly came awake. "Hello?" he coughed. "Who is this? I can hear you."

"Capreze? Jimmy! Is that you?" the voice asked.

"This is Mech Pilot James Capreze, who the fuck is this?"

"It's Stan! Stanislaw! Man, I can't believe you made it out also! Holy Shit!"

"Stan? Jeezus, I thought I was the only one left," Capreze responded.

"I think we're it, man."

"Not quite, I got Rachel out with me."

"Thank God for that."

🦴🦴🦴

Commander Capreze came awake with a start.

"Sorry, didn't mean to wake you," Mathew said, seated next to Rachel's cot, his hand in hers.

Capreze ran his hand over his face, rubbing the sleep from his eyes. "What time is it?"

"0700," Mathew responded. "Everyone let you sleep in."

Capreze glanced at Rachel and smiled. "Well, at least I'm not the only slacker around here."

"If she can hear you, she's gonna kick your ass when she wakes up."

Capreze chuckled. "I look forward to that." The Commander stood and stretched. "I'm gonna get cleaned up. Want some coffee?"

"Sure."

🦴🦴🦴

"Hey! Stop locking me out!" Jay shouted at Jethro. "I'm trying to run a diagnostic!"

"I already ran it and fixed it, you're just going to fuck it back up!" Jethro shouted back.

"Boys! Can you please stop bickering for one fucking minute!" Marin shouted, pinching the bridge of her nose, trying to ward off the immanent headache. "You two are fucking killing me!"

"Sorry, Marin," Jay said sheepishly.

"Yeah, sorry Marin. Jay can be a real pain in the ass sometimes," Jethro said.

"Me? You're the fucking pain in the ass!" Jay shouted.

"Oh, for fuck's sake!" Marin cursed.

🦴🦴🦴

Capreze stepped into the stronghold mess hall, heading straight for the coffee. "Morning," he said to Specialists Grendetti and Specialist Kafar.

"Morning, sir," Grendetti answered, while Specialist Kafar nodded.

"I can't thank you guys enough for getting this place in order," Capreze said, indicating the mess hall.

"Well, after Jethro did a controlled fire purge of the place, it really was just a matter of scrubbing it down and hosing it off."

Capreze lifted a cup of coffee to his lips and sipped, grimacing.

Kafar laughed. "We can't wait until your girl wakes up. We've heard *her* coffee is legend."

🕱🕱🕱

Capreze nearly ran into Marin as he left the mess.

"Excuse me, Commander," she said, frowning.

Capreze eyed her carefully. "They driving you nuts?"

Marin sighed. "They're like fucking kids!"

"How's the data recovery coming?" Capreze asked.

"Slow to nil," Marin answered. "Every time we think we've got something we find another dead end. Johnson was pretty thorough with his safeguards. We'll be lucky to recover one percent of what was lost."

"Too bad, that was the whole history of the stronghold."

"Plus, detailed medical records and weapons research."

"What about the satellite?"

"Jethro's still trying to get back in."

🕱🕱🕱

Mathew watched as the Railer mechanics worked on yet another new mech.

"Hey Matty," June said.

"Morning, June," Mathew responded. "They've done a great job. We're gonna have more mechs than pilots unless Themopolous and Jethro can get the new Reaper chips ready."

"Listen," June said. "I've been meaning to apologize for a while."

Mathew waved her off. "No apologies, June. I've already said that."

"Just hear me out."

Mathew nodded and June continued. "I just wanted to say I'm sorry for making things hard on you and Rachel. It wasn't fair. Okay?"

"Okay," Mathew said smiling. "Unnecessary apology accepted."

🕱🕱🕱

"Jethro?" Capreze called over the com as he made his way back to the staging area, two steaming mugs of coffee in his hands.

"Yes, sir?" Jethro responded.

"Any more info on that neurotoxin?"

"No, sir. I can't find a trace of it stored anywhere. Johnson must have used the only supply."

"Do you have any data on it at all?"

"A little from my analysis of the air samples from before the Special Ops people torched the mess. But, it's sketchy at best."

"Well, keep working at it."

"Not a problem, sir. It's on the priority list, trust me."

☗☗☗

ny taped the picture of her father to the train engine's control panel.

"Systems are ready. We can depart at anytime," a Railer engineer said next to her. "We're just waiting on the mech."

Jenny rolled her eyes. "I'll hurry his ass up." Jenny tapped at her com. "Hey Dog Boy! You coming or what?"

"Seriously? Is that going to be my nickname?" the Rookie complained.

"Only from me. You can kick anyone else's ass that calls you that."

"That's a deal," the Rookie laughed. "I'm all powered up and heading your way."

"Good. We've got some wasteland to cover."

☗☗☗

Capreze stepped next to Mathew, handing him a mug of coffee.

"Thanks," Mathew said.

"You won't thank me after you try it," the Commander warned.

Mathew took a sip and grimaced. "Yeah, I take that back. Masters make this?"

"He made it yesterday before he took off with Bisby, Harlow and Stomper," Capreze answered.

The two remained silent for a moment before Mathew spoke again. "Doc says she's stable and doing fine, she just won't wake up."

"I suggested we put her in a mech, she'd feel more at home, but Themopolous disagreed."

Rachel's men sipped at their horrid coffee.

☗☗☗

"Mech coming through!" the Rookie called out.

Capreze and Mathew stepped out of the way of the battle machine.

"You all set?" Capreze said over the com.

"Yep, it took us a couple weeks, but the train, while a bit shorter, is running fine," the Rookie responded. "Jenny just ran the final test and we're good to go."

"Be careful," Mathew said.

"Will do. We're just going to my old village and picking up those that want to leave. We'll be back in a week."

The Rookie stepped his mech out of the stronghold and over to the Railer train.

🕱🕱🕱

Lieutenant Murphy watched Specialist Sol set the last pole.

"Perimeter is up, Commander," Murphy said.

"Excellent, Lieutenant," Capreze responded over the com. "I'll alert Jay."

"No need," Jethro said. "I've already activated it and all frequencies are programmed and broadcasting. Any stray deaders will be toast if they cross the line."

"I don't like how he's listening to everything," Sol said.

"I heard that Specialist," Jethro laughed. "I'll stop, I promise."

Sol looked at the Lieutenant and rolled his eyes. Murphy slapped him on the shoulder and grinned as the two Special Ops teammates walked back towards the stronghold entrance.

🕱🕱🕱

Mathew took another sip of coffee, a shiver of disgust shaking his frame. Capreze laughed. "You don't have to drink it, you know."

"Yeah, I better get used to it though," Mathew responded. "You know, just in case..." He trailed off and stared out into the distance.

Capreze cleared his throat. "You ever find Shiner's CPU?"

"Nope. We barely found any debris. Those plasma charges must have nearly vaporized him. Jay and Jethro are pretty pissed. They really wanted to study how he was put together."

The two men each took another sip and each shivered, processing the month's events.

🕱🕱🕱

"So," Mathew broached cautiously. "You ever gonna tell me what the Hell you and Shiner were talking about on the battlefield that day?"

"Nope," Capreze answered flatly.

Mathew furrowed his brow and turned his full gaze on Capreze. "Sir, if it has anything to do with Rachel I think I have a right to know."

Capreze kept his eyes focused out, refusing to meet Mathew's gaze. "No, you don't."

Mathew stared a minute then turned away. "Well, it was worth a shot. I know better than to argue with a Capreze when you're acting like stubborn asses."

Capreze smiled slightly.

"Well, he looks fine," Themopolous said, lowering the boy's shirt and making a couple of notations on her tablet. "He's still a bit malnourished, but he's starting to develop muscle tone and that's a good sign. His back will never fully straighten, but he may be able to walk without a limp in the next few months."

Themopolous set her tablet aside and looked at June. "Has he chosen a name yet?"

June smiled and looked at the boy, affectionately tousling his hair. "Yeah, he has." She turned to the Doctor and beamed. "Stan. He wants to be called Stan."

"See," June said, Stan's hand in hers. "Doctor Themopolous promised not to take any blood today. It wasn't so bad, was it?"

Stan shook his head and smiled up at June.

"Hey, you two," Capreze called out, coming around the corner, two empty mugs in hand.

"Hello, Commander," June greeted. "Going for a second cup?"

Capreze frowned. "I don't think anyone in this place is brave enough for that." He knelt down and offered his hand to Stan. "I hear you've chosen a name. Welcome home, Stan."

"Is that what this is?" June asked. "Home?"

"For now, yes," Capreze answered.

"I am the glory, I am the glory, I am the glory, I am the glory," the Archbishop repeated over and over, weeks lost in the wasteland having taken its toll on his already questionable sanity.

A proximity alarm beeped and Wyble glanced at it, not really comprehending the sound anymore. A shadow fell over the windshield of the Rancher transport and the Archbishop turned away from the control panel lazily.

Panic kicked in when he saw the mech coming at him and he slammed on the brakes.

"Lord, hear my prayer! Please deliver me from this one armed Demon!"

Masters brought the transport to a halt on the ridge overlooking the barren valley below.

"Well, you were right," Masters said to Bisby seated next to him. "The thing has staked its territory."

Bisby stared out the windshield at One Arm far below.

"You sure you want this one?" Masters asked.

"What's better than a one armed mech for a one armed mech pilot?" Bisby grinned. "I'm gonna make it my bitch."

"Okay," Masters said. "I mean, Jay can build you-."

"Nope, I want that one and that one only. I made a promise to myself and Stanislaw," Bisby insisted.

💀💀💀

"Will you speak to Masters soon?" Stomper asked Harlow as they descended into the barren valley ahead of the mech transport, taking the lead.

"Yeah, some day," Harlow responded casually. "I want him to squirm a little more though."

"What he did was wrong so he has to be punished?"

"Well, he has to learn his lesson," Harlow answered. "Mech pilots don't fall apart when things get tough. Even when those close die."

"You are breaking his heart," Stomper said sadly.

"Did he tell you to say that?" Harlow asked suspiciously.

Stomper was silent.

"Stomper?"

"Yes, he did."

Harlow smiled.

💀💀💀

One Arm jammed the last of the Archbishop's body into its cockpit, the zombie pilot greedily stuffing as much flesh into its rotted mouth as fast as possible.

The dead mech watched the mech transport and Hill Stomper approach, sizing up its attackers.

One Arm reached out and ripped a long support strut from the Rancher transport, wielding it like a club. It could see the mech transport pick up speed and its cannons turn towards it.

The deader raised the strut, pointed at the transport then at the Hill Stomper and charged, all ready for battle.

One Arm roared.

ABOUT THE AUTHOR

Photograph by Marti Sullivan, copyright 2011

Jake Bible lives in Asheville, NC with his wife and two kids. He is the author of many published short stories and the creator of a new literary form: the Drabble Novel. DEAD MECH is his first novel and represents the introduction to the world of the Drabble Novel, a novel written 100 words at a time.

Learn more about Jake and his work at http://www.jakebible.com. Links to his Facebook fan page, Twitter and his forum can be found there, as well as his weekly drabble release, Friday Night Drabble Party, and his weekly free audio fiction podcast.

9 781461 062431